LOVE POTION #666

Twice Bitten: Book Four

CRYSTAL-RAIN LOVE

ISBN: 9798570532243

DEDICATION & ACKNOWLEDGEMENTS

In loving memory of Zoe.

2005-2019

I miss you growling at and biting me, and I even miss your toxic farts. I miss getting up no less than ten times a night to let you out just so you could turn and walk right back in. Mostly, I miss the way you sat silently, judging us, and treated us like the peasants we were, but despite our utter unworthiness of you, you protected us fiercely because nobody was going to hurt your people. Be a good girl in Heaven, and don't bite any angels!

Thanks to Greg and Christle for all the help with editing, beta-reading, and most of all: Keeping me sane!

Thanks to all the wonderful readers who have sent such nice messages and left such wonderful reviews.

CHAPTER ONE

"What's a sweet thing like you doing here all alone?"

I looked at the inebriated man disturbing my peace. Other than the rotund beer belly, he was rather gangly, with a scruffy smattering of facial hair, and a roadmap of busted capillaries spread out over his nose.

"Don't," I said as he started to slide onto the barstool next to where I sat. I'd seen him down enough alcohol to know he was going to be a problem.

"I'm just trying to be friendly," he said, a hint of offense in his tone.

"So's the lady," Gruff, the bartender and owner of the establishment, said as he planted his large, barrel-chested body in front of us. "Trust me, you don't want her to have to get forceful."

"Oh, I don't know about that," the man said as he reached out to cup my chin. "I like it when women get a little force—"

I grabbed his wrist as I stood, twisted his arm behind his back, and slammed his head down on the bar before I let him fall to the floor. Blood spilled from the gash I'd just inflicted over his right eyebrow.

"Yeah, she doesn't like when overzealous dudes try to

touch her," an amused voice said from behind me just before my dragon-shifter friend-slash-bodyguard appeared at my side. "I don't either."

"I have this handled, Daniel."

"I see that. I'm just helping you out with the cleanup." He bent down, picked the groaning man up, and hoisted him over his shoulder.

"You're lucky," Gruff told the man. "She usually goes for the balls."

I rolled my eyes. Stab one wererat in the testicle, and people never let you live it down. "Give me a rag and I'll clean this up."

"I got it," Gruff said, spraying the bar top down with a special cleaner that contained bleach before wiping the blood up with a towel. Another of his employees rushed over to clean the blood that had dripped onto the floor and followed Daniel in case of further drippage as he carried the man out of the building.

"Sorry," I muttered.

"No worries. It was getting far too peaceful in here. My patrons expect a show every now and then."

I looked around, noting the patrons didn't seem that bothered or impressed. Gruff's Bar and Grille catered to truckers passing through the small West Virginia town, and locals who knew the business's rough and rowdy reputation. It was also popular among every paranormal being in the vicinity. They didn't mind blood and violence so much. Some, like me, even fed on it.

"Do you ever get sued?" I asked the burly werewolf.

He looked at me and chuckled, a rare occurrence for the usually humorless man. "A few have threatened, but the promise they'd get eaten puts a stop to that nonsense."

I raised my eyebrows, but said nothing. I'd seen a tiger shifter eat a man before, so as far as I knew, werewolves could do the same if they truly wanted to. I already knew of one who worked as a detective back home in Louisville, who had covered up a murder by chewing on the deceased's body, passing the incident off as a wild dog attack.

A soft sigh escaped me as I thought of home. I grabbed my drink and carried it over to a table near the back of the room, where I could put my back to the wall and watch the whole floor. My drink wasn't alcohol, of course.

I'd really only ordered alcohol in a bar once, the fateful night about three and a half months ago when I'd first set foot into The Midnight Rider. That was the night I got bit, first by an incubus, then by the vampire who tried to save me from becoming a succubus. Despite Rider's best effort, I held on to a little of what the incubus gave me. I became a hybrid. Half succubus, half vampire. Some would say I was also a full hot mess.

Selander Ryan and Rider Knight were the two sires who fought over me. Well, Rider fought for me. Selander just wanted to use me to hurt Rider. Turns out Rider and I were soulmates, and we'd been united together in a previous life. His evil, dick-wad, half-brother, Selander, knew this and lured me to The Midnight Rider that night just to make Rider's life hell. He'd made mine hell too, and he wasn't finished yet, despite the fact Rider had killed him. Oh, he was still around in his own evil way, toying with us from the pits of Hell.

I'd claimed Rider as my true master, making him my dominant sire. We'd hoped doing so would be enough to turn me full vampire, but no luck. I was still a hybrid, and I've come to realize I'm always going to have a bit of succubus inside me no matter what I do. I seemed to be managing it better now, thanks to Nannette, a nurse who worked for Rider. Okay, I guess she's my friend too, although she'd probably slug me for saying so. Either way, she came up with the idea of varying my cocktail, so to speak. Bagged blood and live blood, both male and female, and a little violence kept my succubus side from trying to run the whole damn show.

I'd traded in my bagged blood for bottled, easily acquired at Gruff's. Any vampire or other blood-drinking freak in the paranormal community could order a very bloody mary from any bar Rider owned, and he owned quite a few, and seemed to be buying up more every day. For live female blood, I had my very own donor. Live male blood was a bit trickier, because of the venom I secreted when my succubus side wanted to come out and play, so I usually drank straight from Rider, who was powerful enough to handle the venom's effects, and if we did end up having sex because of the venom, it wasn't as bad because odds were we'd do it anyway. But Rider was back in Louisville, and I was in Moonlight, West Virginia.

I'd always thought of soulmates as perfectly matched, sickening in love couples who lived on cloud nine without a single worry in the world. That wasn't the case at all. Rider was my soulmate, and I loved him beyond words, but we had our issues. One of those issues was that he could be almost suffocating in his need to protect me. In all fairness, I had been hunted by more than one bad guy since being turned, and Selander Ryan was still out there, aching for revenge.

Then there was the Bloom. What an absolute nightmare that had been. Rider had gotten a little help curing me of that affliction, but the way he'd done it made it hard for me to be around him, so I'd decided to leave. Rider had offered me a few job options, and I'd chosen the one that led me to Gruff's. My donor, Angel, came along as my own personal live female blood supply, and my two bodyguards, Daniel and Ginger, were assigned to work alongside me. That's right. The three of us were security for Gruff's, but Daniel and Ginger were also tasked with watching over me. Like I said, Rider was extremely protective of me.

The assignment at Gruff's gave me just enough controlled violence, even if I tended to kick the crap out of horny guys more than I actually did any real security work.

I got enough action to keep my succubus and vampire sides in check, but to tell the truth, it had been boring.

I took a drink of my very bloody mary and scanned the bar, looking for anything entertaining. It was a weeknight and the dinner crowd had come and gone without incident. Those who remained looked to be mostly local couples. No one brought their kids to Gruff's at night, not with its reputation for late night drunken brawls and more recently, a few cases of truckers gone missing after stopping in.

The stools at the bar were taken by truckers passing through, and a few local women who came looking to hook up when they got lonely. Judging by their carefree demeanor, the truckers didn't seem that worried about the others who'd disappeared during the last week. Of course, two of them gave off shifter vibes, and one practically had his nose sandwiched between a woman's breasts. That might have been another reason why people didn't bring their kids to Gruff's at night.

A couple played one of the arcade games near the front, a trio of guys took turns tossing darts at the dartboard near them, and I knew Angel and Ginger were playing pool under the guise of Ginger watching the pool room. It was going to be a long, quiet night.

Daniel stepped back inside, instantly found me, and headed my way. I noticed more than a few women turn their heads as he passed, including a few employees who I knew had the hots for him. Despite his unique, multi-colored hair, Daniel was a good-looking man. He was handsome, tall, fit, and full of boyish charm. He regularly dressed in worn-out jeans and T-shirts, most of which featured rock bands or movies, giving him a very easy-going appearance, but he was no slacker when it came to my protection.

"You didn't let that guy drive himself home, did you?" I asked as he took a seat next to me.

"Nope. Too much blood in his eyes to see." He

grinned. "The cab service was already outside picking someone else up, so I tossed him in with that dude."

I nodded. Gruff might look like a heartless badass with his big, barrel chest and thick beard, but he employed his own cab driver to hang out in the lot and take drunks home on his dime. Then again, being a werewolf who ran a business employing several paranormals, maybe the free cab rides for patrons were less about doing the right thing, and more about staying under the radar. The fewer drunks he released to get pulled over, the less he had to deal with cops.

Daniel scanned the room. "Kind of a slow night. Braining that poor bastard was probably all the fun you're going to have tonight. I'm surprised you didn't go for his balls."

"I don't always go for the balls."

He raised one perfectly arched golden eyebrow.

"I don't. I've never gone for yours."

"Not yet."

I rolled my eyes and took another drink. "Do you regret me taking this assignment and dragging you out here with me?"

"No. Where you go, I go. It's that simple. This is what you wanted."

"I wanted a job. This is glorified daycare."

He frowned. "You wanted to work security with us. This is a security job. Not all the jobs involve stabbing wereanimals or scaring the piss out of gangbangers."

"I'm a security guard with my own security detail. That's not normal, and Rider sent me to Bumfuck, West Virginia, where clearly nothing happens."

"We're in Moonlight, West Virginia."

"We're in Boresville."

"Uh, did I not recently burn through a small army of lycanthropes to retrieve a vampire friend of Rider's? That was something."

"For you," I pointed out. "You got to fly in and rescue

them. All we did was keep Jadyn company."

"Yeah, but you got to pulverize some dude's balls that night, and you have to admit that thing Christian did was pretty awesome."

I didn't know about awesome, but it was strange, and highly curious. Rider's vampire-witch friend, Seta, had helped us with the Bloom situation. Hell, she had saved Rider's life, and maybe my sanity, if I were being honest. Being turned into a hell-hussy at random intervals was a real bitch. He'd told me he'd owe her, and apparently she'd called to collect the previous week when she'd asked Rider to help protect her friend, Christian.

The vampire and his friend, Jadyn, had fallen under attack from lycanthropes and a dark witch just outside of Moonlight. Daniel had flown in and used his dragon fire to char most of Christian's attackers before bringing him and Jadyn back to Gruff's.

"He was definitely interesting," I said, recalling how he'd forced my succubus side down when it had threatened to come out, and the reaction I'd had to drinking his blood. I still felt light-headed just thinking about it.

"No shit. I'm still trying to figure out how he pulled a flaming sword out of nowhere. Rider tell you anything about him?"

I shook my head. As my sire, Rider and I were always connected, and we could speak with each other within our minds, even while states apart, but we hadn't been speaking much since I'd left Louisville. I felt him there, in the back of my mind, like a whisper on a breeze, but I'd hurt him by leaving. I didn't know what to say to him across the distance, and he didn't care to have anything to say to me.

"If Rider were speaking with me, he wouldn't have sent the order to retrieve Christian to you."

"I'm the only one of us who could fly in and grab his boy up."

I looked at him, and he sighed.

"Communication goes both ways. You could talk to him. You're the one who left, Danni. He probably thinks you don't want anything to do with him."

"I told him I wasn't leaving *him.* I just needed some space." I took another drink, making a face as the blood went down my throat like an overly thick milkshake. I'd let it start to congeal.

"Yeah, in guy-speak that means 'I'm leaving your ass, but taking my sweet time about it just to watch you twist.'"

"Well, that's not what I'm doing," I snapped as I set my bottle down on the table harder than necessary. "I just need some time to deal with what he did."

"He saved your life and got rid of the condition that turns you into something you hate every once in a blue moon."

"He tore my heart out of my chest. Literally."

"He put it right back." Daniel grinned before scanning the bar.

"If you'd ever had someone rip your heart out of your chest, you wouldn't find it so amusing. It was terrifying, and he didn't even give me a heads up."

"I was there, Danni." All amusement left Daniel's eyes as he returned his focus to me. "You know what I didn't find amusing? Crashing into that building to find your sister and that shifter-bitch about to kill you. You gave Shana chance after chance, but Rider does one little thing you don't like to save your life and you leave him. Shit, they had to block me with magic when they pulled that stunt because they knew I would have jumped in and ruined everything, defending you, but once he put your heart back and explained what they had done, I had to agree with it. He did what needed to be done, and he did it for you."

"Well, I'm sorry if I can't just get over it. I was floating around in the afterlife with that weird Jon guy who nobody seems to know much about, yet Rider trusted him to protect me."

"Clearly, Rider knew enough about him to know he'd keep you safe. For what it's worth, Rider didn't want to tear your heart out of your chest, but he'd rather do that than let you die or become something you hate every time the Bloom rears its ugly head."

"I know. It's just hard to deal with. I'd hoped some distance and a little adventure would help me get over it, but every time I close my eyes, I still see my heart beating in his hand." I handed off my nearly depleted bottle to a passing busser. "And technically, I didn't leave. He offered me the choice of Baltimore, Pigeon Forge, or to stay in Louisville and work from there. This job is just like the ones Ginger normally works. She reports to Rider in Louisville, even if the actual work takes her away from the city from time to time."

"You left, Danni."

"Fine, I left." I huffed out a breath. "Since when did you start taking Rider's side, anyway?"

"You will always have my loyalty, sweetheart, but you'll also always have my honesty. The man saved your life and freed you of the Bloom. I'm not going to act like he didn't just to agree with you, even if he is an uptight douche-bat."

"Douche-bat?" I laughed.

He shrugged. "I'm going to do another walk around outside, check the lot. Those missing truckers might have just been a coincidence, but best to stay watchful just in case."

"Call me if you see or hear anything remotely interesting. I'm bored with smacking around skeevy guys. I'd kill to be in a real fight, maybe even get to put a blade in someone."

"Oh shit. Someone might have beat you to that," Daniel said, his gaze on the front doors as he rose out of his seat.

I followed his gaze to see Rob, one of the security guards from Gruff's own staff, stumbling through the door. His hands cupped his crotch. His mouth moved, but he couldn't seem to find words. Blood gushed out of his mouth, and pooled between his fingers to pour onto the floor before he fell to his knees on the hardwood, and spread his hands, revealing more blood. A hush fell over the room, then the screaming began.

"Still too boring for you here?" Daniel asked as we rushed forward.

CHAPTER TWO

We moved through the panicked crowd of freaked out staff and customers as quickly as we could without revealing our inhuman speed, and dropped to our knees on either side of Rob's body as he pitched forward. Daniel grabbed his shoulders to keep him from slamming face-first onto the floor.

"What the fuck happened?" Gruff asked, kneeling next to me. His other staff, all some form of paranormal being or knowledgeable of the paranormal, ushered the customers out.

I shook my head as I looked down at the crotch area of Rob's pants. He was dressed in all black, making it hard to see anything, but my vampire nose could have pinpointed where the blood was coming from even if I couldn't see it. "I think someone stabbed him in the no-no's," I said.

"Oh fuck," Daniel exclaimed, staring in grotesque horror at Rob's mouth as the bulky human attempted to speak, but only made garbled noises. "Whoever did this took his tongue."

The click of a picture being taken alerted us to some asshole standing a few feet away, photographing Rob with his iPhone. A second later, Gruff leaped at the man, grabbing his iPhone and smashing it under one of his massive boots before tossing the man over to another of his staff to be removed from the building.

"Call the paramedics!" Gruff bellowed, knowing that as a human, Rob couldn't heal himself from the damage he'd taken. "How the fuck did this happen?"

Daniel and I looked at each other as Gruff rejoined us. The building cleared of customers. Most hadn't needed to be asked to vacate once they saw the bloody man fall to his knees in the center of the floor. Gruff's was a rowdy place, but this was excessive.

"Holy shit," Ginger said, joining us, Angel on her heels. My eighteen-year-old donor came from a screwed up family and had seen some shit in her time, but I felt this might be too much.

"Take Angel to the cabin," I ordered. "Stay there with her until we know what happened, and be careful. Whoever did this, did it from outside this building. They could be anywhere."

"Maybe I should take her back to the poolroom instead then?" Ginger suggested. She looked a total rebel in her tight ripped jeans, white Rolling Stones T-shirt with the big red Jagger lips and tongue, black leather boots and jacket, and her spiky dark brunette pixie cut, but she didn't bristle at my sharply barked order, knowing me well enough to know I was worried about Angel's safety and mental well-being.

"That's fine. Just keep her away from all this."

Ginger nodded and grabbed Angel by the shoulders, turning the young Latina girl away from us, seeming to break Angel's trance as she did.

"Is that guy gonna die?" Angel asked as they walked away.

I hope not, I thought, as I turned my attention back to Rob, and saw Daniel sniffing along his neck and chest, careful to avoid the blood.

"I don't smell any kind of shifter scent on him. I didn't

see anyone lurking around when I took that guy outside and put him in a cab. Rob was on the door, and he seemed fine."

"Maybe we should lay him down," I suggested as Rob coughed, spraying blood on Gruff's flannel shirt.

"If we lay him down, he might choke on his blood," Daniel pointed out.

"Ambulance should be here soon," Carrie, one of the late night servers, called out from the door, where she stood to watch Gruff's security staff search the lot. Tears filled her eyes.

"They better get here fast," Gruff barked as we watched Rob struggle to speak, unable to form words without the use of his tongue, and held him up, hoping that helped him in some way.

"He could be turned," Daniel suggested.

Rob made loud panicked noises and twisted his head from side to side as he fought to get out of our grasp.

"Nobody will turn you," Gruff promised him, before looking over at Daniel. "Rob's a good guy, and an ally, but he's made it clear he never wants to be turned."

"There's so much blood," I whispered, knowing Gruff would understand. It had pooled under Rob, spreading out to cover our knees, but it no longer poured. It trickled. Rob struggled to keep his eyes open.

"You hang in there, Rob," Gruff ordered as the sound of sirens cut through the night. "The ambulance is almost here. You just hang on."

Rob slowly reached out and used his index finger to draw in his own blood coating the floor. He'd just managed to draw a rudimentary sketch of a stick-figure woman in what looked like a long dress or shirt with long hair, before he released his last breath and died, the paramedics right outside the door.

The police had arrived immediately after the paramedics. We gave them and the paramedics room to work, helping however we could without drawing attention to the fact we weren't your average bar and grille staff.

Gruff's was known as a rough place when it got crowded with truckers, and there had been a few knife fights scattered throughout its time, but nothing like this had happened there.

Well, to the police's knowledge, nothing this bad had happened. Gruff and his people usually handled things themselves and cleaned up well, but when Rob had stepped inside the building while it was occupied by human customers, he'd made it hard to cover things up. The police had been called before anyone on staff had even thought about calling for the ambulance.

The paramedics tried to resuscitate Rob, but were unable to. Once we learned what had really happened to him, we figured he may not have wanted to be saved. Rob hadn't been stabbed. Someone did something much, much worse to Rob, and the only clue he'd been able to give us was a rough sketch of a stick-figure woman with long hair.

"Wait. You're telling me some woman bit off Rob's dick?" Ginger said, balling up my discarded jeans as I used wet wipes to clean the blood off my knees. We'd moved to the ladies' room for me to clean up while the police finished interviewing the other staff. Daniel and I had already gone our round with them.

I tossed the wet wipes away and pulled on the clean jeans Ginger had retrieved for me while I'd been questioned. "He drew a woman, but I don't know if whoever attacked him was human. I'm not sure a human could actually bite a penis off, and I overheard the medical examiner say it looked like it had been bitten off, but he didn't say by what. He just took a peek. He'll look more thoroughly when he gets Rob back to the morgue." My stomach dipped. Poor Rob. I hadn't known him well, but what little I knew about him, he didn't seem like the type of guy who deserved to die in such a horrific way.

"Maybe it wasn't a bite," Ginger suggested. "Maybe

they used a serrated blade or something."

"La la la la la la la," Angel sang as she shoved her fingers into her ears.

I finished tying my boot laces and patted her head. "How about we quit talking about this and you take Angel back to the cabin? Gruff's people didn't see anyone lurking around outside, and if they were, I'm sure they ran off when the cops showed up."

"No fair. You two get to hunt down the phantom penis chomper, and I get babysitting duty."

"I resent that statement," Angel said. "I'm a fully grown adult."

"You don't get fully grown adult status until you can listen to people talk about masticated dicks without sticking your fingers in your ears and singing the la la song," Ginger replied.

Angel stuck her tongue out, and I pulled her down from where she'd been sitting on the sink.

"Angel shouldn't be left alone until we figure out who did this, and what else they are capable of. You'll still be working security detail, just at the cabin instead of here." I sighed. "This is my chance, Ginger. We all know Rider sent us here because he thought this was going to be an easy job. He clearly doesn't have any faith in me, but now something has happened. We have a seriously disturbed predator on our hands, and I can help find whoever it is. I *need* to find them. I need to show Rider I can be a real asset to his company."

"Yeah," she muttered. "I don't think you impressed him that much with your wererat capture, considering you rolled around in baby shit and all."

I groaned. "Exactly. So, you understand?"

"I understand that part of my job is making sure nothing happens to you, because if it does, Rider will kill me."

"Daniel will be with me, and you know I wouldn't do anything to get either of you in trouble with Rider."

She gave me total bitch-face. "You knocked my ass out with hawthorn oil the last time Rider put me in charge of you, ran off, and nearly got yourself killed *on my watch.*"

"But did Rider kill you though?"

She bit her tongue and seethed for a moment before huffing out a breath. "Fine. Please try not to die or get maimed. I was lucky not to face Rider's wrath the last time you pulled a stunt. I don't want to push it."

"You're the best." I gave her my brightest smile.

"I know. Come on, Angel."

We collected our things and stepped out of the bathroom to see Daniel leaning back against the wall, his bloody jeans in hand. "Thanks, Ginger."

"No problem," she told him as she opened the plastic grocery bag she'd put my soiled jeans in so he could toss his in with them. "Apparently, I'm just the laundry and babysitting service tonight. Don't do any stupid shit tonight because if anything happens to her, it's your ass, not mine."

She moved down the hall, every step full of attitude as Angel followed along.

"What crawled up her ass?" Daniel asked. "All we did was have her bring us clean jeans. I thanked her."

"She's a bit miffed that she's stuck watching over Angel while we look for whoever attacked Rob."

"She'll get over it. The cops finally left. Gruff is waiting for us in his office."

I followed Daniel down the hall that ran along the back of the building until we reached Gruff's office. His office was small and brown, from the wood-paneled walls to the dirt-brown carpet. He had a chocolate leather sofa wedged against the wall, and a dark wood desk, which he sat behind, tapping away at the computer in front of him. He hadn't bothered changing clothes. Rob's blood spray still marked his shirt. He looked up at us and grunted. "No one saw a damn thing. I got the security feed here."

"You see anything?" Daniel asked as we both rounded

the desk, one of us on either side of Gruff.

"Yeah, we got a shot of Rob leaving his post, but can't see why." Gruff punched a button on the keyboard with one of his sausage-like fingers and the video rewound. He hit the play button, and we watched Daniel and Rob on-screen. There was no sound, but it was clear the two were talking casually. "He didn't mention anything weird, anyone lingering around?"

"No," Daniel answered. "He asked what had happened to the guy I brought out, and I told him. We had a chuckle about it. The other guy in the cab was that local guy who wears the trucker hat with the big bass on it and gets drunk off his ass every night. Rob said he'd been puking for a good ten minutes before he could get him in the cab."

"Yeah, that would be Upchuck. I saw the puking." Gruff scrunched his nose.

We watched as Daniel walked inside the bar, leaving Rob alone at the door. The cab pulled off, leaving the lot vacant except for the vehicles and Rob. Something caught Rob's attention. He looked off to the side as if he heard something. He stared into the distance a moment, then walked off, leaving his post at the door. We watched him cross the parking lot and step out of the frame into the surrounding woods.

"He might have heard something he thought warranted leaving his post," Daniel said.

"Maybe someone called for help?" I suggested.

"He should have said something instead of just wandering off," Gruff snapped as the video continued to run. "He was a big guy, and he knew how to fight, but he was human. I'm even more stringent on rules with humans than the rest of my people because they're more likely to die when they fuck up. He knew damn well not to do something that stupid."

Gruff fast-forwarded until Rob reappeared back on the screen, struggling to make it back to the building, leaving a trail of blood behind him. There was no point watching any longer after Rob made his way inside. We knew what came next, and I didn't think anyone wanted to watch the life fade from Rob's eyes again. I knew I didn't.

Gruff stopped the video. "This is what we know. He noticed something right after you left him, Daniel. Whatever it was, he felt the need to inspect it without telling anyone. Not even ten minutes later, he came back missing his tongue and his dick." The burly werewolf slammed his fist on the desk. "What the fuck kind of monster takes a man's dick?"

They both frowned and looked at me.

"I might have a tendency to punch or stab men in the testicles, but I've never taken one's penis," I told them.

"What about the blood trail?" Daniel asked, moving on.

"Grady and Ronnie followed it into the trees. It ended in a big-ass puddle of blood. They figured that's where Rob got butchered. They didn't find anything else. Whoever or whatever did this wasn't there, and didn't leave any tracks." Gruff pushed back in his chair, rolling it far enough to allow him to look at both of us at the same time. "We never got a good look at Rob's wounds. We stepped back and let the human responders do their jobs when they arrived, but I listened in. The medical examiner said it looked like some kind of bite, and the police pretty much chalked it up to an animal attack. I know you said you didn't pick up any kind of shifter scent on Rob's body, and I know he drew a woman, but I'm having a hard time picturing an animal or a woman just biting the guy's dick off. I can't even really imagine Danni doing that."

"Why the hell would you?" I asked, and my voice might have gone up a few octaves.

"We need to see that wound," Gruff continued, ignoring me and my indignation.

"I can get into the morgue," Daniel assured him. "I'm sure they have security cameras though, even if this is the boonies. I'm not that tech-savvy and neither is Danni.

We'll have to do this old school and just knock out the guards and break all their shit."

"Or you could just let Rider's computer nerds handle the security cameras," Gruff told him. "I'm going to forward our video feed to them anyway, see if they can catch anything we might have missed. I'll tell them to help you out with getting in and out of the morgue unseen."

My heart did a little hiccup. "You're going to tell Rider about this?"

Gruff looked at me as if I'd lost my mind. "Honey, my name might be on this building, but I pay rent to Rider. You bet your sweet ass when something this big happens here, I report straight to him. I already called it in, but I had to talk to Tony. Rider was out with some new chick, a Lisa or Laney or something. Anyway, he'll know soon enough."

The blood seemed to drain out of my body, replaced by ice as Gruff's words sank in. Suddenly, it made sense why I hadn't heard from Rider since I'd left.

"You all right?" Gruff asked, leaning toward me. "You look pale all of a sudden."

"She's fine," Daniel said, turning me toward the door. "We're going to check out that trail before heading over to the morgue to get a look at Rob's wounds. Rider's tech team knows how to contact me."

Yeah, they knew how to contact me too, and so did Rider, but why would he when he was busy with some woman?

CHAPTER THREE

I quietly sulked until we exited the building and I saw the empty lot. Rob's blood still stained the pavement, reminding me a decent man had died and finding the responsible party was more important than the ever-growing crack in my battered heart.

Daniel gave me a wary side glance as we crossed the lot, careful to avoid stepping in any blood. The police had done their thing rather quickly, packed up, and left, convinced they were dealing with an animal attack. They hadn't even left crime scene tape behind. In Louisville, we'd have called that shoddy police work, but in Moonlight, it seemed to suffice, and I wouldn't complain. I didn't know what the hell had happened to Rob, but my gut said the police wouldn't figure it out. They were doing us a favor by sucking at their job and leaving the real investigative work to us.

"Why are you looking at me like that? Still wondering if I could bite a man's penis off? Rude, by the way."

Daniel's mouth turned up a bit at the corners. "You've developed a reputation for testicular brutalization."

"It's a pretty big jump from that to what happened tonight."

"Not really. You're pretty scary when you get really pissed." He gave me another wary side glance as we entered the wooded area outside of the view of Gruff's security camera.

"What? Why are you looking at me like that?"

"I saw your face when Gruff mentioned Rider, and he was right. You did go a little pale."

"I don't want Rider to take me off this job," I said, knowing where Daniel was headed. I'd had my fair share of jealous outrages and pity parties since we'd met, thanks to severe self-esteem issues, but I'd been working with Nannette, and I liked the stronger version of me I was becoming. I refused to spill all my worries about Rider, what he was doing, and who he was doing it with. I was tired of people thinking I was that pitiful woman. Worse, I was tired of *being* that pitiful woman. "You know how overprotective he can be, and he doesn't think I'm capable of handling something like this. He sent me out here because he thought this was a simple job, and he still sent me with two guards of my own."

"He sent you with two guards because you're his favorite person in the world," Daniel told me as we continued to follow the blood trail, using our keen eyesight and the moonlight to see the dark blood in the grass. It had dried enough it no longer glistened, but I could still smell it, which was a good thing. Even my vampire eyes were having a difficult time seeing it in thicker patches of grass.

"Also, Selander Ryan hasn't stopped hunting you and just because the Bloom has been transferred over to your sister doesn't mean you're no longer a complicated woman. Nannette's blood cocktail experiment has been working pretty well, but you still have flares. Your eyes turned red the night Christian was here. If he hadn't forced your succubus side down, who knows the damage you could have done?"

"Yeah, yeah, yeah, I know. I'm a hot flaming mess of

drama and the world's biggest pain-in-the-ass." We'd reached the spot where Rob had apparently been butchered. A puddle of blood stained the earth, its coppery scent pungent in the still air. It might have called to me if I needed sustenance, but I'd been drinking well, and despite having fangs and a few kills under my belt, I wasn't a big enough monster to desire the lost blood of an acquaintance who'd clearly suffered. "Poor Rob."

"Mmhmm," Daniel murmured, his eyes seeming to focus everywhere at once as he circled the puddle, searching the woods for clues.

I also took a look around, not that I was sure what in particular I was looking for. My security expertise was pretty much just beating people up. I'd gotten fairly decent at kicking ass. Actually unraveling a mystery wasn't one of my strengths, but it was as good a time as any to learn. "What exactly should we be looking for, Scooby?"

"Scooby? Seriously?"

"Would you rather be Fred?"

"Fred's a douche."

"Fine, then. Sherlock?"

"Nerd."

"Well, then, who do you want to be?"

"I'm already the best specimen of man anyone could possibly be, hon."

I rolled my eyes. "Of course you are. So, what are we looking for?"

He stopped circling and looked back in the direction we'd come from, hands on hips. "Tracks, broken twigs, an escape route… Something that explains what the hell happened, how it happened, and where the freak who did this went to after."

I looked around, trying to see something to answer those questions. "We know Rob saw something because he looked this way and started walking."

"And he didn't walk defensively," Daniel pointed out.

"No, his shoulders were low, his walk casual."

“And that tells us what?”

“He wasn’t threatened by what he saw… so whoever did this is someone who doesn’t appear threatening.”

“Exactly.” He walked over to me and ruffled my hair playfully before crouching down at the edge of the blood puddle. “What else do you know?”

“Rob wouldn’t leave his post for just anything. Whoever did this had to have lured him somehow, or appeared to be in trouble, but if they appeared to be in trouble, he would have notified others on the staff that he was leaving his post to check it out, so I’m sticking with the lure theory.”

“Yup.” Daniel leaned forward and inhaled, smelling the blood.

“Is it all his?”

He nodded before stretching out to smell the foliage around the puddle, then stood, leaned his head back, and scented the air. “I can’t smell anything but human, which makes no sense. Rob was human, but he knew how to fight. He also carried a knife on him. There is no way a human would have overpowered him without a major struggle and loss of blood. He would have gotten some cuts in or broke skin with his knuckles, at least.”

I took a closer look at the area. “I don’t see any damaged tree limbs, any broken branches, any smears in the puddle, no evidence of a fight.”

“Look who’s learning this investigative stuff.” He grinned, but it didn’t last long, given the circumstances. Humor was a fleeting thing when standing over a puddle of blood that had once belonged to a decent guy. “Someone lured him here with the intention of taking two very important parts of him. I don’t think they intended to take anything else, because they would have. This puddle is too perfect. The only other blood splatter is what he left walking back.”

“If he fought, blood would have sprayed everywhere,” I said, understanding what he was saying. “They only wanted the tongue and the penis, then they left him… but how? There's no tracks."

Daniel looked up. "They could have gone that way."

"You think the person who did this flew away? You said you only smell human here."

"That doesn't mean a human did this. Maybe it's some kind of being that doesn't have a smell. Hell, maybe it's a damn ghost."

I stared at him for a moment. "Okay, I know I shouldn't be weirded out by that, given the fact I have fangs and drink blood, but a ghost? I'm not saying they can't be real, but you think ghosts are flying off with men's penises now? Why would a ghost want Rob's penis?"

"I don't know. Does he have a dead ex-wife we don't know about?"

I resisted the urge to slug him. "Not funny, Daniel."

"I'm serious. Scorned women can be psycho, and think what you want, but taking a dude's junk is a personal statement." He expelled a breath as he took a last look around. "Whatever or whoever did this, they're gone now, and didn't leave us many clues here. Let's see what his body tells us."

Moonlight was a pretty small town. It didn't take long for Daniel and me to reach Main Street, where the small jail, courthouse, and medical center were all bunched together in-between little diners and mom and pop stores. The area wasn't exactly a tourist destination, and people who lived inside town limits tended to stick to themselves, especially the ones of the paranormal persuasion.

We'd been advised the morgue was in the basement level of the medical center, and it was guarded by a night watchman, as well as monitored by security cameras. Currently, we sat in Daniel's truck in the medical facility parking lot, waiting for Rider's tech team to give us the go ahead to enter.

"Haven't heard from Rider yet?" I asked, glancing over at Daniel, who sat staring at his cell phone's screen, waiting for the message telling him we could get to it to appear.

He shook his head, cutting me a look.

"What?"

"If you're curious what he's up to, why don't you just ask him?"

I huffed out a breath and stared out the window at the two-story medical building. "I never said I was curious what he was up to, and the sooner I contact him, the sooner he can try to pull me off this job."

"Sure."

"What's that mean?"

"Nothing." A message bubble popped up on his screen and he clicked the phone off. "All right. The tech team just gave me the go-ahead. They looped the video feeds inside the building, so if anyone is monitoring right now, they won't see us at all. We still have to deal with the security guard in the morgue, but that shouldn't be too hard. Let's go."

We exited the truck and walked over to the building. The plan was to walk in like we belonged there, and deal with any trouble if it came along. The front door was unlocked, with no intercom for after-hours visitors. We stepped into a small lobby with an unmanned information desk. I couldn't imagine such lax security back home, but Moonlight was the type of place where people slept with their windows open to feel the breeze. Just the thought gave me the willies. If we tried that back home in Louisville, we'd wake up with all our electronics missing, and maybe a kidney.

Daniel scanned the lobby, his eyes slightly narrowed. "There's a woman on shift, but she's in the break room getting coffee. Let's try to avoid her."

"Holy cow, you're able to see that from here?" I said, looking around, but I couldn't even determine where the breakroom was from where we stood.

"No, I'm a dragon, not a gargoyle. I can smell her perfume and the coffee. The rest is just the power of deduction. Come on."

Daniel raised a finger to his lips as we moved down the hall to the left, past a room with a sign indicating it was the breakroom. We took a right at the end and I followed as he pushed through a door leading to the stairwell. "Cameras aren't picking us up, but people can still see us. The stairs are a safer bet than the elevator. We don't want to announce our presence to anyone who may question us being here at this hour."

I nodded my agreement as we took the stairs down to the basement. We paused at the bottom long enough for Daniel to peek through the small window, then he opened the door and scented the air before stepping through.

The basement was dark, lit by flickering, low-wattage overhead light. "I feel like we're entering a horror movie," I whispered.

"You're a vampire," Daniel whispered back. "If a monster jumps out at you, just drink it."

Yeah, right. Like my dragon bodyguard would even let me have all the fun. I stayed quiet as we moved down the hall. MORGUE was painted on the wall in faded block letters with an arrow underneath informing us we were headed in the right direction.

"Are we sure only the security guard is here?" I asked. "Rob was just attacked earlier tonight. Wouldn't they still be doing the autopsy?"

"The tech team hacked in and viewed the security feed before creating the loop. The examiner made sure the body made it here safely, then went home. The old guy was yawning while at Gruff's, and since he suggested this was an animal attack, I don't think anyone is in a rush to do the autopsy."

I shook my head, wondering how many people easily got by with crimes in the boonies given how poor the handling of such events seemed to be.

We reached the morgue doors and stopped. Daniel peered in the narrow window, and frowned. "Stay here," he whispered before disappearing in a cloud of rainbow-colored sparkles.

I envied his ability to dissolve into nothingness and move from place to place without being seen as I stood outside the morgue, glancing around nervously. Yes, I was a vampire-slash-succubus, but the flickering lights were disturbing, especially when paired with the knowledge my partner had just entered a room full of dead bodies.

I jumped a little as his deep chuckle entered my mind. *Well, this is going to be easier than I thought. We just need to be quiet.*

No sooner had Daniel's words filled my mind, the door opened to reveal him. He jerked his head to the left, motioning for me to enter.

I stepped inside and looked around. I saw a vacant desk to my left, and a large multi-body refrigeration unit lining the opposite wall. Metal examination tables and rolling supply carts filled the space between. What I didn't see was a night watchman. I looked at Daniel and raised my eyebrows.

He inclined his head toward a door in the back. "Dude fell asleep on the toilet," he whispered.

I scrunched my nose at the unwanted image. "Sure he's not dead?"

He appeared to think about it for a moment. "It did smell pretty bad."

"Ugh." I moved toward the coolers, my eyes already stinging. The morgue didn't really stink, but the air was thick with the strong scent of chemicals. "Let's hurry this up. Maybe we can make it out before he wakes up."

"The guy's older than dirt. If he does wake up, it'll probably take him a year to get his pants up, then another one to trudge out here."

"Good to know. Where do you think Rob's body is at?" We'd reached the coolers and I noted each drawer was labeled only with a number.

"Not sure. I guess we just start opening them."

"You go right ahead." I stood back and grimaced a little.

"Is the scary blood-sucking vampire afraid of dead bodies?"

"She's not afraid of punching you in the balls."

Daniel chuckled. "Hell, we all know that about you."

"If you must know, I don't know if the bodies are covered or just out on full display. I'm not comfortable looking at people's personal areas without permission. It just seems wrong."

"I'm pretty sure anyone in here is too dead to care," Daniel said as he grabbed the handle on one of the units, "and Rob's personal area got taken." He opened the door and pulled a tray out, revealing someone zipped in a body bag. "They're in body bags. You can unzip as far as you're comfortable until we find him, unless you're just scared."

"Bite me." I walked over to a drawer at the other end of the cooler, ignoring Daniel's chuckle, and opened it, revealing a vacancy.

"Not him," I heard Daniel say as he zipped the bag up and pushed the body back inside before moving to the next cooler.

I'd already opened another drawer and pulled a body out. I took a breath and slowly unzipped the bag, revealing an elderly woman's pale face. She stared at me with blank eyes, sending a chill down my spine.

"Found him," Daniel said from behind me.

I zipped the old woman's bag up, giving her back her dignity, and rolled her body back into the cooler before turning to see Daniel unzipping Rob's body bag all the way. It appeared Rob had been undressed, his clothes in a clear bag near his feet, and covered with a thin sheet, which Daniel lifted to look under. He gagged and turned his face away.

"Now who's bothered by dead bodies?"

"I'm not bothered by the deadness so much as the dicklessness." Daniel took a moment to gather himself, then turned back toward the body I could now see better that I'd moved over to stand on the opposite side of it. "Without all the blood in the way, I can see the damage better. I've seen less mutilation in horror movies."

My stomach took a dive as I looked at the ragged cavity where Rob's genitals had been. I could understand why the examiner had thought an animal had attacked him. The hole was nowhere clean enough to have been done with a blade, but I couldn't imagine a wild animal leaving such a ragged hole behind either. "I'm no expert, but that doesn't say animal bite to me."

"Me neither," Daniel agreed, his face turning green. "There's no way in hell any man would just stand there and allow something to do this to him either. Grab me a tongue depressor."

I walked over to the utility cart and looked around until I found the instrument he requested, and brought the wooden stick back to him. His lip curled as he took it, but he forged ahead and slipped the tool into Rob's mouth, opening it to reveal the tiny stub of what remained of his tongue. It looked like a beet-red alien worm that had spent time inside a blender.

I turned away, one hand clamped over my mouth as I moved toward a wastebasket marked with the biohazard symbol, and struggled to keep the contents of my stomach down.

"You all right over there?"

I took a deep breath in through my nose and willed myself not to vomit. "Yeah. The tongue hit me worse than the missing genitals."

"Knowing your affinity for nut punches and testicle stabbings, I'm not surprised."

"I'm so glad you can find amusement in this."

"This is the most horrifying wound I've ever seen and I'm pretty sure I'm going to have nightmares over it, so it's either joke to make it through this examination or run out of here screaming."

"Yeah, I can understand that," I said, bracing myself to turn around and face the gory mess inside Rob's mouth.

"The M.E. won't be back until morning to do the actual autopsy, but he's pretty much already declared it to be an animal attack," a deep voice said from beyond the morgue.

I turned and met Daniel's gaze. Without a word, he zipped up the body bag and rolled Rob's corpse back into the cooler as I looked around for a place to hide. I thought about jumping in the cooler, taking up one of the vacancies, but had no idea if the door could be opened from the inside. I wouldn't die from refrigeration, but it still wasn't a place I wanted to be stuck for however long it took for an unsuspecting staff member to find me. Then there was Daniel. Even if he could dissolve into sparkles, he couldn't get through a sealed metal door in that form, so it probably wasn't a good spot for him to hide either.

He grabbed me around my waist as the handle on the morgue door turned and shoved me into a very narrow closet, wedging himself in with me before pulling the door closed. A mop handle was poking me in my rear, so I wiggled a bit to ease myself of the discomfort, eliciting a hiss from Daniel as I inadvertently rubbed myself against his nethers.

Sorry, I whispered telepathically as my face filled with heat and footsteps sounded on the morgue floor.

He didn't respond, but relaxed the fingers that had clenched tight around my hips in an effort to stop my gyration. I noticed his jaw remained clamped tight.

"Carl must be in the bathroom," the same deep voice said. "Poor old guy has a tendency to fall asleep trying to drop a deuce. I told my wife to just shoot my ass and take the insurance money if I ever get that damn old I can't even crap right anymore."

"There's no need to disturb him," another man said,

his voice smoother. "I just need to take a look at the body, if you don't mind."

"Uh, I'll just stay out here until Carl returns. The M.E. won't mind letting you look, but you understand someone needs to be with you to ensure the body isn't tampered with before the autopsy."

"Suit yourself."

I held my breath, noting Daniel did as well, as we heard the cooler door open and the bag unzip. Daniel's heart steadily beat against my cheek, remarkably calm for someone who was just almost caught sneaking into a morgue. I felt pretty revved up myself, although I wasn't sure whether it was due to the possibility of being discovered, or the fact I was smooshed against a body that was surprisingly cozy despite all the hardness, particularly the *really* hard part poking my stomach.

I was deeply in love with Rider, and despite our distance, neither of us had said the words that we were over, but I was half succubus, and the closeness to a very attractive man was teasing the succubus part of me into a frenzy. I took a deep breath, held it, and wished with everything in my heated body that whoever the hell was in the morgue would do what they had to do and get the hell out before my itchy fingers did a little investigating.

"Hmm, looks like the M.E. left out a tongue depressor," the second man murmured, and I thought I picked up a little suspicion in his tone, but that might have just been a bit of paranoia on my end.

"It was late when they brought the body in," the deep-voiced man said. "He was probably too tired to notice. Aren't you going to put on some gloves?"

"Oh, of course." I heard the sound of latex gloves being handled, and other movement, then the man spoke again. "Let's just take a look inside here."

I heard a powerful gag followed by running feet. A door opened, followed closely by a greater gag, and then running in the other direction. Daniel's stomach tickled me as it shook with his silent laughter about the same time we heard the morgue doors open and deduced the man with the deep voice had forgotten about security protocol and left the other man behind.

I told you the bathroom stank, Daniel said in my mind, still laughing silently. *Now that I think about it, Carl may have died of his own fumes.*

I shook my head, never ceasing to be amazed by the grossness of men's humor.

"I suspect Willis will be throwing up for a while," the man beyond the utility closet door said. "Come on out, vampire, and … Imortian?"

CHAPTER FOUR

It's a werewolf, Daniel said in my mind. His sense of smell was incredible.

One we know?

He shook his head as he turned the doorknob and somehow managed to squeeze out of the closet, rubbing against me in a way my succubus side enjoyed a little too much. Geez, maybe I should call Rider. I immediately shoved that thought aside. Rider was off playing with some new woman, and apparently having such a good time, he didn't feel the need to check in on me.

I straightened my wrinkled V-neck and stepped out of the small space, biting back my irritation as Daniel moved to ensure I was blocked by half of his body. I suppose there are worse things than being protected, but I didn't like being presented as weak in front of some random shifter.

A cute random shifter, I noticed as I looked around Daniel to see the man standing by the open cooler, Rob's body exposed before him. He was tall and fit, like most shifters, had a lot of scruff and warm amber eyes. His nose was straight, his light brown hair a little on the messy side, but cut just short enough to lend him an appearance of professionalism. He wore jeans with a blue button-down shirt and a brown leather jacket that matched the brown leather of his hiking boots. I appreciated the view, but focused mostly on the badge clipped to his belt and the familiarity I couldn't quite put my finger on.

"You're a cop?"

"Close enough," he answered. "Private detective."

"A private detective who likes to give the impression he's the actual law," Daniel said, nodding toward the badge. "Is that thing even legal?"

The detective grinned. "The badge makes people comfortable, gets them to open up much easier than cracking skulls."

"You crack a lot of skulls?" I asked.

"My fair share," he answered. "Mostly, I bullshit, but that can take time I don't always have."

"I wouldn't recommend bullshitting with us," Daniel warned. "We knew Rob, and I don't recognize you as being on Gruff's payroll, so you better have a good excuse for sniffing around his body."

"I'm here for the same reason you are," the man answered. "I'm investigating this attack. This isn't the first time I've seen this sort of thing, but I've never seen it here in the states."

I peered closer at him, feeling I should know who he was. "You look familiar, but I can't place you."

"I believe you know my brother," he answered before zipping up Rob's body bag and rolling him back into the cooler. "There's nothing you'll get off this body that I haven't already seen on three others. Also, there's probably only so much puke in Willis. He'll be back soon, and I'm sure you'd rather slip out of here peacefully than beat the crap out of an innocent guy just doing his job. Meet me back at Gruff's and we can start hunting down this monster together."

Daniel and I looked at each other, strengthening our

telepathic focus. *Did Rider send this guy?*

You know as much as I know, Daniel responded.

I pulled out of Daniel's mind and directed my gaze at the werewolf. "Who's your brother?"

"Aaron Grissom."

The familiarity now made sense. The man before me heavily resembled the detective, the real detective with a real badge, who'd been first on the scene when Angel had been forced to kill a man. Grissom was a good guy, going so far as to take a few bites out of a deceased man's body to fake a dog attack, ensuring the man's death investigation wouldn't lead to her. I trusted Aaron, but I didn't know this guy, and he seemed awfully trusting of us, given we'd just met and hadn't even exchanged names yet.

"Who sent you here?"

"No one," he answered. "I work for myself."

"And you know what did this?"

"I have a pretty good idea, which I'll be glad to share when we're not so rushed. I got in here with a badge. The staff trusts badges. They speak to people with badges. They don't speak to people who sneak in, so if you don't mind…"

I folded my arms over my chest. "We're supposed to believe you'll be willing to include us in your investigation if we leave? You don't even know us."

"A pretty little vampire hybrid who hangs out with a rainbow-haired Imortian shifter?" He grinned. "Sweetheart, we've all heard of Danni the Teste Slayer."

I fought the urge to roll my eyes as Daniel stifled a laugh.

"I'm a little surprised to find you here since last I heard, you were part of Rider Knight's nest and living in Louisville, but whatever. I'm going to find whatever the hell is doing this sick shit. You can work with me, or you can find something else to do, but I'm not walking away from this."

"Bossy sonofabitch, isn't he?" Daniel muttered.

I grinned. "Yeah, but we're used to that, and sounds like he already knows more than us, so we might as well not butt heads with him. You ever going to introduce yourself, werewolf?"

"Holden," he said with a tip of his head. "Holden Grissom, and you, Danni Keller, don't have a lot of time to get out of here unseen."

He was right. My vampire ears had just picked up the sound of a toilet flushing.

"Tony said Holden Grissom checks out." Daniel locked his cell phone and set it on the table.

Gruff's was closed, but Gruff didn't care if we used his place for the meetup with Holden. He kept a couple of staff on duty during the time the building was closed in case any paranormals in need stopped by after hours. I'd taken a few of those shifts myself. Gruff lived nearby, but spent many a late night or early day sleeping on the leather couch in his office. That was where he could be found now, and where I suspected he'd be sleeping until we solved Rob's murder. Thc big, hairy guy was taking the man's death hard.

"I figured he would," I said, pushing the words out through the ball of disappointment trying to clog my throat. Moonlight and Louisville shared the same time zone. It was getting close to daylight in both places, and Rider generally preferred to be safe within the walls of The Midnight Rider before dawn, so why the hell had Tony taken Daniel's call instead of him? "Hopefully, with his help, we'll get this all figured out soon, and give Gruff some closure. I think the big guy's blaming himself."

"I think Rob was to him what Rome is to Rider."

"That close of a friend?"

"I was thinking more like a pet, but sure, let's go with that."

I grinned despite the hollow ache in my chest. No matter how I felt, Rome and Daniel's brotherly constant ribbing of each other could always give me a chuckle. My amusement didn't last long though. That hollow ache was pretty powerful, and growing stronger by the day. "I'm pretty sure I'm Rider's pet."

Daniel stared at me, his eyes sympathetic, but the front door opened and Holden stepped inside Gruff's before he could say anything. Daniel stood and moved to my side of the booth, sliding in next to me as Holden crossed the floor, giving the werewolf no choice but to sit across from us.

The werewolf looked around the otherwise empty room as he slid in opposite us. "Sorry for the delay. I wanted to check the morgue records to see if anything else similar to this case came in recently, and question the medical facility staff further. I've always found the night staff at such places to be far more loose-lipped than the employees who actually get a decent night's sleep every now and then."

"Learn anything useful?" I asked.

He shook his head. "Nothing but gossip, typical in towns like Moonlight. Of course, with a decent amount of paranormals in the community around here, there's bound to be rumors and little things people think they may have seen or overheard, but nothing pertinent to this case."

"How did you know to come here so soon after Rob was attacked?" Daniel asked.

"Just because I'm a bit of a lone wolf, it doesn't mean I don't still hang with the pack sometimes. Carrie told me. She knows I investigate these types of incidents."

"You live around here?" I asked.

He shook his head. "I just wrapped up a case in Pennsylvania. I visit Carrie sometimes when I'm passing through. I stopped by earlier this afternoon to crash at her place. Hell, I was still snoozing when she got home and told me what happened."

I raised my eyebrows, realizing he and Carrie were knocking boots, or sniffing butts, or whatever the hell werewolves liked to call it. Good for Carrie. I remembered the poor girl had made a play for Daniel not long after we'd arrived, but Daniel was all business, and had shot her down. Nicely, of course, but let's be honest. All rejection sucked. Holden was a cute guy, not a bad alternative at all, but while I was happy for Carrie, I wasn't overjoyed for me. Holden was a threat to my chance at solving something big and proving I was capable of more than just stabbing jerks in their balls and providing comic relief for Rider and his staff.

"Carrie didn't tell you we were already investigating this?"

"Carrie never mentioned either of you," he answered. "She was a little worked up about her friend and co-worker dying. Look, I've heard enough about you from my brother and other contacts I have in the community to know you're part of Rider Knight's nest, and you've built a pretty big reputation in a very short time as someone no guy wants to end up in an interrogation room with. Your friend here is a dragon shifter, which is enough to tell me I don't want to step on his toes if I don't have to. I'm not taking business from you, and I'm not your enemy. I'm not sure where the distrust I sense in you is coming from, but we're on the same side. I want to find this monster and kill it."

"We all do," Daniel said, casting a frown in my direction. "You said you've seen this type of attack before. Where? What did this to Rob?"

"Malaysia, five years ago." He took a breath. "It doesn't make a bit of damn sense that it would be happening here, but the wounds are the same. This thing lures men just so it can bite out their tongues and drink their blood while ripping their genitals off."

"What thing?" I asked once I finished wincing at the image his words had put in my mind. "What is it?"

"A pontianak."

Daniel and I shared a look, his suggesting he was as

clueless as I was. "I thought that was a car."

"A pontianak," Holden repeated. "Not a Pontiac. Pontianaks have been around for centuries, but I've never heard of one outside of Southeast Asia. Even there, attacks are few and far between. They lure men, eat their tongues immediately, drink their fill of blood, and rip out the genitals to save for later."

"They actually eat the dude's junk?" Daniel asked.

Holden nodded. "I hunted one in Malaysia five years ago after three men were found attacked. Pontianaks hibernate for years, feed, and then go back into hibernation, usually for at least a decade. They're damned hard to destroy."

"How did you?" I asked.

"I didn't." He looked away. "The damned thing went into hibernation and I didn't find it. They're described as female vampire ghosts. They can appear in spirit form or take on the appearance of a human woman, even a woman you know personally. In human form, they imitate speech, movement, everything. They take on vampire form during the attack. Not vampire like you," he clarified. "They have far nastier fangs and their tongues are long and thin. Their hands are clawed, allowing them to rip the genitals out effortlessly, but not without a great deal of pain, as you can imagine. Then they just evaporate into thin air, disappearing until they attack again."

"How the hell do you catch and kill something like that?" Daniel asked.

"You can burn them in physical form," Holden answered, "which makes you a good guy to have on the team. Also, legend has it they don't attack women, so Danni, you'll come in handy as well. If you can get hands on the evil bitch, you might be able to put her down. It's said that if you grab their hearts, they can't turn back into their spirit form. You'd have a better chance at that than we would."

"So you're so willing to work with us because you need

us."

"I'm willing to work with you because I failed to kill one of these things before and I have to live with that. I don't know that I can live with letting another continue to terrorize innocent men."

The pain I saw in Holden's eyes told me there was more to the story, but the set of his jaw warned not to ask. He'd given us the information he'd deemed necessary for the moment, and I had to admit it was good information. We knew what had killed Rob, and we knew how to destroy it.

"How do you actually hunt these things? You said the one you were hunting went back into hibernation. How do you know that?"

"The attacks stopped. As for how to hunt a pontianak, you hang out in locations they're known to look for prey. You won't find them in a big city. They stick to rural areas, small towns, and they love heavily wooded areas. Rumor is, they dwell in caves or burrows."

"In Malaysia or Indonesia," I reminded him. "If it's changed countries, could it change its habits?"

"Well, it's still sticking to the same diet," Daniel pointed out.

"I have no idea why one would pop up here in the states, let alone in West Virginia of all places, but it's here. It attacked a man the same way those evil beasts have been attacking men for centuries. It's the same monster, just a different country." He glanced at the clock over the bar. "They hunt at night when they're most powerful, another part of their vampire side. It's almost daylight, so all will be safe, but it will hunt again when the sun goes down. Are you with me, or am I doing this on my own? Either way works for me, but it would be nice to have some backup."

"We're in," Daniel volunteered for us. "It's getting close to Danni's bedtime, so I say we all get some sleep and convene again after we're all refueled. Maybe you should wait here until the sun actually comes up. We should probably tell all the men on staff to stay inside during the night as well."

I saw something that looked a lot like raw pain flit across Holden's eyes before he blinked and sniffed. "If only it were that easy."

He pulled a cell phone out of his jacket pocket and handed it to Daniel. "Put your number in. I'll get in touch with you tomorrow."

"How do we know you won't hunt this thing without us?" I asked.

"I'm not looking for this thing because I want the accolades that come with killing it," Holden answered, "which I'm starting to suspect are what you're after. I'm hunting it because it needs to be destroyed, and I'm not so cock-sure of myself that I think I would have a better shot alone so if somebody can help me, I'm going to accept the help. I really don't care which one of us takes the thing out, but I hope we can all agree we should back each other up so someone can."

"Maybe I asked the question because I'm concerned you might do something reckless and get yourself killed," I shot back at him once I finished gawking. The nerve of the guy, insulting me as if I were some sort of attention junkie.

He simply raised his eyebrow as he took his phone back from Daniel, slid it into his jacket pocket, and stood. "The pontianak never kills twice in one night. I'll be safe going back to Carrie's, where I'll be staying until this is over. I'm not sure we want to cause a panic in the area, but Gruff should know not to have any men watching the front door at night while that thing is hoarding food."

"Hoarding dicks," Daniel muttered as if that needed to be clarified, his nose scrunched.

"Yeah," Holden said, nodding. "I'll tell him tomorrow, unless you beat me to it. Get some rest."

"We'll walk out with you," Daniel said, standing up. He pulled me along with him.

We walked Holden to his car, a black Impala, not the

same year as the one owned by my fictional boyfriend, Dean Winchester, but a newer model, which may have lacked the same level of badassery, but was still a nice ride. We said our goodbyes and waited until he'd taken off before getting into Daniel's truck.

"What was all that attitude about?" he asked me as we headed toward the cabin.

"What?"

"The attitude, Danni. We had no clue what killed Rob, then this guy comes along and just lays it out for us, and you're giving him shit."

"I wasn't giving him shit."

"Yes, you were. You're acting like this is a competition for who can kill the monster first and he totally called you out on it."

"I thought you were supposed to be my bodyguard," I reminded him.

"I am your bodyguard."

"Well, you didn't seem like much of one when you let Holden snap at me."

"I'm supposed to protect you from people who try to kill you, not guys who call you out on your pissy attitude," he said as he pulled the truck to a stop in the driveway next to Ginger's Mustang and cut the engine.

My mouth dropped open as I gawked at him. He simply stared back at me in complete boredom before sighing and stepping out of the truck.

I got out as he rounded the front of the truck and slammed the door closed. "Fuck you, Daniel!"

"As nice as that offer is, I think I'll pass," he said, stepping into my personal space.

I started to snap back at him, then registered what he'd said. Did he say it was a nice offer? Did he want to…? I practically felt the succubus side of me start stripping in anticipation, and knew I'd entered the danger zone. I turned to walk away before I gave in to what the demon side of me wanted, but Daniel grabbed my arm and pulled me back.

"You're not mad at me, Danni. You're upset with Rider. You can either man up and hash your shit out with him or suck it up, but you can't take your issues out on me or Holden." He released my arm and walked to the front of the cabin. He opened the door and stood there, waiting. "Bring your ass on in here and let's go to bed."

My stomach did a little flip. Lower parts of me may have had a little reaction too. Why'd he have to say *let's* go to bed? Why'd I have to leave Rider back in Louisville, knowing part of me was a horny little devil? Ugh.

I averted my eyes as I walked past him and made sure not to inhale his scent, afraid any little thing might awaken my succubus side even more. I just needed to go to sleep. My eyelids were already heavy thanks to the sun about to rise.

"About time," Ginger said from where she sat on the couch in front of the TV currently playing some old black and white horror movie. "I didn't want to go to sleep until you got back. What's up? Anyone else lose any genitals tonight?"

"No," I said as I passed behind her, headed for my room. "I'm exhausted. Daniel can fill you in on everything."

I hurried into my room and closed the door, knowing Ginger had to be more tired than me. As a hybrid, I could stay up easier in the daylight than she could as a full vampire, but even I struggled with staying awake as the sun first came up. Already, I heard her entering her own bedroom, skipping on the gossip to get to her bed before daylight zapped the last of her energy.

I kicked off my shoes and peeled off my jeans before crawling under the thick plaid comforter covering the bed I'd been sleeping in for the past few weeks. Alone.

I missed Rider. I missed falling asleep in his arms and waking up next to him, smelling his fresh rain scent before I even opened my eyes. As often as I'd complained about them, I missed his mental intrusions. I missed his voice speaking from inside my own head, missed his deep chuckle when I amused him. I missed knowing I was his.

There was a soft rap on my door and it opened. Daniel poked his head inside. "Good. I was afraid you'd be asleep already. We good?"

I smiled despite the sadness filling my heart, touched to know someone still cared to check on me. "We're good. I'm sorry. I've been in a mood."

He stood in the doorway, biting his lip for a moment, before speaking again. "She's no one."

"Who?"

"Whoever the woman is that Gruff said Rider was with. I know it's bothering you. She's no one."

I fought to keep my eyes open. "You know who she is?"

"No."

"Then how do you know she's no one? I left. Why wouldn't he replace me?"

"Because you don't replace diamonds with glass, and I don't need to know her to know that next to you, she's no one."

My heart fluttered a little as the power of the sun sealed my eyes closed and dragged me into a deep sleep, safe from where I could give in to the foolish desire to thank Daniel for his sweet words in a way I would be sure to regret later.

CHAPTER FIVE

I was in a dark room. Sensual music filled the air, wrapping around me, coaxing my hips into a gentle sway. Light flickered. Fire, I realized, recognizing the shadowy outline of torches along the walls. My nostrils flared as I caught a hint of sulfur wafting past my nose. Crap.

"Selander?" I called out, dread unfurling in my gut. The last time I'd gone to a dark place lit by fire in my dreams, it had been Selander Ryan's doing. As one of the men who'd sired me, we shared a connection. He could call me to any place of his choosing in my dreams, even after his death. He just really sucked like that.

A deep, throaty chuckle laced with a hint of growl rumbled through the room as a large, hulking shadow formed before me. It was far enough away I didn't feel in immediate danger of being snatched, but it was big enough to make my legs shake. It was far too big to be Selander Ryan.

"Not Selander," it said, its voice echoing off the walls and testing the strength of my bladder as my blood ran cold. Whoever it was, he sounded like a demonic James Earl Jones.

Yeah, it definitely wasn't Selander. Selander was a big

guy in normal terms. Six feet tall, broad-shouldered, and strong despite a general slimness. This dream intruder gave new definition to broad-shouldered and stood closer to eight feet tall. I couldn't make out features as he appeared solid black and smoky, but he did have a shape. I made out heavily muscled arms, a narrow waist, and a human form, even if the legs seemed to fade in and out of existence.

"Who are you?"

"The man of your dreams." He chuckled again, amused by his joke.

"I highly doubt that."

"Are you sure?" A tendril of shadowy smoke lashed out from the dark figure to slither between my legs. Dressed exactly as I'd been when I'd fallen asleep, the thin cotton of my underwear didn't protect me from the feather-light intimate stroking. I gasped and nearly fell to my knees, eliciting another deep chuckle from the man as he pulled the shadow tendril back into himself. "You spend a lot of time fighting half of what you are. Wouldn't it be easier to just give in to it and let yourself reap the rewards of your nature?"

"There are no rewards to my nature."

"Ah, Danni, you can lie to yourself, but not me. I see you. I smell you, the sweet aroma of fear and loathing, of desire and shame, rage and sorrow. You are a smorgasbord of delicious emotion I will very much enjoy devouring."

"What the hell are you?"

"Interesting word choice." The torchlight intensified as he threw his head back and laughed, a full-bodied guffaw that shook his massive shoulders. I made out a hint of blue tint to his skin before the torchlight died down and cloaked him in shadow once more. Again, I smelled sulfur.

"You're a demon."

"*You're* a demon," he replied. "A sex demon ashamed of her own nature. Oh, what fun I will have breaking you."

"Tough talk for a shadow," I said. "It's easy to screw with a person in their head, but why don't you step outside the dream world and try to mess with me then?"

I sensed him smile in the darkness as he folded his arms. "I don't have to. I don't have to do anything but whisper a little encouragement and watch you destroy yourself."

"You can try," I warned him, "but I'm stronger than I look."

"Oh, I know all about your strengths," he said, drifting closer. "And your weaknesses."

He shrank down to six feet and seemed to cast off the shadows as he stepped before me, his rainbow-colored hair shining in the flicker of firelight.

"You're not Daniel," I said, looking directly into gray eyes ringed in brown, so like his own. The silver-looking hoop I knew to really be imortium gleamed in his nostril as it flared.

"I can smell your body's reaction to me," he said in Daniel's voice. "We can do as we please here, Danni. No one ever has to know."

"You're not Daniel." I said the words as heat pooled between my thighs and I swayed toward him involuntarily, drawn to him like a magnet. His chest was bare, revealing the honey-colored treasure trail disappearing into jeans that would be so easy to unsnap and discard.

"You know I am." He tucked a piece of my hair behind my ear, his knuckles gently brushing against my face. His mouth curved in a smile as he stared into my eyes. "I don't know how I got here in this realm with you, but it's just us now. We can give in to our desire, Danni."

I shook my head even as my hands settled over his chest, feeling the hard pectoral muscles underneath. His heart rate picked up. I saw the vein in his neck bulge as blood pumped furiously through it, calling to me like a siren. My mouth watered as my fangs lowered from my gums. I angled my head to lick the skin covering that delicious pulse point.

"Danni!"

I whipped my head around to see Rider storming toward me, dressed all in black. Somehow, his blue eyes seemed even darker than his clothes as he glared beyond me.

"Didn't take you very long at all," he growled as he reached my side and grabbed Daniel by the throat.

"That's not Daniel!" I exclaimed, coming back to my senses. "Wait. You're not... This isn't real."

"It's as real as when my brother brought you to that room outside Hell," he snapped. "This time, he brought you a plaything. I knew you wanted to fuck him."

My mouth dropped open as my heart slammed against my ribcage. I looked between the two of them, noting the pure hatred in their eyes as they glared at each other.

"Kill me if you want," Daniel said, half choking out the words as Rider's hand squeezed tighter around the column of his throat. "It'll be worth it just knowing you know she wants me. She's always wanted me as much as I've always wanted her."

"Say goodbye to your boyfriend, Danni."

"Rider, no!" I grabbed his arm as panic set in. "This was a demonic trick. You can't kill Daniel!"

"You're right," Rider said, loosening his grip as he turned his fiery glare on me. "You're the one who betrayed me."

He flung his arm out, easily knocking my hands away, and reached into my chest to pull out my heart.

My breath caught in my throat along with a silent scream as I stared at my heart in his hand, and watched it beat as all the fear I'd felt the first time he'd done the same thing to me filled the hole it had left in my chest.

"Demon whore," Rider whispered... and crushed my heart.

I sat up in the bed, screaming. Pressure invaded my skull, and I immediately threw up my mental walls in reflex.

A heartbeat later, Daniel barreled through my door, his

eyes alert, seeming to search the entire room at once before settling on me where I sat in the bed, clutching the covers to my chest. "What is it?"

I looked around the room, realizing where I was as I struggled to shake off the chilling fear that had settled over me. "It was a dream."

"Fuck," he muttered as I heard more footsteps running toward my room. "Give me a fucking heart attack, why don't you?"

"What happened?" Angel poked her head around Daniel to look into the room.

"Danni had a nightmare," Daniel told her. "I thought we told you to hide if you ever heard the sound of major shit going down, not run toward the shit."

"Clearly, there is no major shit going down right now." Angel stuck her tongue out at Daniel and walked away, back to whatever she'd been doing before I scared the hell out of everyone. Well, everyone but Ginger. The sun was still up and Ginger was a heavy sleeper, especially when she stayed up all the way to the ass-crack of dawn.

"Sometimes I want to make that brat stand in the corner and think about her attitude," Daniel grumbled.

"I heard that," Angel called from the kitchenette.

"Go bake something!" he yelled back at her. "You could use the practice."

I heard a growl, and a moment later, Daniel ducked as a wooden spoon flew over his head. It hit the wall next to the window and clattered to the floor. He let out a sigh and looked at me. "We really should do something about that girl."

I didn't respond, still trying to shake off the nightmare, which it had to have been. Rider wouldn't have crushed my heart, and Daniel… "It was a nightmare, right? It didn't really happen. You and I …"

I heard my cell phone vibrate inside the pocket of my discarded jeans. I hadn't even bothered to plug it in to charge before getting into the bed. Daniel frowned at me as he moved across the room and retrieved it. His frown deepened as he looked at the screen. "It's Rider."

That explained the pressure I'd felt in my head the moment I'd awakened screaming. Damn, I knew I was scared, but not so terrified he'd felt it all the way in Louisville.

"Talk to him," Daniel ordered as he handed me the phone.

I took it and stared at Rider's name on the screen. No picture. Rider wasn't big on pictures.

"Talk to him unless you want him to come down here and kick everyone's ass before dragging you back to Louisville," Daniel said.

I huffed out a breath and thumbed the little phone icon before raising the phone to my ear. "Yeah?"

"What the hell's happening out there?" Rider's voice tumbled through the phone sharper than I'd expected, causing me to wince as I held the phone away from my ear.

"I'll give you some privacy," Daniel said, picking up the wooden spoon Angel had thrown at him before walking back out of my room, closing the door behind him.

"Danni!"

"I'm here," I said as I moved the phone back to my ear. "You don't have to yell. I'm part vampire, remember? Good hearing."

"Then why am I still waiting for an answer?"

"I don't know, maybe because you're giving me way too much attitude right now," I snapped as my eyes watered. I sniffed and fought back the tears. I wasn't about to start blubbering just because the first time Rider thought to reach out to me, it was to yell at me.

"I'm giving you too much attitude?" He scoffed. "I felt you, Danni. You were terrified, and you shut me out of your mind. Do you have any idea what goes through *my* mind when that happens?"

"I didn't know you cared so much."

He was silent for a moment, and I could sense him stewing through the phone. "You know better than that, Danni. You wanted space, so I gave it to you. I didn't ask for this separation."

My heart lurched. Separation sounded like divorce. Not that Rider and I were married, but we were together, although lately, with the distance, it didn't seem like it. "I asked for space, not complete silence."

"You requested a job that took you away from me, and you never checked in. The last time we spoke, you were upset about the way I handled things with you and your sister. I was giving you time, waiting for you to reach out when you were ready. When I felt your terror, I couldn't wait any longer. What happened?"

I closed my eyes and took a deep breath. "Nothing. I just had a nightmare."

I felt him pressing against the wall I'd put up, searching for an opening. "Let me in, Danni."

"It was just a bad dream," I said, knowing better than to give him access to my mind. What had happened in my dream hadn't been real, but the temptation I'd felt had been. I quickly shoved the thought down in case my wall gave out. If Rider had even an inkling that I'd desired Daniel for that fraction of a second, one man would end up dead at the other's hands.

"Was my brother there?"

"No," I answered, shivering as I recalled the shadow man. He'd seemed so real, but couldn't be. Selander Ryan could get into my dreams because he was an incubus, and my sire. We had an actual connection. I had no connection to whatever the man in my dream had been. "It was just a dream."

"Our kind isn't known for having just dreams."

"Yeah, well, last week I dreamed I was floating down a chocolate milk river on top of an Oreo cookie, so I don't know what to tell you."

He laughed softly. "Are you sure it was chocolate milk?

It might have just been the Ohio."

"True." I grinned. We had a disgusting river back home.

"You'll be able to eat all the human food you want eventually," he said, analyzing my dream, "but until then you have to stay on top of your diet. It's been a while since you drank from me. Nannette said you need to so we can keep our bond stronger than the one you have with Ryan."

"Are you coming here?" I perked up at the thought of seeing him, as did certain areas. Succubi were sexual creatures, and even though I was only half succubus, that side of me was hungry for more than blood. If I could take the edge off with Rider, I could quit feeling things I shouldn't feel around Daniel.

He was silent for a moment, and I knew before he spoke I wasn't going to be happy.

"I think it's time for you to come back home."

I took a deep breath in through my nose, willing myself to stay calm. Pissing him off wouldn't help matters at all. "Why?"

"This was supposed to be a simple security assignment, filling in until we got someone else in permanently. I have people I can put in those spots now."

"Put them somewhere else. This is my job. Daniel, Ginger, and I are doing fine here."

"Is that why someone was killed last night?" I heard him take a hard breath and knew he, too, was struggling not to let his temper show. "The job changed, Danni. I've spoken with Holden. There's a monster out there killing men. I sent you to break up fights, not hunt vampire ghosts."

"You sent me to play security. You never believed in me enough to put me in a real job."

"Danni."

"It would just kill you to believe in me, wouldn't it?"

"I do believe in you, but I also know…"

"You also know what?" I snapped as he trailed off.

"You haven't been part of this world that long. You have to work your way up to some things, but you're so headstrong and stubborn, and you don't listen when people are trying to protect you."

"Control me."

"*Protect* you."

"I don't need your protection. I need your faith!"

"I need your respect!" he snapped back. "If you want to work the big girl jobs, you need to act like one. That means following my orders and not fighting me. It means listening to others who know more than you so you don't put them or yourself in danger. It means acknowledging that you need more than luck and a decent right hook to come out of some fights alive. Shit, Danni, it hasn't even been half a year since you were turned. You don't even really know what the hell you are yet. I shouldn't be letting a hybrid out of my sight at all, but I let you leave the state. Maybe I believe in you *too* much."

I clenched my free hand into a fist and sucked my teeth, biting back the words I wanted to spill, words I knew would only piss him off, and have him coming to snatch me up in a heartbeat.

"I need you to recognize me as your boss if you want to work for me," he continued, his voice at its normal volume once more. "I sensed your terror from that nightmare, which tells me it wasn't just a simple dream. I've asked you what the dream was. I'm going to ask you one more time as your employer who needs to know what the hell is going on, and if my people are safe. What was the nightmare?"

"It was you!" I huffed out a breath. "It was you, all right? You pulled my heart out of my chest and this time you crushed it. You killed me."

Despite the distance, I felt his entire body go still. Silence stretched out as I chewed my lip, waiting for his response. When it finally came, it didn't come with the anger I'd expected.

"You just can't let that go, can you?" His voice was soft, tired.

"I'm trying to. That's why I'm here."

"I would never hurt you. You have to know that by now."

I thought I did. He'd killed his own brother to save my life. Well, he'd kind of killed his own brother. He'd assigned Daniel to watch over me despite not liking it at all, and he'd lost men in order to keep me safe, but I couldn't shake the image of my heart in his hand. This wasn't the first time I'd dreamed of him pulling my heart out of my chest. It was just the first time it had seemed real, not a memory, and the first time he'd actually crushed it.

"I can't deal with this right now," I said, pushing back the covers. "I know you think I'm not capable of this, but you sent me here on a job and it isn't finished."

"I'll put you on another job, Danni. I have others more suitable for this kind of work."

"Like your new employee you've been spending so much time with?" I snapped, standing up. "Send whoever you want, but don't get mad when I send them back to you broken. I'm doing this job. You might not think I have what it takes, but like you said, I'm stubborn. I'm hunting this monster down and killing it, and I'll go through anyone you try to replace me with. And I might not know exactly what I am yet, but I know *who* I am. I'm Danni Fucking Keller. I don't get replaced!"

I hung up, wishing I'd been talking on a landline instead of a cell phone so I'd have the satisfaction of slamming the phone down. Instead, I had to settle for a throaty bellow as I kicked my jeans across the room, tossed the phone on the bed, and gave my pillow some good, solid punches. The nerve of the man!

"Everything all right in there?" Daniel called from the living room.

"Leave me alone!"

"All righty then. Good chat."

I yanked open a dresser drawer and pulled out clean underclothes before snatching up a black T-shirt and dark jeans, then stormed into the bathroom. I'd taken the only bedroom with a private bath, leaving the other three to fight over the common one, although I was nice enough to share when necessary.

I expelled a string of rather creative curse words as I peeled out of my clothes and stepped into the shower. My skin grew red under the hot stream of water mixing with my angry tears as I continued to mutter curses. Anger soon turned into regret as I turned the curse words on myself. Damn me and my temper. After the way I'd ended that call, I didn't have to worry about Rider sending someone to replace me.

He was going to come and drag me back himself.

CHAPTER SIX

I entered the living area to find Angel icing a cake in the kitchenette and Daniel sitting at the table, working on a laptop. He looked up at me and grinned. "Feel better now that you've exorcised all those filthy words out of your system?"

"You heard me?" I plopped down on the sofa and put my feet up on the coffee table.

"Ireland heard you," Angel said, never taking her eyes off the mound of chocolate buttercream she spread across the top of what looked like a yellow cake. My mouth watered. Why'd it have to be one of the best cake and icing combinations ever? I couldn't wait to eat cake again without puking.

"I had no idea you were so creative," Daniel said. "I especially enjoyed your use of hobbit-fucking, rat-balled, shit-brained, son of a flea-infested, five-cent, donkey whore. I have no idea what any of that meant, but I liked it."

"I said hobbit-fucking?"

"You said hobbit-fucking."

"Wow. I don't know what any of that means either. I was a little peeved."

"Yeah, I kind of figured that." He chuckled. "I'm guessing you and Rider still have some issues to work out."

I heaved out a sigh. "He's going to come here and try to drag me back to Louisville. I pissed him off."

"Well, you inferred he fucks hobbits, so I can't say I'm surprised. You might have also inferred he has fleas and I think there was something in there about hoping his new friend, how did you put it… *sucks it all the way off and nails it to a dartboard?*"

"I didn't say any of that to him," I clarified as I rested my head on the back of the couch. "That was just me venting after I hung up on him. He talked to Holden and now he wants to send replacements for us."

"Correct me if I'm wrong, but this was never supposed to be a permanent job."

"He wants us off of this because of the attack."

"We're headed back to Louisville?" Ginger stepped out of the bathroom, freshly showered and dressed in ripped black jeans and a dark purple T-shirt, both of which fit her slender frame like a glove. Her hair was styled in its usual spiky fashion and her makeup was bold, complete with purple lipstick. "Daniel filled me in on the pontianak stuff. Somebody else is going to get all the fun of finding that thing?"

"Not if I can help it," I muttered as she walked over to the kitchenette and dipped her finger into the bowl of icing. "I told Rider I'll send any replacement he sends back to him, broken."

Ginger choked a little on the icing. "Oh boy."

"I'm guessing that didn't go over so well," Daniel commented.

"I hung up before he could reply, but you know what this means. He's going to come for me himself. I have to kill this pontianak before he gets here."

"*You* have to kill the pontianak? You have to be the one to do it? What exactly are you trying so hard to prove?"

"You wouldn't understand, Daniel. You're a badass, fire-breathing dragon. On your very first day working for him, Rider assigned you to guard me, and he's sent you on other jobs. Ginger gets jobs all the time. He sent you in solo to pick up his friend when they were facing a whole army of shifters. Everyone in the nest knows this. They don't question whether you can handle a job or not. Despite all your joking around, Rome respects you. No one messes with you two, but I am constantly getting tested." I felt my eyes burning and sniffed, willing the tears not to fall. "I'm a joke, and I'm tired of it."

"You're not a joke," Daniel said.

"Oh yeah? Then why is most of the nest wearing Danni the Teste Slayer T-shirts?"

"Hey, that title was given to you out of respect," Ginger said, placing her hands on her hips. "Those T-shirts are a commemoration of the moment you became a legend."

"To you," I said, not wanting to hurt her feelings. "To others, it's a gag. I'd rather be known for being someone who goes in and gets the job done because she's skilled and talented, not because she's gotten a few lucky shots in on testicles."

"Hey, The Rock has The People's Elbow, and you have the Sac Attack," Ginger said. "I don't see the issue."

"You do know Rome calls me Puff the Magic Dragon?" Daniel said. "We all have nicknames. Sometimes people give you nicknames and tease you because they like you. No one thinks you're a joke, Danni."

"No one thinks I'm a real member of the nest either. I'm Rider's pet." I wiped the wetness away from my eyes. "I'm his pampered, spoiled pet that he gave a cake job to just to appease. If he takes me off this job because the stakes have gotten higher, that just proves it. I just want to do this job, Daniel. I want to actually catch and take out a threat without rolling through garbage or doing something else to give everyone something to laugh about. I just want to prove to him that I'm just as capable as any of his other…" My voice broke, forcing me to take a moment to collect myself.

"Danni, are you afraid Rider's going to replace you on this job, or that he's going to replace *you*?" Ginger asked softly as she walked over to the couch and sat next to me.

I closed my eyes and focused on breathing until I calmed down enough to speak without falling apart. Once I was composed, I opened my eyes and sat up straight. "I just really need to do this."

Daniel shared a look with Ginger before he sighed, picked up the laptop, and carried it over to the coffee table. His spicy, masculine scent washed over me as he lowered himself onto the couch, his hip touching mine and sparking little fires inside me. I leaned into him a little before I realized what I was doing, my body acting on its own, and jerked back, muttering a curse.

"What now?" he asked, looking at me in confusion.

"Nothing," I said, shaking my head. I felt Ginger's gaze on me and turned to see her watching me with suspicious eyes.

"Well, I don't know that we can catch and destroy this thing before Rider gets here, but we can work this job with all we have until he does, and then see what happens. I've been researching."

"I didn't know you knew how to read," Ginger teased.

"Bite me, Ginger Spice." Daniel clicked a link and opened up a web article with a black-and-white image of a young woman in a white gown. Her long hair obscured her face, but the clawed fingers were enough to give her a monster-like appearance. "So, according to what I've found, these things are pretty common in folklore all over Southeast Asia. There are different variations to the lore, just like there are with vampires, witches, and shifters, but most of it says they actually rip out men's stomachs. Figures we'd get a version who likes to take something far more precious."

"What is it with men and their adoration of their penises?" Ginger asked.

"What is it with women and their excitement when they find clothes with pockets?" Daniel replied.

"It's hard finding women's clothes with pockets. Is it hard finding your wee wee?"

"Guys," I interrupted. "Can we stick to this case, please?"

Daniel narrowed his eyes at Ginger for a moment, then turned his attention back to his laptop screen. "It says they lurk in forests, watching. They're supposedly created when a woman dies while pregnant, giving birth, or after being victimized by a man. Some of the stories I found say they give off the scent of a frangipani flower, but start to smell like a rotting corpse when you're really close. I can't find anything about how they lure men, just mixed stories over whether they lure specific men to them or if they just kill any man who looks them in the eyes."

"Like Medusa?" I asked.

"I guess, but they don't kill as easily. I, for one, would rather go by way of being turned into stone than having my junk snatched off. It says men in Southeast Asia will avoid looking women in the eye lest they accidentally set their gaze on a pontianak and have their organs ripped out."

"Did you really just say lest?" Ginger asked.

Daniel flipped her off and scrolled down the web article he had pulled up on his laptop. "It's hard to say if the attacks are random, or if they go for specific men, men who resemble the fathers of the children they were carrying when they died, or while giving birth to, or the men who killed them."

"If it's the latter, that doesn't say anything good about Rob," I pointed out. "Do you think he may have lost a wife or girlfriend pregnant with his child?"

"I'm pretty sure he didn't have kids," Daniel answered, "and he was a good dude. I can't see him hurting a woman. We saw Rob look off and then walk in the direction he looked. I'm still searching to see if there's anything about how they might lure men."

"What about the flower thing?" Ginger suggested. "Maybe it's like a perfume. She releases the scent and that lures her victims to her."

"Love Potion Number Six-Six-Six," I murmured, and shuddered. "It makes sense, and could explain why it changes to a rotting corpse smell once you're really close to her."

"That actually does make sense," Daniel agreed.

"Hey, I have good ideas. Don't seem so surprised."

I patted Ginger's shoulder. "We know you do. Now we have to figure out if that's how Rob was lured, and if it was random or if this pontianak hunted for him specifically."

"I'm not finding anything definite here," Daniel grumbled. "Most of the sites read like fan pages. There is a crazy amount of women out there who think of this thing as some kind of superheroine."

"Well, of course they do," Ginger said. "Men treat women like objects and don't pay any consequences. Hell, how many young athletes have been caught in the act of raping girls and got off because prison would ruin their promising futures? No one cares about the young woman whose life was ruined, and that's in this country where our justice system is supposed to be the best. The pontianak is the heroine some women need. She's like Rosie the Riveter, but way more awesome. She's Wanda the Whacker."

"I'm not sure whacker is the word you want to use," I advised, getting a much different image in my head than Ginger was going for, "but I see your point."

"I kind of like this thing's style."

"You have issues," Daniel told her. "We're not letting a monster run loose, ripping off men's genitals."

"I know, I know. I'm just saying I appreciate the pizzazz. Anybody can cut a throat or shoot a gun, but tearing off a wiener really makes a statement."

Daniel shook his head and closed the laptop. "From all accounts, it appears these creatures only kill men, so Angel will be fine. We can all track this thing. Out of the four of us, you and Ginger are actually the best options we have to track it."

"Yes!" Ginger pumped her fist in the air.

"As long as you remember to kill it, and not ask for its autograph," Daniel told her.

"I'll try my best."

"You still need to stay inside with all the doors and windows locked," Daniel ordered Angel, who'd been sitting at the table, eating cake and listening in. "And call us immediately if you hear anything weird. Unless you want to hang out at Gruff's tonight."

"Nope. There's a *Blade* marathon on tonight, and I know the drill," she said before sliding a chunk of cake into her mouth.

Daniel fished his phone out of his pocket and looked at the screen. "We're supposed to meet Holden in about half an hour to go over how we're going to track this thing. I think you're about due for your live female blood requirement if you want to take care of that before we leave."

I looked at Angel. "I know. Maybe I'll get lucky and some of the chocolate will flavor her blood."

"Good luck with that," Ginger said. "It's blood, not breastmilk."

"Yeah, I know, but a girl can dream." I watched Angel eat and lived vicariously through her as she swallowed the dessert. My body may have only craved blood, but I was an emotional eater, and my emotions wanted cake, damn it.

And my nether regions wanted to start a bloody war, I realized as Daniel inadvertently brushed against me as he got up from the couch and I caught a whiff of warm-blooded male, sending a tingle straight to a place I should not be tingling.

Crap.

CHAPTER SEVEN

Daniel's my friend. I don't fornicate with my friends. I'm still with Rider. All fornication matters should be taken care of through Rider. But Rider's not here… I looked over at Daniel, taking in his profile as he drove the short distance to Gruff's. We could have walked, but never knew when we might have to go somewhere farther than we anticipated, and we really didn't want to risk leaving a vehicle with Angel. She'd wanted to travel, and being stuck in either a cabin or Gruff's Bar and Grille in the small town of They Don't Even Have A Mall Here, West Virginia, wasn't what she'd had in mind. It wasn't wise to tempt her with a way out.

I quickly realized I should have ridden with Ginger in her Mustang. Ginger didn't tempt my succubus side. Ginger was full of estrogen. My succubus side craved testosterone. I no longer suffered from the Bloom so I could control my urges, but that didn't mean they weren't there, strong as hell and steadily chipping away at my willpower. But Ginger had an errand to run right when I needed her, which figures. The universe was really giving me the blues.

"You all right?"

"I am A-Okay, *mi amigo*. Why?"

The corners of his mouth curved upward and his brow wrinkled a little as he stared at me a moment and shook his head before returning his focus to his driving. "You're kind of rocking a little bit, and you just called me *mi amigo*."

"It means my friend." I forced myself to sit still and look out my window, away from the enticing view of Daniel's chiseled jawline… or chiseled other goodness I knew was hidden under his black Metallica T-shirt. "You are my friend, aren't you?"

"That I am."

"Okie dokie then. Friends are great. Friends are the best."

"Glad we got that settled," he said as he pulled into a space in Gruff's lot, cut the engine, and turned toward me. "Is there anything you want to tell me?"

Oh crap. Had I drunk from him often enough that our bond had strengthened to the point he could read my thoughts? Or were my emotions so out of control I'd been broadcasting my thoughts? "Am I leaking?"

His eyes widened a moment before he frowned and looked down at my lap. "I hope not."

"I mean telepathically."

His frown deepened as he met my gaze.

"Am I broadcasting my thoughts?"

"Nooo…" He said slowly as he shook his head. "If you were, what would those thoughts be?"

I opened my mouth, but no words came out. One of his golden eyebrows arched quizzically as he awaited my response. It was a sexy arch. *Oh, good fugging grief.* I rolled my eyes, and he leaned forward to sniff me.

"What are you doing?" I jerked back, practically ramming my back against the door, as the mouth-watering scent rolling off his skin as he dipped his head to smell me made me all warm and melty.

"Sniffing for weed."

"Hardy har." I reached behind me, struggled with the door handle for a moment, but finally got it open. "Drugs have no effect on vampires," I told him as I slid out of the truck.

"Well, something's made you go goofy." He got out and joined me. "You're acting weirder than usual."

"Usual? I'm not weird."

"Sweetheart, you're a great big bucket of the what-the-fuckness." He grinned and ruffled my hair. "But it just makes you even more loveable."

"You love me?"

His eyes warmed as he held my gaze, causing a fluttering in my stomach, and he closed the distance between us, reaching for my hand as he opened his mouth to speak…

Squealing tires broke the moment, and we both turned our heads to watch Ginger's Mustang come to a screeching stop in the parking space next to Daniel's Ford F-150.

"We all love you," Daniel said, shoving his hands into his jeans pockets. He shook his head as Ginger emerged from her vehicle, a black shopping bag with no logo or lettering in hand. "That's a good way to damage your tires."

"What do you think money's for if not getting shit fixed?" she asked as she walked to us, grabbed my hand, and practically dragged me to the front door.

"What—"

"We need to have a girl moment before we meet what's-his-face and figure out the game plan for tonight. It won't take long."

"Like a girl on girl moment?" Daniel asked, following us into the building. Despite the previous night's incident, Gruff's appeared to be business as usual inside, although I noticed far more men than women customers. There were no children at all.

"Please," Ginger said. "I'm not that lucky."

He laughed. "The sun just went down. This thing will probably hunt soon."

"Get started without us," Ginger told him as we saw

Holden sitting at the bar, his hands wrapped around a mug of steaming coffee. "This is important, but we'll be super-quick."

"What's going on?" I asked as Daniel split away from us to join Holden, and Ginger continued to pull me toward the back. "What's in the bag?"

"Hopefully, the thing that will save us from mass bloodshed," she told me as she led me to the back hall, turned, and took me to Gruff's office. We'd already seen him behind the bar and knew it was empty inside. "I've noticed how you've been looking at Daniel."

"What do you mean?" I feigned innocence as she closed the door and led me to Gruff's desk.

"Danni, please. I thought you were about to take a bite out of the man's ass when he stood up from the couch earlier, and you keep squirming around him like your lady parts are itching to get at him."

I scrunched my nose. "Ew."

"Ew, yourself. You're the one in heat."

"No, I am not. Rider and Seta worked that spell, so I don't go into heat anymore."

"You know what I mean." She reached into the bag. "Even if you don't go into full-blown succubus heat, you still have the sexual appetite and Rider isn't here to feed it, so your wicked little hormones have latched onto Daniel. I don't need to tell you why that's a bad idea, so I got you this."

Ginger removed her hand from the bag and planted a ridiculously huge penis on top of Gruff's desk. My mouth dropped open as I looked at the monstrosity. "What in the … Why?"

"I knew you were too vanilla to have ever used one of these before you hooked up with Rider, and word around the bar is that once you and Rider started doing the nasty, you two never came up for air long enough for you to have use for one of these, but now you do." She smiled at me, seeming to await my gratitude. "It's a vibrator, hon.

It's a penis without the stupid man attached."

"That is not a penis."

Ginger looked at the freakishly large pornographic monument, then looked at me. "I might be a lesbian, but even I know what one of those things looks like. Surely, you *have* looked at Rider's thing before he shoves it up in—"

I raised my hand, shushing her. "It's green."

"Yeah, that's because it glows in the dark. They had one that was flesh-colored, but honestly, those things are so ugly I don't know how you straight women can do it."

"And you thought this was better-looking?" I studied the toy. It was lumpy, unrealistically large in both length and girth, and made of a rubbery material I suspected was supposed to feel like flesh. I would continue to assume because there was no way I was touching that thing. It looked a little like a booger, and I was terrified of what would happen if the little button I saw on the side was pressed. "I appreciate the thought, but even if that would work, there's no way I could even get that …" I shuddered, unable to complete the sentence.

"Oh, sure you can. Give it a whirl and I'll just stand outside and guard the door."

"That's a definite no. Even if I did use that thing, it wouldn't help my situation. Succubi are sex demons, but it's the testosterone we really crave. That thing won't do anything for me, except maybe frustrate me even more."

Ginger placed her hands on her narrow hips and studied the enormous dildo. "What if you rub it on Daniel? Get his man scent on it, like how breastfeeding mothers rub bottles on them to get the baby to drink from them when they can't nurse?"

"Are you crazy? I'm not rubbing a giant green penis on Daniel!" I threw my hands up in the air. "And that wouldn't work anyway. This is insane. I just have to keep it together until Rider gets here."

"You damn sure better, because if you bang one out

with Daniel, forget about the awkwardness after; Rider will skin that poor dragon and serve him up to the rest of the nest for snacks."

The office door opened and Gruff barreled through, Daniel and Holden right behind him. All three froze as their eyes locked onto the oversized penis atop the desk.

You didn't lock the door? I asked Ginger, using our telepathic link.

Oops. She quickly tossed the black bag behind her, and it landed on the other side of a file cabinet, out of view. Neither of us moved, both frozen in place.

Gruff recovered first, and lumbered past us and around the back of the desk, where he lowered his sizeable self into the desk chair. He sat back and stared at the vibrator as Daniel and Holden neared us. Daniel stopped at my side, staring straight ahead at the cause of my mortification as Holden stood between him and Ginger, looking at the floor.

"Daniel," Gruff said, still eying the big green monster. "Is Max sneaking those funny mushrooms into the meat sauce again or am I really seeing Godzilla's pecker on my desk?"

Daniel's mouth twitched a moment before he could respond. "No, you're really seeing it."

Gruff nodded. "I see. Do we want to know why Godzilla's pecker is on my desk?"

Again, Daniel took a moment to gather himself. "It's probably best we ignore it."

"Yeah, that ain't possible," Gruff muttered, still not having lifted his gaze from the damn thing. "Would either of you ladies like to claim ownership of this pecker?"

Daniel's entire body shook with barely contained laughter as Ginger and I both declined. My face flushed with so much heat, I expected my head to explode in a giant ball of flames at any moment.

"Sadly, this isn't even the weirdest shit I've found in here," the burly werewolf said as he leaned over and picked up the small wastebasket by his desk. He grabbed a stapler and used it to knock the vibrator into the wastebasket. Unfortunately, he used too much force, and the rubbery vibrator hit the bottom of the empty wastebasket, turned on, and bounced right back out.

"Shit! It's attacking!" Gruff ducked as the violently vibrating—and now glowing—sex toy flew over his head, then jumped from his seat just in time for it to hit the wall behind him and bounce back, hitting him in the rear. "Sonofawhore! It's trying to have its way with me!"

Daniel completely lost it, doubling over in laughter as the green penile missile zip-zapped around the room, bouncing off walls and other hard surfaces as Gruff and Ginger tried to catch it without getting pegged by the thing. I just stood there with my mouth hanging open, wishing the floor would open up and swallow me.

Finally, Holden snaked his arm out as the thing flew overhead and caught it. With an unbelievably straight face, he found the button, switched it off, and carefully placed it inside the wastebasket before returning the receptacle to its spot and helping Gruff and Ginger straighten the items that had been knocked over along Gruff's desk and filing cabinets.

Daniel straightened as he got his laughter under control, wiped the tears running down his red cheeks with the backs of his hands, and wrapped an arm around me before he planted a kiss on my temple and whispered in my ear, "Don't think you're not telling me the story behind this."

"I'd rather die," I muttered, earning a snort of laughter out of him. On the bright side, my utter humiliation seemed to have dampened my libido. Daniel's close proximity, even the press of his lips against my temple, were bearable, at least for the moment.

"The video," Holden prompted as Gruff fell back into his chair and sighed heavily.

"What? Oh, right." Gruff shook his shaggy head as he

pulled his chair in closer to the desk and tapped away at his keyboard. "I take back what I said before. This was definitely the weirdest shit I've ever had happen in this office. Here it is."

Holden and Daniel edged around the desk to view the monitor, their eyes narrowed on the screen as they focused. Part of me wanted to join in, but the other part of me was still too embarrassed to move and thought if I just stayed quiet and still enough, they'd forget I even existed, which I wouldn't mind at all.

"Right there." Holden pointed. "You can barely see it, but he took a quick sniff."

"Yeah," Daniel agreed. "I see it this time. I didn't even think to look for that the first time I watched this."

"So I was right about the Mad Whacker luring men with the scent of franky panky flowers?" Ginger asked, lighting up.

"Frangipani flowers," Daniel corrected her. "It looks like it, and it's a pontianak, not a Mad Whacker."

"Thanks, Gruff." Holden stepped back around the desk. "As you know, the online lore about these things is varied, and not many have seen pontianaks and lived to tell about it, which makes it even harder to get good intel on them, but knowing how they actually lure men is a good thing. The more we know, the more we can protect others from them."

"So, what are you gonna do?" Gruff asked. "Should all the men wear nose plugs?"

"It hunts in rural wooded areas," Holden answered. "Any man foolish enough to be outside at night during a pontianak hunting season should definitely plug his nose."

"So… that would be you?" Ginger asked.

Holden folded his arms and lowered his gaze to the floor, twisting his lips as he thought. "No," he said a moment later, and looked up, taking the time to make eye contact with each of us before he spoke again. "If the pontianak lures men to her, that tells us she isn't going to just walk up to her target. No, she lures the prey to where she is. We'd be wasting time hunting her without a way for her to lure us."

My stomach took a dip as I realized Holden's intention. "You're going to use yourself as bait."

He nodded. "Having two women on board can make this work. We'll go out in pairs. Daniel and I are the bait. You girls are the hunters."

"I'm with Danni," Ginger and Daniel said at the exact same time.

"Uh, guys, we need these pairs to be male and female," Holden said. "Ginger, you'll go with me."

"No offense, Holden, but I'm sticking with Danni."

"I don't think you understand the issue here," the detective said. "This thing hunts men. We need an actual guy to be bait, and a woman to take the thing out."

"Go with Holden," Daniel told Ginger. "I got Danni."

"No." Ginger threw a worried look my way, knowing how I'd been struggling with my hormones. "I don't think that's a good idea."

"Why the hell not?" Daniel looked between the two of us, suspicion in his eyes before he turned his gaze to the wastebasket.

"Who did you hunt these things with before?" I asked Holden, remembering the pain I'd seen in his eyes earlier when discussing his previous hunt for one in Malaysia. "You've done this bait thing before, haven't you?"

I saw the pain flicker again as he held me in his gaze, his jaw tight.

"Look, you've probably noticed Ginger and Daniel are a bit protective of me. Well, I'm protective of them too. They're my family and I don't just dangle part of my family out as bait if I'm not one hundred percent certain I'm getting him back whole. Tell us how you hunted these things before and what happened, and don't leave anything out, or we're not leaving this office."

I think I'm sufficiently embarrassed enough not to be horny for anyone for a while, I telepathically told Ginger now that I'd moved Daniel's suspicion off me and redirected his attention to Holden's past hunting experience.

I still don't think you should be alone with him or any other man until you get some from Rider or figure out how to make that vibrator work for your special needs, she shot back.

I recoiled a bit at the thought of the gross vibrator, which of course Daniel noticed, but fortunately Holden started talking before he could say anything.

"I had a friend with me when I hunted the pontianak in Malaysia," he said. "Jeff and I practically grew up together, and he was one of very few humans I trusted with my secret. No, I didn't use him as bait, but the pontianak got to him and killed him anyway. We split apart, not very far, but out of each other's eyesight."

He sat on the edge of Gruff's desk and lowered his gaze to the floor, seeming to stare past it into another place and time. "He didn't even scream. I wasn't that far away, but I had no clue my friend was being killed while I was walking a circle, searching for the damn thing. Then I found him, too late to save him, and the monster was gone."

"That's why this is personal for you," I said.

He nodded. "Danni, I'm not suicidal, and I wouldn't willingly risk Daniel's life either, but these things are hard to find. They're quick, and they don't make a lot of noise. Jeff and I screwed up hunting one by ourselves. We were its prey, and we didn't stand a chance. I could have just as easily been the one to die that night."

"You could easily die tonight," I told him. "You said it yourself. They're quick, and they don't make a lot of noise."

"Vampires are quick too." He looked at me and Ginger. "We know Rob smelled something and left his post. Was he in a trance? Maybe. Maybe the thing just got him so quick he didn't have time to fight back. Was he specifically chosen or just in the wrong place at the wrong time? We don't know that either. What we do know is that thing is hunting in those woods and it doesn't attack women. You and Ginger are more than just women. You're paranormal women with speed and the ability to self-heal. Daniel and I really don't have much choice but to be bait, but the two of you can make sure we don't die."

"Four against one are better odds than two against one," I pointed out.

"We'll cover more ground if we separate."

"Like you and Jeff did?" I ignored the flash of guilt that passed over his face and continued. "Ginger and I are fast, and we do self-heal, but we aren't invincible, and we don't know what all this thing can do. It doesn't leave tracks, kills in a blink, and is supposed to be some sort of vampire ghost. No matter how fast we are, we can't grab something if it isn't corporeal, so you're still taking a hell of a risk putting your lives in our hands. We go out as a group, and that's final."

He stared at me for a while, his gaze boring into my own, but I didn't blink or back down.

"Fine," he finally said. "Gruff, you should inform your staff and customers to be careful, but try not to cause a panic or encourage any looky-loos. Stick with the excuse the humans are giving for last night's attack. Wild animal on the loose."

"You know this is West Virginia," Gruff said. "Tell some yahoos there's a dangerous animal on the loose around here and they're sure to run off into the woods with their shotguns, trying to get that thing's head to stuff and mount over their fireplace."

"Tell them it likes to eat dicks," Daniel suggested. "That should hold them off."

Holden glanced at his watch. "Let's head out to the woods and hope we get lucky. What weapons do you girls have?"

Ginger and I both pulled switchblades out of our pockets.

"That it?" he asked.

"Well, we have fangs and claws, super strength, and speed," I replied.

"And a pet dragon who breathes fire," Ginger added.

Daniel gave her the finger, and she blew him a kiss.

"Follow me." Holden led the way out of the office, Ginger on his heels.

Daniel walked alongside me as I followed them out. "So, are you going to tell me what exactly you two were—"

"Never."

He chuckled. "I'll get it out of you eventually."

"Keep trying and the pontianak won't be the only woman you have to worry about."

"I always knew you'd come after my junk one day, teste slayer."

Taking his statement an entirely different way than he'd intended, I stumbled. Daniel grabbed me about my waist before I could face-plant into the floorboards, and righted me, but not before drawing the attention of Ginger and Holden, who both looked back and eyed me curiously.

"Everything all right?" the werewolf asked.

"Yep, all good. I'm just a little clumsy."

Holden shook his head and continued on, clearly wondering if a klutzy vampire was a good idea for this mission. Ginger also shook her head and sighed, and I didn't need to telepathically converse with her to know she worried I was going to go completely hulked-out horny while in the woods with Daniel. I was worried about it myself as the heat from his hands warmed not only the part of my body they touched, but far more sensitive areas as well. So much for humiliation killing off my lust, I thought as I maneuvered out of his hold. "I'm good now."

Daniel watched me curiously, but said nothing as we continued out of the building, into the parking lot where we congregated by Holden's Impala. It might not have been the same year as Dean Winchester's Baby, but his trunk did hold a small arsenal.

Holden looked around to make sure no humans lurked about, then handed Ginger and me sheaths that went around our thighs, and a blade apiece to slide into them. These blades were sharper and much deadlier looking than our switchblades.

"If you can cut the pontianak, cut her, but try to get her heart so she can't go back into ghost form and disappear," Holden instructed. "Daniel, your fire and your dragon form are your weapons. If you see her, shift and take her out."

"The fact that I could start a huge wildfire aside, shifting into my dragon form right on the spot could take out a lot of trees."

"Then do your best to direct your fire at the pontianak, and any trees you crush when you shift will grow back. Will your dick?"

"Possibly," he answered, "but I'm not crazy about finding that out."

"Me either," Holden answered as he grabbed a pretty badass machete and closed the trunk, "so let's go kill this evil bitch before she can get her claws in us."

CHAPTER EIGHT

We entered the woods, taking the same route Rob had taken to his death. His blood still stained the foliage.

"Will she hunt the exact same location two nights in a row?" I asked.

"She'll hunt these woods," Holden answered, "but she could be searching for prey in any part of it."

"Or luring men from areas around it," Ginger said, looking over at me. "Maybe we should have gotten a larger group together, covered more ground, but in fours like Danni suggested."

"I asked Gruff," Daniel said. "He can't spare the manpower. We were already sent here because he was running short on security, but he's got Angie on the door, watching the lot and the edge of the woods in case this thing tries to lure a man from there."

"And some other pack women who live in the area have offered to keep an eye out on the edges of woods by them. They'll call me if they see anything," Holden advised.

"I thought all the werewolves in the area worked for Gruff," I said.

"Not all, and when I say pack, I use the term loosely.

Gruff's pack is a pack of rogues. They left the packs they were born or brought into, not wanting the true pack life. Still, they come together when necessary to defend themselves against hunters and the like."

"And the pontianak is a threat against the pack because it can take out the males of the pack?"

"Anything that draws attention to the area and possibly the paranormals living in it is a threat."

We reached the location where Rob had been killed, and carefully avoided stepping in the circle of dried blood that had drawn bugs.

"Maybe this should be cleaned up," Ginger suggested.

"You're welcome to," Daniel told her, earning a raised middle finger. "I guess there's not much of a crime scene cleanup crew out in this area."

"The locals think this was an animal kill, and it happened in the woods," Holden said. "They'll just leave the blood for nature to clean up itself eventually." He looked around the area. "I spoke with the sheriff today. They've put out a warning about an animal attack and small towns like this spread gossip like wildfire, so people should stay out of the woods. Plus, Gruff is warning people in case any hunter types think about taking the supposed wild beast out themselves. If we're the only ones in the woods, that should make us far more appealing to the pontianak."

"What about the police?" I asked. "Sure, they were awful at investigating Rob's death, but if they think there's an animal out here dangerous enough to kill Rob, why aren't they out here hunting it?"

"Because I offered my services as an expert marksman."

"More of that bullshitting you were telling us about?"

He grinned. "Nah, I am pretty damn good with a gun, but I won't be using one with this monster. It would just be a waste of bullets."

"So, are we just going to stand here all night and hope

she finds us?" Ginger asked, already looking bored.

"Pontianaks are violent monsters, but they don't lack intelligence," Holden answered. "They're smart enough to have gone centuries undetected by most, so I don't expect this one to just walk up to us while we're standing around, clearly waiting for her to pop up. My original plan was for us to split up and each take a side of the woods, casually walking from the outer edge to the center, then back out again."

"But we're not doing that," I said, folding my arms, "because splitting up would be stupid and dangerous."

"Just being out here is dangerous," Holden said, "and I prefer daring to the term stupid, but yes, I have altered my plan because of your thoughts on the matter. We'll walk together, but we still need to try to appear casual, and it would help if we spaced out just a little. Daniel and I won't leave your line of sight, but we should walk far enough ahead of you that the Pontianak doesn't see us clustered together and go elsewhere looking for easier prey."

Daniel moved closer to me. "Are you absolutely sure this thing wouldn't attack a woman?"

"There has never been a report of a woman being attacked by one," Holden said. "Hell, there's a story of one grabbing a man while he was in the act of forcing himself on a woman in Indonesia. Killed the man and never touched the woman. It *rescued* the woman."

"Man, I really dig this chick," Ginger said.

"Tell me again why we've brought her," Holden said, watching her warily.

"Because we need all the womanpower we can get and when it comes down to it, Ginger won't let a monster take our tongues or dicks," Daniel told him. "If she did, Rider would fire her."

"Yeah, I've heard how he fires people. I don't imagine many risk that." Holden assessed Ginger while she gave him a cute finger wave, shook his head, and started walking. "Keep us in sight, girls, but give us a little room."

Daniel waited a while to let Holden get a bit of distance between them, then followed along, about three feet to his right and ten feet behind. When he got about ten feet ahead of us, he looked back and gave us a look that said we'd better move our asses.

"He knows we're supposed to be protecting him, and not the other way around, right?" Ginger asked with a grin as we started to follow. We didn't bother distancing ourselves from each other since, supposedly, the pontianak wasn't interested in us. We only had to keep our distance from the guys, which we carefully did, making sure we didn't lose our visual of them.

"He's still my personal bodyguard no matter what other job he's working, just like you are, however I'm pretty sure Rider is harder on him than you when it comes to my protection."

Ginger snorted. "Please. If anything happens to you while we're here, Rider will have both our heads in the breakroom. Actually, I take that back. There'd be nothing left of us to put on display if you were killed on our watch."

Daniel glanced back at us and I did a little twirl with my finger, gesturing for him to turn his head back around and watch where he was going. "I don't think he's grasped the concept of appearing as if he isn't directly with us."

"You know, I sense a clear lack of his belief in my ability to keep you safe," Ginger said, and shook her head in feigned disappointment. We continued on in silence for a few minutes, glancing around, searching for a lurking vampire ghost, before she spoke again, her voice very low. "So, how are you doing now? Still got that dragon fever?"

"I do not have dragon fever," I practically growled, careful to keep my voice low. I was pretty sure Daniel's hearing was right up there with vampire hearing. "Daniel and I are good friends. I don't think of him in that way."

Ginger simply raised her eyebrows.

"Fine, I may have noticed he's an attractive man," I

conceded, "and lately I might be a little…"

"Hot in the crotch?"

I rolled my eyes. "For lack of a classier way to put it, yes."

"Hey… Are you saying I'm not classy? I'm classy. I got class out the ass."

I laughed, unable to hold it in. "I see that. I'm half succubus, which is like being half…"

"Super-Ho?"

I gave her my best bitch face. "You really enjoy finishing my sentences in the absolute worst ways, don't you?"

"Hey, I'm just helping you out when you seem to struggle with words. You're welcome."

"I'm not thanking you for calling me a ho," I told her.

"Half, and I said Super-Ho. That's better than just a regular raggedy ol' ho. You get a cape and super ho powers like, you know… the ability to scale tall penises, super turbo thrusting, and, of course, your venom."

I glared at her as she batted her eyelashes innocently. I felt my traitorous lips twitching, and the next thing I knew, I was laughing. "I can't stand you."

"You love me. If your succubus half wasn't repulsed by estrogen, I could totally get you to cross over to my team. The Super-Ho thing is a compliment, by the way. I mean, hello, you can totally weaponise sex. That's pretty badass. You should embrace your power."

I sighed as I thought over what she said. It was kind of empowering if I thought of my curse as a weapon, but the reality was it didn't make me feel powerful at all. It made me feel helpless. "I don't want to use sex as a weapon. I just want to be a regular woman in a regular relationship."

"Well, sweet-cheeks, I hate to be the one to break it to you, but neither you nor Rider are what you would call regular people. Hell, you're fighting against your very biology by being in a monogamous relationship with him. That's why succubi generally travel in harems and serve a master incubus. It's easier for them to just do what their bodies want."

A chill ran through me, Ginger's words reminding me of whatever the monster was in my dream had said. "So that's it? Because I got bit by an incubus, I have to be a single woman constantly on the prowl for new lovers? I can't be with the man I love?"

"No, I'm just saying that it's never going to be easy for the two of you, especially since you have a pretty broad stubborn streak and he's just as bullheaded. For example, why are we here, Danni?" She spread her arms out, indicating the woods. "You are head over heels in love with that man, and he had no problem giving you everything you needed, yet you chose to take a job putting you in another state, knowing damn well that you would need sex."

"I didn't know how soon I'd need it," I muttered, "and I needed some time away to think, and to just be my own person."

"Well, now you're here, and you're thinking about dragon dick," she scolded me. "Hopefully you're right about Rider being on his way here because if you go much longer, judging by the rate you're drooling over Daniel, you'll go from thinking about dragon dick to full-out community dick, and then it's going to be really fun making sure you don't get some poor idiot killed because I can tell you something about your boyfriend. Rider Knight isn't the super-friendly sharing type. He isn't going to be happy if you get freaky with some other guy. He's going to kill the guy, and he's going to kill me for letting it happen. And what is this be your own person crap? What does that even mean?"

Are you two watching out for this thing? Daniel spoke in our minds. *Every time I peek back there, you two are running your mouths.*

Maybe if you'd quit watching us and actually appear as if you were alone, the Mad Whacker would show herself, Ginger replied.

We got this.

We've got you covered, I responded, my tone much nicer. *Ginger and I having a conversation makes it look less like we're watching you. That's what we want, remember?*

I felt him sigh. *All right, then. Just be careful and stay alert. If you get hurt or I lose my junk, I'm not going to be happy.*

Wow. You actually mentioned us getting hurt before you mentioned your junk? We're so honored, I replied playfully.

You should be. My junk is extremely valuable.

Ginger rolled her eyes as Daniel eased out of our minds, cutting off the telepathic communication.

"Well?" she prompted after a moment of silence other than the crunching of leaves under our feet. "Explain this finding yourself thing."

I started to answer her, then realized I had no clue how to. Hell, I didn't even know what I wanted, so if I couldn't tell myself what it was I wanted, how could I tell anyone else? All I knew was I wasn't happy, and the more I thought about it, the more I confused and irritated myself. "Geez. No wonder I get told I'm a spoiled brat so often."

"Who says you're a spoiled brat?" Ginger asked, her brow furrowed, "and where did that come from?"

"Rider and Nannette, mostly," I answered. "They have a point."

"How so?"

Again, I couldn't really put the answer into words. "I don't know. I just know I bitch and complain a lot. For so many years of my life, I felt like I wasn't good enough. I never got the guy, I never compared to my perfect sister. My mother could never just say she loved me. She just pointed out my flaws. Rider is easily the sexiest man I have ever laid eyes on, and there's no arguing he's extremely powerful."

"None," Ginger agreed.

"You'd think being known as Rider's woman would make me so happy I wouldn't care about anything else. I actually got the incredibly hot and powerful guy. Not my sister. Me. I'd never have to work again if I didn't want to. Rider would buy me a house, a car, anything I want. My very existence has brought so much trouble to him, and he could have easily let Selander Ryan have me, but he's done everything in his power to keep me safe, even when I've made it so hard for him just by being my usual self." I huffed out a heavy sigh. "I don't know why the hell I'm here, Ginger. I don't know why I can't get past what Rider did to save my ass yet again. I don't know why I can't just be happy being his girlfriend and letting him take care of me and keep me safe. I don't know why I need him to see I can take care of myself. Am I just being ridiculous?"

"No," Ginger answered quickly, clearly not having to put much thought into her response. "You've shown you want to work, to earn everything you have, and honey, there is no shame at all in that. You clearly love the man or you wouldn't be fighting your succubus half so hard, and any idiot can see the man loves you. Any idiot can also see he's extremely overprotective. Hell, whether you're in love or not, you have to breathe sometimes, right?"

"You don't think I'm being a spoiled brat about everything?"

"If you were a spoiled brat you'd be back in Louisville on a shopping spree with Rider's money, and for what it's worth, that removing your heart thing would have freaked the hell out of me too. Yes, he saved your life by doing that, but I'm not going to tell you to get over it because I've never been through something like that and couldn't possibly imagine how badly you wanted to piss yourself in that moment." She slung her arm over my shoulders. "And there's nothing wrong with wanting Rider to see you as a strong fighter who can handle herself. I understand why he wants to ensure your safety, but I also understand why just lounging around his place and being protected twenty-four hours a day, seven days a week, would be a pain. There's nothing wrong with wanting to be more than just the big, bad master vampire's girlfriend, to actually be known for who you actually… Oh. Now I get that being your own person thing."

I started to smile, but my stomach rolled and I grimaced as a nasty smell wafted past my nose. I quickly scanned the trees as I willed the contents of my stomach to stay down.

Ginger picked up the smell too and stepped away from me, scanning the trees as well. "That's not fucky pucky," she said.

"What?"

"Franky panky, fuddy puddy…" She snapped her fingers as she thought. "Foggy poggy."

"Frangipani?"

"That. That's not that."

I looked ahead and noted Daniel and Holden had both just stopped and were turning, searching the trees.

"Doesn't the pontianak smell like a rotting corpse when she's really close?" Ginger asked.

We shared a panicked look before running toward the men. We didn't see a vampire ghost, but if she was close, we didn't want to give her the space to attack and flee. Holden motioned for us to stay back, but we ignored him, not stopping until we reached Daniel.

Holden glared at us. "You're supposed to wait for her and rush in when she shows."

"Well, her funky-ass smell is already here," I snapped. "Isn't that the smell she gives off right before she attacks? She's a ghost, remember? How do we know she's not right here and we just can't see her?"

Daniel covered his groin with his hands. "Shit. I'm not feeling so good about this anymore."

"Me neither," I said, blade in hand. Ginger had grabbed hers as well and I could tell by the way her body was coiled to strike, she was as anxious and ready to lunge at anything that suddenly appeared as I was.

Holden kept a six-foot distance from us, not crazy enough to go off too far, but still dangling himself out there as bait. If the pontianak was as quick as we thought she was, she still stood a good chance at getting him and escaping.

"Um, guys," Ginger said, "I think maybe we've been hunting the wrong kind of flesh eater."

We followed her gaze to see shapes emerge from deep in the trees. They limped and shuffled as they drew closer, bringing their sickening smell with them.

I blinked a few times, sure I was seeing things. "Am I seeing what I think I'm seeing?"

"Zombies," Holden said, his voice full of disbelief. "Actual zombies, which technically don't exist."

"Well, I see at least a dozen of them that would argue with you about that," Daniel said, removing his hands from his groin to grab his dagger. "So one of those nasty bastards took Rob's dick?"

"I guess he was one of those men whose brains was in his dick," Ginger said before laughing, and quickly slapped her hand over her mouth before saying a muffled, "I know, I know. That was bad. I'm going to Hell for that one. Sorry, Rob."

"No, a pontianak killed Rob. That was a pontianak attack," Holden said.

"So explain the zombies," Daniel told him.

"I can't." Holden shook his head as he took his own blade out. "Zombies aren't real. I don't know what the hell is going on in this town, but I think we're missing a big piece of the puzzle."

"Maybe this is a prank," I suggested, stepping forward. "Those could be costumes."

We watched the horde as it continued to draw closer to us, bringing its sickening smell along with it. I counted sixteen people approaching, male and female. They didn't walk very well, and were covered in dirt, blood, and other grime I didn't even want to try to identify. Their mouths snapped open and shut and they groaned as they got closer to us. They reached toward us with skeletal, filthy arms. A few eyeballs dangled like pendulums beneath the sockets. One man was missing an ear, a woman had what looked like intestines hanging out of the bottom of her nearly shredded blouse, and some of those hands reaching for us were missing a few fingers.

"Hell of a makeup job," Ginger said. "I don't think anyone in Moonlight has that kind of artistic talent, or could produce that smell."

"Smells almost as bad as burned assholes," Daniel murmured, effectively drawing our attention away from the freakish monsters approaching as we all turned and stared at him, our mouths agape.

"What?" he said, noticing the way we stared at him with our noses scrunched in disgust. "I was in Hell. You smell some bad shit in Hell."

"Hold on." Ginger raised her index finger. "You were in Hell? Like, actual *Hell*?"

Daniel's eyes widened as he looked over her head. "Talk later, kill now!"

I turned to see the zombies had suddenly picked up speed and were headed right for us, hungry mouths snapping viciously.

CHAPTER NINE

We all reacted at once, rushing toward the zombies, walking dead, undead, or whatever they were so we could meet them head-on rather than stand there and get attacked. Daniel shoved me behind him and took the lead, pissing me off. He and Rider didn't seem to get along sometimes, but there were moments they acted just like each other. Those were usually moments that really ticked me off.

With sixteen zombies and only four of us, it didn't really matter who was in the front. There were plenty of monsters to go around, and as soon as Daniel grabbed one, I took the opportunity to take my frustration out on a decaying man wearing a soiled uniform shirt. I couldn't make out the name of the business, but the name stitched over the pocket of the dead man's shirt was Stu.

"Sorry, Stu," I said as I dropped to the ground and spun with my leg out, sweeping the feet out from under Stu and two other nasties close to him. I immediately plunged my blade into Stu's forehead, slicing right through to his brain. I got a quick flash of what I imagined Stu had looked like at some point in time before becoming a nasty, rotting corpse, and hoped I hadn't just offed a decent guy, but what could I do? He was kind of dead already and I was pretty sure he wanted to eat me.

I pulled the blade out of his skull just as the second man I'd taken to the ground with my leg sweep latched on to my arm with his cold, wet, and utterly disgusting fingers. Of course it was my right arm, and I was right-handed so that was the hand holding the dagger I needed to stab him with.

I bit out a curse, got to my feet as quickly as I could while the bastard's rotting mouth opened, preparing to bite down on my arm, and I swung around, bringing the whole dead dude with me. Thanks to my vampiric strength, I was able to lift him off the ground effortlessly before slamming him into a tree, breaking his hold and crushing his skull in the process.

I took a quick look around as I caught my breath, and saw Daniel doing his shimmering in and out of existence thing as he quickly moved about, dispatching the dead to their second and hopefully final resting place. Holden was holding his own, showing real prowess with his blade, and Ginger was doing pretty decently, even though she had a lot of gunk on her.

I barely had time to feel sorry for her before I felt claws dig into my hair. I reached back purely by reflex, grabbed a pair of shoulders, and flipped my assailant over my head, nearly screaming as what felt like a thick, cold river splashed down my back, neck, and head. I stood there, gasping as the woman's body hit the ground, the cold, slimy substance oozing down my back, through my clothing… and then the rage set in.

I stomped on the woman's face, my boot sinking into the depths of her skull as I let out a guttural growl. Someone clamped their bony dead hand on my arm. I shrugged the hand off, turned, and thrust my index and middle fingers into the stinking sonofabitch's eye sockets before I called upon all my vampiric strength and yanked hard enough to snap his neck bones and tear through his rotten skin, detaching his head from the rest of his putrid body, and then I used that head to take out another zombie.

I growled, roared, kicked, punched, and stabbed anything that got close to me, and when it was all over, the four of us stood over a heap of broken bones, spilled guts, and other atrocities I hoped I would somehow eventually find a way to forget, and I still had my fingers shoved inside a dead man's eye sockets.

Holden and Daniel had some blood and filth on their T-shirts, and on their blades, but were otherwise not so bad off. Ginger's clothes were a mess, and I imagined I looked like Stephen King's *Carrie* after she'd had the pig blood dumped on her at the prom. The three of them were staring at me, and Daniel was grinning.

"What?" I snapped.

The corners of his mouth twitched. "Nothing, just, uh, noticed you took out a couple of dead fuckers with another dead fucker. Kind of badass, kind of crazy as hell. Completely Danni."

He laughed, and I tossed the head at him.

"Hey!" He dodged, but the head hit his arm, and he flung it away. "Don't be throwing dead fuckers at people. That's nasty as hell. What's the matter with you? Shit, he's still chomping!"

We all looked at the head where it had landed on the ground and saw it chomping at Daniel. Holden walked over to it, crouched down, and put a blade in its brain.

A chunk of something red and squishy dropped from my head and landed on the ground with a plop. I shuddered, wondering how much more gunk was on me, and hoped no one would tell me.

"I still say a pontianak attack fits Rob's death," Holden said, "but something bigger and stranger than just that is happening here. Pontianaks shouldn't be in America, and zombies just don't exist outside of Hollywood. This doesn't make sense.

"I don't think we're going to make much sense out of anything while we're cold, wet, and covered in shit that smells like infected ass," Daniel told him. "You can come back to our cabin with us. We all definitely need to clean up, especially the girls, and then maybe once we're clean and dry, we can figure something out."

Holden rose, flicked the gunk off his blade before sliding it into its sheath, and looked around. His eyes said it all, and despite how disgusting I felt, my heart went out to the guy. "Honestly, Holden, if a pontianak was out here, I don't think she'd want your stuff anyway. It now smells like the ass-end of something that crawled up something else's ass and died."

Daniel and Ginger laughed. Holden's mouth twitched. He didn't laugh, but I did get a grin out of him. He heaved out a sigh and slowly nodded.

"Let's go," Ginger said, heading in the direction of Gruff's, where we'd left the vehicles. "I think I got some viscera in my cleavage. I'm riding back to the cabin with you guys."

"You're riding in the back," Daniel told her as he and I started to follow, Holden taking up the rear.

"I'm not that messy," she said.

"The hell you aren't, and if you weren't, you'd take your own car back."

Ginger didn't turn around, but raised her middle finger in the air. "You're messy too."

"Just my shirt, and that's easily rectified," Daniel commented as he grabbed the ends of his T-shirt and pulled it over his head, the cool night air not that big of a deal to a hot-blooded dragon shifter.

I'm not sure whether she heard the rustle of fabric, realized by his words what he was going to do, or heard my sharp intake of breath, but Ginger slammed into me just as Daniel's shirt cleared his body and my fingertips were half an inch away from his hard abs and that honey-colored trail I found myself desperately wanting to follow.

I stumbled back as Daniel's head whipped around, nearly ran into Holden, but with Ginger's help, managed not to fall.

"Danni and I should walk in the back," Ginger quickly said as she kept a firm grip on my forearm. "Just in case the pontianak is out here. You two walk ahead so we can keep an eye on you. Now."

Daniel blinked a few times, shook his head, and walked on. Holden directed a curious look my way, dropped his gaze to Ginger's tight hold on my arm, frowned, but passed us without a word.

"That was close," I whispered.

"You better appreciate me," Ginger whispered back, "because I don't know what the hell is all over you, but now I have my hand wrapped around it."

I looked her over, noting the blood and guts coating her clothes, boots, and skin. "You're not so pristine yourself."

"I'd stick my tongue out at you right now, but I'm terrified I might taste something."

I laughed a little, then I noticed Holden look back at us, wondered what the man must think of us after the scene he'd just witnessed and the even worse scene in Gruff's office, and the laughter grew until tears streamed down my face, and Ginger joined in.

Daniel glanced back at us, shook his head once more, and turned, continuing to wipe his skin clean with the unsoiled parts of his T-shirt as we continued on to Gruff's.

Once we'd reached the lot, Daniel grabbed a clean T-shirt from his truck to put on, thankfully covering his impressive chest with dark cotton baring an image of Inigo Montoya.

"You know the drill," he said to me as he pointed to the back of his truck.

I rolled my eyes but climbed into the truck bed as he got in the cab and started the engine. Ginger followed me and we both took a seat on the hard bed, our backs against the outside of the cab, our filth-covered heads resting against the glass. Ha! Let Daniel clean that, I thought, although I really couldn't blame him for making us sit in the back like stinky dogs who'd just waded out of a swamp.

Ginger huffed out a breath as the truck moved and looked over at her Mustang. "I hate that the jackass got to put me in the back. He's probably loving this."

"It's not so bad," I told her, "and don't take it offensively. This isn't the first time he's made me ride in the back. At least I'm not covered in actual shit this time."

Ginger looked over at me and sniffed. "Don't be so sure."

I raised my heavily soiled arm to my face and sniffed. "Yeah, you might be right. I really wanted to work a job without getting covered in gunk or pulverizing a testicle."

"Well, you've been halfway successful so far."

"Yep, but what will tomorrow bring?" I asked as we continued to the cabin, Holden following us in his Impala. Silently, I wondered where I'd even be tomorrow, and hoped I at least had time to clean the gunk off me before Rider showed up, took one look at me, and hauled me back to Louisville.

The ride to the cabin was short and uneventful. Ginger and I jumped out of the truck bed the moment Daniel parked and hurried into the cabin. Ginger, I knew, wanted to reach the main shower before Daniel could, and I wanted to reach my shower before anyone got any ideas about using it. We both removed our boots outside the door, and entered the cabin to find Angel lounging on the couch, watching one of her movie marathons. She took one look at us, scrunched her face up, gagged, and ran to her bedroom, muttering about the smell of shit and armpits.

Not needing any further clarification that we were beyond disgusting, Ginger and I parted ways to scrub ourselves clean.

I didn't bother to grab clothes, figuring anything I touched would immediately become unwearable. I walked directly into the bathroom, kicking the door closed with the bottom of my foot, the underside of my sock being the only clean part of me, then peeled off my clothes and discarded them in the wastebasket before removing the bag and tying it in a tight knot. I'm sure the clothes could have been salvaged, but as long as I knew the innards of the walking dead had splashed all over them, I couldn't wear them so into the trash they went.

I stepped into the shower, slid the frosted-glass door closed, and turned the water on full-blast, turning it up as hot as I could stand, and stood there watching red and brown gunk slither down the drain. I did this for several minutes, letting the water knock most of the gunk off me as I tried not to cry, suddenly feeling a little like a failure. Sure, I'd helped kill a bunch of monsters, and Ginger had gotten messy too, but I, of course, had come out the nastiest. Typical Danni, I thought. My one saving grace was that Rider hadn't yet seen me covered in filth, but he always heard the stories. Everyone heard the stories. I was sure he'd be arriving, and he'd hear the zombie story too. While hearing about it, he'd hear that we'd gone out looking for a pontianak and hadn't found it.

I'd wanted so badly to track and kill the monster. Yes, I'd killed more than just one monster, but I agreed with Holden. Something very odd was going on in Moonlight. Zombies didn't kill Rob. The ones we took on hadn't been going for groins or tongues, and I couldn't imagine a zombie taking two pieces of Rob and letting him go. He would have had to kill it to get away, and we'd have found the body, or at least parts of it. And then there was the obvious problem. Zombies weren't real.

I grabbed a rag and a bar of soap and worked up the biggest lather in creation before I worked the suds over my body, making sure to get every nook and cranny. Then came the hair. I used at least half a bottle of shampoo, scrubbing it deep into my scalp, rinsing and repeating until I didn't see a speck of discoloration in the water going down the drain, then I conditioned it, rinsed, and just stood there, my face to the water, letting its heat and the steam it filled the space with take me away for a moment.

My thoughts drifted to the last time I'd shared a shower with Rider and my legs grew weak, to the point I had to brace myself with my hand against the wall. Images from that time spent with him flashed through my mind and suddenly the fact he would be arriving to take me back didn't seem as bad, not as long as he took me in a completely different way first… but what if he hadn't been able to leave immediately? What if I had to go another night without him, another night of aching for him? Daniel's image appeared in my mind. I saw him taking off his shirt, saw his muscles ripple under his flesh. I felt pressure in my gums as my fangs threatened to drop at the thought of sinking into that flesh.

"Daniel's my friend," I said, needing to say the words out loud to knock the idea of doing anything with him out of my sex-crazed skull. Yes, Daniel was incredibly good-looking, and he oozed charm the same way Rider oozed power, but he was my buddy, my pal. I couldn't, and wouldn't, let my damned succubus hormones ruin what we had.

There's another option…

I whirled around, sure someone had spoken to me, but I was alone with only my thoughts and the hot water raining down around me. Still, I'd heard the words whether they'd come from my own conscience or not.

Holden wasn't a bad-looking guy. He was tall, fit, and had a nice smile, warm eyes, and an air of mystery, maybe a hint of tortured soul. Even better, he wasn't close to any of us. If there was anyone in the area I could pull into the shower with me and…

"What the hell?" I twisted the shower knobs, turning the water off, and grabbed a towel.

I wrapped the towel around me, stepped out, and forcefully used another towel to dry my hair, my anger with myself causing me to rub my hair much harder than necessary. Fortunately, vampires were built pretty solid all the way down to their hair follicles and fingernails. Otherwise, I might have rubbed all my hair out. Once my hair was reasonably dry, I balled the towel up and used it to wipe away the steam coating the bathroom mirror. I gripped the sink and glared at my reflection in the mirror.

You are not one of Selander Ryan's sex slaves, I thought to myself. *You are a hybrid. You are part succubus, part vampire, but you are always you. Danni Keller. Danni Keller is stronger than her demons.*

The porcelain under my hands seemed to groan, and I loosened my grip, sighing in defeat. I could give myself the ultimate pep talk, but my body still ached. How was I going to make it another night without doing something I would regret the rest of my life?

Suddenly, the air shifted. My knees went weak again as a familiar tingle started in my core and spread out to more intimate places, my body's reaction to the awareness it was going to get what it desired. I breathed out a sigh of relief, and braced myself for the drama I sensed just beyond my door, because I felt his anger just as well as I felt his proximity.

I took a deep breath, walked the few steps across the bathroom, and opened the door to find my sire standing in my bedroom, facing the door, waiting for me. He wore a silky black button-down shirt with the sleeves uncuffed and rolled up to expose his forearms, black pants and shoes, and his blue-black hair was in its usual style, gathered into a ponytail at the nape of his neck. A few strands had slipped free and fell over his face, accentuating the sharp planes. If the muscular arms folded over his chest didn't clue me in to his mood, the way his sapphire blue eyes had darkened to the point they almost appeared black and slightly glowed with the golden color of his power as they bore into mine would have.

"You hung up on me," he said in the dark and eerily calm tone he used when truly angered. "Don't ever fucking do that again."

My temper rose. This was the problem Rider and I had. He thought he could tell me what to do because he was my sire, my master, and I didn't like that. I did, however, like the way his angry eyes warmed as they traveled down from my eyes to the towel that I'd knotted over my breasts. The heat in them warmed my blood, and I found myself before him.

"I'll do whatever the fuck I please," I growled, ripping open his shirt. I shoved him backward onto the bed, climbed on top of him, and let my fangs drop. "Starting with you."

CHAPTER TEN

We moved in a blur of hastily discarded clothes, biting, clawing, thrusting, kissing, licking, and drinking. One moment I was on top of him, wrapped in a towel, the next my towel was nowhere to be found, his shirt was shredded, his pants around his ankles and my back was against the wall on the complete other side of the room as he thrust in and out of me, his fangs raking down my throat.

"I'm supposed to be punishing you," he growled.

"Punish me harder," I whispered in his ear before sucking the lobe between my teeth.

"Fuck," he gasped, before thrusting inside me hard enough to knock the framed art off the wall. I heard something else break, but didn't care as I felt the buildup of what I knew was going to be an explosive, desperately needed orgasm. It built and built, and built… and then I heard a scream. I realized it was me as I seemed to leave my body and travel to another plane of existence, where the very atmosphere was complete euphoria, but then I tumbled back down.

I needed to go back to that place.

I found myself on top of Rider again, his back on the

hardwood floor, my nails deep in his shoulders as I moved faster and faster, trying to get back to that euphoric plane. Then we were rolling, slamming into things. I heard things crack and shatter, heard Rider's whispered words, growled curses, and gasps as we alternated positions, fighting for dominance. I tasted copper and salt as my mouth found blood and sweat, each taste fueling the passion I felt for this man who frustrated me more than any other, but I couldn't get enough of.

I felt the buildup, the release, the fall, the buildup, the release, the fall, over and over until finally I reached that euphoric plane and the comedown was a light float back to earth instead of a freefall. I lifted my mouth from Rider's neck, swallowed the mouthful of blood I'd taken, and discovered myself on top of him in the bed where we'd first started, both of us glistening with sweat, chests heaving, bodies still joined together as they had been for hours, judging by the time I saw on the alarm clock on the nightstand.

The lamp on the other nightstand had fallen over and smashed. The walls were bare, the art on the floor, the glass in the frames shattered, the dresser had been moved several inches from where it should have been, Rider's pants hung over the headboard, having been taken off at some point I couldn't remember, and pieces of his shirt could be found all over the room.

"Hello," Rider said.

I looked down at him and felt myself frown. "What?"

He grinned. "I said hello. People usually greet each other with a hello, but I'm not really complaining about this welcome."

"You wanted a hello?" My blood warmed as I remembered the greeting I'd received after stepping out of the bathroom. "Maybe you would have gotten one if you hadn't started off cursing at me and giving me an ord—"

He sat up, quickly shifting my weight so I sat easier in his lap, and pressed his index finger against my lips. "The last time I spoke to you before that moment, you had one hell of an attitude. Also, I was worried about you and you hung up on me. That angered me."

"I wouldn't have said the things I said or hung up on you if you hadn't angered *me*, if you'd quit trying to control me."

"Protect you," he said before letting out a tired sigh. He gently ran his thumb over my bottom lip as his mouth curved slightly upward. "I think we both know the only way I could truly control you would be to use my power as your sire to force your will, and I hope you know I love you too much, smart mouth and all, to ever make you my slave."

I lowered my eyes, the recent lustful feelings for Daniel, and even Holden, filling me with guilt. "I know you want to keep me safe. I just need you to believe that I can keep myself safe too."

"Mmhmm," he murmured, then wrapped his arms around me, holding me in a snug cocoon. "It seems you were in need of something else too. I'm not so vain as to think this impressive display of erotic athleticism happened because you were so overjoyed to see me. How long?"

Shit. I forced myself to meet his gaze before he suspected more than I was afraid he already did. "Not long."

He narrowed his eyes. "There was venom in your bite, Danni. You won't go through the Bloom anymore, but you still have to feed your succubus side."

"I know," I said, a little irritation slipping through, although I wasn't irritated with him. I couldn't hold it against him that he knew me so well. No, the irritation was all self-inflicted.

"You didn't come to me."

I closed my eyes against the pain in my chest, the guilt I felt hearing the sliver of heartbreak in his voice that I knew he'd tried not to let slip. It took every ounce of emotional strength I had to make sure my eyes weren't wet when I opened them again. "I would have. I knew you were coming to me. The minute I hung up on you, I knew you'd come here to drag me back."

He winced as if I'd struck him, but it was so quick I would have missed it had I blinked. He loosened his hold on me and rested back against the pillows, raising his arms to fold underneath his head. "I'm not dragging you back."

"What?"

"I'm not dragging you back," he repeated, staring up at the ceiling.

I slid off of his lap to lie next to him, supporting my weight on my elbow as I leaned over him, resting my palm over his heart. "Why?"

He lowered his gaze from the ceiling to look into my eyes. "Do you want me to?"

"No. I want to stay and complete this job, but I thought for sure you were going to make me go back."

"The thought crossed my mind," he admitted. "Several times, in fact."

"What changed?"

"Your brother-in-law's body was found. Your sister's hasn't been, of course, but your mother has been to my bar several times looking for her, and has sent the police. Fortunately, Aaron Grissom has been assigned to Kevin White's homicide and your sister's missing persons case. He's running interference, but your mother has the tenacity of a pit bull."

"Don't I know it," I muttered, groaning silently inside my heart. I knew my mother would eventually discover my sister missing, and I'd have to deal with her, but Shana's new husband being found dead was going to make dealing with her even more problematic. "Where did they find him?"

"You don't want to know, babe."

I grimaced as my stomach turned. Never in a million years would I have ever believed my sister to be the type of woman to marry a man, then seduce another man into killing him, even after she'd been turned into a vampire, but she'd confessed the truth to me herself.

"How is Shana doing?"

"She's exactly the same as you last saw her, and she will stay that way."

I took a moment to absorb that. My sister was pretty much a vegetable, a comatose vessel used to keep me from going through the Bloom. It was hard not to feel bad about that, even if she had tried to kill me. Of course, she'd been turned, and as Rider had tried to warn me, she was a bad turn. It should have never happened, but I'd forced his hand, guilted him into doing what he knew would blow up in our faces.

"Does Aaron know where Shana really is?"

"He knows she's not dead, but he doesn't know all the details. With her husband found dead, he can pretend to look for her and, after a suitable amount of time, convince your mother she's dead. Especially since he's also supposedly looking for you."

"I'm a missing person again?" I sighed. It was the second time since I'd been turned that my mother had declared my sister and I abducted and blamed Rider. "How have you not been arrested?"

"Deceit, persuasion, and a touch of magic," he said, and he probably meant it literally. He had powerful witches and who-knew-what-else in his pocket. If he wanted to be president, he'd probably just have to place a call and it would happen without him even having to run a campaign.

"I'm surprised you don't want me to come back and deal with her."

"You said you needed time to deal with everything that happened with Shana. I figure coming back to deal with your mother isn't going to be conducive to that. She was told we'd had an argument after her last visit to my bar and I haven't seen you since. I will buy you as much time as you need." He ran his index finger down my cheek. "I'd rather you be elsewhere than here chasing monsters, but I spoke to Holden and Daniel while you were in the shower. I know Holden thought you were after a pontianak and wanted to go off in twos to lure it. You refused to do it, and made sure you went out as a group, which was safer. It was a smart decision to avoid unnecessary risks."

I lowered my gaze, knowing part of that decision had been based on the fact I needed Ginger with me in case I tried to seduce one of the men.

"You can stay and finish this job, but I will keep tabs on you, and my reports won't be coming from just Ginger and Daniel, but others whose loyalty to me you haven't tampered with." I met his gaze again, picking up on the anger slipping back into his tone. His eyes darkened. "And if you hang up on me again, you'd better just pack your things and start praying for mercy because I will come back, and there won't be enough succubus venom in the world to help you seduce me out of my fury or stop me from *dragging* you back. Do you understand?"

I bit my lip and nodded.

"You will not take any unnecessary risks. Say it."

I forced down the reply I wanted to say straight from my gut as he went back into his controlling mode, and repeated, "I will not take unnecessary risks."

"And if your succubus side gets hungry for more than blood and violence..."

"I'll tell you."

He studied me, and I got the feeling he was weighing my words for honesty.

"I'll tell you, Rider. I didn't break up with you, you know, and I'm not out here looking to hook up with random men."

"Good to know. One wonders when their woman leaves and can't be bothered to communicate with them."

I glared at him as I remembered part of the reason our last call had gotten so volatile. "You know, you could have reached out to me at any time instead of checking up on me through Daniel and Ginger as if I were a child who needed watching, but I guess you were too busy having fun."

"You think I've been having fun since you left?"

I sat up and wrapped the sheet around me. "That's the way I heard it."

"I have no idea what you're talking about." He sat up and leaned toward me. "On that call, you mentioned a new employee. You were so busy flying off the handle on your rant, I didn't think much about it. What exactly do you think I've been doing while you've been gone? I thought you'd grown less jealous since you started working with Nannette."

"I'm not jealous," I replied, my voice even, and I actually meant it. I was angry, and hurt, but for the first time I could remember I wasn't wondering if he found someone prettier or sexier than me, and wanting to lick my wounds because I thought I wasn't good enough. I was just angry that if he had been fooling around with someone, he'd gone behind my back. Yes, I knew that might be a little hypocritical coming from me with my recent lustful thoughts about Daniel and Holden, but I was part succubus and fighting the demon side of myself. And I hadn't done anything except *think* about other men. "Gruff called you, and Tony said you were out with a woman. If you're seeing other women, I think I have a right to know that."

"Tony said I was out with another woman?" His tone dripped with incredulity. "He actually said I was out with a woman? What were his words?"

"I don't know. It wasn't my call, and it's not like he wouldn't cover for you if I'd been the one to call."

"He wouldn't have covered for me because there's nothing to cover. I have some new employees and some are female. I haven't slept with any of them, at any point in existence. I don't know what Tony told Gruff, but I assure you it was misconstrued."

I thought about that and supposed it could be true. It

did seem a little odd that Tony would just say Rider was out with some woman if there'd been anything sexual going on. Rider's people respected his privacy, even if it was out of fear of what he'd do to them if they revealed his secrets, and Tony wasn't a blabber anyway.

Rider muttered under his breath and grabbed his pants from the headboard. "Not that I didn't enjoy the last couple of hours, but I'll need to get back to The Midnight Rider soon, and I still need to go over some things with Daniel and Holden, and introduce you to Lana."

"Wh... what?" I shook my head, not sure what part of what he'd just said to start with, especially since I was pretty sure he'd just said the name of the woman Gruff had been told he was out with.

"I have to get back soon." He stood, pants in hand, and picked up a scrap of his shirt that had been twisted up in the bedsheets. He shook his head and tossed it aside. "That wasn't a cheap shirt. I'll have to borrow one of yours, or Daniel's."

"No!" I blurted, the thought of him borrowing a shirt from Daniel because I'd destroyed his sending heat straight to my cheeks, then I remembered all we'd done, and all the noise those actions had produced, and the heat spread. "Oh man. Everyone had to have heard us."

"Pretty sure everyone here knows we have sex, and they won't say anything unless they want to never be able to say another thing the rest of their lives."

"Take one of my shirts. I'm sure I have a loose T-shirt that will fit you."

He eyed me suspiciously, and I saw his jaw tic. "Any particular reason why you're so bothered by me taking a shirt from Daniel?"

"Hey, if you want a T-shirt that has The Goonies or He-Man on it, go for it." I stood, still wrapped in the bedsheet, and walked over to my dresser to grab a T-shirt for him.

"You have a point," he conceded, walking over to get

the shirt, not concerned by his nudity. That was Rider. I, on the other hand, could never do the just-walking-around-freely-with-all-my-stuff-jiggling thing. Of course, Rider didn't jiggle. Rider was all hard muscle and sinew. Next to him, I felt like the Pillsbury Doughpire.

"Tony told Gruff you were out with a woman whose name started with L, by the way." I handed him the shirt. Actually, I might have shoved it into his chest. "Who is Lana, and why is she here?"

"I brought a few people to help you." He placed his index finger over my mouth as I opened it to say something he definitely wouldn't have liked. "I'm going to forget your threat to break anyone I send to replace you, and I suggest you forget it too. I'm not replacing you. I've brought you help, not because I don't believe in you, but because it sounds like none of you know what you're really dealing with yet. Lana is good muscle to have around, and Christian is very knowledgeable."

"You brought Christian?" I asked as he removed his finger to take the shirt.

"Yes."

"I thought he was in danger. That's why you had Daniel retrieve him and we watched him until you sent Rihanna to transport him and Jadyn to The Midnight Rider."

"He was in danger, but the threat has been neutralized."

I frowned, remembering what Daniel had told me. "Daniel said a small army was after him."

"Daniel saw a portion of the army after him. We took out the rest."

"You took out a whole army?"

"A lot has happened since you left. There have been losses. None you were close to," he quickly said, apparently picking up on the sudden fear that gripped me. "Look, if I was out with Lana when Gruff called Tony, I was out with her, Rome, and whoever else. There's been a lot going on, and it's all been bloody."

I immediately imagined Rider in the middle of a supernatural battle and felt my heart race. "I hope you've been taking your own advice about not taking unnecessary risks."

He angled his head sideways and studied me. "Does this concern mean you've forgiven me for what I had to do to work the spell?"

The image of him in battle was replaced by the memory of him removing my heart, and just like that, the storm of emotions was back.

"Shit," he muttered, picking up on my sudden change in mood, then let out a mirthless laugh as he moved toward the bathroom. "The real shit of this is I could easily have the memory of that moment removed, but I'm not doing that. I would never do that, and *I would never fucking hurt you.*" He stopped at the bathroom door, facing me. "Sometimes you have to make choices you don't want to make, sometimes you have to do things you don't want to do, to save those you love, and sometimes you keep things from them in order to protect them. I'm sorry I didn't tell you beforehand. I honestly didn't think you'd think me capable of killing you. I sure as hell didn't think you'd still think that to the point of having nightmares."

He stormed away into the shower, leaving me to consider his words. I didn't doubt that he could have the memory of my heart in his hand erased. Rihanna was a powerful witch, and he'd used her before to clean up the gruesome scene I'd made of my former boss's death. No doubt it would be costly to erase a memory, but he had money. In fact, I highly suspected I only knew the tip of the iceberg when it came to Rider's income sources. However, he also had honor.

The man could erase my mind of every negative thought toward him. He could turn me into a living puppet if he wanted, but he wouldn't. Despite the darkness inside him, Rider was a good man… so why the hell couldn't I just get over what he'd done?

I walked to the bathroom and leaned against the doorjamb, watching him as he showered. The lines of his face were tense, even his muscles seemed taut with anger. He didn't take any of it out on me though. He let it simmer rather than hurt me, and I knew I frustrated him as badly as he frustrated me, yet I also knew no matter what, he'd be there when and if I needed him.

"Are you going to just stare at me or join me?"

My body reacted instantly, my traitorous body that didn't give a damn whether my mind needed some time to sort things out.

"Ah, hell," I muttered as I joined him in the shower. I told myself that after the close calls I'd had around Daniel and Holden, I might as well get what my succubus side needed while I could. My mind would have plenty of time to try to figure things out after Rider went back to The Midnight Rider, including the real reason he wasn't dragging me back with him. My gut told me my mother and the investigation into Shana's disappearance wasn't the real reason.

Rider was still keeping something from me.

CHAPTER ELEVEN

"So, what's the deal with Christian anyway?" I asked as I laced up my shoes and watched Rider slather on the specially made lotion he provided his nest with. Regular human sunblock just didn't cut it with us.

"What do you want to know?" he asked, setting the bottle of lotion on the top of the dresser he'd moved back into place for me before pulling on the black T-shirt I'd given him. It was loose on me, but fit him like a wetsuit.

"Daniel said he had a flaming sword that he pulled out of nowhere, and it disappeared right back into nowhere when he was finished using it," I told him as I stood from the bed and smoothed my light gray T-shirt. I wasn't sure if we'd even attempt going back out before dawn, but I was dressed for it, just in case. "What kind of being has the ability to do that? We know he's a vampire, but I drank from him and his blood was unlike anything I've ever had before."

Rider's eyes narrowed on me.

"I thought Nannette would have told you I drank from him. I told her when I reported in to her."

"I know you drank from him. Daniel reported it to me right after, and the effect of it. Christian is older than even

I am, and he was more than just a vampire, which was why you reacted the way you did to his blood."

"Was? You say that like whatever he was, he isn't anymore."

"Christian was an angel, but he gave it up to be with the woman he loves. He's human now. Well, I highly suspect he's a guardian, but we're still figuring things out."

I stood still, blinking, trying to choose one thread to follow out of the many Rider had just dangled in front of me. Angels were real? Christian had been an angel? I drank an angel's blood without disintegrating? No wonder it felt as if the darkness inside me had fled from him. How did he give up being an angel? What was a guardian? Who did Christian love? Jadyn? It had to be Jadyn. Daniel had said he was sure the vampire, err… angel, had the hots for her. Wait…

"He was a vampire though. How could he have been an angel if he was a vampire?"

"That's a long story, one you'll have to ask him, because I need to get back before Kutya misses me too much and destroys my room."

"Who the hell is Kutya?" I asked, my blood suddenly boiling, "and what's she doing in your room?"

Rider went very still, his eyes widening a bit as he took in my obvious ire, and then he started laughing.

"Oh, this is funny? You lied to me about seeing other women and it's funny that I'm mad?" I folded my arms, resisting the urge to throw a punch at him as I pictured a tall, statuesque blonde waiting for him in his bed, or shredding his bedsheets since apparently she was the type to wreck his room if he left her for too long "I hope you enjoyed tonight because it's the last time you'll ever have the pleasure of being with me."

"That's a shame," he said, the corners of his mouth twitching as he slowly crossed the room to stand before me. "I think we finally figured out that reverse donkey cowgirl thing right around the time we broke the lamp.

The shower was fun too."

"This really is just a joke to you?" I heard the crack in my voice and part of my anger turned on myself for being weak in front of him. I refused to cry. If Nannette had taught me anything, it was that I didn't need him. I loved him, and it hurt to think of him with anyone else, but being with him didn't define me, and losing him wouldn't destroy me, no matter how much it hurt. Still, the backs of my eyes burned with the need to shed tears, but I wouldn't give him that. If he could replace me so quickly, he didn't deserve the satisfaction of knowing how deeply he'd cut me. "Go to—"

"Kutya isn't a woman. He's my dog." He angled his head to the side as he watched me open and close my mouth, trying to form words, but I couldn't. The thought of Rider having a dog was enough to process, but I also had to wrap my mind around the name. "Now, where exactly were you about to tell me to go to?"

"Oh, you know exactly where I was about to tell you to go," I said, and he surprised me by laughing in response. "You really got a dog?"

"It's more like the damn dog claimed me, but yes. I killed the man abusing him, and now he won't leave me." Rider studied me as the tension in my shoulders evaporated and tipped my chin up with his fingertips. "I didn't mean to tease you or make you think I'd been with another woman, but I'd be lying if I said I'm not a little happy to still spark such a response from you. You still love me."

"Of course I still love you," I told him. "I think you're a controlling, overprotective jackass, but that doesn't mean I don't love you."

He smiled as he grabbed my waist and pulled me against him. "So, does that mean I can look forward to still receiving the pleasure of being with you?"

"Maybe," I murmured, sliding my hands up his chest until I reached his shoulders and laced my fingers together behind his neck. "If I get to give the dog a good name."

"The dog already has a perfectly good name." His response came with a bit of offense that made my mouth drop open.

"You're the one who named him Kutya? He didn't come with that terrible name? Wow. Even Rome could have given that dog a better name."

"Rome wanted to name him Notorious D.O.G."

I burst out laughing. "All right, maybe Rome couldn't give him a better name, but I can. What kind of dog is he?"

"The kind that has a name."

"Kutya sounds like the name of a female assassin… or another way of saying a female body part. You gave a boy dog the nickname of a woman's lady parts."

"Kutya is a perfectly acceptable Hungarian word, not a nickname for lady parts, and it has no gender."

"What does it mean?"

He released me and walked away as he muttered, "Dog."

"What? Wait a minute. You're telling me you got a dog, and you named it *Dog*?"

"I named him Kutya," he argued, turning back toward me.

"Which means dog. That's like naming me Woman. The poor little thing needs a real name."

"Poor little thing, my ass. He's half German shepherd and half Doberman pinscher. He's already big, and still growing."

My mouth dropped open on a gasp as I pictured how big and gorgeous the dog had to be, and his new name came to me. "What a perfect dog to name Dean."

"No." Rider held his hand up. "That is exactly why you're not naming him. I'm not having a dog named after Dean Winchester."

"But—"

"No."

I sulked. "Sammy?"

"No."

"Win—"

"No." He huffed out a breath. "No *Supernatural* names."

I smiled. "Jensen."

"No naming him after the actors either," Rider said.

"Castiel."

"I said no, Danni."

"Charlie," I tried, hoping to slip one past him.

"I don't get the reference, but I'm sure it's *Supernatural* related, so no."

I thought for a moment. "Assbutt?"

He stared at me, looking the picture of disappointment dipped in bewilderment and coated in defeat, and sighed. "Why are you like this?"

After quickly shooting down my other suggestions, Rider led me out of the bedroom. My face warmed as we stepped out, aware that anyone who'd been in the cabin when Rider and I had our sexcapades would have heard us, but to my relief, we didn't enter a room full of people staring at us, which of course was what my brain had pictured.

The door to Angel's room was closed. I hoped she'd gone to sleep hours earlier with her earbuds in, as she sometimes did, although I had trouble imagining her not nosing around any new people. She was a curious girl.

Ginger sat at the dining table with Holden and Christian, who appeared to be busy doing something on the laptop he had open in front of him. He looked up from it and smiled. "Hi, Danni."

I smiled back, fighting through the embarrassment crawling over my skin in a heated flush as I wondered how long he'd been in the cabin and what all he'd heard. It would have been bad enough when all I'd known about him was that he was a vampire and a minister, but now I knew he'd been an angel. I really hoped I hadn't screamed out any certain names in vain while Rider and I had been going at it so intensely, I'd lost track of time. Apparently I hadn't been smote, so I hoped that meant I hadn't. "Hi, Christian."

Holden glanced at me for a moment before returning his attention to whatever they'd been looking at on the computer screen. If he'd heard anything, he didn't seem bothered by it, but then again, he'd walked in on Ginger and me with a giant green penis so it would probably take a lot more than overhearing me having sex to get any kind of reaction out of him.

"Where are the others?" Rider asked as we reached the middle of the room.

"Daniel went out a while ago," Ginger answered, looking at me as if trying to convey some sort of message, but whatever it was, I didn't get it. "Rome and the new girl went out after him."

"He went out there alone?" I rushed over to the window and looked out, seeing no one. "We haven't actually ruled out the pontianak, have we?"

"No," Holden answered, sounding more than a little miffed. "Fortunately, the woman followed when he went out. I was in the bathroom or I wouldn't have let him go."

Good luck stopping a dragon, I thought, but didn't say anything. Holden already appeared a little put-out, and I suspected it was because he'd gone out looking for a pontianak, but ran into a pack of zombies instead, and now it appeared as if Rider had brought in someone else to be the brains of our team. The private detective clearly didn't like having his hunches doubted or his toes stepped on.

"What are you thinking?" Rider asked, his focus on Christian.

"Black magic, occult, demons…," Christian answered without looking up from the computer screen. "I've just started looking into it, and there are several possibilities, but I'll get it narrowed down and we'll clean up whatever this mess is."

"Keep me posted on all developments, even the theories."

"Of course," Christian replied.

"And let me know right away if you need more help."

"You don't think we're capable of handling the situation?" I turned toward him, folding my arms as I shot him a look that clearly said what I'd truly been asking. He didn't think I was capable of handling the situation, not without the helpers he'd provided, which I knew were babysitters and bodyguards.

"I think we don't know what the situation is," he replied, his tone warning me not to push him, as he walked over to stand behind Christian, looking over the man's shoulder at whatever he was working on.

I moved to the couch and dropped down onto it, not missing the duffel bags resting on the coffee table. Christian and the mystery woman, Lana, were going to be staying with us.

"It's going to get cramped in here," Ginger muttered, plopping down next to me on the couch before she put her feet up on the coffee table. She'd dressed in sweatpants and a T-shirt after her shower, and hadn't bothered with any makeup. Judging by her attire and the fact she only wore socks on her feet, she didn't plan on going back out anytime soon.

"I guess we'll have to work out some sort of arrangement," I said. There were four of us and we had four bedrooms, but now two people were adding to our numbers. "I guess Angel can bunk with me, and Christian can room with Daniel. The Lana chick will take Angel's room."

"You want the new chick to have her own room?" Ginger asked incredulously. "You're giving up your privacy so she can have some?"

"Well, I'm certainly not going to have Angel share a

room with some woman I don't know, and no offense, but if I have Angel share a room with you, she'll think I'm trying to pass her around to all my vampire friends for feeding."

And what happens if we stay here longer and Rider has to come back and feed your needs? She asked through our telepathic link. *We all know what was happening in there.*

I groaned and lowered my head into my hands, hiding my suddenly warm face. *Everyone heard?*

I suspect Rider used some of his power for soundproofing, but we did hear some furniture moving… and whatever the hell you were doing when it sounded like you were about to break down the wall.

"Geez," I muttered, and glanced over at the men, most of my attention on the former angel.

Christian was tall and lean, but he was a strong lean. I suspected his dark pants and cream-colored sweater hid quite a bit of muscle. He was actually similar to Rider in looks. They both had silky dark hair, although Christian's was cut short, and now had a streak of white through it, and blue eyes. Christian's eyes seemed to radiate warmth though, whereas Rider's eyes could stop a heart when they darkened with anger. Christian was an attractive man, but he'd never triggered any kind of response out of me, not like Rider, who only had to exist to make me melt.

He's still a minister, Ginger spoke into my mind, correctly guessing where my thoughts had gone. Of course, I was staring right at the guy. I lowered my gaze into my lap before he or Rider noticed. *But have you noticed he's no longer a vampire now?* Ginger continued.

I nodded. *Did he tell you why?*

Yup. Did Rider fill you in?

Christian was an angel and somehow gave it up, and now he's human.

Trippy, huh?

Do you think it's possible to have our vampirism reversed?

Ginger shook her head. *No. He was a special case for sure. I have so many questions for that guy.*

You and me both. I sensed the sun's nearness. *Where did Daniel go? Why would he go out there when there could still be a pontianak loose?*

Ginger gave me a look as if I'd said something stupid.

"What?"

She glanced over at Rider, who'd leaned down to see the laptop screen closer, and was into whatever the men were talking about. They appeared to be discussing different paranormal entities who liked to mess with people.

"What?" I repeated.

It's one thing knowing the woman you're in love with has someone, she said across our telepathic link as she returned her attention to me, *but it's a totally different thing to hang around when you know she's getting her brains boinked out by that man in the very next room.*

I sat stone still for a moment, replaying her words, sure I'd misheard them. *You're saying Daniel went out there because Rider and I …* I shook my head. *No. Daniel's my friend. My best friend. He's not in love with me.*

She gave me the stupid look again. I was starting to really not like that look. *Danni, I like you a lot, but you can be really slow on the pickup sometimes.*

He's not in love with me. I glanced over at Rider to make sure he was still focused on his discussion with Christian and Holden, and hadn't picked up on the fact Ginger and I were having a private telepathic discussion. He tended to get suspicious when we communicated this way around him. He still had his head bent down, going over whatever they were looking at on the screen. *I'm not going to share Daniel's personal business without his consent*, I told Ginger through our link, *but I know he was very much in love back in Imortia. He's still in love with her.*

He's not in Imortia anymore, Ginger replied. *Why do you think he's so damn protective of you, Danni?*

It's literally his job.

Ginger laughed a little as she shook her head. *Yeah, well, you didn't see the man's face when he left out of here, or the slump in his shoulders. Be careful with him, honey. Despite the cocky attitude and laid-back personality, I get the feeling you could do some serious damage to that one.*

Ginger stood and stretched. "Since it doesn't look like anything major will be happening soon, I'm going to bed, if that's all right." She directed the last part of her statement to Rider, because when he was in the vicinity, he was in charge. Hell, he was in charge when he wasn't in the vicinity, but we had a little more leeway when we had distance.

He looked at her and nodded his approval before letting his gaze rove over to me, where it narrowed a little. I decided to get up and move to the table, join the guys, before he suspected we'd been having one of our private conversations.

"Stick the new girl in my room," Ginger said as she headed that way. "The bed's mine, but she's welcome to the floor, unless she wants to get cozy." She winked at me as she disappeared into her room.

"Is Lana… um, her type?" I asked as I reached the guys.

"I think anyone female and willing is her type," Rider responded as he held a chair out for me, showing off his gentleman skills. "If you're asking me if Lana's into women, I have no idea what her preference is. I'm running a security firm, not a matchmaking service."

"Your matchmaking service worked quite well for me," Christian said, raising his left hand, which I noted sported a very shiny gold band on an important finger.

"You were already matched when Rihanna flashed you into my office," Rider replied with a small eye roll. "And I suspect it was Porter who lit a fire under your ass on that situation, not me."

"Who's Porter?" I asked, wondering just how many new people Rider had acquired since I'd left.

"No one you ever need to know," Rider replied rather

tersely as Christian opened his mouth to answer me. The former angel closed his mouth and returned his attention to the laptop, seeming to hold back amusement as he gave his head a small shake.

"You know the women in your nest generally don't get along with me," I reminded him. "Unless they're like Ginger."

"Eliza and Nannette aren't like Ginger, and you get along with them just fine."

"You know what I'm talking about." I fixed him with a hard stare. Rider was well aware that many of the female members of his nest had given me a hard time from the moment I'd entered his life and it had become obvious to his organization that I was special to him. Most of the women just glared at me, but one had gone so far as to help my sister try to kill me. Ginger had been assigned as my female bodyguard because, as a lesbian, I could trust her not to take me out of the picture in order to worm her way into Rider's bed. Rider could trust her too, because despite her flirtations, there was no chance of me returning the attraction. My succubus half would never allow it.

Rider took my hand, pulled me up from my seat, and led me outside, where the sky had just started to lighten.

"It could be dangerous for you out here if the pontianak is near," I told him as he walked to the railing and leaned against it, still holding my hand.

"You'll protect me."

I raised an eyebrow. "You mean the big, bad vampire king thinks the lowly hybrid can protect him?"

"I'm not royalty, sweetheart, just a mean bastard who isn't afraid to get his hands bloody and advertises that fact often enough to discourage anyone from trying me, and just because I'm protective of you doesn't mean I'm ignorant of your abilities. Besides, I figure you're not going to let some vampire ghost have all the fun of slaughtering my genitals."

"Why? Because that's my thing?" I slipped my hand out

of his and walked away a few feet. "That's what you all think of me, isn't it? I'm just a hothead who stabs men in the balls. Good for a laugh, but not worthy in a real fight."

"I didn't say that."

"You didn't have to. You sent *help*, which I know is just another way of saying babysitter." I turned toward him and folded my arms. "You know, when I track down whoever or whatever is behind what's happening here, and put an end to it, you'll see I'm capable of more than just giving you and your men something to laugh about."

"This attitude right here is exactly why I worry about you," Rider said. "Why do you think you have to prove something, Danni? Why do you have to be where the danger is? Why can't you just be happy staying where you're safe?"

"Where is that? Stuck in your room over the bar? I love you, Rider, but I want more out of this undead life than keeping your bed warm, and occasionally being brought down to interrogation to play with your captured prey and give your people something to talk about."

"I'm sorry your life with me is so unsatisfactory," he muttered, looking toward the tree line as figures emerged.

Daniel was in front, the set of his jaw showing he wasn't in a good mood. Rome followed from a few feet back, dressed in his usual attire of all black, and next to him was a slender, yet curvy in all the right places blonde bombshell in faded jeans that fit like a second skin, a brown long-sleeved T-shirt with a deep vee, and matching hiking boots.

"I brought you out here for a warning," Rider said, closing the distance between us. "You don't know what the hell is happening here so you will follow Christian's lead since he's probably seen more weird shit than all of you put together, and do not attempt to break Lana and send her back to me like you threatened. She might actually eat you."

CHAPTER TWELVE

"You brought a woman who might eat me? And you're leaving her here?"

Rider grinned as he wrapped his hand around the back of my neck and planted a kiss on my forehead. "I forbid her to eat you, but please don't give her a hard time. You know, it's not easy for me being so far away from you, especially when I know you're up against an unknown threat. Take the help and save me the heartburn."

"Vampires don't get heartburn."

"They do when they fall in love with your stubborn ass." He removed his hand from my neck and placed it along the small of my back.

"Cute." I watched the three approach, my attention mostly on the woman whose gaze appeared to be on me. Her walk was fluid and graceful while still giving off a predator vibe. "She's very pretty."

"Pretty disgusting," he said softly, "but she's good on a battlefield."

I looked up at him. "You can admit she's pretty. I know I've had my moments, but you don't have to say a gorgeous woman is disgusting because you're afraid I'll be jealous."

"You'll see what I mean," he said with a soft chuckle before stepping away to address the others as they reached the cabin. "Everything all right?"

Daniel looked over at the new woman, who raised a golden eyebrow in his direction before returning his attention to Rider. "Yeah. Everything's great."

I didn't miss the tone in his voice indicating everything was not that great, and judging by the subtle furrowing of Rider's brow, he'd noticed it as well. "Is there something I should know about?"

Daniel and the woman exchanged looks again before she spoke. "Apparently, I do know Daniel. When I knew him from Imortia, he had another name."

Holy crapoli. The new woman was Imortian, which explained Rider's comment that she could eat me, and why she gave off an energy similar to Daniel's. Similar, but not exact, so I had no idea if she was a dragon shifter or something else. Also… what was this about Daniel having a different name? Oh, I was definitely going to ask about that.

"Are you two going to have any issues working together?" Rider asked, his voice heavily implying that if they had issues, they better get over them quick.

"None," the woman said.

Daniel shook his head, his jaw still clenched tight. He had yet to look at me, and when he looked at Rider, he seemed to look through him. Rome hung in back, his meaty arms folded over his chest, observing. He gave a polite nod when he saw me looking at him, but said nothing.

"Good," Rider said. "Daniel, I was just telling Danni that Christian will be in charge. Your job has not changed. You're just looking to Christian for instruction as he researches and hopefully figures out whatever the hell it is you're dealing with here. Any questions?"

"No."

Rider stared at him for a moment before turning to me.

"Danni, this is Lana, who I'm sure you've just realized is originally from Imortia. Lana, this is Danni."

"The Teste Slayer," she said, immediately raising my hackles. She grinned. "Your reputation precedes you, and I have to say, I like your style."

"I can do a lot more than stab testicles," I said, and she arched one of those perfect eyebrows as Rome grinned widely behind her. Hey, if she wanted to take the statement as a threat, she was more than welcome to.

Behave, Rider said through our link.

Who, moi? I replied through the link.

He cut a warning glare my way, but the brief twitch at the corner of his mouth took the sting off it. "Ginger has graciously offered to share her room with you, Lana. Daniel, Christian will need a place to rest."

"No problem," Daniel said. "I got the room with the two twin beds anyway. Christian's a good guy."

I didn't miss the way he directed a dark look Lana's way, and wondered if he was implying she wasn't a good guy. He'd told me about his life in Imortia, and filled me in on the realm in general, but he'd never mentioned Lana. I knew he'd been engaged, but had lost his fiancé immediately after she'd accepted his proposal, and I knew the Imortian queen had punished him for trying to avenge her death. I had no idea what his relationship with Lana was, but she seemed to be another unhappy reminder of the realm he'd left.

And if she hurt my friend, I would either knock her ass back to Imortia or cut her down where she stood. I didn't give a crap what kind of shifter she might be.

"You know, I get the impression you don't think I can take the new girl," I told Rider after Daniel and Lana had gone inside, he'd wrapped things up with Holden and Christian, and now we stood next to his SUV, Rome waiting in the driver's seat to take them back to Louisville.

"If I didn't have the ability to toss people around without even touching them, I probably couldn't take the new girl, so don't take it personally."

"So, what is she? Dragon? Gargoyle?" I tried to remember all the different types of Imortian shifters I'd been told about, excluding those I didn't think would eat people, like unicorns, but the sun was on its way up and its pull made my brain a little slow.

Rider appeared to consider answering for a moment, then grinned. "Nah, it'll be more fun to let you discover on your own if the need arises for her to shift. I hope she doesn't have to, and not just because she'd only have to shift if you were in danger. I'd love to be there to see your reaction to it the first time."

"I could just ask her."

"She doesn't like talking about it, so I wouldn't recommend it." He looked up at the lightening sky and reached out, taking a lock of my hair between his fingers. "You didn't put on any lotion. You need to get inside before the sun rises fully."

"You can't stay any longer?" I asked, suddenly missing him terribly although he stood right in front of me and I was still irritated that he'd brought two more babysitters, and then there was the whole heart thing I wasn't done grappling with, but I loved him despite all that, and what could I say? Him leaving me to travel to another state was a lot harder to take than me leaving him to go elsewhere.

"I'd never leave you by choice," he answered before dipping his head to kiss me goodbye. "I have to go now. Get inside before you burn, and get some sleep."

I nodded as I flexed my fingers, fighting against the urge to grab him by the front of his shirt and pull him into the cabin. Not for sex. That appetite had been sated, thank goodness. I didn't want him to leave me. I still wanted to prove I could take care of myself without his constantly looking over my shoulder, and I still needed time to come to terms with what he'd done, but I didn't want him to leave.

"Go on, Danni. I can't drive away from here until I know you're inside, safe and sound."

It was then that I noticed the subtle bags under his eyes. As a vampire, he'd never look as bad as a human without sleep, but no amount of blood or healing powers could erase the tiredness in his eyes as he looked at me. I remembered the weeks we'd spent apart after he'd killed Selander Ryan. He hadn't slept, said he couldn't without me. This was the first time since then that we'd spent any real time apart. "Promise me you'll sleep too."

"That's why Rome's driving," he said, but I saw the truth in his eyes. He would try to sleep, and he might get a little rest, but he wouldn't sleep well. He couldn't. Damn it.

"You don't have to worry about me, Rider. I can take care of myself, and you've left plenty of guards to watch over me."

"I won't apologize for protecting you," he said, "and I'll never feel that you are safe enough, but if you need space, you have it as long as things here stay under control. I need you to go inside before the sun comes up though."

I nodded. Standing outside at dawn without any of the special sunscreen we used, allowing myself to get burned wouldn't do anything to prove I was capable of protecting myself from danger. I started to kiss him out of habit, but the memory of my heart in his hand bubbled up to the surface, and I stopped. "Be careful. Get some real sleep."

"You too."

I stood there for a moment, holding his hand, still fighting the urge to pull him along with me, if only to make sure he slept. I was upset with him, but that didn't mean I wanted him to suffer. "You're sure you can't sleep here, then leave at nightfall after a good rest?"

His tired eyes warmed over, and he smiled. "No, I have to go now, but it's nice to know you care."

"I've never stopped caring. This isn't a breakup, right?"

"You would know the answer to that, Danni. You

would be the only one to ever leave." He kissed my forehead, grabbed my shoulders, turned me around, and gave me a push. "Cabin. Now. You're running out of time."

I was. My skin was already warming, but if I looked back at Rider, I'd have trouble moving away, so I didn't look back. I made my way to the cabin.

"And Danni," Rider called out as I reached the shelter of the covered porch, and had one hand on the front doorknob. I turned to see him sitting in the passenger seat of the SUV, his door still open, watching me. "Call me immediately."

"I will," I told him, knowing what he referred to, and opened the door, hoping our recent sexfest had sated my succubus side for a while because I didn't think I could go through another visit from him if it meant him leaving me again.

I entered the cabin, closed the door, and leaned against it, listening to the sound of his SUV's tires rolling over gravel, and felt as though the big machine had driven right over my heart.

"Are you all right?" Christian asked, looking up from where he still sat, working at the dining table. Lana sat next to him, watching me curiously. Holden exited the bathroom, grabbed his jacket, and pulled it on.

"I'm fine," I answered, offering a little smile when I noticed the deep concern in his thoughtful blue eyes. A huge yawn escaped me as the sun rose fully. I hoped the sun managed to pull Rider into a deep sleep as Rome drove him back to Kentucky.

"That sounds like bedtime," Holden said. "Get some rest. I'm going to grab some too, and meet back up here later."

"Are you sure you don't want to stay here?" I asked. "At least until we know what's going on?"

"Thanks, but it's getting a bit crowded here, and Carrie will expect me."

"Right." I moved away from the door so he could leave. "Be careful out there, and thanks for everything."

"It's my job," he said as he passed me and left the cabin.

"I kind of feel like he's upset the pontianak we were hunting turned into a zombie horde."

"I'm not sure if the amount you fought qualifies as a horde," Christian replied, "and I think it's more along the lines of he's upset Rider sent me in. From what I've gathered, Holden is used to working solo or with a very small amount of partners, and he's always the one to call the shots."

"Ah, so the angel is stealing his thunder." I studied Christian, imagining him with wings and a halo as I tried to figure out how an angel became a vampire. I'd been bitten twice in the same night by two very powerful beings, but I was pretty sure angels didn't become angels from a bite, and it seemed they would be immune to a vampire's bite.

"You have questions about me, don't you?"

"Soooo many questions," I replied, earning a grin from the former angel. The Imortian just stared at me, her gaze boring into my skin.

"Perhaps I will have answers after you've gotten some rest."

"Geez. Rider really did send you to babysit me."

The Imortian grinned, triggering a flash of anger in me. "Am I amusing to you, Imortian?"

Her grin turned into a full smile, her warm brown eyes sparkling. "No offense meant, vampire. I'm simply trying to figure out your power."

I stood still for a moment, a little surprised. That hadn't been the response I'd expected. "My power?"

"As I stated before, your reputation precedes you. I can't help but be intrigued by the woman whose presence calms that surly beast."

"What sur… You mean Rider?" I looked over at Christian as she raised her eyebrows and gave a subtle nod, and noticed the way he hunkered down in his chair as he shot a look at Lana, a look that told her to be quiet. "Why are you so interested in whatever power you think I have over Rider?"

The amusement that had lit her eyes left. "It was a compliment, vampire, and I'm here to fight beside you, not against you. I am not one of the many twits who desire to be the boss's mistress." She looked over at Christian as she rose from the table. "Wake me when you need to sleep and I'll take over the watch."

Christian nodded as the woman stepped away from the table, eyeing me with a hard gleam in her gaze as she passed on her way to Ginger's room. She stepped inside without knocking and closed the door behind her.

"I think you offended her," Christian said softly, and sighed. "She's a good person, Danni. You can trust her. She has no desire for Rider and holds no ill will against you."

I walked over to the seat she'd vacated and sank down into it.

"You really should quit fighting against the sun's pull and get some rest. We don't know what we're up against here, and not all monsters need to wait for nightfall to hunt. Get sleep while you can, especially during the hours your body craves it most."

I yawned again, almost as if Christian's mention of my body needing the day sleep drew it out of me. My eyelids grew heavy, but I fought against the pull. "I'm a hybrid. I don't need the day sleep as badly as other vampire newbs."

Christian frowned at me. "I might no longer have all my powers, but I can still recognize a fib."

His mention of powers reminded me of the first time I'd met him at Gruff's, and the effect he'd had on my succubus side. "You were able to keep my succubus side from overtaking me because you're… you *were* an angel."

He nodded.

"But you didn't know you were an angel?" My eyes

closed, but I forced them open just as Daniel emerged from his bedroom. "How is that possible?"

"That's a story for after you've slept," Christian answered as Daniel crossed over to the kitchenette and grabbed a bottled water out of the fridge. The dragon shifter eyed me as he opened the bottle and drank. "All you need to know right now is that I'm looking into what's happening around here, and Lana can be trusted."

I looked at Daniel, noticing the way his body tensed at the mention of the woman's name. He crushed the now empty water bottle and tossed it into the recycling bin.

"Get some rest, Danni. We will have plenty of time to talk about whatever you'd like after you're rested, and hopefully I'll know more about what we're up against here."

"Danni doesn't do well with orders," Daniel said, walking over to us. "Even when you're telling her to do something she already wants to do anyway."

"Hey!" I said as he scooped me up out of the chair and slung me over his shoulder. "Put me down."

"I intend to," he replied, walking toward my room. I looked at Christian to see the man staring at us, his mouth hanging open and curved up in amusement as he shook his head before returning his attention to whatever he'd been doing on the laptop.

"Go to sleep," Daniel said, dropping me on top of my bed. "You can barely keep your eyes open."

"Wait," I said, stopping him before he reached the doorway. "What's wrong?"

He turned toward me and took a deep breath, blowing it out slowly. "Nothing."

"I know you, Daniel. Something's wrong." I noticed the way his gaze slid over my room, his nostrils flaring as he took in what all had been damaged. Rider and I had cleaned up the best we could, but without a little witch help, we couldn't repair the things we'd broken. I felt my cheeks flush with heat. "Are you … upset with me?"

"No," he answered, his gaze snapping back to mine. "Why would I be upset with you?"

I thought about what Ginger had said earlier, but couldn't bring that up with him. If there were any truth to Daniel having feelings for me deeper than friendship, discussing them would be awkward, especially discussing them in the room I'd so recently been with another man in, a man he worked for and respected, no matter what barbs they traded, and a man I loved deeply. "I don't know." I shrugged and removed my shoes. I'd dressed in leggings and a T-shirt after my shower with Rider, and opted to just leave those on. "You just threw me on my bed." The heat in my cheeks intensified as I realized what I'd just said. I wanted to smack myself on the forehead.

"I didn't throw you," he said, his voice a little strained, or maybe I was imagining things. I was struggling hard not to give in to the pull of day sleep. "I dropped you, and only because you're being your usual stubborn and overly curious self. Christian will be here for your interrogation when you wake up. We all need to rest. It's been a shitter of a night."

"Daniel," I called again as he turned to leave me.

He stopped, his shoulders tense, and turned halfway. "Yeah?"

"I can tell there's something upsetting you, and I can tell you're not thrilled Lana is here. You can talk to me."

He stared at the floor a moment, thinking. "I know," he finally said. "Don't worry about me. I'm good, and you don't have to worry about Lana. She's not your enemy."

"Is she yours?"

He raised his gaze to meet mine and shook his head. "No. No, she's not. Go to sleep, Danni."

"Fine," I said, "if you tell me why she knew you under another name. Is Daniel not your real name?"

He ran his hand down his face. "It's my name here."

Interesting. I knew he'd entered our realm without a last name and had chosen Steelheart when the Imortian

Agency had assigned him to the first wolf pack he'd been with, primarily because he'd been listening to Steelheart in the waiting room. I'd thought Daniel was his actual name though. "What do they call you in Imortia?"

"Dead, probably." He turned to leave.

"Daniel."

He released a breath full of frustration and turned back to face me. "How about I make you a deal? You don't ask me about my birth name anymore and I won't ask you about that green monstrosity in Gruff's office."

My cheeks went from warm to raging inferno. "Deal," I muttered.

He looked back over his shoulder, looking out the door to see what Christian was doing. The man was totally focused on the work he was doing on the laptop, and didn't even raise his head. Daniel walked over, bent down, and kissed the top of my head before straightening. "It's nothing against you. Get some sleep."

"Fine. You too."

He nodded and headed out of my room, but stopped at my door. He turned toward me, his gaze not really connecting to mine, and lowered his voice. "If your succubus side starts wanting more than blood and violence, and you're too stubborn to contact Rider, tell me or Ginger so we can. You don't want to do something you'll regret, and Christian's just a guy now. He can't fight against your venom, and if you bite him, I can't stab him to break him out from under the effect without seriously hurting him, maybe even killing him."

I pulled my knees to my chest and wrapped my arms around them, embarrassment filling the pit in my stomach. "Okay."

He stood there for a moment, as if he wanted to say something more, but didn't. He simply nodded and left, pulling my door closed behind him.

I muttered a curse and got under the covers, cursing again as Rider's midnight rain scent wafted all around me. I didn't know whether to feel sad or ashamed, and curiosity about so many things ate away at me. Fortunately, the sun was stronger than my will, and I succumbed to the need for day sleep before my curiosity could totally drive me crazy.

I smelled sulfur.

"Shit," I muttered as small flames spread a little light in the darkness. Torches, I realized, attached to the walls. I craved their warmth as a bitter chill invaded my body. I was back in the dark place, and could feel the presence of the dark figure with the blue-tinted skin. I'd fed my succubus side, damn it. I'd given it violence, sex, and blood. Hell, I'd given it the blood of my sire. Drinking from Rider should have strengthened our bond and strengthened me. So why the hell was I having another nightmare? Unless it wasn't just a nightmare.

A deep laugh rumbled through the dark space, echoing off the walls. It had to be a cavern. The smell of sulfur clogged my throat as another smell came from the depths of the darkness, causing my eyes to water. It was salty and sweet, cloying. I strained to see, but the torchlight didn't land on anything.

I heard a moan, a gasp, and a grunt, almost as if I'd intruded upon… Oh no. The sounds intensified, gaining in number, growing in volume. They surrounded me. Groaning, gasping, grunting, and heavy breathing mixed with the sound of flesh slapping against flesh. My knees grew weak as wet heat pooled between my thighs.

The laugh I'd heard before drew closer until the large shadow figure from my previous nightmare stepped close enough for me to see his outline. "That little taste your vampire sire gave you could never satisfy you, Danni, not when your very DNA desires this."

The torchlight grew brighter, revealing naked men and women as far as the eye could see, covered in blood, thrusting into and against each other, biting, licking, and suckling whatever they could get their mouths on.

There appeared to be no less than three men for every woman, every succubus, I realized, and the succubi were having the time of their lives. One reached out her hand to me, smiling enough to reveal curved fangs. "Join us sissssssssssster."

Unholy hobbit-fucking hell… I'd been pulled right into Satan's orgy.

CHAPTER THIRTEEN

The shadow figure stepped closer. I tried to shut out the sloppy sounds of what was happening around me and focus on him. "Are you the devil?"

He cocked his massive head to the side. "Do you see horns?"

"No. Does the devil actually have horns?"

He shrugged his oversized shoulders. "The devil is whatever you make him to be, or so I have heard. He is very much like your realm's Santa Claus. He only exists if you believe."

"So you're telling me there's no devil, no such thing as Satan or Hell?"

"Oh, Hell is very real. The red character with the pointy tail and pitchfork is not. You know Hell exists, Danni. You've spent time just outside its walls."

I shivered, reminded of the times Selander Ryan had brought me to him after Rider had killed him. I also remembered he'd been able to do that because of dark magic he'd worked prior to his death. He'd used a symbol called a soul stitch. I looked around the room I now recognized as a cavern, searching for a symbol, trying to ignore the activities surrounding me… and the shameful pull toward those activities. My succubus side was aroused, and wanted to join in on the festivities.

"Feel free to join the party," the shadow figure said, a lilt of amusement to his voice.

"Fuck you," I snapped, "and not in the sloppy way happening here."

"But you seem to like it so much."

I clenched my teeth, closed my eyes, and shook my head. I could call out to Rider. Clearly, I was sleeping and had been pulled into this horrible place, just as I'd been pulled into that room outside Hell by Selander Ryan. Rider could pull me out. He couldn't have made it that far from me. He could turn around and … No. I wouldn't prove myself capable of taking care of myself if I called on him to save me from a dream. That's all this was. A dream.

I opened my eyes, fixed my sights on the shadow figure, and marched toward him. I couldn't find a symbol on the dark walls or amid all the sweaty gymnastics happening around me, but maybe he had a symbol on him. At the very least, if I could get past the shadows and lay eyes on the bastard, I'd know what I was dealing with.

Unfortunately, as I neared the shadow figure, it shrank down to six feet and morphed into Rider.

"Take his face off of you," I snapped, stopping a breath away. "Quit hiding behind masks."

"Danni, Danni, Danni," he said, his voice matching Rider's to perfection. "I'm trying to help you."

"Show yourself."

"I can be whoever you want me to be," he said, reaching out to touch me. I stepped back, and nearly tripped over a trio of men who'd rolled over, attached to a succubus who writhed in pleasure between them. I turned my face away, mortified by the vulgar sight of them, and disgusted by the shiver of delight running up my spine having viewed them. "I can help you release your inhibitions and be what you were truly meant to be, Danni.

I can do it with this face and body, or the dragon's. Perhaps you want the werewolf?"

"How do you know so much about me?" I asked. Selander Ryan had been able to get into my thoughts because he'd sired me along with Rider. He had access to my mind, but this *thing*, this shadow creature, shouldn't have been able to read me so easily, and he shouldn't have known anything about me in the waking world.

"I am an avid reader." He smiled wide, and it was like looking right into Rider's face, except for the eyes. Even at his angriest, Rider's eyes never bore that much darkness. I noticed a sparkle and looked deeper. It felt as though I were falling right into his gaze, and that's when I realized what I was seeing was a small galaxy, a whole other world buried deep in the creature's left pupil.

"What the hell *are* you?"

"I told you. I'm anything you want me to be." He grabbed me and pulled me tight against his body. "What do you want me to be, Danni? How many faces and bodies do you want me to wear? What do you want me to do to you?"

I started to melt against him, but the swirling galaxy in his pupil reminded me this was not who I belonged to. I was with Rider, and I wouldn't hurt him, not even in a dream. I shoved the creature wearing the Rider costume away, but toppled backward, falling into a pit of naked, writhing bodies.

Suddenly, they were on top of me, beside me, under me, all around, and the succubi had left, giving me all the men. All the muscular, sexy, lust-filled men. They crawled over me, wrapped their arms and legs around me, and nibbled at my exposed flesh, quickly ripping away my clothes to give them more access, and I did nothing to stop it. There were so many, and the succubus side of me was on fire with need. Tears spilled from my eyes as the shadow figure, back to his large, shadowy form, hovered above me, laughing.

"Yes, Danni, yesssssssss."

Scorching heat sizzled through my chest and I screamed, sure my body was going to explode. I heard the shadow figure roar in pure rage before he and what felt like the entire world disappeared into a bright, blinding light, and then I was in my bed again, my back arched off the mattress, my lips peeled back in pain as a streak of white-hot lightning poured into my chest. I'd been screaming in the dream, but couldn't make a sound now, the pain too much.

The light disappeared with a cracking sound, and I fell back onto the bed. Christian stood over me. Tears poured from my eyes, but I didn't sob. I barely breathed.

"Danni. Are you all right?" Christian sat on the edge of my bed and placed his hand over my heart. I expected pain, expected a bloody, burned hole in my chest, but there must not have been any damage.

I looked at him as I slowly started to breathe again, the rush of pain subsiding. "That light… It came from your hand."

He nodded.

"Rider said you were an angel, but he also said you weren't anymore."

Christian nodded again.

"What the hell are you now?"

"I'm not sure, but I'm thinking I might have kept a bit of my angel power."

"Ya think?"

"Drink," Christian said, handing me a glass of warmed blood.

We'd moved to the living room, just the two of us. Apparently I'd only screamed in my dream, so no one else had been disturbed, and it was early morning, so even Angel still slept. I looked at the blood, relieved to not see any clots, but still not thrilled. Fresh blood straight from the vein was best, but my donor was asleep, and I sure as hell wasn't going to attempt drinking from Christian after my succubus side had gotten all riled up in the dream. I took a sip, grimacing a little. Man, I couldn't wait until my stomach could handle chocolate again. I needed hot chocolate, cupcakes, and donuts. Comfort foods.

"Rider said something about you possibly being a guard or something."

"A guardian," Christian said, sitting in the armchair rather than taking a seat next to me on the couch. I was thankful for the space. It wasn't always easy to tell what I might do after my succubus side was aroused. "Possibly. I chose to give up my grace. I don't remember everything, but I remember I was told I'd no longer be an angel or a vampire. I was given the chance to live out the rest of my life as a human man. I suppose it's possible I'd keep a little grace, enough to be a guardian. I was created as an angel, after all. I wasn't born a human man."

I shook my head, so confused. Yes, I'd just been brought out of a hellacious dream in a completely crazy way, and needed to figure out who the shadow creature was and how he knew so much about me, but at the moment the answers I craved most were about the man who'd somehow shot lightning into my chest without causing any damage at all to me or my clothing. "You're going to have to walk me through all this. When Daniel first brought you here not even a month ago, you were a vampire on the run from a group of lycanthropes and a witch. He saw you use a flaming sword that you'd pulled out of thin air, and it disappeared when you were done using it, but you had no knowledge of how you'd done that and no knowledge that you'd been an angel?"

"That's right," he said, nodding.

"Even though you were able to push back my succubus side when it tried to take over after that guy at the bar pissed me off?"

"I always knew I was good at fighting demons. The

power of prayer was my greatest weapon, and still is."

"Well, I guess so, given you have a direct line to God."

"We all do," he said. "But a person has to still have absolute faith to strengthen that connection."

I thought about that, wondering if there was enough faith in the world to save someone like me.

"You didn't choose to be half succubus, Danni. It's not about what you are as much as it is about what you do."

Oy. I'd just gotten quite a naughty tingle in a dream where I was practically buried under a pile of naked men, and before that I'd broken quite a few things in my bedroom while fornicating heavily with a vampire known for literally ripping people's organs and bones out, so I still wasn't feeling that optimistic about ever entering the pearly gates given what I'd been doing lately. "How were you a vampire if you were born an angel?" I asked, moving the topic back to him. I had enough problems in my life without worrying about what the afterlife held for me.

"I wasn't born," he answered. "I was created as an angel back in the beginning."

"The beginning of wha… Ohhh… you mean *the* beginning."

He nodded. "I don't remember Heaven. That was taken from me when I chose to become human, but I wasn't stripped of my knowledge of what happened this time. You see, I was created as an angel and spent many centuries in Heaven with my brothers and sisters, but one of my brothers became jealous of me when he realized I would ascend to the rank of archangel."

My eyebrows shot up. "Impressive."

Christian shrugged. "My brother's jealousy got the best of him and to sum up a long story, he arranged for me to get dragged down to earth by use of very dark magic, my grace nearly stripped enough to make me an easier target for the men he had in place to beat me. They were supposed to kill me, but didn't succeed. They did succeed in beating me into amnesia. I lost all my memories, and this was worsened when my brother later sent a vampire to turn me and again, beat me severely, ensuring my memories didn't come back. I woke up as a vampire inside a cabin with another vampire who'd found me and took me under his wing. Fortunately, he is a much better man than my sire was."

I tried to wrap my mind around the story. "But you were still an angel? I mean, that sword you pulled out of nowhere was like some kind of angel weapon, right?"

"I was an angel without my full grace and without my memory. I had no idea who I had been prior to that moment I woke up and discovered I'd been turned into a vampire. I didn't even know my own name, so I gave myself one. I did know I served God, and I continued to serve God as best I could."

"Even though you had fangs?" I smiled.

"I lived primarily off of bagged blood, and when I drank from the living, they were predators. I protected the weak and the innocent, and I shared the Word of God with all."

"You must have been turned a long time ago, but you didn't know to pull that sword until the day Daniel was sent to help you. How did you know to draw it then?"

He smiled, his eyes warming with love. "Jadyn. It turns out Jadyn is a guardian, and her presence awakened my grace."

"This grace… It was like some sort of angel autopilot?"

He chuckled softly. "I guess it was in certain moments. An angel's grace is an angel's source of power. Jadyn descends from a fallen angel, so she has a small amount of grace, just enough to make her a guardian."

"What is that? A guardian?"

"Guardians are a special kind of protector. Jadyn is a guardian of beasts, so her powers are specifically attuned to animals. She can hear and speak to them, and she was once able to heal one when she reached out to me and borrowed from my grace, but that was before I became human. It was Rider's dog she healed, actually."

Christian grinned at me, and I realized my mouth had fallen open sometime during his explanation, and I was gawking. I shook my head. "I'm sorry. By hear and speak to animals, you mean like barks and purrs or…"

"She can hear their thoughts, and communicate with them in a way most cannot, no matter the species."

"Wow. That's pretty freaking awesome. What kind of guardian are you?"

He frowned. "I'm not sure. As you know, it hasn't been long since I learned I was an angel, and then gave that up. I was granted the knowledge of what happened this time so I wouldn't be bumbling around, completely ignorant to my origin as I was after my brother betrayed me all those centuries ago, but a lot of knowledge of Heaven itself was taken from me. I remember the sister who helped me, and the brother who betrayed me. I remember the battle that was fought against him, my vampire sire, and their army. I wasn't told I would be a guardian, so if I am, I'm really not sure what specific kind I am, nor do I remember very much about them. I would have to research guardian types or figure it out naturally."

My chest tightened a little as I latched onto what he'd said about a battle and remembered what Rider had told me earlier. "Rider gave you an army to take into that battle, didn't he?"

Christian held my gaze for a moment before nodding. "He and his people fought alongside me, for which I will forever be grateful, but there were lives lost in the process. I try to find solace in the fact that those losses protected others who are part of something very important, others who will save so many more lives than what were lost on that field."

Okay, I'd been thinking this battle was just two large groups of people in a street fight, but words like battle and field being tossed around had me picturing something much grander, and wondering what the hell Rider had been up to while I'd been gone. "What others?"

Again, he held my gaze for a while before speaking. I could almost see the wheels turning in his mind, debating what I could be told. "It's best you don't know anything," he finally said. "All who know are in danger of revealing those who need to be protected to the enemy."

Ugh. Seriously? I knew Rider was keeping something from me, and I was so over it. "Great," I said. "More secrets that Rider thinks he has to keep from me because he thinks I'm not capable of—"

"Rider only knows about what I'm speaking of because he figured it out on his own," Christian said, cutting me off before I could really go into a hissy-spiel. "He figured it out while figuring out what I was. I wouldn't have just offered that information to him, and he will not share it with you, not because he doesn't trust you, but because he has been warned of the danger and has seen with his own eyes, the lengths that the evil ones will go to in order to win. The battle he fought with me was only a sliver of the greater battle between good and evil that has been raging for several centuries, foretold by prophecy older than even he."

Damn, I thought. I didn't know Rider's exact age, but I knew he'd been around a very long time. Christian, of course, had been around even longer, since the beginning of all. I went over what he'd just told me in my mind, focusing on how Rider had stumbled upon this information himself. "You're part of this prophecy thing too?"

Christian nodded. "And I would give my life in a heartbeat to protect the others involved. I'd rather you not have to, so forgive me, Danni, but I will not tell you any more about it."

I sighed. "Fine. I'll just add it to the pile of secrets and mystery already filling space in my brain, and wait until my head explodes. I guess I can file that Porter person y'all mentioned earlier away in there too."

Christian practically erupted into laughter, bending over and gripping his knee.

"What in the world is so funny?"

"Sorry." He straightened back up, still laughing. "Jacob Porter, or Jake, as he likes to go by, is a very good friend of mine. He's really about as close to a brother as one can get without sharing blood. He is also one of the deadliest slayers to have ever walked this earth."

"Wait a minute. I know enough about slayers to know they are supernaturally gifted hunters born to kill pretty much any and every paranormal being in existence. How could one of the supposedly deadliest ones be like a brother to you?"

"Jake is special. He's still a killer who craves bloodshed though, and is very dangerous to all paranormal beings."

"That makes no sense." I shook my head a bit, then froze. "Rider said Jake Porter was the one who lit a fire under you to…" I looked at the wedding band on Christian's ring finger. "You married Jadyn?"

He nodded.

"Wow. That was quick."

"Didn't seem that quick to me." Christian smiled. "I suppose it was, but when you know, you know."

"She's the reason you gave up Heaven after just rediscovering who you really were. Wow, that's some kind of love."

"I have no regrets."

"Rider mentioned this Jake Porter guy as if he'd been with both of you. Was he part of this battle you mentioned Rider helping you out in?"

"Yes. He and Lana teamed up during that."

This just kept getting more and more confusing. "A slayer and an Imortian, who would qualify as a supernatural being, teamed up together to help you, still a vampire at the time, and Rider, a pretty damn powerful vampire himself, in a battle. He didn't try to kill Lana, Rider, or Rider's people?"

"Actually, things got hairy near the end and the bloodshed he'd inflicted on the other side brought the bloodthirsty killer out of him. He came very close to attacking Rider, but Jadyn was there, and I'd warned her he might fall prey to the darkness inside him if he drew enough blood during the battle. You see, a slayer is practically another type of beast."

"And Jadyn is a guardian of beasts."

He nodded. "She calmed him before he and Rider could engage. I honestly don't know which of the two would have won. Both are extremely powerful men."

"And that's why Rider didn't want to tell me about him? It seems like he'd want to warn me of someone so dangerous." Christian started laughing again. "Okay, seriously. What gives? What is so funny?"

"I'm sorry. It's just so amusing to me, given how otherwise confident and powerful Rider Knight is."

"What's so amusing?"

Christian wiped his eyes and gathered himself, expelling a deep breath as the last round of chuckles had been spent. "Rumor is, you're practically enraptured by a certain character on a certain TV show."

I frowned, wondering what that had to do with anything. "Dean Winchester?"

Christian's mouth spread into a wide smile as he nodded and softly chuckled.

"And?"

"Jake Porter has gotten confused with the actor several times, no doubt in part his attire and mannerisms are very similar to the character he plays. It appears the all-powerful master vampire Rider Knight… is a bit jealous, and scared of the woman he loves taking one look at the slayer and falling head over heels."

"You're telling me there's a man out there who looks and acts just like Dean Winchester?" I leaned forward, looking for a cell phone on Christian's person. "Do you have a picture of him?"

"No, I don't. Jake isn't big on pictures, like most who live in the shadows. He's a slayer, Danni."

"Yeah, a slayer who looks like Dean Winchester, who's kind of a slayer too."

"Maybe it wasn't pure jealousy that made Rider less inclined to tell you anything about Jake Porter." Christian shook his head. "Jake is family to me, but he's still a slayer, still a danger to you, no matter who he looks like."

"But he looks like Dean Winchester," I practically whined. "Ugh. What are the odds there'd be a man who looks like Dean Winchester and he's genetically designed to kill me?"

"He's married, too, and I thought you were in love with Rider? He's certainly in love with you."

"I am in love with Rider." Still, a girl could scope out a Dean lookalike as long as it was lookie no touchy. I rested my head along the back of the couch and looked at the mysterious man sitting near me. "I really am. Tell me, how has he been doing? I noticed he seemed tired before he left, and Lana said something about him being a surly beast."

All remaining humor fled Christian's eyes as he released a soft sigh and folded his hands together. "He doesn't sleep, he's extremely short-tempered, his mood souring more and more every day, and according to Jadyn, his new dog adopted him because it sensed his pain."

I felt my eyes burning and took a moment to grit my teeth and breathe deep, getting my emotions in check, knowing if I opened my mouth to speak too soon I would open up the floodgates.

"I don't tell you this to make you feel bad, only to give you an honest answer. He is a good man, and I have been worried about him. Jadyn and I had hoped the dog would help him sleep, but he still gets very little rest."

Damn it. "Please don't think I'm being cocky when I say I know he doesn't sleep well when I'm away from him."

"Your telling of the truth is not cockiness. It is easy to tell his mood and lack of sleep is due to how greatly he misses you being with him, and he worries about you quite a lot. I can imagine how hard it is for a natural protector such as himself having to entrust others to protect what is most valuable to him in this world."

"So why did he leave me here? I know him well enough to know that no matter what I say, he would drag me back with him if he thought I was in danger, or he would stay to protect me. He wouldn't leave others to do it, not even Imortians and a former angel who has some freaky lightning power. He gave me a reason, but it was weak. You know the truth, don't you?"

Christian stared at me a moment, and I could see in his eyes he knew something I wasn't supposed to know.

"What aren't you telling me, Christian? What is Rider up to back in Louisville?"

Christian sighed. "I honestly don't know why he decided to not take you back to The Midnight Rider. As for what he's been up to, I'm sure he told you about having to fend off your mother while Shana's disappearance and her husband's murder are investigated, and you're aware he has the witch who helped set up your sister's attack on you. He's trying to get to Selander Ryan through her, but she's a tough witch to break, and Seta isn't available to help him. He's using a lot of witch's net to keep Trixell contained, and he's getting help from Rihanna and Malaika. I believe you've met Malaika."

"Kind of." I recalled the witch helping Seta when I'd gone into the Bloom and nearly killed Rider. She'd helped keep me alive while Seta had done what I could only describe as a bit of magical surgery. "She helped us once."

"She's helped me many times. She's a good person, and a good witch, much like your friend, Rihanna, but neither of those witches have Seta's power. If they can't get Trixell to crack or keep her contained, Rider may have to bring in Jake."

"And what, he doesn't want me there to ooh and ah over the Dean Winchester lookalike? That's why he's letting me stay here?"

Christian shook his head, his mouth set in a grim line. "I don't know. I'm not sure he'll even bring Jake in. It was just a thought. Maybe he doesn't want you there in case something goes wrong with the witch. Maybe he has an entirely different reason."

"What do you mean?" I swallowed, and to my own ears, it sounded like an incredibly huge gulp. "What could go wrong with the witch?"

"That's his monster to deal with," Christian said, leaning forward. "We have our own monster issues right here. Thankfully, I was able to sense the demonic presence invading your mind while you slept and could make it release you. Tell me everything so I can figure out what we're dealing with here, and how to destroy it before more people die."

CHAPTER FOURTEEN

"You can tell me, Danni. I will not judge you."

"You're, like, a minister."

The side of Christian's mouth curved up. "And a good minister does not judge. I'd like to think I'm a good minister. I also used to be a vampire for many, many years. Centuries, actually. I have seen a lot of evil, darkness, and depravity, and I have seen some truly good people rise up out of that darkness. Whatever happened, whatever the demonic presence made you feel, I promise I will not judge you. I already know you're a good person."

"How?"

He tapped his chest with two of his fingers, right over his heart. "I can feel it."

"Angelic superpower?"

He grinned. "Something like that. I sensed the presence while you slept, and I sensed its hold over you. I knew you were trapped, but I couldn't see or hear what was happening. You're going to have to tell me."

I took a deep breath and let it out on a groan. "I'm really tired of demonic scumbags toying with me."

"I can imagine. Do you know who or what this one was?"

I shook my head. "No clue. Apparently you're aware of

Selander Ryan and who he is to me."

Christian nodded. "Just so you know, Seta never divulged anything about you or your situation to me, other than you were the woman Rider Knight cared for. I did, however, sense your sister's presence when Rider gave me shelter under The Midnight Rider and you could say I demanded answers. He also demanded answers about me and the situation I was in, and we shared information. Respectfully, of course, and only enough to help one another protect our loved ones."

"I know, and it's okay. I know Rider wouldn't share any information about me with anyone he didn't trust completely, and if it wasn't necessary. I had some reservations about Seta at first, but—" I flashed back to the moment she worked the spell, and instructed Rider to remove my heart, and felt my breath seize in my lungs. I quickly shoved the memory back down into whatever hole it kept popping out of, and continued. "I know Rider would never trust a woman so much if she were a blabbermouth."

"Are you cold?" Christian asked, his eyes narrowed. "You just shivered a bit."

"No, I'm fine. Really." I remembered I had the glass of blood and it would congeal if I let it cool too much, so I forced myself to drain the glass. The last swallow went down a little thick, and I fought not to grimace as it made its way to my stomach. I set the glass on the coffee table, pulled my legs up, and tucked them underneath me before continuing. "So you know Selander Ryan is my other sire, and he has gotten to me in my dreams before, from Hell, no less."

Christian nodded. "It wasn't him this time?"

"No. I thought it was at first because I smelled sulfur and the place in my dreams looks like a really dark cavern lit by torches embedded in the walls. It's a place that looks like it could be part of Hell, like the last place Selander Ryan brought me to in my dreams with him was."

"You said dreams, plural. This morning's dream wasn't your first visit with this entity?" He sat forward. "Rider brought us here after you'd had a nightmare. This entity was in that one too?"

I nodded.

"Why didn't you tell Rider?"

"Because I thought it was just a nightmare." I looked down at my hands as I fiddled with one of my nails. "Did Rider, uh, tell you why I came here?"

"The only information about you that Rider shares with me is what is absolutely necessary for me to know to ensure your safety. I wasn't told why you're here other than you're working a job, but I don't need any angelic superpowers to know there's tension between the two of you. The pain in him isn't just from a physical separation either, so I know something happened between the two of you to cause a rift."

"You said you sensed my sister and asked Rider about her. You know about the spell he and Seta worked?"

"He told me of the Bloom. The spell put your sister in a suspended state and she will now bear the Bloom during the time it should normally cycle through your system."

I nodded. "Do you know *how* they worked the spell?"

"I wasn't given details. I've witnessed Seta work several spells though. I know some are just words, and other spells require ingredients or actions."

"To work the spell, Rider took my heart. He literally reached inside my chest in that freaky, magical way he has, and he took my heart out. He didn't tell me he was going to do it. He just did it. One moment I was fighting my sister, who was doing her damnedest to kill me, the next we were across from each other, completely immobile, and Rider took out our hearts. I saw my heart beating in his hand."

"That had to be frightening," Christian said, his voice very soft.

I continued to fiddle with my nail, not ready to look at

him. I wasn't sure why, but it felt like it would be harder to get through the story if I actually looked at him and read whatever I saw in his expression. "When Rider killed Selander Ryan, he removed his heart from his chest, and he crushed it. I saw it all."

"And when he removed your heart for the spell, you thought he was going to crush yours too?"

I nodded. "It didn't help matters that during the rest of the spell, I was floating around in the afterlife with some guy I barely knew. Do you know some guy named Jon who can float around the afterlife and actually take spirits where they're supposed to go? Seta knows him."

"We've not met. I am close to Seta, but she interacts with many people I am not familiar with."

"He protected me from soul eaters. I thought I was dying." I realized I'd gotten off track and cleared my throat. "Anyway, the thing that visited me in this morning's dream was in yesterday morning's dream. It was a shadow figure, a big shadow figure. He was at least eight feet tall with massive shoulders, a big, bald head, and had a voice that kind of boomed through my chest when he spoke. I thought that dream was just a nightmare because he transformed into Rider and he took my heart. He crushed it."

"That's why you were terrified to the point Rider could feel your emotional reaction from such a distance."

"And that's why I thought it was just a nightmare," I explained. "I came here because I needed some space after what Rider did. It might seem stupid to still be so bothered by him taking my heart out, but he didn't tell me. He just did it, like he just does everything, and—"

Christian reached over and took my hand in his. No longer able to fiddle with my nail to avoid looking at him, I made eye contact and saw complete compassion and understanding in his blue gaze.

"There is nothing stupid about being frightened. You know Rider is capable of removing and crushing a heart.

You've seen him kill in that way before. You trust him, so it is perfectly understandable you would have been completely shocked when he did that as well as frightened when he removed your heart and you had no idea why or what his intention was." Still holding my hand, Christian moved to the couch, sitting next to me as he threaded his fingers through mine and squeezed before covering our joined hands with his other one. "Am I correct that when this shadow figure came to you the first time and took on Rider's appearance, and crushed your heart, you thought it just a nightmare because that scene has been playing on a loop in your mind since Rider and Seta worked that spell?"

I nodded and felt a cool trickle fall from my eye. "And I've dreamed it before. Not of him crushing my heart, or the shadow figure, but the memory of what happened that night has played in my dreams. I just want to get past it. I still love Rider. I still trust him. Why can't I stop seeing him do that?"

"Because you haven't dealt with it. I don't think you need space from Rider, Danni. I think you need to talk to him. No yelling, no fighting, but no holding back, either. You need to talk to him, and he needs to listen, and vice versa. The two of you need to do this as long as it takes until you get to the root of the real issue and come to an agreement on how to resolve it. Clearly, he didn't crush your heart. You still love each other, and you weren't afraid of him when he was here earlier. What he did isn't what's bothering you. It's how he did it."

"He didn't tell me," I said, wiping the wetness off my cheek with my free hand. "He wanted to protect me, and he had all the power to do what he needed to do, so he just did it. He always has the power. He can do whatever he wants whenever, and he doesn't have to tell me anything. He has all the control, and I have all the… terrifying uncertainty of when he's going to use his power to do whatever he wants without telling me again," I said, feeling a weight in my chest come loose.

"You just did a decent job talking that out with yourself," Christian said, giving my hand a squeeze before he released it and sat back against the edge of the couch, turning toward me. "Now you just need to have the same discussion with Rider, but first, we need to deal with our issues here. This shadow man took on Rider's form and performed an action he knew frightened you. That means this entity has access to your thoughts and fears."

"That would explain his comment about being an avid reader. He read me, but I don't think he's a vampire or anyone in Rider's nest who I'd be linked to through him. Do you know what type of entity can do that?"

"Sadly, there are multiple beings who have the ability. Some only read memories, some only sense fears, and there are some who have access to pretty much everything. I know whatever it is, it's demonic, which was why the holy light I used weakened its hold."

"You used holy light on me?" I nearly shouted as I ran my hand over my chest again in case I'd somehow missed the damage the first time. "Are you nuts? I'm a flippin' creature of the night, and half demon at that. You can't use holy light on me!"

"What is all the commotion out here?" Daniel stepped out of his room, let out an enormous yawn that threatened to set off a chain reaction, seeming to remind my body it too needed some shut-eye, and frowned as he looked between the clock on the microwave and me. "Why are you awake so early?"

"Christian still has angel juice and tried to turn me into a southern fried bat," I answered.

Christian chuckled as Daniel's frown deepened, his brow furrowed in confusion. Between it and the disheveled state of his rainbow-colored hair, he was kind of adorable as he placed his hands on his hips and gave his head a disoriented little shake. "I feel like I'm missing something."

"All is well, Daniel. Go back to sleep. I'm awake to

watch over Danni, and she'll be going back to sleep soon."

Daniel stood there for a moment, blinking, then let out another huge yawn. "All right," he said through the tail end of the yawn, "but former angel or not, anything happens to her, I'll kick your fluffy ass." He turned, stumbled back into his room, closing the door all but a crack. I heard him land on his bed and imagined he must have fallen face-forward onto it.

"He cares a lot for you," Christian said, grinning as he stared at the door, clearly not offended by Daniel's threat.

My face flushed a little, remembering what Ginger had told me. "Yeah, he's a good friend, and about as protective as Rider, but fortunately, not quite as controlling."

Christian looked over at me and held my gaze for a moment, something in his eyes making me feel as though he knew something I didn't. He cleared his throat and turned his torso to face me again. "You're not evil, Danni. Holy light won't kill you or do any physical damage. I wouldn't have used it on you if I thought it would injure you."

"It hurt," I told him as I absently rubbed the center of my chest where he'd directed it. "Burned like fire."

"I'm sorry," he apologized. "I could have contacted Rider to pull you from the dream, but I sensed time was of the essence, and I just went with my gut instinct. I didn't even know I could do that until I did it."

"You did the right thing," I told him as I remembered what had been about to happen right before he'd rescued me. "There was no time to waste."

He angled his head to get a better look into my eyes, which I'd lowered. "I sensed the succubus in you rising. What was about to happen, Danni? Please trust me so I can help you."

I forced myself to meet his eyes, looked deep into them, seeing only sincerity, and spilled everything. Maybe it was the fact I knew the man had been an angel, maybe it was the ridiculously kind way he looked at me, but once I started talking, I found I couldn't stop. I had to break off eye contact to get through the embarrassing parts, but I didn't leave out a single detail of the dreams, not even the way I'd been aroused by the vulgar acts that had been happening around me in the cavern.

I even told him how badly I'd wanted Daniel, and had started to desire Holden as well before Rider arrived and sated me.

"This entity knows your struggle to keep your succubus side caged, and it desperately wants to set it free."

I nodded my agreement and fought to keep my eyes open. Having spilled the secrets and fears I'd been holding back, I was completely spent. "Do you know what it is, and why it's doing this to me?"

Christian leaned back, a faraway look in his eyes as he ran his finger back and forth over his lips, thinking. "It seems to enjoy toying with you. That it can affect you to the point your succubus needs remain after you wake speaks to its strength. I think it's doing this for amusement, and it could be feeding. Some demonic entities feed off fear or chaos."

"Does any of what you said narrow down what the entity is?" I asked, stifling a yawn.

"If I were to go off appearance and your dreams alone, I'd say it was a djinn."

"A genie? Like the smoky people who live in oil lamps and grant wishes?"

"Genies are a type of djinn. There are good djinn and evil djinn. The entity in your dreams would definitely be an evil djinn, if it were indeed a djinn."

"Can djinn take on the appearance of people I know?"

"Yes."

"Are they freakishly huge with blue-tinted skin and the ability to appear as shadow people?"

"Yes."

"So why—" I yawned, and felt my eyelids drifting closed as my head lulled forward. I quickly snapped it back up. "Why aren't you sure this is a djinn?"

"Because it's highly strange that a djinn would randomly invade your dreams around the same time you're tracking a monster that attacks exactly like a pontianak, a monster not even native to the vicinity, and in the same area where you killed zombies, that don't exist, by the way."

"Are we sure zombies don't exist? Because, I mean, I killed some." I opened my eyes wide, forcing them to stay open. "They were all bloody and smelly and juicy and everything."

"Yeah, it's a mystery," Christian murmured as he stood and walked over to the table where he unplugged the charger from his laptop before tucking the computer under his arm, and returned to me. "Time for you to go back to bed."

"I can't. That thing will get me again."

"No arguing." He put his hand under my armpit and hauled me up, then walked me to my room. "I haven't been human long enough to forget the importance of day sleep. Give in to it. I'll be right here watching over you, and if I sense that entity bothering you, I can do what I did earlier or contact Rider to pull you out."

"No," I mumbled as I crawled into the bed. "I don't want to disturb Rider in case he's sleeping. He needs sleep. Use the holy light. Just don't turn me into a french fry."

Christian chuckled as he lowered himself onto the bed next to me and opened the laptop. "Sweet dreams, Danni."

CHAPTER FIFTEEN

I came awake slowly and stretched my body, feeling more rested than I had in weeks. As my back arched off the bed, getting the full benefit of the stretch, I opened my eyes and frowned, noticing new décor hanging on the wall at the head of my bed.

"I hung that a few hours ago."

I jerked, realizing I wasn't alone, and turned my head toward Christian's voice as my back crashed back down onto the mattress. He sat next to the bed in a chair he'd brought in from the dining table, still dressed in the same clothes he'd been wearing when he'd sent me back to bed. He had one leg pulled up so his ankle rested over his opposite knee, and he leaned back in the chair with his arms folded over his midsection. His eyes were alert, but a little red-rimmed.

I sat up and looked at the dreamcatcher. I'd seen hundreds of them in stores, but none like this one. The hoop and the webbed design woven through it appeared to be silver. The few beads caught within the web were some kind of pearlescent stone, not the normal plastic beads I usually saw on dreamcatchers, and a silver ribbon had been tied to the webbing, a blood red rock shaped similarly to a human heart affixed to the fabric. Three darker ribbons hung from the bottom of the hoop and affixed to those ribbons were more of the pearlescent stones and large black feathers. "You didn't get that in any store near here."

"I had it delivered."

I had a feeling the dreamcatcher had been witch-delivered, which meant it was definitely not some generic retail product, and had a far more useful purpose than décor. It was the real deal. "So, is this some type of magical dreamcatcher that catches and kills the djinn or whatever?"

"It's more of an alarm system," he said, dragging a hand down his face as he yawned.

"Geez, Christian, did you get any sleep at all?" I asked, instantly feeling a pang of guilt. It was bad enough Rider wasn't sleeping well due to me leaving. Now I'd caused another man to skip out on his needed rest.

"No, I didn't want to risk it in case the entity returned and you needed me, but it's all right. I'm going to crash after I get everyone updated." He sat up, both feet on the floor, and stretched. "I've been tumbling around some thoughts all day, and I have a theory. Get up, do whatever you need to do, and I'll be out there with the others when you're ready."

He stood, grabbed the chair, and took it out of the room, closing the door behind him to give me my privacy. I swung my legs over the side of the bed and stood up, studying the dreamcatcher. I reached out and touched it with my fingertips, feeling a little zing of electricity. Yep, this was definitely not your regular run-of-the-mill dreamcatcher.

Since I'd showered the night before, I just freshened up, brushed my teeth, did a quick finger comb of my hair, and changed out my clothes for a pair of jeans and a black long-sleeved T-shirt after slathering on the sunblock. Night hadn't fallen yet, and I wasn't sure what my plans were going to be for the day. I swiped on a coat of cherry red lip gloss, pulled on my black on black Adidas, and left my bedroom to join the others.

Angel sat at the dining table, wearing lounge pants and a BTS T-shirt, eating a bowl of ramen noodles. Holden sat across from her, finishing off a sandwich piled high with ham, turkey, and roast beef. Just the smell of the meat made my sensitive stomach want to purge, so I was thankful when he shoved the last bit of it into his mouth and gobbled it up. His face was scruffier than the day before, but he was dressed in fresh jeans and a hunter green flannel shirt, so he'd definitely cleaned up since he'd left earlier in the morning.

Daniel sat at the table, facing me, but staring down into the mug of steaming coffee his large hands were wrapped around. The lower portion of his face was covered with honey-colored growth, and it was the first time I'd known him not to be clean-shaven. His eyes were a little squinted as if he hadn't gotten much sleep, but he was dressed for the day in jeans and a Def Leppard T-shirt.

Lana stood in the kitchenette, her hip leaning against the sink. Her arms were folded under her breasts, which were covered by her long-sleeved olive-green shirt that molded to the contours of her hourglass shaped body, just like her dark jeans. She chewed her plump bottom lip as she watched Daniel.

Christian, who stood near the table, caught my eye and tilted his head, gesturing for me to join them, so I walked over to the couch and took a seat beside Ginger, who rocked her normal punk rebel look in black skinny jeans, a black T-shirt with a big middle finger on it, and a cropped black leather jacket. Her lips were painted crimson, and her eyes lined in black.

"I hope you all weren't waiting long for me," I said.

"I just got here about fifteen minutes ago," Holden said, leaning back in his chair. "I didn't sleep too great."

None of them looked as if they'd slept well, except for Angel, who merrily went about eating her noodles as if the cabin hadn't filled with even more freaky creatures. I supposed she was getting used to our paranormal world.

"You haven't inconvenienced anyone," Christian said as he shoved his hands into his pockets, "but I wanted to get everyone together so I could go over this with everyone at the same time, then catch some sleep."

"You have an idea what the hell is going on around here?" Holden asked.

"I think I do," Christian answered. "Holden, you weren't wrong about the pontianak. What happened to Gruff's employee had all the signs of a pontianak attack, except for the location."

"So you think the pontianak is still out there hunting?" the werewolf asked, perking up a little.

"I think there could be a similar attack, but I think there might be more than pontianaks and zombies to worry about."

"Zombies aren't real," Holden said, scratching the scruff along his jaw. "I know we killed some freaks that sure as hell looked like zombies, but this shit isn't adding up. You got an explanation for it? I tossed and turned all morning trying to come up with something, and nothing's clicking."

"That's because we don't have all the puzzle pieces," Christian replied, "and the ones we have don't fit completely. The attack on Rob was straight out of the pontianak playbook, but the location is illogical. From your description of the monsters you slaughtered last night, you killed a bunch of zombies, but that entire incident is illogical. I was told some truckers have been reported missing after stopping at Gruff's, and we don't know what's happened to them, but it could be related to these incidents, and the incident with Danni," he added, glancing at me.

Every head in the room turned toward me, except for Daniel's, and my heart stopped. I looked at Christian and he gave his head a very subtle shake, and winked.

"I had to wake Danni from a bad dream early this morning," he said, recapturing everyone's attention. Daniel, I noticed, didn't really look at either of us as he picked up his coffee mug and took a drink. Lana glanced his way, but returned her attention to Christian as he continued speaking. "As was explained previously when I arrived and those who met me before could tell I'd been a vampire before and no longer gave off the vibe, I used to be an angel. I gave that life up to become human, and I was supposed to have been stripped of my vampirism, and my grace, which is what gives an angel power. Rider has suspected that I might be a guardian, and this morning pretty much solidified that. I sensed a demonic entity attacking Danni as she slept, and fortunately I have some grace left because it enabled me to wake her and pull her free of the entity's clutches."

"What kind of demonic entity?" Ginger asked, moving closer until we were hip to hip. She slid her arm through mine. "Is Selander Ryan back? What happened?"

"It wasn't Selander Ryan." I looked at Christian. "Right? We're sure it wasn't him?"

"Selander Ryan is an incubus, and an incubus does have the ability to travel and attack people through dreams, especially when there's a connection between the incubus and its prey. However, it can't create a pontianak or zombies, so we can rule out Selander Ryan."

"What are you saying?" Holden's brow furrowed. "You're saying whatever attacked Danni is creating monsters and unleashing them into the world?"

"And what do you mean by attack?" Ginger asked. She looked at me. "What kind of attack, Danni? What happened and why didn't you tell us?"

"You were sleeping," Christian answered, saving me from struggling to come up with a response I could comfortably share with everyone in the room. "I woke Danni as soon as I felt the demonic presence, which was before it could hurt her. There's nothing to worry about. It was handled."

Ginger relaxed a little, but still stuck to my side. "Oh. Well, it's a good thing Rider sent you here to help then."

Christian nodded, and made eye contact with me before dipping his head just a fraction, a discreet little nod to let me know he would keep the humiliating parts of my nightmare to himself.

I released my pent-up breath, careful not to release an obvious sigh in the process, and caught Daniel looking at me, but he lowered his gaze the moment I made eye contact. Strange. I felt a little exposed, but wasn't sure why. Deciding it was just paranoia on my part due to the fear I'd had of Christian telling everyone all of what we'd discussed that morning, I squashed it down.

"Based on Danni's physical description of the entity that invaded Danni's dream, I would say it was a djinn, and not the good kind, but the odds of a djinn attacking Danni the same time these other types of paranormal beings are being spotted aren't that good. It doesn't feel right."

"So the thing that attacked Danni in her dream isn't causing the other incidents?" Holden asked.

"What's with the dreamcatcher you put in her room?" Angel asked as she stood with her bowl, collected Holden's plate, and took the dishes to the sink. "Are you going to catch the demon thing?"

"If the entity invading Danni's dreams is a real djinn, the dreamcatcher will work to prevent it from returning. If, as I suspect, the djinn is just another illusion being created by the real monster preying upon this area, the djinn will return and the dreamcatcher will work as an alarm, notifying whoever is watching over her of its presence. This way, she's protected even if I fall asleep while she's asleep and don't sense the entity."

"Man, these things aren't illusions," Holden said. "We were really slicing and dicing whatever the hell those zombie-looking bastards were."

"And Rob really died," Daniel said, looking up at the

former angel. "In an extremely horrifying way I wish was just an illusion."

"I have no doubt you really fought against something in the woods, and a monster did attack and kill your friend, but I don't think everything is quite as it seems. It doesn't make sense that these particular beings would be here."

"So what do you think is causing this?" Daniel asked.

"Have you ever heard of a trickster?"

"Like on *Supernatural*?" Angel asked before I could.

Christian raised his hand, palm out. "Please, forget everything you've seen on television. In actual lore, have any of you heard of a trickster?"

"You mean like Loki from Norse mythology?" Holden asked, folding his arms as he leaned back in his chair, starting to look like he wasn't buying what Christian was selling. "Brother of Thor?"

"Norse mythology is all fiction," Christian said, "but the tale of Loki was inspired by actual tricksters, so you're close. A trickster is not some mythical god of mischief. It's a demon, and a powerful demon at that. It can take on the form of anyone or anything it wants. It can read through people's memories and find their fears. It likes to toy with people, and it likes to create chaos and fear."

"Like letting monsters loose in a small town," I said, catching on.

Christian nodded. "The pontianak and the zombies fall into that category, but invading your sleeping mind to mess with you is personal. If I'm right, and a trickster is behind what's happening here, it's specifically targeted you for some reason."

Again, every head in the room turned toward me, including Daniel's. The tiredness in his eyes fled, replaced by the protective fire I usually saw burning there. I wished some of that fire could find its way into me because my blood had run cold. "A powerful demon has a vendetta against me?"

"More likely, someone else, and they're using the

trickster to do their bidding."

Like Selander Ryan, I thought. Gah, I was so sick of that demonic pain-in-my-ass. Why couldn't the evil bastard just rot like everyone else did when they died? No, he was living it up in Hell, rubbing elbows with tricksters and imps and Charles Manson, greasing palms and making deals.

"Not who I'm sure you're thinking of," Christian said. "Tricksters don't do favors, especially not for lesser demons who've died and gone to Hell. The only way to get one to do one's bidding is to summon it to the physical realm and bind it."

"You're saying someone summoned a trickster," Holden said. "Someone in this general area has trapped a demon capable of creating monsters and is getting their kicks, letting that thing have its fun?"

"Not exactly." Christian held up his finger while he let out an enormous yawn. The poor guy was ready to drop. "Sorry," he said after finishing. "I think what's happened can be compared to when a foolish person uses a Ouija board or holds a séance, hoping to reach out to a beloved one who has passed, and ends up drawing an evil entity into their home instead. Whoever summoned the trickster probably had no idea what he or she was in for. Summoning spells aren't for amateurs, and any tiny thing done even the slightest bit off can have severe consequences. This person may have tried summoning a genie or a witch. Even if they did intentionally try to summon a demon, they were probably trying for a lower-level demon."

"So some idiot went playing around where they had no business and brought an uber-demon out of Hell," Lana said, sounding more than a bit peeved. "And since the demon had to be summoned, this means whoever did it has to already be here in the physical realm?"

"Correct," Christian said.

"And then they sicced the demon on me?" I asked.

"It would seem like it, however, they may have not done so intentionally. Like I said, that whole god of mischief thing was inspired by tricksters. Are you familiar with the short story, *The Monkey's Paw*?"

"Yeah," I answered, trying to remember the details. "We had to read it in school. There was a monkey's paw that you could wish on or something, but every time someone made a wish, even though they got what they wanted, something horrific happened to make that wish come true. I think one of the wishes was for a specific amount of money and the person who made the wish got it, but it was an insurance payout after their child died in a freak accident."

"Tricksters work similarly to the way the monkey's paw worked in that story. They'll grant a wish, but not in the way the person making the request wants. Even worse, if someone has bound the trickster, that person doesn't actually have to ask for a wish to be granted. The trickster knows their desires and fulfills wishes the person might not even know they've made in their hearts."

"So if Danni just bumped into someone who happened to have bound a trickster and that person thought 'Wow, what a bitch, I hope she falls,' the trickster could like… shove her off the top of a building?" Ginger asked.

"It really concerns me how easily such violent thoughts come to you," I told her.

"I'm just trying to understand how this works. To understand an evil entity, you gotta kind of go to the dark side, ya know?"

"That is a scenario that could happen," Christian said, "but again, tricksters don't really do things *for* people. Any action it takes, even if that action indirectly fulfills what the summoner wants, will be for its own amusement, and tricksters are amused by creating chaos, creating fear, and toying with people similarly to how a cat toys with a mouse."

"So it won't push me off a building," I said. "That

would be too quick with too little a reward. It wants me scared or otherwise tormented."

"Yes." Christian nodded. "And although it's highly likely whoever summoned it brought you to its attention, intentionally or not, it's messing with you because it wants to."

"Great. Being the source of a demon's shits and giggles is just what I need." I took a moment to breathe. "You said intentionally or not, so there is a way to intentionally pinpoint someone for it to go after."

Christian nodded. "If the summoner can mark a target, it can put the trickster on that target's scent, so to speak. Tricksters can enter a target's mind easier if they've made a physical connection, whether that be through blood, saliva, or a deep scratch."

"I know that has to suck," Holden said, "but the upside is if this is what's actually happening, we have a starting point to investigate. The pontianak and zombie attacks were too random to piece together a connection, and I'd assumed the missing truckers could have fallen prey to the pontianak, but no bodies turned up. But if this thing is toying with you, we can look into that and hopefully trace this thing back to whoever summoned it."

"Exactly," Christian said, "and actually, I think I may have found some of those missing truckers." He moved over to the laptop on the table and tapped a few keys before turning the laptop so Holden could see the screen. "I had a hunch, so I pulled up some recent missing persons reports matching truckers who'd gone missing after visiting this area. Recognize any of them?"

Holden looked at the screen and I saw recognition dawn in his eyes before he let out a soft curse. Daniel leaned over to look at the screen and closed his eyes before turning his head away.

I moved over to the table, instinctively knowing what I'd see, and not wanting to, but I had no choice. My legs moved on their own until I reached the table and looked over Holden's shoulder to see the faces of the missing people staring back at me. The first my eyes latched onto belonged to a man named Carl Green, a father of three from Arkansas, and a man whose eye sockets I had rammed my fingers into before using his head to take out other men whose faces stared back at me from the screen. And there was Stuart Woodson, who I knew went by Stu because that was the name embroidered on his shirt when I'd sank my blade into his forehead. Stu wasn't even out of his twenties, and according to the information given to the police department, he only drove trucks on the weekends because during the week he tended to his bedridden mother.

"There were women too," I said, wiping at my eyes. "I remember stomping on a woman's face, crushing it."

"You didn't know," Holden said as Daniel reached over and gave my hand a squeeze before quickly dropping it and leaning back in his chair, looking as pissed off, disgusted, and devastated as I felt.

"I searched for the truckers since I had a hunch they were involved in the zombie attack," Christian said softly, "but I'm sure the women have been reported missing as well, all from here or surrounding areas."

"I'll look into it," Holden said. "I'll go to the station and try to get a full report of just how many have gone missing since the first missing trucker was reported, and talk to the police, figure out what they know. Explain this to me. Did we kill innocent people last night?"

"Anyone who died was killed because of the trickster, not because of you," Christian said in a stern voice that warned there would be no argument with him on this statement. "Those people might have already been dead to begin with, or depending on how powerful this trickster is, they could have been created out of nothing but the demon's imagination and made to look like the missing people. Tricksters like to mess with people's minds, remember? They like to taunt people, and nothing is more fun to them than making people hate themselves."

"Focusing on whether or not you actually killed innocent people isn't going to do anything to make sure no one else dies," Lana said. She removed a switchblade from her pocket and started twirling it in her hand. "How do we end this thing?"

"It's not easy," Christian said, "but it is possible. You have to find it. The trickster can take on the form of anything, but it can also project itself like a hologram. It can possess people as well. It can die like a mortal if you stab it with a silver blade, but the hard part is finding it, since you will never see its true form until the silver has entered its body."

"So it can hide in plain sight," I said, "by wearing other people's faces."

"Basically," he answered. "You have to stab it in its heart, which can be more difficult than it sounds because you will have to stab it no matter whose face it is wearing. This thing is a master imitator, and can survive for eons because people aren't likely to go for a kill shot if they think there's even the slightest possibility they may be killing someone else."

"Speaking of kill shot," Holden said. "Do silver bullets work?"

"Only if you hit dead center in the heart," Christian said.

"You said something about the summoner binding this thing," Ginger said. "What does that mean? Is it stuck somewhere, like in a trap?"

"That depends on the binding," Christian answered. "It could be caught in a physical trap using an occult symbol and blood magic, or if the summoner was really stupid, he or she could have bound it to themselves, meaning as long as they live, it goes where they go, and they can't send the thing back to Hell without dying. Also, if the binding is deep enough, you may have to kill them to stop the trickster."

"So even if the idiot didn't mean for anyone to die, they'll fight tooth and nail to keep that thing hidden," Lana said, "just to save their own skin."

Christian nodded. "If Danni is visited in her sleep again, we'll know for sure this is a trickster at work, but I'm pretty sure about it already, so I would recommend not wasting any time. You need to find the person who summoned it." He yawned. "I need to get some sleep and I'll dig further. While I rest, I think it best you give an appearance of normalcy. That means those of you assigned as security at Gruff's should go to work, but keep an eye out for anything strange, particularly try to figure out who would have something against Danni, no matter how slight. Holden, you can investigate, and Lana can assist. Danni's been spending most of her time at Gruff's since coming to this area, so those of you on security there really need to keep an eye out. If she was intentionally targeted by the summoner, that means the summoner might be a regular or even an employee, and she may not be the only person in the area targeted. Rob could have been a specific target."

"We need to look into who you and Rob both had physical contact with," Holden said, turning toward me. "Has anyone bled on you, scratched you, gotten their DNA into you in any way?"

I thought over all I'd done since arriving to work at Gruff's and shook my head. "I mean, I drink from Angel, and I drank from Christian when he was first here."

"I didn't summon anything," Angel said, raising her hands. "I won't even enter a house that has a Ouija board in it. I'm not stupid."

"I know it wouldn't be Angel," Ginger said. "She'd sic a trickster on Daniel before she'd ever sic one on Danni, even if it were on accident, just for his comments on her baking and music."

"Is Angel in danger?" I asked. "She's just a human. Can this thing attack her?"

Christian looked at the teenager, who'd pulled herself up on the kitchen counter and had gone a little pale listening to us. "Anyone in the area could be harmed or killed by the trickster. She needs to be armed with silver, just in case. Everyone has silver blades? I can have them sent if not."

"I have more than enough to share if they don't," Holden said. "And I have silver bullets."

"Will imortium work?" Lana asked, looking at her blade, which appeared silver to me, but I knew enough about imortium to know it looked like silver to anyone who'd never set foot in Imortia or been born of Imortian blood.

"I have no idea," Christian answered. "I would go with silver rather than risk the chance of using a weapon that has no effect on the trickster."

"All right." She closed the switchblade and shoved it into her pocket. "I'll need one of those silver blades, Holden."

"All right. Danni, if I can have a moment?" Christian walked toward the room he shared with Daniel, and I followed him.

I hadn't actually been in the room since we'd first arrived. It was small with two twin beds, clearly meant to be a kids' room, but the beds were big enough to accommodate a six-foot man's stature, even if he didn't have much room to roll around in. Daniel had taken the room, giving the nicer ones up to us girls, but looking at the smaller bed now, I felt kind of bad about that.

"I informed Rider of my theory," Christian said, closing the door to give us a bit of privacy. "I didn't tell him any specific details about your dreams, just that the trickster may be causing you to have nightmares. You may want to reach out to him. This trickster will use everything at its disposal to toy with you, including any issues you have with those close to you."

I wrapped my arms around myself and nodded. "That's

why it took on Rider's appearance and made him crush my heart. It knows my fears."

"And desires," Christian said, his voice barely a murmur as he moved his eyes toward the door, where Daniel resided beyond.

"Christian, I don't—"

"I'm not judging you, Danni, so you don't need to try to convince me you are not attracted to Daniel. I've been a minister for centuries. I know how to listen to people in a way others don't. I see things others don't, things others sometimes can't even see in themselves. Denying what you truly feel will give this entity power. It will try everything to break you by using your own fears and emotions against you. Try not to feed it."

I expelled a breath. "That doesn't sound easy."

"It's not. I understand not wanting to share your private thoughts with the others, and I respect that, but you have to be honest with yourself, and it would help to be as honest as you can be with the others you love."

I scrubbed my hands down my face. "All right."

"I know this is hard and scary." He squeezed my shoulder and stifled a yawn. "This thing is choosing to attack you while you sleep and are most vulnerable to its mind intrusion, so you should be safe from it while you're awake, and you know Daniel and Ginger will watch your back. Just try to think of how any DNA could have gotten into your system, or who might have a grievance against you, no matter how small."

I nodded. "I will."

"Good." He gave my shoulder another squeeze before letting go and lowering himself onto one of the twin beds, clothes and all. "Now get out of here and let me sleep. And call Rider."

"Yes, sir."

I stepped out of the room, closing the door behind me. "I'll be back in a moment," I told the others as I walked to my room, grabbed my cell phone from the nightstand, and pressed the button to connect me to Rider.

CHAPTER SIXTEEN

I closed the door for a little privacy as Rider answered before the first ring had finished. "Are you okay?"

I grinned. That was Rider. No hello, no casual inquiry into what I was up to, just an immediate need to know if I was all right. "I'm good. Christian told me he filled you in on what he thinks is happening here."

"He did." He went silent, and I could sense him wanting to ask me about the dreams, but something held him back.

"Did you sleep well today?" I asked.

"I'm fine," he said, avoiding a direct answer, not that I really needed one. I could hear the tiredness in his voice. "You? I mean, after you spoke with Christian this morning?"

I sighed as I sat on my bed, leaning back against the headboard. "I know Christian told you about my dreams and that he thinks this demonic entity is toying with me. I didn't call for you because it didn't seem like I was in immediate mortal danger. It was just … messing with me."

"I know. One moment." The line went so quiet I knew he'd muted the call on his end. "Sorry," he said a moment later. "Just had to handle some business. What do you need, Danni? Do you need me to come help, or do you want me to stay here?"

My mouth dropped open, and I just sat there, stunned into silence.

"Danni?"

"I'm sorry. I thought I'd called Rider Knight. I don't believe you and I have met, stranger."

He let out a soft chuckle. "I'm trying, Danni. I can tell you it's not easy. I really wanted to bring you back with me this morning. Hell, I never wanted to let you go in the first place."

"So why didn't you make me come back?" I asked. "I mean, I appreciate it, but I really expected you to declare this job far too dangerous for me and find a reason to lock me away."

He went deathly silent for a long enough stretch I thought the call might have dropped.

"Rider?"

"Am I really that bad?" he finally asked, his voice low, and completely resigned. Not a hint of anger. He almost sounded defeated, which completely threw me for a loop. I was about to apologize for calling the wrong person again, and actually mean it. "I know I have a temper, and I need to be in control. It's been my duty to protect for so long, and I've fought against a darkness you've only seen the tip of. I've grown used to calling the shots, making the decisions, and I honestly never cared if I pissed anyone off because at the end of the day, it was the result that mattered, not the means. I've survived so long because I'm a controlling, bossy sonofabitch, and if being that way keeps you safe… I just want you to be safe, Danni. If I'm an asshole the way I go about protecting you, or I make you miserable, I am sorry. The thought of losing you is just—"

I heard a deep bark and a whine that grew closer, and imagined Rider's dog rushing to his side to comfort him. My mouth fell open. My eyes watered. "Rider…"

"Yeah, I know. I sound like a damn needy jackass, but you know what? I don't fucking care. I love you, Danni, and it was bad enough when I found out you were dreaming about me crushing your heart, but knowing this damn thing is screwing with you by making you see me do that, knowing that it's my face and your fear of me that is helping it get to you… That's eating me alive. I can't be responsible for something hurting you. I just can't." He took a deep, shuddering breath. "Tell me what the hell I have to do to fix this, to make you not be afraid of me. What do I need to say or do for you to know I'm not the monster in your dreams?"

"I know you're not a monster." My chest ached. I knew Rider loved me, and his love and need to protect me had always been intense, but I'd never heard such vulnerability in him before. "I think you just said a lot, actually, and I'm not miserable with you, Rider. I love you too." I thought about the conversation I'd had with Christian after he'd awakened me from my dream. "Can I be honest with you, and you just listen?"

"Yes," he said softly, without a moment's hesitation.

I went over my conversation with Christian, and the conversation I'd had with Ginger before the zombies showed up. I went all the way back to conversations I'd had with Daniel, Nannette, and Eliza, and I took a breath as all the jumbled pieces started to come together.

"I'm not the same person I was when we met. I've changed, and I'm still changing, but I remember who I was. I was weak, needy, and I honestly didn't like myself very much. I always felt expendable. You're the first real love I've had, and just as I was accepting this, Auntie Mo dropped the soulmate bomb on me. It felt like maybe this love wasn't real, that you didn't have a choice to love me, you just did because we were created to be together, and it just seemed like… I don't know, like it was a cheat, that it was all too easy, like the decision to be together wasn't even ours. That probably sounds so stupid." I groaned and lowered my head into my hands, struggling to find the words. "Rider?"

"I'm here. I didn't want to interrupt, and that doesn't sound stupid. I think I understand what you're saying. Go on."

"Okay." I sat back up and took a breath as I organized my thoughts. "Whether or not it was a cheat how we came together, I love you. I've always known in my heart that it's been real for me, but I've had to *trust* that it's real for you, and trust hasn't always been easy for me. I went from a woman with no confidence at all, no belief I'd ever find love, to being told I was loved by a man so far outside the realm of what I thought was within my league.

"I know I haven't made anything easy for you, but you've never given up on me. You've stayed with me, a massive standing wall, no matter how hard I've pushed against you. You didn't give up on me when I went through the Bloom and almost killed you. You turned my sister when your every instinct told you not to, and you lost some of your own people over me. You killed your own brother to save me. Yet, when I saw my heart in your hand, all I could think of was that my life was literally in your hand and I didn't know if you were going to keep it or end it, because I didn't know if your love was a choice you made, or just something you had to feel because we were supposedly made for each other. I didn't know if you wanted to love me, or resented the fact you had to because it was predesigned."

I wiped my eyes, realizing I'd started crying. I suddenly felt lighter, as if a huge weight had been lifted off my shoulders, and the muddled confusion in my head had finally arranged itself into something that could be processed.

"I just realized that. It's been rolling around in my head and heart for so long, but I finally can make sense of it. With Nannette's help, my self-esteem has gotten better since we met, but even though my confidence is stronger, I could never shake the questions in the back of my mind: How strong could a love be that just happened so quickly? How real could it be? How could anyone love the mess I was?

"That's why I'm here now. I need to prove I'm strong enough to not need to be saved, and I need to be on equal footing. I want you to choose to love me because you respect me, and because you want to share your life with me, not because fate threw us together, and you feel obligated to protect me. I need to know you won't perform a spell like that on me without telling me again just because being your soulmate and fledgling means you can do whatever you want to me. I need to be your respected partner that you share plans with, not your property you can boss around and expect to just be okay with it."

I grabbed the top sheet off my bed and used it to dab my eyes while I waited for Rider's response. The only thing I heard was a series of whines from his dog. "Rider? Are you mad?"

"No," he answered, sounding a bit choked. "I'm just processing. I don't really know how to respond, other than to tell you I honestly don't give a fuck about any of that soulmate shit. I love you, and I'd love you even if we weren't soulmates, and I am truly sorry if I've failed to show you that."

My heart, which had felt so light with the relief of letting go of all that I'd been holding in, filled with regret, picking up on the hurt in his voice. "I didn't mean to imply…" I sighed. "I'm sorry if I—"

"No, Danni. Don't apologize for telling me how you feel. You never have to do that, and you damn sure don't have to prove anything to me. I'm sorry you've been harboring all these doubts, and that I had any part in that. I love you because you're you, and I do respect you. I'm working on the controlling thing. I really am, but just know it's not because you're my property. It's because you're my heart and soul… and you have no idea how much I didn't want to perform that spell, but I couldn't lose you. I'll die before I lose you."

I willed myself not to start crying again. "You know, I think we talk better with each other over the phone. We should do this more."

He chuckled. "Eh, I think it's more that I just miss the hell out of you, and I'm not the only one. I asked Tony about that call he had with Gruff. Turns out the jackass insinuated I was with a woman hoping it would be relayed to you and you'd come back to mark your territory. I think all the guys miss you and your interrogation prowess."

I laughed. "You didn't punish Tony, did you?"

"Not painfully, but when Kutya has to go out, he's the designated pooper scooper."

I shook my head. Never in a million years did I think I'd hear Rider Knight utter the words *pooper scooper*. "I think the guys just miss having someone to laugh at."

"Danni, no one here laughs at you because they think you're a joke. They laugh because they like you, and they respect the hell out of you when you get in that interrogation room."

The mentions of interrogation reminded me of Trixell. "Is everything going okay there? Christian didn't give me a lot of information, but he said the witch that helped Shana set up the attack on me wasn't very forthcoming."

"Yeah, she's a pain, and as much as I wouldn't mind killing her, we need to know what she knows so we can figure out what Ryan is up to. Rihanna and Malaika have been helping. I'll get her to crack."

"And my mother?"

"Grissom's handling her. You have enough on your plate where you're at. I have everything under control here."

"And there's nothing you're not telling me? You're being very good about letting me stay here. Too good."

"Hey, I told you I'll still drag your ass back here if the

danger gets too high so you might not want to sing my praises just yet." He was quiet for a moment, almost as if he were hesitating to continue. "I left good people with you, and it sounds like my hunch about Christian being a guardian was correct. I know you think I don't believe in you when I assign people to protect you, but I do believe in you. I'm just more experienced and know how things can go sideways, especially when you're still learning the ropes of this world. You're strong and you're determined, but you're stubborn, which can be an issue. Please be careful, Danni."

"I will," I promised after an initial moment of surprise that he managed to say all that without being bossy or demanding.

"This is hard for me, but I want you to be here because you want to be here, so I'm trying real hard to let you do what you need to do. Just please understand that you have nothing to prove to me, or to anyone else, nothing at all. I would never ask you to prove anything to me, and Danni… I would never hurt you."

I sighed. "Yeah. Yeah, I know. The heart thing… It just freaked me out, but I realize now it wasn't just about that moment. It was all the stuff in my head."

"I know. I'll never crush your heart, Danni. Literally or figuratively."

"And… if something ever happens where you have to save my life, but in a way like…"

"I will always save your life no matter the cost, but I promise you I will make every effort to let you know what I have to do beforehand. Let's make a deal. I'll work harder to be more open with you, and to include you in major decisions regarding your safety, if you'll be more open to understanding that I am as powerful as I am for a reason, and sometimes I have no choice but to make immediate decisions. Any choice I do make, however, will always be in your best interest."

"Okay," I said, nodding, although he wasn't there to

see me. "And I guess if I'm going to work for you, I do need to recognize you as my boss."

"Holy shit. Can you wait a minute? I need to get something to record this on."

"Funny." I chuckled. "You know, I'm less inclined to fight with you when you actually listen."

"Yeah. I'm less inclined to bark my orders when you listen to me. Interesting how this works."

"Yeah, I wonder if other people know about this listening stuff?"

He laughed softly before letting out a sigh. "I miss you, and I really wish you were here with me, but I want you to do whatever you need to do so that when you return here, you know it's your decision. I'm not going to order you back here, and I'm going to fight my every instinct to carry you out of there and lock you away where I know you're safe. Just promise me you'll remember what I said about not needing to prove yourself. If Christian, Daniel, or any of the others tell you something, listen to them. You're a fighter, Danni, and you're smart, but they have the experience. It's not a pissing contest. It never has been."

I thought about what he said, and for the first time I didn't immediately want to rebel against him, because he wasn't bossing me around and what he said made good sense. I might be stubborn, but I wasn't a fool, even if my temper made me act like one sometimes. "I promise. I'll stay safe, think before I act, and Rider… I'm coming home after we destroy this thing."

By the time I finished my conversation with Rider and emerged from my bedroom, Holden and Lana had left to do some digging at the police station and medical center, but the werewolf had left silver switchblades for our use.

"You don't hesitate, you just sink that blade right in the heart if anything attacks you," Daniel instructed Angel as he handed her a blade. He'd shaved while I'd been in my room, but still had a tinge of red rimming his eyes. "And that's only if you can't get to Christian. If anything weird happens, if you even think something feels off, you wake him up and you call us."

"Yes, sir, Captain, sir," Angel quipped, taking the switchblade. She flipped it open and studied its sharp point.

"Smartass," Daniel muttered. "We could drag you to Gruff's with us."

"Isn't that where the last dude died?"

"Do something with her," he said, speaking to me for the first time since I'd awakened.

"This is serious," I said to the girl as I snapped a silver switchblade closed and slid it into my back pocket before grabbing a black hooded sweatshirt off the coatrack next to the front door. I shoved my arms inside and zipped it halfway. "You heard what Christian said about this thing. It's dangerous and it can attack anyone in the area. A lock on the door isn't going to keep it out if it wants to get in and get to you."

"I know," she said as she walked over to the couch and slumped down onto it. "But all the windows are locked, right?"

"Yes," I assured her. "Ginger just went through and double-checked them all."

"You'll be all right, kid." Ginger squeezed her shoulder as she passed behind the couch, zipping up her leather jacket. "Christian might not be a vampire anymore, but he can still fight. You have a weapon, and we're not that far away."

"I'm not a kid," she grumbled. "You know, when I said I wanted to travel and see new places, I was thinking along the lines of Disney World."

"Yeah, I know," I said. "Maybe we can take a vacation after this job."

Her eyes brightened. "And LEGOLAND?"

"We'll see."

"Funny how she's so adamant she's not a kid, but all the places she wants to see are kiddie locations," Ginger muttered as she neared me.

"Hey, I want to see those places too," I admitted, and looked at Daniel, expecting him to jump on board, but he stood by the front door, arms folded, staring off past me.

"I'm heading over. I'll see you two there," he said as he opened the door. "Be careful."

"What's with him?" I asked.

"Not sure," Ginger answered, grabbing her keys, "but he looks like he didn't sleep a wink."

"I don't think any of us slept that great," I commented as we exited the cabin and locked up.

"I did. I dreamed of Wonder Woman, and boy oh boy, did she have some wonders."

I chuckled as we stepped down from the porch. "You better watch yourself. What if Wonder Woman had been the trickster?"

"I would have died happy," she said as we crossed over to her yellow Mustang and got inside. She put her keys in the ignition and brought the vehicle to life. She nodded her head forward, gesturing toward something in the distance. "Whatever's crawled up his butt, he's still in protective mode."

I looked ahead and saw Daniel's truck paused on the dirt road ahead of us. He waited for Ginger to pull off before he took his foot off the brake and headed toward Gruff's. "That's odd. Why would he wait for us to leave if he said he'd meet up with us there?"

"I don't know. He usually drives you wherever you need to go too, even if we're all going to the same place. Did you two get into it about anything?"

"No," I answered, thinking back to the last time we'd really spoken. "I asked him about his name and he didn't want to tell me what it was, but he didn't seem upset about it."

"His name?"

"Crap," I muttered. "Don't say anything to him, but apparently Daniel isn't the name he went by in Imortia."

"Interesting," Ginger said, a devilish gleam in her eyes as she navigated the dirt road.

"Ginger, don't tease him. He'll know I said something, and for whatever reason, he doesn't want to discuss it."

"Fine," she said, managing to raise her hands in a gesture of surrender without removing her thumbs from the steering wheel. "Maybe he's still upset about Rider's alone time with you. I'm telling you, that man was seriously bummed."

"We're just friends," I told her, and ignored the eye roll I received in response. "Whatever it is, it's weird. He didn't even ask for details about my dream with the trickster."

"Yeah, about that… Christian said the thing likes to toy with people. Was this morning the first time you dreamed of it, or is it what set your hormones all aflame in the first place?"

"Uh, let's just say it didn't start the fire, but it definitely fanned the flames."

"But Rider's visit set everything back as it should be?"

"Pretty much." I bit my lip. "The trickster is definitely trying to draw out the succubus in me, but I think I'm good. Rider said I had venom in my bite when we…"

"Bumped nasties?"

I gave her a look. "Anyway, that was then, and I didn't feel the slightest bit uncomfortable when you were sitting so close to me on the couch earlier, so I think my vampire and succubus sides are balanced back out again. If my succubus side was flared up, I would have been totally chilled being that close to a woman."

"Well, I'm glad to hear your super-ho powers are manageable again, especially now that Christian is rooming with us. Can you imagine the amount of Hail Marys you'd have to say if you jumped the bones of a minister-slash-former angel?"

I cringed at the thought. "And apparently he's married

to Jadyn now too."

"Yeah, I heard, and she talks to animals. Girl, you mess with her man and she might send a whole flock of birds to scratch and peck your eyes out, whoop your ass Hitchcock-style." She pulled into a parking space in Gruff's lot and turned the car off. "Geez. Look at how many cars there are. It's going to be one of those nights."

Yep, I thought as we exited the car just as Daniel slipped inside the building, not waiting for us. "Hey, did you find out anything about Lana? Apparently, she and Daniel knew each other in Imortia."

Ginger shook her head as we walked toward the building. "I was asleep whenever she came to bunk down in my room, and we didn't really get to talk today. Why? Do you think she's the reason for Daniel acting off today?"

"I don't know. Maybe," I said, hoping that was the case, because I couldn't imagine why he'd be deliberately distancing himself from me, but it sure seemed like he was.

CHAPTER SEVENTEEN

"How's it been today?" I asked Angie, the blonde werewolf on the door as we approached.

"Not bad," she said, "but you know the real party doesn't start poppin' until the sun goes down." All three of us looked up at the blazing ball in the sky, which had only started its descent. "So, have you figured out anything about Rob's attack yet? I mean, Gruff told us about the Pontiac thing, but we haven't heard anything else. Did you catch it?"

"Pontianak," I corrected her. "No, we didn't, and we're not entirely sure that's what got Rob, but we're still on the case."

She glanced toward the woods. "Shouldn't you be out there then? Gruff ordered us to stay out, but if you need the help—"

"No, it's best everyone else stay out of the woods while we're looking into this." I looked at her and thought about the fact she'd been put on the door because she was female, and we'd been working off the assumption a man-killing vampire ghost was the only thing going bump in the night. She was outside alone most of her shift, up for easy grabs. "I'm going to talk to Gruff about doubling up on the door, but be careful either way. The pontianak might not be the only thing preying around this area."

"Sounds like you know something you're not sharing."

"Believe me, I don't know nearly as much as I wish I did, just that something unusual is happening in the area, so if you see or hear anything strange, let us know."

"Even if it sounds batshit crazy," Ginger told her.

Angie frowned at this. "Uh, sure, but it's been boring as hell out here so far. Of course, with the amount of people inside, things are bound to pick up. I can handle myself pretty good though."

I had no doubt about that. Even humans who had no idea werewolves existed would give pause before confronting Angie. She was muscular without losing her femininity, and between the clunky shitkickers on her feet and the *try me* look in her eyes, nobody would confuse her with a timid pushover.

The screaming guitar riffs of eighties hair bands blared over the noise of clinking dishes, arcade machine games, and multiple conversations filling the space as we pushed through the front door and entered Gruff's.

The sweet scents of perfume and musky colognes mixed with sweat and the salty, spicy aroma of fried foods, sizzling grilled steaks, and other foods that teased me with their delicious smells.

"How long was it before you could eat anything you wanted?" I asked as Ginger and I moved to the middle of the room and looked around.

"Anything at all? About five years."

"Please, just kill me now."

She laughed. "You might get lucky and get over the sensitive stomach issues soon, being hybrid and all. Hell, you already stay awake during the day far easier than the rest of us. Some new turns don't see daylight at all their first couple of years, and none can avoid going dead to the world at the crack of dawn, but you don't suffer as much from it."

"My ass can still go crispy in the sunlight without this lotion Rider provides us," I reminded her, "and I'd trade my resistance to full day sleep for a dozen doughnuts."

"You shouldn't even be hungry though. Eating human food is just a pleasure for us, not a need. You shouldn't crave it."

"It's the emotional tie I have to it," I explained. "Guzzling down a bag of blood satisfies my thirst, but it doesn't comfort me like chocolate or junk food."

"Poor thing." Ginger slung her arm around my shoulders and smacked a kiss on my cheek.

"Hello, ladies," a ruddy-faced man with about three days' worth of unkempt facial hair, glassy eyes, oily hair tucked under a trucker hat, and a rotund gut encased in a T-shirt that may have once been white and looked only slightly better than his oil-stained, holey jeans and busted work boots approached us, bottle of Miller in hand. "Need some meat for that sandwich? I got just enough space in the back of my truck, and the shocks are good."

"They'd have to be to haul your ass around," Ginger replied.

"And they say all the good guys are taken," I muttered as the man's face grew redder.

"Bitch," he spat out, swaying a little. Clearly, he wasn't on his first bottle of beer. "I was trying to do you flat-chested dykes a favor, and give you a taste of a real—"

Ginger rammed her fist into the center of the man's face hard enough for the sound of his nose breaking to be heard over the tunes blaring from the jukebox. Before he could fly backward, she grabbed the collar of his shirt, and maybe some of his chest too, and hauled him to the door before literally kicking his ass out of the building.

Men and women alike whooped and hollered, raising beer bottles and glasses, and some stood to give an ovation, always thankful for a good show at Gruff's. Some just sat staring with their brows drawn together and mouths hanging open, no doubt wondering how such a thin woman delivered such a solid punch and tossed the large man out by herself. One group of similarly trashy-looking men at the bar lowered their gazes and slunk down. If I was a betting woman, I'd put my money on them being the guy's buddies.

"That's where I find my comfort," Ginger said, brushing imaginary, or I guess it could be real, dirt from her hands as she returned. "The audacity of that asshole."

"I know. You're not flat-chested."

"Honey, both of us are completely titless compared to his man boobs, but I was talking about the fact he actually thought he could get *two* women." She took a quick look around and prodded me toward Gruff's office. "Daniel's not out here and neither is Gruff, so they must be in his office."

"You'd think Daniel would have waited for us at the door since we arrived right after him."

Ginger shrugged. "I already told you what I think. He's been in a sullen mood since Rider dropped in for a booty call."

"Rider brought Lana when he came. Those two clearly have a history, and it doesn't seem like a happy one. I don't know why he wouldn't talk to us about it though."

"Yeah, well, he's a guy," Ginger said as we reached Gruff's office. "Half the reason I only do women is because men are dumbasses."

"And the other half of the reason?"

"Their genitals look gross and they never stop farting."

I shook my head as we knocked and entered Gruff's office. Sure enough, Daniel was already inside, standing in front of Gruff's desk with his arms folded over his chest as the big werewolf leaned back in his desk chair.

"Ladies," Gruff said by way of greeting. Daniel merely glanced at us, but said nothing. "Daniel was just filling me in on the zombie apocalypse you busted up last night. I was hoping you'd be in shortly to corroborate because I'm starting to think all his checkers done rolled off his board."

"There were zombies," I said, "or at least what looked and moved like I imagine zombies would look and move like."

"And they smelled even worse," Ginger said, plopping down onto the leather couch.

Gruff looked at me for a long moment, just blinking, then gave his head a slow shake and muttered, "Godzilla peckers and zombies. This whole week is giving me flashbacks of that bad acid trip back in my senior year."

I wasn't sure how to respond to that, so I moved along. "Since it seems like you all got started without us, wanna catch us up?"

"Just zombies so far," Gruff said. "You're going to have to explain to me how that's even possible because last I heard, zombies weren't a thing, and they make no sense. How the hell is a person gonna walk and rot at the same time?"

I glanced over at Daniel, but he seemed satisfied to just stand there now that I'd arrived, so I took Gruff through the whole trickster spiel Christian had given us. "I think if you're going to have someone keeping an eye on the lot, it should be two sets. We haven't ruled out the pontianak still being a threat, but we do know there's a demon capable of creating any kind of monster it wants using this area as its sandbox. Women aren't necessarily safe out there alone either."

Gruff nodded as he watched me over his thick, steepled fingers. "You're right. Fortunately, Rider brought the new, permanent people with him when he came up here last night, so I have the manpower to stretch. I still have you all here until this shit is taken care of. So, you have this Holden and Lana pair off questioning the police and medical personnel. If one of you can watch the lot with Angie, that would help."

"I'll do it," Ginger said. "Sounds like it's gonna be a big hair band night on the jukebox, and I'm not in the mood."

"You love classic rock," I told her as she stood.

"Yeah, but I don't like off-key drunk rednecks yodeling along, and it always reaches that point on nights like these." She gave us a finger wave and left the office.

"I knew something happened out there last night because Rider had the new people clean up whatever mess you left behind. I'd hoped it was whatever got Rob, but sounds like it wasn't."

"What we fought last night didn't target specific body parts," Daniel told him. "They tried to chomp on any part they could get a grip on, and they didn't lure us or do any kind of mind mojo that would have prevented us from fighting back. The pontianak theory still lines up best with what happened to Rob."

"Shit," Gruff muttered. "At least he didn't have family to give explanations to, but I'd sure like to see whatever killed him die, whether it's the pontianak, trickster, or whatever the hell got him. He deserves justice. He was a good kid."

"Rob didn't have any family at all?" I asked.

"Nah. His parents died when he was a kid, and he lived with an uncle that was a mean drunk. He ran off from home soon as he hit eighteen and ended up washing dishes at a diner I ran in Alabama. He barely had two pennies to rub together when I met him, but he was a hard worker who didn't complain about anything. I gave him a place to stay until he could get on his feet."

"And he came here when you got this place?"

"I think we all became his family." Gruff let out a hearty laugh. "He damn near crapped his pants the first time he saw me shift. I was taking him home after we'd closed the diner and these punks came up on us with guns and knives. We fought them off, but I got shot. I had no choice but to shift shape or else bleed out right there where I stood. I don't know who screamed louder, Rob or the sonofabitch I took a chunk out of."

"Rob still came here and worked this bar and grille, knowing most of your employees are werewolves, and a portion of the population around here are some form of paranormal beings. Why did he seem so freaked out about being saved the paranormal way after he was attacked if he got along just fine with everyone?"

"You get along great with Ginger. Do you wanna hump women because you're good friends with a chick who likes chicks?"

"Well, no," I answered, "but hell, if it saved my life, I might kiss her."

Gruff barked out a laugh. "Yeah, I reckon so. Rob worked for me for enough years, we were real good friends. He'd really needed some help when we first met, and I gave it to him. I fed him, gave him a job, and helped him get his footing in the real world. I don't hire just anybody. He knew I and the others on staff were good people. He respected us, and the vampires and other paranormals he came across, and kept our secrets, but he didn't want to be like us. He was born human, and he had no desire to change that. I respected that."

"I'm going to go out and keep an eye on things," Daniel said. "I'll let you know if we need anything, or if Holden and Lana have anything new for us when they check in." He barely glanced at me before moving to the door and letting himself out.

"You know, I reckon part of why Rob didn't want us to have one of you try to turn him was because he missed his parents. When you lose your parents that young, I don't think you really fear death as much, not even when you get cheated out of life like he did." He sighed. "So you said this demon your friend suspects of being behind everything can just create monsters at random, but it can target people too. Do you think that pontianak targeted Rob or just got him because he was the one on the door that night?"

"I don't know," I said, taking a seat in the rickety chair in front of Gruff's desk. It was short, hard, and wobbled a little. I got the feeling Gruff didn't want to make it comfortable for his employees to come into his office, sit across from him, and chat awhile. "Christian said someone had to summon this trickster demon, and this person could target people unintentionally in any number of ways. To target intentionally, they'd have to find a way to get the trickster's DNA into that person, and those attacks would be more personal, more specific to the victim's fears. It's hard to say if the pontianak attack was a targeted attack or the demon was just having fun and Rob was in the wrong place at the wrong time."

"He seemed to be lured by it."

I nodded, thinking. If the monsters weren't real, but just a creation of the trickster's doing, I wondered if they had to adhere to the exact same lore. The pontianak was already outside its normal hunting ground. Maybe the trickster created it to send after Rob because it just liked the way the monster killed its victims. Maybe Rob didn't have to be abusive toward women or didn't have to have lost a wife or girlfriend in childbirth. "Rob was single, right?"

"Yeah. I mean, he got around like most men of his age, but he wasn't what I'd call a womanizer. Werewolves tend to get a little frisky around the full moon, and I'm sure he's helped some of the unmated singles around here satisfy their needs, but he's never been serious with any of our kind. He had a girlfriend he was serious with about a year ago. Human. She went off to law school. I think they kept in touch, but other than her, I can't think of anyone who sticks out as special to him. Why?"

"Just wondering. The pontianak lore suggests they go after men who've had a mate die in childbirth, or men who abuse women. He didn't strike me as the second type, and I didn't know about his personal history well enough to rule out the first."

"No way Rob ever hurt a woman, or had a pregnant girlfriend. I'd have heard about it. He was like family, and Rob's responsible. If he got a girl pregnant, he'd have married her immediately. That's the kind of guy he was."

"Did he have anyone who would have had it in for him? If he was intentionally targeted by whoever summoned the trickster, that could explain why he didn't fit the description of the type of man that monster usually goes for."

"I can't think of anyone and believe me, I've been trying since the attack happened." He scrubbed his meaty hand down his face and scratched his beard. His eyes grew glassy, and I knew the tough-as-nails guy was having a hard time keeping up his image of being a burly badass. Rob really was like a family member to the childless man. "I can't recall any personal fights, just regular occurrences of kicking out assholes when they got too wasted to act decent. I can say the same thing for you. I haven't heard anyone complain about either of you."

I thought about that. Maybe Rob and I had kicked out the same person… except, how would we have both been exposed to the person's DNA? I didn't recall having been scratched by anyone I'd kicked out, and I damn sure hadn't swapped spit or blood. I hadn't used my fangs on anyone but Angel, Christian, and Rider since I'd left Louisville. "Well, if that changes, let me know."

"Will do, and Danni? Watch your ass. I know you're tough, but if this thing can make any kind of creature it wants, it might not have balls to destroy."

"I don't always go for the balls. I've fought women too, you know."

"Just sayin'. Be careful. I don't want to find out anything's happened to you, and not just because Rider would kill me and every sorry sonofabitch within a hundred-mile radius."

"Aww, Gruffy. I knew you cared."

"Don't start that shit now." He pointed to the door. "Get the hell out of my office and kill something. And don't be calling me any pansy nicknames."

"But Gruffy…" I laughed as his cheeks reddened, and

walked around his desk to wrap him in a bear hug from behind, laughing harder as he bit out a choice selection of expletives, and tensed up. "It's so nice to know I was right, and you're just a big mushy marshmallow on the inside."

"I'm gonna show you a marshmallow if you don't get off of me, demon woman. Get on now."

"You're such a sweet-talker, Gruffykins." I patted his bushy head and walked away before the poor guy had a complete fit. His face was already the color of a ripe strawberry.

"And don't be bringing any more peckers into my office," he said as I reached the door. "Play with all the peckers you want on your own time."

"That was Ginger's pecker," I told him as I made my way out, leaving him flummoxed. As I walked away from the office, I felt a little better, knowing I'd given the man a bit of humor after having to ask him about Rob. Despite his steel exterior, he was in mourning, just like any other man would be who'd lost the equivalent of a son.

I shook my head as I passed a couple grinding against each other outside the bathrooms, the man's tongue so far down the woman's throat he was probably licking her kidneys, and continued on to the dining area. A group of guys played air guitar and sang horrifically off-key with the Guns N' Roses song blaring from the jukebox, and I laughed to myself. Ginger knew what kind of night it was going to be, and she had bailed just in time.

With little else to do in Moonlight, not even the threat of a penis-eating animal was enough to keep the rowdy townies at home, and then there were the truckers. I spotted more than a few of them at the bar. Either they hadn't gotten the message that some of their associates had gone missing after visiting the area, or they just didn't care.

I saw a couple help their children into jackets and herd them out the door, having just finished dinner. They were the last family I could see, the rest having already vacated the premises. It was an unspoken policy that when the sun went down fully, the animals came out to play, and I felt the energy increase in my body telling me the sun had fully set.

Daniel sat at a table in the rear of the massive room, his back to the wall so he could see everything happening between where he sat and the front doors. He looked at me, but his gaze flicked right past as he continued to scan the floor. I was going to need a drink, or at least something to wrap my hands around so I wasn't tempted to go for his throat if I was going to talk to him, and try to weed out what the hell was going on with him.

I slid in between two men sitting at the bar and leaned forward to get the bartender's attention. One of the guys gave me a thorough up and down, but something in my eyes on his trip back up caused him to swallow hard and turn around. Then again, maybe it was the don't-fuck-with-me-right-now growl that had escaped me. Oopsie.

"Need a drink?"

I turned toward the voice and saw Carrie grabbing a longneck out of the cooler. The petite auburn-headed werewolf looked more harried than usual, which made sense given the amount of customers.

"My usual," I replied, although I knew she was fully aware of what I drank.

She moved over to where the bottled blood was kept warm and grabbed one for me, which I was thankful for because the werewolf on bartender duty was busy flirting it up with a brunette on the other side of the bar.

"Here." She uncapped the bottles and handed them to me. "Can you take that one to Daniel since I figure you're headed his way?"

"Sure," I said, taking the bottles. I frowned, noting the hard set of her jaw. "Everything all right?"

"Everything's great, I mean, for taking orders from drunk assholes and uptight, overly picky jerks who could have stayed home and made their own food on what should have been my night off." She sighed. "It's not like I had anything else to do anyway, so I might as well make some money."

"That sucks," I said as she grabbed a pitcher and started to fill it with Dr. Pepper from the fountain, "but at least Holden's in town. I heard you two were a thing."

"I'm sure you'll see more of him than I will," she muttered as she finished filling the pitcher and came around the bar, growling a very wolf-like growl at a trucker who'd come close to copping a feel as she squeezed past. He wisely retracted his hand and let her pass unbothered.

Poor thing, I thought. I couldn't handle her job. If I was forced to deal nicely with the type of people who frequented Gruff's in a place with the atmosphere of Gruff's I'd probably have a much worse nickname than Danni the Teste Slayer.

I took the two bottles and made my way to the table where Daniel sat, careful to avoid running into any couples gyrating on the floor. Gruff's was such an odd place. It was like Gruff couldn't decide if he wanted to open a restaurant, seedy bar, or fight club, so he just tossed everything together and ran with it.

I set the beer in front of Daniel as I slid into the chair next to him and took a pull off my own bottle. The blood was fresh enough not to be revolting, but I'd rather have had a chocolate milkshake. "Am I imagining things, or are you avoiding me?"

Daniel glanced over at me before taking a drink of beer. "Nah, we're good."

"Really? Because you've barely spoken to me all day. I mean, I know I might have been prying when I asked you about Lana and your name before we went to bed this morning, but I thought we were friends. Friends talk to each other."

"It's fine, Danni. I'm not mad about you asking about any of that, and we're friends. We're good friends."

"Then why are you avoiding me? You've barely spoken

to me or even looked at me. You drove here alone and came in without us. You left Gruff's office without me, and when you found out something tried to attack me in my dream, you didn't even ask about it. You still haven't. It's like you don't even care what happened."

"I know what happened, Danni. I heard you." He muttered a curse and took a long draw from his beer, draining half the bottle before he set it back down hard on the table and wiped his mouth with the back of his hand. "I heard you this morning when you were talking with Christian, after I'd gotten up and went back to bed. My door was open and I … I heard you tell him about the dreams and everything that happened in them. I heard you tell him about me and Rider, and the way the demon made you want to…"

Heat climbed up my neck to flood my face as Daniel faltered. I ran everything I'd told Christian through my mind, remembering how I'd been so comfortable with him I'd just spilled everything. *Everything.* Oh, hell. "Daniel, I… It was just a dream."

He bit out an almost disgusted sounding laugh. "Yeah. You know, I kind of thought there were a couple moments when you…" He shook his head angrily and took another drink. When he set the bottle back down, his grip tightened until his knuckles turned white. "The Bloom was horrible, and I'd never wish that back on you, but at least then I knew that any flirtation was your succubus side trying to take you over. It's harder now to…" He shook his head, his lip curled a little. "If anything like that happens again where the succubus part of you makes you desire things you don't actually want, tell me. I'd never forgive myself if I let you do something you didn't actually have any desire to do."

I sucked in a breath, realizing he'd picked up on my attraction to him before, and he'd thought it was genuine, untainted by my demon half, only to learn a demonic entity had entered my dreams and revved up my succubus appetite. Although he'd behaved himself, erred on the side of caution, he'd allowed himself to think I might actually be interested in him as more than a friend. He was hurt now, but worse, angry with himself because if I was understanding correctly… he would have given in to his own attraction and taken me to bed, only to feel as though he'd taken advantage of me later when my succubus side had been sated, but I was still very much in love with Rider. Ginger had been right. Daniel had feelings for me.

Crap.

CHAPTER EIGHTEEN

"Daniel, you are the best friend I've ever had."

He winced as if I'd raised my hand to strike him. "Don't, Danni. It's… It's nothing. I shouldn't have said anything at all. We're good."

I watched him finish his beer, and didn't feel as if we were good at all. Worse, I now had a jumble of confused feelings to deal with myself. I loved Rider with all my heart, but I'd be lying if I said the knowledge of Daniel finding me attractive didn't spark a little flare inside my heart. He was a great guy. Funny, sexy, and even though he had a protective streak in him, he didn't hold me back. If I wasn't in love with Rider…

But I *was* in love with Rider, so I wouldn't even contemplate the thought of what it would be like to be with Daniel, no matter how tempting. Curiosity killed the cat, and I was pretty sure it would do just as much damage to the vampire-succubus hybrid.

"You see anything out of the ordinary tonight?" I asked, trying to move past the awkwardness now enveloping us.

"No, it's just a normal rowdy night at Gruff's," he said. "I'm gonna go grab another beer. Carrie and Jenna look a little swamped with actual customers to have to bother with me. Want anything?"

Yeah, I wanted to go back to earlier that morning and move my conversation with Christian out of his earshot, I thought, but I didn't say anything. I raised my bottle of blood, showing I had what I needed, and shook my head.

"Be right back."

I watched him as he made his way to the bar, my eyes traveling the length of him, paying special attention to the way he filled out his jeans in a way most men couldn't. No pancake ass on that man, I thought, then muttered a curse, realizing I was ogling him. It was bad enough lusting after the guy when my succubus side was all worked up, but now that there was no denying he was attracted to me, I was looking at him like he was an option. I was already in a relationship. I didn't need options. I needed to do my damn job and get back home to the man I already had waiting for me.

With that in mind, I scanned the room, not entirely sure what the hell I was even looking for. I tried to sort out the puzzle pieces in my head. So far there'd been missing truckers, followed by the attack on Rob, which we were pretty sure had been a pontianak attack. Holden had joined us after that and the following night we'd gone out hunting the vampire ghost only to stumble upon a group of zombies, and two days in a row I'd been visited by a demonic entity we now thought to be a trickster posing as a djinn. Why had it posed as a djinn?

"You having a deep thought there, or did you try to eat human food again?" Daniel asked, returning to his seat, a new ice-cold longneck in hand.

"Funny," I muttered, but was relieved to have Daniel joking with me again. He really was the best friend I'd ever had, and losing that friendship would hurt about as bad as losing a limb. "If it is a trickster behind everything, why do you think it would pretend to be a djinn? Why wouldn't it pretend to be Selander Ryan since an incubus can invade my dreams and obviously I'd fear him as much, if not more than I'd fear some creature I'm not even familiar with?"

Daniel kept his eyes on the room as he considered my question, eventually shrugging before starting on his second bottle of beer. "That might be a question for Christian, but he did say tricksters love to create chaos and to toy with people. You've already been through a Selander Ryan dream invasion. Maybe the added confusion of not knowing what exactly you were up against made the whole deal sweeter for it."

"Maybe," I murmured, thinking about it, and how the entity had stayed hidden in shadow. I'd just barely seen the blue-tinted skin and other djinn features. Even while pretending to be something else, it had stayed hidden, really making me work to figure out what it was. If Christian hadn't been with us and I'd researched what I'd seen on my own, I would have thought the entity was a djinn and not looked any further because it had seemed to be really trying to hide the fact it was a djinn. The thing really went the extra mile to make one question the reality in front of them. I shivered, just imagining how badly it could screw with a person's mind.

"You all right?"

"Yeah," I said, and finished my bottle of blood before it could cool down enough to be all thick and gross. I glanced over as Daniel took another long pull of his beer. "How many of those can you drink before I have to take your car keys?"

"I don't know," he answered. "Five hundred and thirty-two?"

"That few, huh?"

He grinned. "This stuff doesn't even come close to what we drank in Imortia."

"Do you miss it? Imortia, I mean."

He was quiet for a moment, and I didn't miss the sadness that flitted through his eyes. "What I miss isn't there anymore, and what I've become isn't welcome."

I instinctively reached over and squeezed his hand. I sensed his body become completely still as he looked at my hand on his, and I withdrew it, silently cursing myself. Just because he was talking and joking with me again didn't mean there wasn't an awkwardness still between us.

"After all this time, are you sure the Imortian people wouldn't welcome you back?"

"Are you trying to get rid of me now?" He gave me a sideways glance.

"Never," I replied, "and if you returned I'd be heartbroken, but I don't like that you think you'd be treated badly or that you're still holding on to guilt over how you were given the ability to shift. It wasn't your fault."

He went quiet as he stared off across the room, not really looking at anything, and I imagined he was probably remembering the first time we'd met Christian. Jadyn had been with him, and she'd sensed the dragon soul inside Daniel. It had freaked Daniel out, but I'd noticed the relief in him when she'd told him the dragon didn't blame him for the loss of its life.

"The new Imortian queen is a dragon shifter, and not all of us who were forced to become shifters as punishment came here. Some stayed, and from what I hear, the Imortian people are becoming more accepting, understanding it was not our choice to kill such beautiful creatures to gain power. There are still those who won't even look at us, but with time, they too should learn to put the blame where it truly belongs. That's not the reason I can't see myself ever returning."

"You miss her," I said, knowing his fiancé, Salia, was the reason for the sadness I'd seen in his eyes.

He nodded, but didn't say anything, and I didn't say anything either when he finished the bottle of beer in front of him.

Not wanting to push him further, feeling more

questioning would be the equivalent to poking an open wound with a salty stick, I reminded myself I was on a job. I scanned the room again as I tried to look for anything not normal, not that it had been an unusual night when Rob had been attacked.

Carrie and Jenna, a Wiccan with an affinity for piercings and dark makeup, weaved through the people gyrating on the dance floor to deliver drinks and food to people filling booths and tables. The bartender on duty flirted with women between filling mugs of beer and sliding bottles down the bar top. Truckers, some I'd seen before, and some new to me, mostly sat at the bar, but some would move to the dance floor after getting friendly with local women looking for a little fun.

Not all the people were paranormal, but they all sure seemed in the mood to howl at the moon as the jukebox played a steady stream of rock classics and a few country tunes. A group of men cheered over by the arcade games as one apparently beat out a high score on Mortal Kombat, and I heard similar noises coming from the poolroom.

A man with a handlebar mustache sidled up to a woman in a very tight, very low hot pink halter top sitting at the bar and got the collar of his shirt snatched by the man sitting on the stool next to her. The two exchanged words, but Mustache raised his hands and was let go. A heartbeat later, he zeroed in on another woman and started working what I was sure were corny pickup lines on her. It was indeed just another night at Gruff's, nothing out of the ordinary at all, except somewhere in that crowd was probably someone who either purposely or accidentally set me up for some trickster mind games, and for the life of me, I couldn't figure out who.

I heard a crash and swiveled my head in unison with Daniel's as we looked over to a booth in the opposite corner of the room where several women had been gathered. I'd noticed them earlier, laughing and drinking as they passed wrapped presents and decorative bags to a redhead wearing a costume tiara with a shiny number twenty-five on it, although anyone with halfway decent eyesight could tell she was probably closer to forty than twenty. Glasses had spilled over and broke as Carrie practically dragged another woman out of the booth.

"The hell?" I said as I watched the werewolf haul the woman into the hall that led to the poolroom, bathrooms, and Gruff's office, her grip on the lapel of the brunette's red leather jacket tight enough she'd probably damaged it with her nails.

"I'm pretty sure that was Carrie's cousin, Pauline, she just dragged off," Daniel said.

"We should check that out." We got up at the same time and headed toward the hall the two had disappeared into. "How do you know Carrie's cousin?"

"She invited me over for dinner not that long after we arrived here. I think she's been staying with Carrie."

The woman was pretty, and so was Carrie. They hadn't been the only two women I knew of who'd either flirted with or taken the initiative to ask Daniel out since he'd come to work for Rider, but I hadn't heard of him taking any women up on any offers. I'd thought it was because he was busy working, guarding me, or because he still mourned the loss of Salia, but now that I knew he had feelings for me, I wasn't sure what to think.

"Uh, call me if you need me," he said as we reached the hallway and saw Carrie drag her cousin into the women's bathroom. He walked with me to the bathroom, but waited in the hallway as I entered, stepping aside before I got mowed down by two women hurrying out.

"You don't know who the hell you're messing with!" Carrie snapped at her cousin as she shoved something into the pocket of the money apron tied around her waist. Whatever it was, it formed a lump in the pocket. She swung her head toward me, realizing someone had joined them, and released her grip on her cousin's jacket. Sure enough, she'd torn the leather. "What?!"

I raised an eyebrow as I folded my arms over my chest and stared at her. Carrie and I were cool, but the tone had to go.

"Shit," she muttered. "Sorry. We're just having some family business."

I looked at the brunette and watched her wipe tears from her eyes as she glared daggers into the family member who'd just dragged her away from a party as if she were a child. "Are you all right?"

"I'm fine." She straightened her jacket, adjusted the lapel to cover the tears, and stormed past me, pulling the door open hard enough it slammed against the wall before she marched out.

"What the hell was that about?"

"Like I said, family business," Carrie answered. She raked her nails through her hair and bit out an expletive before moving over to the sink and turning on the water. I watched her rinse her face with the cool water and take a moment to collect herself, just letting the droplets run off her skin, before she grabbed a paper towel and patted her face dry. "It's been a long night already."

"Looks like it," I said as I watched her redo her ponytail and tuck in her black T-shirt with the Gruff's logo on the front. My eye went to the lump in her apron pocket. "What's that?"

She covered the lump with her hand. "Nothing, just some perfume. My favorite, actually. My cousin's been staying with me, and she won't quit taking my stuff. Maybe I overreacted, but I'm just tired. I really needed a night off. I guess I snapped."

I unfolded my arms and dropped my security guard pose. "Yeah, I get that. I have a sister. She liked to take my stuff without asking too." Hell, she'd tried to take my life, but that was more information than Carrie needed to know. "I assume someone didn't show to work tonight?"

"Maryjane," she said, nodding. "She was new, and human. She probably got freaked out after … after Rob."

"Were you and Rob close?" I asked, picking up on her struggle to say his name, and the way she wrapped her arms around herself. "Holden said he found out what happened to him from you."

Her entire body stilled a moment before she nodded. "We weren't super close, but we worked together for a few years. It was horrible the way he died." A sheen of tears covered her eyes. "He didn't deserve that. It shouldn't have happened. Oh, look at me. I'm a mess. I'm sorry. I just really need a break." She grabbed another paper towel and blew her nose.

"It's fine. Sometimes we need to explode a little, and what happened to him was awful. We are going to find the thing that did that to him and we're going to get justice for Rob."

She stared at me through her reflection in the mirror over the sink. "Do you know who, or what, it was?"

"We're still investigating," I said, not wanting to give too much information out to others. "Do you know if Rob was involved with anyone?"

She blew her nose again and threw the paper towel away. "I don't know of anyone he saw after his last girlfriend left for law school. She was human. He only committed to his own kind." She tightened her ponytail and took a breath before doing a quick wash of her hands. "I'm good now. I just needed a little stress break. I really hope you can stop what's happening around here without anyone else having to die."

"We're working on it," I said as she moved to leave, "but making sure no one gets killed in the bathroom is a distraction, so let's find another way to manage stress, all right?"

"Sure," she said, exiting the bathroom.

I walked out right behind her, nearly running into her as she saw Daniel leaning against the wall and came to a stop. She released a deep breath and continued moving down the hall.

"Everything cool?" he asked, straightening as the bathroom door closed behind me. "I didn't hear any ass-kicking."

"It was just a family spat," I said as we started walking away from the bathrooms. "And what sounded like a lot of stress and emotional buildup that just blew up under the pressure of working on a desperately needed night off. Have Holden or Lana checked in yet? Carrie's working tonight because another server didn't show up. I hope she really did just freak out over seeing Rob stumble in here after the attack and isn't another missing person."

"No check-ins yet," Daniel answered, his jaw set a little tight.

"Okay, what is up with you and Lana? There's clearly some bad blood or something between the two of you." I nearly stumbled as a thought crossed my mind. "Is she an ex?"

"No," he answered, the word practically leaping from him as we stepped out of the hall and made our way back to the table we'd vacated. We passed the birthday girl's table, and I noted it had already been cleaned up, and Carrie's cousin was nowhere to be found, probably having left after her fun night had been ruined.

"Okay, so that was a pretty adamant no. Why was that no so adamant?"

"You're not going to drop it, are you?" he asked as we reclaimed our seats, but there was no anger or irritation in his tone.

"Nope, but only because I care."

"And here I thought it was because you were such a massive pain in the ass." He grinned, taking the bite out of his comment.

"You…" I paused, realizing I was about to tell him he knew he loved me, something I easily said to him as a friend without attaching any deep thought to it, but now that I knew he had feelings for me, or at least an attraction, it didn't seem like a good idea to say it. "Just tell me. We all have to work together, and I don't think she's part of the crew Rider dropped off here to stay, so she'll be with us after we wrap things up here and head back to Louisville. I need to know if I'm supposed to like her or hate her."

He frowned. "Why would you have to hate her?"

"Your enemy is my enemy."

"She's not my enemy." He sighed, reached for the beer he'd left on the table, felt the weightlessness of the bottle he'd already drained, and set it back down. "She's not a bad person at all. She just brings back bad memories. It's not her fault, and neither is any awkwardness between us."

"You were friends?"

"She was Salia's friend." He took a deep breath, staring forward. "She was Salia's best friend. They were like sisters. She was there when …"

"You don't have to say it," I told him, realizing what he was referring to. "Was last night the first time you've seen her since… you lost Salia?"

His jaw clenched as he shook his head. "I wasn't the only one who tried to avenge Salia. Whereas I leaped forward and tried to kill the queen right then and there, she took the time to gather others. She took things further. Not only was she avenging Salia, but she brought others together, helping form a rebellion to rise up against the queen. She was captured and punished for her effort, and the next time I saw her after being taken by the queen was in Hades."

Daniel had told me how he'd become a shifter, and how he'd still tried to kill the queen who had taken his beloved's life, even after the queen had killed a dragon to bond its soul with his, giving him the ability to take on its shape. She'd tortured him until she was sure she'd broken him, then forced him to be her own guard, and he'd unleashed his dragon fire on her the moment the opportunity presented itself. Sadly, she hadn't underestimated his vengeance, and had taken precaution against dragon fire with a spell to protect herself. Daniel's second attempt on her life had been the act that had gotten him thrown into Hell.

"Damn. That wicked queen really loved using Hell as her own personal jail cells, didn't she?"

He nodded, and I didn't press him on any details about Hell itself. I mean, it was Hell, or Hades. I was still a little confused on the difference although he'd tried to explain it to me before. I could imagine how awful his time there had been. "So, what kind of shifter is Lana?"

"I don't know."

I frowned. "How do you not know?"

"She never spoke of it, not that we spent a lot of time chatting in Hades. We were busy outrunning demons and hellhounds, and we couldn't shift forms while there."

"What about after? When you got out? I thought the Imortian shifters rescued from Hades went through an agency for placement here, and they knew all your information."

"I didn't work for the agency or have access to their files. I just went through them like everyone else."

"Right. Wouldn't you have spoken to Lana there? Surely, what you were would have come up. You said you had to go through training in that Njeri realm where time seems like months but is just a day or two, or whatever. That's a long time not to discuss—"

"She wasn't in training with me, Danni. She didn't go through the agency at the same time I did. Lana escaped Hades long before I did."

"You mean she…" Anger rose in me like hot molten lava as I pictured Daniel lost in a fire pit, and worse than alone… Abandoned. "She left you there?"

I caught movement at the front of the room and looked over to see Holden and Lana enter. I rose out of my seat, eyes locked on my target.

Daniel's hand clamped around my forearm before I could launch over the table and take off at a dead run for the Imortian woman. "She had an opportunity to escape a living nightmare, and she took it. I can't blame her for that."

"I can."

"Please, don't."

I looked down at him and saw the pleading look in his eyes. I was baffled. I couldn't imagine the torture and punishment the man had endured, not just what was done to him in Hell, but the guilt he'd lived with, blaming himself for not being able to save the woman he'd loved, but to forgive someone who had shared some part of that with him, and just left him to continue suffering alone?

"Everything good here?"

I whipped my head around at Holden's voice, but my gaze zeroed in on Lana, her brown eyes connecting with mine, holding steady, and my fingers instinctively curled into a fist.

CHAPTER NINETEEN

"All good here." Daniel's grip tightened as he pulled me back down into my seat. I landed hard, and he slid his hand down my forearm until it met mine under the table. He forced his fingers between mine, breaking apart the fist I'd just formed, and held on tight. "Did you find out anything?"

Holden flicked a curious, slightly wary glance my way as he pulled out a chair for Lana and took a seat directly across from me. As Lana lowered herself into the seat next to him, placing her across from Daniel, the dragon shifter moved his leg, resting his ankle over mine as if sensing my desire to kick the Imortian bitch.

Let it go, he said through our mental link.

"I looked into all the missing persons reported in or near the area over the past few months. There was an uptick over the last month, but it didn't grab the local police force's attention because most were truckers or others passing through, not actual residents. In each case, it seemed as though they just vanished."

"The truckers' trucks?" Daniel asked as Carrie stopped next to our table.

She replaced his empty beer bottle with an ice-cold

longneck and scooped up my empty bottle of blood as well. Her mouth was pinched a little as she looked over at Holden and Lana, her eyes darkening as she took in the pretty blonde. "You want anything, Holden, or are you good for the night?"

The werewolf's eyebrows raised subtly, and Daniel and I shared a look, not missing the woman's pissed off undertone. Holden had made his relationship with the server seem casual, but I got the impression Carrie was a little more invested, and not too happy seeing the man she was currently sleeping with spending time with the curvy blonde.

"Thanks, Carrie. Maybe after I'm done working."

She took in a long, slow breath through her nose, her glare cutting into Lana, before she expelled the breath and left, nearly running over a busser making his way over to a table that needed cleaning.

"The trucks were mostly left abandoned along the highway," Holden said, watching Carrie storm off. He turned his attention back toward us once she disappeared to the other side of the room, hidden behind the cluster of people dancing to the music blaring from the jukebox. "Some were abandoned at rest stops just before Pennsylvania and Virginia."

"Did the missing all match the people we fought last night?" I asked, getting my head back into the job. I could always kick Lana's ass later, provided if Daniel would release my punching hand.

Holden nodded. "I was able to match enough of them I remembered seeing to truckers who'd gone missing, including two of the women, to conclude that's where they came from. Some of them, as you're aware, were too far decomposed, or looked like it anyway. None of them have actually been missing long enough to look as bad as what accosted us last night, even if they were killed immediately after they were last seen."

"Adding to the trickster theory," Daniel said.

"Christian said it could possess people and create illusions. It must have done a mix of that to create what looked like a zombie attack."

"I think at this point we can agree it's not just a theory," I said. "Did you find anything the missing people had in common other than being truckers? One of the women was in a skirt, so I doubt she was a trucker."

"The missing are different genders, ages, races, you name it. Most were truckers, but not all. The only thing I found in common is that they all passed through here at some point."

"Here as in Moonlight or here as in Gruff's?" I asked.

Holden reached inside his jacket and removed his cell phone. "I'm not sure, but I have pictures of them all and I'm going to ask Gruff's staff how many they've seen come through here. I'm also including pictures of anyone who died in any sort of freak accident during the past month, or died in their sleep."

My heart lurched to a stop. Picking up on my flare of panic, Daniel squeezed my hand.

"I don't mean to alarm you," Holden said, "and I damn sure don't intend on letting this thing kill you, but we know it's invaded your dreams under this djinn façade. There's nothing to say it hasn't been messing with others in their dreams, and we don't know how long it likes to play with people's minds in their dreams before going for the kill."

"Can it actually kill her in a dream?" Daniel asked, his thumb now stroking my hand, and I wasn't entirely sure if the gesture was supposed to comfort me or calm his own fear. "Can the pain it inflicts damage her body in the living world?"

"I don't know," Holden answered. "This isn't an entity I'm familiar with, but I can't imagine it bothering to draw her into a dream and screw with her if it can't eventually kill her. No matter how much fun it has toying with its prey, death is the endgame. It didn't just scare Rob with that pontianak gag, it really took his life. At some point, it's going to go for a kill. Maybe its goal is to frighten her to death in her sleep."

"Maybe it has tricks up its sleeve you're not aware of," Lana said. She looked directly into Daniel's eyes. "The Njeri realm."

Daniel frowned. "Do you think it has that power?"

"If it's powerful enough to create monsters out of nothing, and we know for a fact it can invade dreams, does it seem that far of a stretch? It clearly possesses the magical talent, as well as the ability to move between realms if it can be summoned from Hell."

Daniel's hold loosened, and he released my hand, bringing both of his above the table as he leaned forward and ran his thumb along his bottom lip as he thought. "The Njeri realm requires sleep. Rob was awake when attacked, and so were we when the missing truckers appeared."

"That was them," she said. "Christian said the trickster can create monsters and place them in reality. Those supposed zombies were clearly people who've gone missing, changed to look like rotting corpses and made to do the trickster's bidding. The pontianak attack could have been performed by someone else who went missing, or the trickster himself. Rob could have been sleepwalking. We don't know, but if you're asking if Danni can be killed in her sleep, the Njeri realm is a good way for that to happen."

"Do you have any clue what they're talking about?" Holden asked me, looking between the two Imortians.

"Not entirely," I said, trying to catch on to what I could, and mostly coming up empty. I had, however, heard of the Njeri realm, even if I didn't entirely understand it. "You're talking about that place you had to go to in order to learn this realm's entire history before you were released to live and work here."

Daniel nodded. "In order to go to the Njeri realm, you

have to be asleep. While your body appears to sleep here, and time basically stands still, you are also living, breathing, and functioning in the Njeri realm."

"Kind of like being in two places at the same time," Holden said, his brow furrowed.

"Exactly like being in two places at the same time," Daniel said. "You're asleep in one realm, although so it feels as though you're only in one place. Depending on whether you have previous knowledge of the Njeri realm, you might not even know you've been taken there."

"I think I've heard of this," Holden said. "Back when the birthrate in packs was dangerously low and the forced breeding law was enforced, it was rumored a human from within a dream defeated the reigning pack leader, banishing the law. He was able to take a moon vow with his mate and become one of us while he actually slept in a prison cell, not even in the same state. I thought it was a myth."

Daniel shrugged. "It's possible that happened. I've lived with a few different wolf packs since I left Imortia, but I don't know their whole history. I do know Zaira, the mother of the werewolf race, has the ability to bring people into the realm, but she's not the only one. The trickster could be another entity with that power. It could kill someone while they slept if using the realm's magic, so it makes sense why he'd do the whole dream thing."

"You're saying these dreams I've been having might not actually be dreams? I could really be in some other realm with that thing, really doing whatever's taking place?" I thought about the orgy that had been raging in the last dream, and how close I'd been to giving in to the disgusting lure of it before Christian had sensed the demonic entity and saved me. My stomach rolled with nausea.

Daniel reached over and squeezed my shoulder. "Breathe, Danni. In and out."

I did as told, slowly inhaling and exhaling, working

through the nausea as I tried to wrap my mind around the concept of an alternate reality where what I did actually happened, even if everything within it was some elaborate mind-trick. "If this trickster is pretending to be a djinn and taking me to this realm, you're saying the people in my dream weren't real, but I still could interact with them, and I could actually die if any of them kill me in the dream?"

"It's possible," Daniel said.

"How does that even work?"

"Do you remember what I told you about magic?"

"It's best to not try to think of it logically, and to just accept it." I shook my head. "You make that sound so easy."

"I come from a realm of magic." He glanced at Lana as he stretched his arm over the back of my chair. "We don't question it. It's just part of the reality we've always known."

"Good. You're all here." Gruff stopped beside our table and leaned toward us before lowering his voice. "One of my servers, Maryjane Maguire, never showed up for work tonight. I wasn't that surprised, given she was here the night Rob died, and this was supposed to be her first shift after. She's a human, and pretty young, so I didn't think much of it that she just up and quit rather than coming back to where she witnessed such a horrible incident, but I just got a call from Upchuck's mother that he never came home last night. That wouldn't be unusual on its own, given he's known to pass out and not come home some nights, but as you can see, he isn't here. If he passed out somewhere last night, he'd have slept it off by now and returned for a drink. He never misses a night here."

"Upchuck?" Holden's brow wrinkled.

"He drinks himself stupid every night and throws up a lot after," I explained, "hence the nickname."

"His name is really Gilbert Shaw, and he lives with his mother down on Roadrunner Bend," Gruff told us. "He's an unemployed drunk, but he's here every night like clockwork. His mother has already checked with the police and he wasn't picked up by them. He's not in the hospital."

"You're thinking the trickster has gotten to him," Daniel said.

"Hell, man, Upchuck would be easy pickings. He's almost always drunk off his ass and seein' shit anyway. He could have been lured somewhere by that pecker-eating vampire, the zombie trucker apocalypse, or anything. Then there's Maryjane. She came here a few months back after a divorce and, as far as I know, she's on her own. Easy pickings too, and she's not answering her phone."

"Give us their addresses," Daniel said, standing up. "We'll look for them. With Rider's new people in place, you have enough security for the regular shit, even on a packed night like this."

I stood as well, the other two table occupants rising with me. "You two should stay here and flash those pictures around," I said, directing my commentary to Holden. I still wasn't ready to play nice with the woman who'd left my friend in Hell, even if he seemed to not hold it against her.

"We can't let you go off on your own," Holden argued. "Last night was zombies. The night before was a pontianak. Who knows what this thing has cooked up for tonight?"

"I think you're going to have a worse fight than what we went through with those zombies," I told him, jerking my head in the direction of the bar where Carrie stood glaring at Lana as she filled a pitcher of beer. "Carrie's had a rough night and I know for a fact her fuse was short already before you came walking in here with another woman. I'm pretty sure if you go out that door with Lana right now, she's going to do something to you that'll make you wish the pontianak got to you first."

Holden blanched a little. "I can't stop this job for—"

"Nobody said you have to stop working the job. Daniel and I will check out these addresses, and look for Upchuck and the server. We need to know how many of those missing or deceased people were here at Gruff's so you can stay here and do what you were going to do anyway."

"That's a one-person job," Lana said. "I can go along to look for the missing people."

"Daniel and I have it covered," I snapped.

"Danni." Daniel gave me a stern look. "An extra person isn't a bad idea."

"We'll take Ginger."

He stared at me a moment before heaving out a sigh. "We'll check on Upchuck. Lana, you and Ginger can go look in on Maryjane, then we'll meet back up."

The Imortian looked at me a moment, her expression not giving anything away, and nodded. "All right."

"I'll text the address to Ginger," Daniel said, typing away on his phone. "There. Call us if you need help."

"Will do." Lana turned and walked away, headed for the front door.

"I'll do what I can from here," Holden said, "but you call me if you need any help. Carrie knows I'm here on a job and that comes first."

"She's having a really rough night," I told him. "It wouldn't hurt to check in with her from time to time while you're flashing those pictures around."

"You're not sidelined, dude," Daniel assured him. "We need eyes in here watching in case any weird shit happens anyway. You're holding down the fort until we get back."

"All right. Watch your back out there."

We assured the werewolf we would, waited for him to head over to the bar to start questioning people, rubbing against Carrie's backside as he passed her at a table, allowing his hand to slide across her lower back as he made his way over. She glanced back at him, then over to our table, seeming to perk up a little.

By the time we reached the parking lot, Ginger and

Lana were already gone, Ginger's Mustang no longer in the parking lot, and Grady, a werewolf who normally worked inside had taken up a post at the door along with a woman I wasn't familiar with, who'd taken Angie's spot once her shift had ended.

"Is that one of the new people Rider sent?"

"Must be," Daniel said as we reached his truck and he opened the passenger door for me. He waited for me to get in before closing the door and rounding the front to hop in behind the wheel. "You know, Rider told us he'd let you stay on this job as long as you worked smart. Ginger and I tend to let you do your own thing and just stay ready to jump in when you need help, but Lana and Christian are likely to report back to him every single thing you say or do, so you might want to can the hostility toward Lana. If you can't work with her, you're going to be the one Rider pulls off the job, not her."

"The woman left you in Hell, Daniel. How can you be so forgiving?" I asked, genuinely confused.

"You've never been there, so I don't expect you to understand," he said softly as he started the truck and pulled out of the lot. "She had a chance to escape, and she took it. We were separated at the time, and had she come looking for me, she could have lost her opportunity to free herself from the constant fear and suffering. I won't resent her for that. If I resented her for escaping Hell, I would be just as evil as the demons and hellhounds who chased and tortured us."

My mind immediately filled with images of Daniel being tortured, most of the images inspired by television shows and horror movies I'd seen. I forced the images out of my mind, unable to bear thinking of Daniel being put through the horrific situations my imagination conjured, and knowing whatever I imagined couldn't be as bad as it truly was because the pain and torment must have been beyond comprehension for Daniel to be so okay with Lana getting away from it while he still suffered.

Roadrunner Bend was about three miles from Gruff's and ran along the edge of the woods. In fact, Upchuck's backyard could pretty much be considered part of the woods. Daniel pulled into the gravel driveway and cut the engine. We sat there, looking at the small brownish white house with the aged aluminum siding and cracked front window held together with duct tape.

"How old do you think Upchuck is?" I asked.

"I'm not that good at guessing ages," Daniel replied. "Imortians don't age like you all do in this realm, but I know he's old enough to be able to hold down a job and have a family of his own if he wanted."

"I guess as long as his mother pays for the roof over his head and gives him beer money, he's not all that motivated."

Daniel shook his head in disgust and opened his door, stepping out into the cool night. I got out and met him around the front of the truck where he stood, scanning the tree line.

"You know, where I come from, a lazy man like Upchuck would be shunned by his family, not coddled. This realm has some strange customs."

We walked up the drive and along the cracked pavement leading to the front porch. The steps groaned under our weight as we stepped up them and rang the doorbell. We waited for a moment, not hearing anything, then Daniel knocked loudly.

"Coming," a voice that had grown raspy with age called out, followed by the sound of shuffling feet.

I could see the impatience growing in Daniel's eyes, until finally the door opened, revealing a short elderly woman trailing an oxygen tank beside her. Daniel recoiled, and my hand instinctually shot out to grab his arm, stopping him from leaving.

The little white-haired old lady adjusted her glasses,

squinting up at Daniel through lenses that looked to be over an inch thick. "I didn't order a clown. Is it my birthday?"

I stifled a laugh. "Mrs. Shaw, my name's Danni Keller and this is Daniel Steelheart. Gruff sent us because you said Up… er, you said Gilbert hasn't come home."

She looked between the two of us, the amount of wrinkles in her face growing as she frowned. "Gruff sent a clown and a waitress?"

"We're security, Mrs. Shaw."

"Security?" She squinted at us again before shaking her head and turning, muttering about what the world had come to. "Come in then, though I don't know what you're doin' here. He ain't here. I called down to him to come up and eat, but he ain't come up. I figured he'd stayed elsewhere, but he didn't show up for lunch or dinner, and now he ain't at Gruff's. I know he goes to Gruff's a lot. He's a good boy, but he likes his women and that place is full of 'em, and he can't tell 'em no." She narrowed her eyes on me. "Are you one of his girlfriends?"

"No," I blurted, and caught myself just short of gagging at the thought. I glanced over at Daniel, figuring I'd see him holding back a grin at the thought of Upchuck being a love interest of mine, but I couldn't see the bottom half of his face at all, given it was hidden under the collar of the T-shirt he'd pulled up over his nose. I admitted the house didn't smell the greatest, but it was bearable. I shook my head and returned my attention to Mrs. Shaw as she slowly groaned her way down onto the busted recliner in the corner of the small living room.

A pair of cats ran into the room, explaining part of the smell permeating the air, and brushed past my ankles as they made their way to the woman and jumped on her lap. I noted the living room was pretty plain, with a brown sofa covered in a neutral-toned crocheted throw, and taupe walls adorned with various prints of cats. A basket of yarn sat next to the recliner and several stacks of books rested on top of an old floor model TV that looked like it hadn't been watched in months, based on the layer of dust I could see coating the screen.

"I'm just security at Gruff's, ma'am. I really don't know your son that well. You said you called down to him today?"

"Yes. He lives in the basement. I didn't see him come in last night, so I called down to him this morning after I made up some biscuits and some gravy, but he didn't come up. He loves biscuits and gravy."

"I'm sure he does," I said. "So you didn't actually look in his room?"

"It's not just a room, it's a basement," she said. "It's where he lives. It's so hard for young'uns to have their own house in this economy and he's good to watch after me with my health." She coughed forcefully, as if the mention of her health reminded her body of its issues, and Daniel cringed next to me.

"How old is Gilbert again?"

"Forty-six."

Oh yeah. Upchuck was a real young'un. I felt sorry for the little old woman who clearly paid the bills with a social security or retirement check while her middle-aged son mooched off of her and spent her money on alcohol, but it wasn't my place to say anything so I swallowed down my opinions.

Mrs. Shaw pulled the two cats against her breast and started stroking them as she worried her bottom lip. "I didn't think nothin' of it before because sometimes he stays out, but when I called up to Gruff's and he wasn't there, I got to thinking… I can't get down those stairs to look in on him."

My eyes widened as I realized what she was saying. Fortunately, the smell permeating the air wasn't the odor of death, but that didn't mean Upchuck couldn't be unconscious in the basement. "Mrs. Shaw, is it all right if we go down to the basement and look around?"

She thought for a moment and nodded her head. "That'd be all right. It's through the kitchen."

I walked in the direction she pointed, leaving her in the small living room as we entered an even smaller kitchen. Once away from her, Daniel lowered his T-shirt and expelled a breath of relief.

"Don't tell me you're still grossed out by old people?" I whispered as we moved toward the basement door in the corner of the room.

"They smell sad and gross," he whispered back. "How can you not be disgusted by them?"

I rolled my eyes as we reached the door, and I pulled it open. "Uh, my memmaw was in her eighties and half paralyzed when she passed, and I loved her very much, just as she was. There have to be some older people in Imortia. I know you said you age slowly once you reach your prime, but you still age."

"Our elders aren't so frail and depressing," he replied as we made our way down the stairs into the basement. "Most of us retain our youthfulness, and those who don't are usually some of the most powerful magic wielders."

"Well, it doesn't usually work that way here, so you need to suck it up, buttercup, and for the record, my memmaw was a warrior woman."

He grinned. "My apologies for offending."

We reached the bottom of the stairs and looked around. Upchuck was a slob and his space had the smell of body odor combined with cheap cologne. My stomach rolled a little as my hypersensitive sense of smell suffered the aroma that blew past me on a cool gust of wind.

Daniel crossed the room, stepping over piles of clothes and discarded beer cans, and pulled the chain on a bare bulb hanging overhead.

My nostrils flared as I picked up the scent of blood a split-second before the light came on, revealing the blood smears on the wall under a window that had been left open.

"Well, that's not a good sign," Daniel said, following my gaze.

CHAPTER TWENTY

I did a quick scan of the room as I crossed over to the wall, but it was such a mess I couldn't tell if there'd been any kind of a fight inside it.

"It looks like he might have been dragged out the window by something," Daniel said, speaking my own thought as we stood near the wall and studied the blood.

It ran in two lines, spilling straight out through the window, which was just wide enough for Upchuck's body to fit. The window was near the top of the basement wall, right at ground level, so pretty much anything could have gotten to it from outside.

I moved aside discarded clothes, bottles, and pornographic magazines, following the blood smear that had poured onto the floor, and found where it began about two feet away from the wall.

"What the hell do you think happened?" I asked. "It's like something reached in and yanked him out."

"I think that's exactly what happened," Daniel said, looking between the open window and the beginning of the blood trail I'd just uncovered.

"That's a pretty damn long arm span," I said. "What do you think could have done it?"

He measured the distance again with his eyes before meeting my gaze and shrugging. "Groot?"

I barely managed to not roll my eyes, but I had to admit it wasn't the craziest idea, given the fact a trickster could create anything it wanted and so far seemed to be getting a kick out of creating creatures. "This thing has been creating mythological monsters so far. It must have created a new monster because I don't think this fits the mythology of pontianaks or zombies. There's a lot of blood. Maybe something actually hooked Upchuck before dragging him up the wall and out of the basement."

"Whatever it was, he wasn't scared of it."

"How do you know that?"

Daniel pointed at the window. "That window isn't broken. He opened it for something, or someone."

"So we could be looking for something that looks like a non-threatening person, but can transform into something with hooks or claws?" I frowned. "I have no idea what that could be."

"Me neither," Daniel said, "but that window is facing the woods and I'm betting there's a blood trail to follow."

"And a killer monster at the end of it," I muttered. "I guess we need to call in the others."

"I'll do it," Daniel said. He closed and locked the window, giving the basement at least a small amount of fortification in case the thing that took Upchuck came back, then pulled his cell phone free from his pocket and headed back up the stairs.

I followed him as he took the stairs two steps at a time, which was pretty effortless with his long legs, and crossed over the kitchen into the living room, and nearly slammed into him as he came to an abrupt stop, the phone to his ear, a look of pure horror on his face as he stared into the living room.

"What is it?" I asked as I reached his side and looked over to see Mrs. Shaw setting a water glass on the end table between her sofa and the recliner she sat in. Her dentures floated in the liquid.

She jerked a little in surprise as she realized we'd returned. "Oh, you gay me a shcare," she said, her lips flapping together as she spoke. "Wash ee dow theh?"

Daniel let out a terrified little mew, as if squelching a scream. I elbowed him in the ribs, hoping to snap him out of it before addressing the woman. "No, ma'am. We're going to go out and look for him now," I told her. I didn't have the heart to tell her we believed her son had been dragged out of the window by some unknown creature, and sincerely hoped we'd find the man alive and possibly avoid giving her any bad news at all.

"All wight then. I'm wowwied about him now. I hope heesh wif a guhfwiend."

I just nodded, feeling no need to tell the woman that her son's reputation for being an unemployed drunk who puked his guts up every night before going back home to his mama had earned him the nickname Upchuck, and didn't make the girlfriend scenario very likely. "We'll see our way out. Lock up after us."

I nudged Daniel, then gave him a shove when that didn't get him moving, and took his phone from his hand. I could hear Ginger saying hello repeatedly before I put it to my ear. "Sending you an address. Meet us here," I said before hanging up.

I managed to get Daniel through the front door and pulled it closed behind me before I texted off the address to Ginger's phone. "What the hell is wrong with you?"

Daniel stumbled down the porch before turning and pointing back toward the house, his mouth opening and closing, but nothing coming out.

"Good grief. Are you really this bothered by a woman's dentures?"

He pointed toward his own mouth before swallowing hard and pointed toward the house again. "Gums," he finally said. "Pink. Pink gums. Wrinkled lips." He gagged and turned away.

"Dude, for real? How are you seriously this freaked out by old people? You need therapy." I watched him as he bent over and gripped his knees before drawing in deep breaths. "Seriously, man, how is this bothering you so much? I guess that big, long crash course you got about our realm never covered the effects of aging. I guess Imortians don't lose their teeth either."

"Why the hell would they?" He drew in another ragged breath, still hunched over. "I mean, teeth can get knocked out in battle, but they don't just all fall out of your mouth and leave you all… *gummy*." He pulled a face. "What else falls out of you people?"

I saw the green tint to Daniel's face and the whiteness around his mouth from where he'd clamped his teeth together so hard, and knew the guy was having a rough time, and I shouldn't screw with him, but the little devil dancing on my shoulder just couldn't help it. "Vaginas."

His entire body stilled as he slowly looked up at me. "What?"

"Vaginas. They can fall out. It's called prolapse. Buttholes too."

His knees wobbled, a full body tremor shook him from head to feet, and little beads of sweat popped out along his upper lip, and I realized I might have gone too far. "Are you all right?"

He raised his index finger, then ran over to the bushes next to Mrs. Shaw's porch and started hurling in them. Yep, I'd gone too far.

I looked off into the woods as he continued vomiting into Mrs. Shaw's bushes, wondering what was out there and how equipped we were to handle it, especially if I'd just handicapped Daniel. We had the silver knives and our own special abilities, but I kind of wouldn't have minded having a gun because whatever took Upchuck, it was big.

"Do you think we should call in Holden too?"

Daniel let out a gravelly response that sounded similar enough to an affirmative that I pulled up Holden's number on his phone and called the werewolf.

"Hey," I said after Holden answered on the second ring. "We're over here at Upchuck's. It looks like something grabbed him from the basement and hauled him out the window, leaving a good amount of blood behind. We're about to head into the woods, following the trail once Ginger and Lana get here. You want to join in? Maybe bring some of those guns I saw in your trunk."

"Yeah, I'll be right… What is that?"

I looked over at Daniel's hunched over form and watched the middle of his body contract with each retch. "That's Daniel. He's throwing up, but he should be empty soon and good to go."

"What happened?"

"Yeah… I'd rather not share the details. I think I've done enough evil mischief for the night. We don't want to waste any time, so as soon as Ginger and Lana get here, we're on the move. If you don't get here by then just follow the blood trail that starts from the window in the back of the house. You guys are pretty good at sniffing out blood too, right?"

"Yeah, I can handle it. Be careful. I'm on my way now."

Daniel had just managed the feat of standing up straight when Ginger pulled her Mustang to a stop along the curb and parked. The two women got out and walked across the lawn toward us, both frowning.

"What's with Dragon-Boy?" Ginger asked, her nose scrunched. "Why do I smell puke?"

"He saw an old woman without her dentures in," I answered as Daniel reached my side, and I handed his phone back to him.

"Dude," Ginger said, "don't be such a wuss."

Daniel just looked at her as he slid his phone into his pocket and took in a deep breath through his nose. He was still a little green, a little clammy, and a little wobbly.

"Are you going to be good to do this?" I asked.

He nodded and started moving toward the back of the house. “Holden’s coming?”

“He’s on his way, but I told him we were going ahead. The longer that thing has Upchuck, the less of a chance we have getting him back alive.”

We explained the scene we’d found to Ginger and Lana as we moved to the back of the house and found the window. We couldn’t see the blood trail easily in the dark grass, but all of us were capable of following it by smell.

“What happened with Maryjane?” I asked as we moved into the woods, following the blood trail and stepping around small trees that appeared to have fallen along the path we followed.

“Her apartment was empty,” Ginger answered. “But it didn’t look like she packed anything. Her car was still parked outside, and a woman a couple apartments down said she hasn’t seen her in two nights, and she had checked on her because she found her car door standing open, but Maryjane didn’t answer the door when she knocked.”

“You think she could have been grabbed while getting into or out of her car?” I asked.

“Could be,” Ginger answered. “It was parked along the edge of the building’s lot, close to the woods. It would have been easy for someone or something to run out, grab her, and make a quick escape back into the trees.”

“Shit,” I muttered, wondering if the same thing had grabbed Maryjane, and how many others it could have taken, and for how long it had been doing it. “There wasn’t any blood?”

Ginger shook her head, both of us watching as Lana stepped away from us, her brow drawn as though concentrating on something. She stopped, looking at the ground, then passed behind us and stopped after about ten feet before doing a zig-zag across from us and stopping again to scan the area. She walked over to a downed tree and started studying it before looking up, searching the treetops.

"What is it?" I asked, deciding to honor Daniel's request to drop whatever negative feelings I had toward the woman and give her a chance.

"Go over there and tell me what you see," she said, pointing toward the spot behind us on our left where she'd stopped to look down at something previously.

The three of us walked over, searching the ground as we did. I noticed a round hole in the ground where she'd been before. "Yeah, that's probably a mole or rat hole. I don't think either of those critters has anything to do with Upchuck or Maryjane's disappearances."

"Walk ahead in a straight line," she said as she stepped around the downed tree and started walking parallel to us, about ten feet over.

We did, and it wasn't long before we noticed a similar hole, then another, then another… I looked over at her, and at the space between us. "Are there similar holes over there?"

She nodded and looked at another small downed tree bisecting the distance between us. Ginger and Daniel looked around, but didn't seem to catch on.

"Either people have been walking through here on stilts, or we're chasing after something big as hell with a lot of spindly legs," I said, pointing toward the closest downed tree, "and that's where its body crashed through." I looked up, knowing when it couldn't crash through a bigger tree or move around it, it would climb.

"Wait a minute," Ginger said, looking around, her eyes so wide they almost looked like they were going to pop right out of her skull. "Are you saying what I think you're saying? Are you saying some big, giant man-eating spider is out here? You better not be saying that because I don't fuck with spiders, especially ones I can't stomp on and smash their nasty little guts."

"What, you're scared of spiders?" Daniel grinned. "It's just a bloodsucker like you."

"Oh, I know you're not trying to say something about

me being afraid of spiders, Daniel, not when you're terrified of animated characters from a kids' movie."

"Those Minions look like living Twinkies with eyes," Daniel shot back. "They can see you, and they talk all creepy and they're so hyper. That shit is fucked up."

"Guys!" I waited for them to cool down and look at me. "Bigger problems here."

"Where would it hide?" Lana asked, still scanning the area. "If it's snatching people and not killing them right away, it's got to be taking them to a lair. If it's a spider, it has to have a web."

"So what, this thing is dragging people off someplace, wrapping them up in a web cocoon and sucking them dry like they're just really big bugs?" Ginger shuddered. "I say we just torch the whole fucking forest. Daniel, get up there in the sky and light it all up."

"We can't burn down the entire woods," I told her. "We'd take out all the animals in it, and there's a lot of buildings practically backed up into the outer edges that the fire could spread to."

"How do we kill this thing then?" she asked. "By the time we get close enough to stab it, it could grab us with one of those legs and eat us, or maybe it can shoot webs. It could catch and cocoon us before we even get close."

"First of all, we're only speculating this thing is a giant spider," I told her as I removed my cell phone from my pocket and dialed the cabin. "It might not be."

Angel picked up on the third ring. "What up?"

"Is Christian awake?" I asked her, hoping he'd have a better idea what we were dealing with.

"Nope, and I know you said this guy used to be an angel, but let me tell ya, he snores like a devil. Want me to get him up?"

I started to urge her to do so, then thought better of it. The poor guy had stayed up to watch over me the whole time I'd slept, despite having been up the previous night researching what we were dealing with. "No, that's okay.

Hey, keep everything locked and stay away from windows. Far away."

"Um… okay. I'm just gonna stay on the couch watching this *Buffy* marathon."

"Good. We'll be back as soon as we can."

I hung up, slid the phone in my pocket, and sighed. "I was hoping Christian would know something, but he's still asleep. I guess we just follow the blood trail and eventually we'll come to it and deal with it then."

"What if the *it* is a *them*?" Ginger asked. "We could be walking into a nest of who-knows-what."

I sighed, growing frustrated. "We don't have much of a choice. What if this thing, or things, has Upchuck and Maryjane? What if they're alive, but won't be for long if we don't get to them? We can't take the chance of letting people suffer."

"We know the zombies had webs on them, and we know this certainly looks like tracks made by a big-ass spider," Daniel said. "And a big-ass spider could reach its leg inside Upchuck's window and snatch him out so it's not that wild of an idea. Lana has a point about a lair. A big-ass spider probably has a big-ass web somewhere. I'm going to go up and take an aerial look for that. You three stick together and stay alert. I can still communicate with you through our link when I'm in my dragon form."

"Shit," Ginger muttered as we watched him climb a tree effortlessly, disappearing into the mass of thick branches that provided a canopy over the forest floor. "Now what do we do?"

I sniffed, picking up the blood trail. "We keep going."

CHAPTER TWENTY-ONE

"I don't guess either of you brought a big can of Raid?" Ginger asked as we continued to follow the blood trail, Daniel's large shadow momentarily blocking the moonlight as he flew ahead of us, having reached the top of the tree and shifting into dragon form.

"No, but the good news is there's four of us," I said, "and Holden is on his way. While we don't want to burn down the whole woods, Daniel can still burn whatever this thing is if he gets a good shot, and we can circle it, attack it from three directions while he looks for an opening from up above it."

"If it's just one thing," Ginger muttered. "We might end up all getting one or two of our own to tango with."

"Daniel flew ahead," Lana told her. "Hopefully he'll get a bead on it first and report back so there's no surprises. If he can get a clear shot, you might not have to confront it at all. He might be able to burn it to a crisp."

I looked up as we continued along the trail, noting how the amount of trees had increased, their limbs and foliage far denser, and wondered if Daniel could see anything moving underneath the cover they provided. I didn't mention my concern to Ginger, however, given I'd never seen her so shaken before. "You really don't like spiders, do you?"

"I'm generally not a fan of anything that can bite me, especially something that can inject venom and suck out juices."

I watched her as we continued walking, one eyebrow raised.

Realizing I was looking at her, and why, she rolled her eyes. "You don't count. The side of you that does all that venom stuff only does it to men. I'm safe from you."

"Thanks," I muttered. "You bite people too and can suck out juices, or else what would you call blood?"

"Tomato, potato," she replied. "You really don't see the difference?"

"Yeah, I see it. I'm just trying to make this seem less scary." Truth was, I wasn't looking forward to dealing with a giant spider either, and might just wet my pants when the moment arrived, but I didn't have much of a choice. Whether it was a giant spider or something else, I couldn't let something live if it was abducting people from their homes and killing them. "Also, I'm thinking of what Christian said. This thing can create monsters, but it can also possess people. What if this spider-monster we think we're looking for is the trickster? I want to kill the bastard and get this over with before anyone else gets hurt."

"And before the creep comes back for you?" Ginger looked over at me knowingly.

"Yeah," I admitted. "I know Christian said that thing he hung over my bed will alert y'all to the trickster's presence when he returns, but if it really is a trickster, it won't stop him from entering my dreams and screwing with me. Honestly, I think I prefer the hand to hand combat with its monster creations over the mental games."

Ginger reached over and squeezed my shoulder. "Okay, we'll track the evil mutant spider and kill it, but only because you're my boo."

I laughed, but the merriment died in my throat as we

heard something shuffling deep in the trees. All three of us came to an immediate stop and jerked our heads in the direction the noise had come from, which was toward our left and several feet ahead.

"What was that?" Ginger whispered, her voice quivering as she grabbed my hand.

I stood perfectly still, not even willing to breathe as I pushed my vampiric hearing ability to the limits, picking up on all sorts of little shuffling noises from all directions, and what sounded like running water ahead. "It was probably a squirrel," I finally whispered back. "It's the woods. There's all kinds of critters running around in it, and besides, if this thing is what we think it is, it would probably come crashing through the woods toward us."

"Yet no one has reported hearing such a thing," Ginger replied. "These are made-up creatures, remember? They might not follow all the rules of reality. It could be gigantic, but move as if it weighs nothing. The damn thing could fly. It could have eaten Daniel or shot a web up at him like Spider-Man for all we know."

"Geez, Ginger, are you trying to terrify us?" I looked up, suddenly overcome with worry. *Daniel? Are you dead?*

I sensed his laughter roll through our mind link. *Would you expect an answer if I were? I haven't seen anything yet, but there's a lot of spaces where the tree covering is too thick to see through. I'm circling around, keeping an eye out. Watch your back. I can't see you either right now.*

"Daniel's fine," I reported. "He hasn't seen anything yet. Let's keep going."

Lana started walking first, and I was more than fine letting her take the lead. Ginger and I brought up the rear, the normally unbothered vampire holding onto my hand like her life depended on it. "Uh, maybe it's best to hold on to your knife instead of my hand," I suggested, feeling my circulation start to cut off. "That way you're better prepared in case this thing jumps out at us"

"Right," she said, releasing my hand and replacing it

with her switchblade, which was open and ready to slice. I looked at her white-knuckled grip on the handle and hoped I hadn't made a mistake in suggesting she take the knife out. As jumpy and hyper-alert as she was, she might hear a chipmunk fart and end up stabbing one of us.

"Shit," I cursed as the trail of blood which had slowed to droplets half-a-mile back came to a complete end. I sniffed, hoping to catch the scent farther into the woods, but it was gone.

"Sounds like water ahead," Lana commented. "It sounds like a stream. Have any of you mapped this area out?"

"No," I said. "We came here as security for Gruff's Bar and Grille, and really didn't even set foot into the woods until after Rob was killed. I've heard some guys at Gruff's talking about fishing, so I know they have somewhere nearby they go."

Lana looked back at us, but said nothing, quickening her step as she moved to the left and started walking closer to the sound of running water.

"You're following the water?" I asked. "What if this thing kept going straight? Should we be getting off the path?"

"I don't know a great deal about spiders," she said, "but if this thing is a monster, it preys on people. If I preyed on people, I'd hang around a fishing hole, not some random spot in the middle of the woods where there isn't even a clear walking trail. We've lost the blood trail, so this is what we have left. Also, there's a small tree this way that's crashed over so it could have come through here."

I looked over at Ginger, and she shrugged. "It makes sense. Also, if we find a stream, there should be a break in this damn canopy of trees. I don't like being hidden from view in case that thing creeps up on us and we need Daniel to shoot a flame up its ass."

"Good point. I just hope Holden will still be able to find us. He should definitely be in the woods by now."

We followed Lana until we came along the stream and stopped. It looked pretty deep and was about twelve feet across, lined along both sides with several jagged rocks and small pebbles. The water ran at a decent speed, headed back in the direction we'd come from, and seemed to start above a hill in the distance.

"I'll just text Holden to tell him we've started following the stream," I said as I dipped my hand into the pocket of my sweatshirt to retrieve my phone, but stilled as I glimpsed something coming over the hill, hidden in the water. "What was that in the water?"

"Where?" Ginger's head jerked around. "It better be a big, fucking fish."

Daniel, get to the stream, I ordered through our mind-link as my gut twisted. I bypassed the cell phone for my knife and flipped it open, noticing the other two women had done the same. We all stood with our feet planted firmly, watching the large, dark shape under the water as it grew closer.

A woman's torso emerged from the water, completely nude, shocking me immobile. I'd expected a giant spider, or hell, Nessie, but not a butt-naked, long-haired brunette. She brushed her drenched hair out of her face, revealing three sets of eyes. The first set was where they should be on a human, and a normal size. The other two sets were smaller and went up at a diagonal into her hairline. All three sets were perfectly round and completely black.

"Not a fish," Ginger said.

Definitely not a fish, I thought as the woman continued to rise from the stream, her humanoid hips fused together with what looked like the bulbous ass end of a giant bug. We all instinctively stepped back as several thin, black legs covered in fibers emerged from the water, and the creature took its first step toward us. A weird, clicking noise came from the monster, causing my teeth to rattle, and she opened her mouth, revealing a vicious looking set of sharpened teeth and two prominent fangs.

"Have I pissed myself?" Ginger asked. "I think I might have, but I can't feel anything below my waist."

"I suggest you find your legs quick," I said as four arms covered in dark hair folded out from each side of the creature's body, each one measuring at least six feet wide from armpit to clawed fingertips.

I'd barely gotten the warning out when one arm whipped out and grabbed Ginger, a spider web immediately forming around her body as she was brought to the giant insect-woman's open maw.

I lunged forward with a battle cry, the silver knife gripped tightly in my hand, vaguely aware Lana ran alongside me. A stream of fire shot down from the sky, connecting to the beast's torso. Daniel had arrived.

The creature screamed as Lana and I skidded to a stop, knowing better than to jump right into the path of fire. Its body writhed as it reared back, arms flailing wildly. It managed to sweep an arm out and knock both Lana and me back several feet. My back hit a tree, and I saw stars as the back of my skull connected with bark. Once my head cleared, I saw Ginger go flying, and the monster ducked under the water.

I got to my feet and ran forward, knowing the horrible creature was just putting the fire out. It rose as I neared it.

"Get down!"

I ducked as gunshots rang out and bullets connected with the monster's chest, causing it to scream with rage and flail again. I looked over to see Holden running toward the bank, both hands wrapped around a gun. I couldn't see Ginger.

"That's a damn jorōgumo," Holden said as he neared, his face lit with what I could only describe as horrified awe.

"A what?"

"A whore spider."

Okay, that wasn't a name I was expecting, and it stunned me for a moment, just long enough for the thing to reach one of those hairy extra arms toward me, a web shooting out of its palm. I ducked and rolled as Holden continued to empty his clip into the thing's chest and Daniel shot another stream of fire at it.

This time, when it reared back, it shot a web up at Daniel, tangling him in a sticky net before swatting at him, sending him flying several feet to crash into the stream. Then it released a rage-filled roar that shook the earth and reached for Holden.

Acting purely on instinct, I got to my feet, surged forward, and sank my blade into its fuzzy arm. It let out a cry before one of its other arms wrapped around my waist and lifted me off the ground.

"Hold on, Danni!" Holden reloaded his gun and started shooting into the spider's chest, again only seeming to piss it off.

I brought the knife down into the arm holding me and started sawing back and forth, adding to the monster's fury. It opened its jaws wide, and I looked at the gleaming fangs as I was brought to its mouth, and I wished like hell I'd stayed in Louisville.

Before it could sink those fangs into me, Daniel flew overhead, somehow having escaped the web and emerging from the water, and buried his claws into the side of the beast's head, yanking it back with enough ferocity the creature let out an ear-splitting screech and dropped me into the water.

I sank down into the stream, somehow still gripping the knife for dear life, and thought about shoving the blade into the monster's giant spider ass, wondering if maybe its heart was in that part of its body, not in the humanoid part that had already taken several bullets. I turned toward it, and bubbles emerged from my mouth in a silent underwater scream as the biggest snake I'd ever seen swam right past me.

I made my way to the edge of the stream and scrambled onto the ground, oblivious to the sharp rocks cutting into my palms as I hurried away from the nightmarish thing I'd seen in the water.

A hand wrapped around my arm and helped me up. It was Daniel, back in human form. He stared straight ahead as he backed me up to where Holden stood, also staring forward, his jaw dropped open wide.

I looked toward the water and felt my own jaw drop as the upper half of the giant yellow snake's body swayed back and forth, it's massive jaws opening even wider as the whore spider's body was swallowed down, inch by inch, head first.

"Not that I'm not appreciative, but do we have to kill that thing next?" I asked as I watched the jorōgumo's body disappear into the snake, then slowly slide down the long column of its massive body.

"Not unless you want to kill one of our own people," Daniel said. "That's Lana."

My jaw dropped for the second time as I looked between the area I'd last seen Lana after the jorōgumo had sent us flying and back to the live-action creature feature happening in the stream. "Lana's a giant snake?"

"Lana's an anaconda," Holden clarified, continuing to stare ahead, mesmerized.

Lana's giant snake form undulated, and we all grimaced as we heard snapping and cracking, the lump in her middle thinning and stretching.

"I thought anacondas broke their prey's bones before they swallowed them down."

"She did that," Holden explained. "She came up from the water, wrapped around it and squeezed while you were still headed to shore."

"So, what is she doing now?" I asked and soon got my answer as Lana lurched forward and regurgitated the monster's broken body onto the ground.

We all jumped backward, away from the slimy mess, as Lana's snake form curved backward and went back down into the water.

"Guess she wasn't hungry," Daniel said.

"Hell, I wouldn't want to risk having to shit that out later myself," Holden said, his nose scrunching as he moved forward to inspect the carnage as Lana pulled herself up from the stream.

"Shit," I said, looking around. "Where's Ginger? Ginger!"

"Somebody get me the hell out of this motherfucking tree!" she screamed back.

"There she is," Daniel said. "Holden, Lana, make sure that thing doesn't resurrect or anything."

We jogged down the edge of the stream, following the sound of Ginger's cursing, until we found her, still wrapped in a web, jerking her body back and forth as she dangled from a tree limb. "Get me down!"

Daniel chuckled under his breath and took a running leap at the nearest tree limb before easily climbing the rest of the way to her, moving like a monkey.

"Did you kill that damn thing?" she called down. "Tell me you killed it."

"Lana kind of ate it and threw it back up."

Ginger blinked at me, processing this information as Daniel reached her and started working on the web. "Is it dead?"

"Pretty sure."

"Good," she said, nodding her head, not that she could do much else.

"Shit," Daniel muttered, pulling his hands away from the web, most of it coming with him, now attached to his fingers. "It's like bubblegum."

"Get me out of this!" Ginger snapped, a bit of a whine in her tone.

"I have to take you into the water. That and shifting shape is how I got out of it. We'll just have to hope the water does well enough on its own." He looked down at me before grabbing Ginger, web cocoon and all. "Go back to the others, and we'll meet you in a minute."

He jumped from the tree, bringing Ginger with him, and shifted into dragon form mid-air before he flew over the stream and dove into the water with Ginger cursing a blue streak.

I returned to where we'd left the jorōgumo carcass to find a pile of ash in its place, and Holden wiping a blade in the grass. "What happened?"

"Found the heart and stabbed it. It went up in a poof."

I froze in place, wanting to jump up and down with relief, but afraid I might be wrong. "Was this thing actually the trickster?"

"Not sure," he said, putting the knife away. "You need to take care of your hands."

I looked down and realized I was bleeding, tiny pebbles still embedded in my palms. I wiped them on my jeans to get rid of the rubble and brought them to my mouth. I really wasn't crazy about licking my palms after they'd been in a stream with a giant monster and who knew what other kind of critters, but thin-blooded vampires couldn't afford to be germaphobes. I licked the wounds, healing them with my saliva.

"Lana went up the hill to look for the missing people," Holden said. "She doesn't seem to be in a talkative mood. I tried to give her props for taking this thing out, but she didn't seem all that happy with the accolades."

I heard a steady stream of cursing and turned to see a soaked Ginger marching toward us, picking at little pieces of web still attached to her, and flinging them away, or trying to. "I am taking five boiling hot showers when we get back to the cabin. I hate spiders!"

Daniel grinned as he trailed behind her, then reached out and touched the back of her neck with his fingertips, causing her to let out a blood-curdling scream before she jumped a foot high and turned around, immediately pummeling him with her fists while calling him some very creative and vulgar words. Daniel laughed, disappeared into rainbow sparkles, and transported himself ahead of us.

"Where's Lana?" he asked, looking around.

"She went up the hill to look for the missing, as should we," I said, grabbing Ginger. "Come on."

"What the hell was that thing?" Daniel asked as we started up the hill.

"A whore spider."

He stopped and turned to look at me, eyebrow raised, corners of his mouth curved up.

"That's what he called it," I said, and pointed to Holden.

"It was a jorōgumo, otherwise known as a whore spider," the werewolf explained. "There are a few variations of the lore, but it's Japanese in origin, and the most common theme is that a spider gains magical powers once it lives about four centuries, which allows it to take on the appearance of a beautiful woman. It then lures men to it and keeps them in its web to feed off of. Some lore says it hangs around rivers and streams waiting for fishermen. Dragging men out of basement windows is different, but I think we've established these monsters aren't sticking exactly to the lore."

"Yeah, not if we're supposed to believe that thing could actually attract men," Daniel said. "Not with an ass like that."

We quickly covered the distance and once we topped the hill, we saw Lana working at a web cocoon with her knife and a stick. There were at least a dozen of them attached to a huge web that stretched out between trees, tall trees that were wider and thicker at the top, offering enough coverage to block them from view.

"Shit," Daniel muttered.

"You couldn't have seen them from the sky," I told him, "and it doesn't matter now. They've been found. Let's get these people unwrapped and see if we can save any of them."

CHAPTER TWENTY-TWO

As Daniel had stated, the webs were like bubblegum. It took what felt like forever to get the people detached from them as we used sticks and leaves to work at the webs, while avoiding touching them with our hands and clothes as much as we possibly could. We'd toyed with the idea of Daniel taking them to the stream like he did with Ginger, but these people had clearly been fed from, and we didn't know what effect taking them into the stream would have.

Ginger had a major freak-out when a leaf fell from a tree and barely touched her neck, but otherwise held it together pretty well, although she looked back over her shoulder no less than four times a minute.

Lana worked in silence, her mouth pulled into a permanent frown, her eyes focused on the job at hand as if she were purposely avoiding making eye contact with us, which got me curious about what Holden had said, and Rider. I recalled him saying she didn't like talking about what she was, and Daniel hadn't known what animal soul she'd been bonded with, as if it were a secret. Whatever her reasoning, she'd come through when we'd needed her, so maybe I didn't hate her.

The longer it took to free the bodies, the more my

hope that what we'd killed had been the actual trickster fell, because it seemed to me that if the trickster had been killed and went up in a poof, so would its frigging webs, but they were still there, and they were a pain in the ass.

By the time we finished, nine of the twelve people were still alive. Those nine people were also all human, which put us in one hell of a pickle.

"Go," Holden ordered as he disconnected the call he'd made to Gruff and shoved his phone into his jacket pocket. "The sun will be up soon enough and we don't need you and Ginger burning alive. Gruff knows the situation, and he's working on a way to get these people help without them exposing the paranormal community to humans."

I started to argue, but Ginger and I had both been in the stream. It wasn't smart to risk the chance our lotion hadn't come off while we were deep in the woods. I looked at the people we'd saved, unconscious but breathing, and the three we'd been too late for, and wished I could stay and see things through to the end.

"All right, but you guys be careful."

"Go with them," Daniel told Lana. "We don't know if that was the only thing out here or not, and if they get attacked, they might need someone who can shift."

Lana held his gaze for a moment, something silent passing between them, then stepped toward us. We caught up to Ginger, who hadn't needed to be prodded into leaving. She'd been ready to leave at the first suggestion of a spider. Her head turned toward every little sound she heard as we made our way back toward where we'd started.

"We should pick up the pace," she said. "We still have to drive back to the cabin after we get out of here."

I looked at Lana, expecting a grin since there was no way she didn't realize Ginger was just being a scaredy-cat, but the Imortian was looking ahead, her eyes distant.

"All right," I said. "Let's get out of here."

We jogged the rest of the way, my shoes squishing with each footfall, and as we reached the edge of the woods, Ginger practically leaped from the tree line. "Hot shower, here I come!"

She skipped to her Mustang, bursting at the seams with joyous relief. Lana and I trailed behind, relieved, I'm sure, but not quite as merry. Lana had her reasons which were unknown to me, and as for me, I couldn't stop staring at Upchuck's house, imagining his mother in there worrying about him.

"He's alive," Lana said, sensing where my thoughts had led. "You helped save him and her relief will come soon. You did well." She passed me and got in the back of Ginger's Mustang, leaving the passenger side for me.

I'd barely closed the door behind me when Ginger floored the gas and took off, more than ready to get to the cabin and wash the remnants of her ordeal off of her.

"I think you can relax now, Ginger. The spider's been squished."

She gave me a look. "You guys think it's funny that I'm scared of spiders, but did you ever think of what might happen if a spider bites a vampire? Huh? Do you want big, bloodthirsty, mutant, immortal spiders feasting on unsuspecting humans while they sleep? They might even turn into bats."

"Okay, now you've just gone goofy. You can't even turn into a bat."

"You don't know what I can do."

"I know you can't turn into a bat. You might be bat-shit crazy, but you can't turn into a bat."

"I might if a spider bit me." She stuck her tongue out at me before refocusing on the road.

I glanced in the back and saw Lana looking out the window, a tiny grin on her face, and smiled. "Just drive, weirdo."

Ginger shot out of her car and into the cabin as if the devil himself were fast on her heels. Although the sun was about to pop out to say hello, I walked in like a normal person, Lana behind me.

"Good morning," Christian greeted us as he poured himself a cup of coffee at the kitchen counter. "Would you like some coffee, Lana?"

"No thank you," the Imortian said. "I'll have enough trouble sleeping without it."

I watched her as she glanced toward the bathroom where we could already hear Ginger's shower starting, and didn't think I imagined the desperation in her eyes.

"I have a private bathroom off my bedroom, Lana. You can shower in there. I have a feeling Ginger wasn't kidding when she said she intended to take five showers. Hell, with the sun rising soon, she might just fall asleep in there."

Lana's eyes widened a little. "Oh, no, that's fine. I can wait."

"Go. I don't plan on going to bed immediately anyway." I swung my arm out, gesturing for her to head to my bathroom. "Go. Ginger's going to be in the other bathroom forever."

"Well… all right. Thank you." She gave a little nod and headed for the room she shared with Ginger to get her things.

"That was nice of you," Christian said, watching me over the rim of his cup as he sipped the hot coffee inside it.

"It's just a bathroom, and we all feel pretty scuzzy after tangoing with that thing in the stream," I said, knowing Daniel had already called him and filled him in on what had happened. "So, do you think it poofed out of existence after Holden stabbed its heart with the silver blade because it was the trickster?"

"Hard to say," Christian answered. "I can't imagine its death being that peaceful. It's a demonic entity. They tend to go out with more …"

"Drama?" I suggested as he seemed to struggle to find the right word.

Lana exited Ginger's room, a change of clothes in hand, and nodded at me as she made her way into mine.

"You could say that." Christian grinned. "We will know for sure if you are visited in your sleep again."

"What if it decides to take the day off from my dreams?"

"It won't," he replied, the grin transforming into a grim line. "This thing has set its sights on you. It won't lose interest until it completes what it started, which I'm sure is a sick game of using your own fears against you to completely antagonize you before it kills you, or tries to kill you. We're not going to make it easy for it to do that."

Christian pushed back the sleeve of his blue Henley, revealing a string of beads tied around his wrist. "Just got these a couple of hours ago. They took a bit longer to make than the dreamcatcher. Everyone is getting one, just in case. Angel was already given hers before she went to bed."

"What is it?" I asked as I unzipped my still damp sweatshirt and peeled it off of me, the discomfort more noticeable in the cabin than it had been when I'd been helping untangle victims from web cocoons, too focused on them to worry about how soaked and disgusting I felt. I felt heaviness in the pocket, and cursed, pulling out my cell phone. "Man, this went in the stream with me. I'm glad I didn't lose it, but I guess I might as well have."

"We might be able to save it," Christian said, opening a cabinet. He removed a plastic food storage container filled with white rice, took off the lid and held it out to me so I could shove my phone in, burying it in the grains. "These bracelets are made of dream beads. The dreamcatcher will keep any actual djinn from entering your dreams if you sleep under it, while alerting us to any other demonic entities. The dream beads work whether you are awake or asleep, blocking your thoughts from demonic entities."

"So you're saying if we are dealing with a trickster, which I'm pretty sure we're all confident we are now, it can still visit in my dreams, but it can't read me?"

"Exactly. It will only have access to what it had prior to you wearing the dream beads, and it won't be able to sense them at all, so it won't catch on." He set the container of rice on the counter and pulled a bunch of the bracelets out of the pocket of his khakis, placing them next to the rice. "Pick one. They all work the same."

I sensed the sun rise as I looked over the selection, my eyelids immediately drooping. I'd expelled a lot of energy, and I needed to rest, but I didn't want to until Daniel returned and I knew what they'd done with the humans. The bracelets all contained the same colors of blood red, burgundy, black, gray, silver, and a few dark blue beads, just in different combinations. I grabbed one, not seeing much difference between them, and slipped it over my hand as I yawned.

"You should get some rest," Christian said, watching me.

"Not until I get my turn in the shower. I'm sure I smell like fish ass."

"I'm not sure that's even a possibility." He laughed, turning his head toward my bedroom as the sound of the water from within my bathroom stopped running. "Shouldn't be much longer until you're able to get your turn, then you need to sleep. I will watch over you. There's nothing to worry about."

I raised my arm, showing off the bracelet at my wrist. "If you truly believed that, we wouldn't need these."

He frowned. "Yes, well, I've been thinking. Some of these attacks could be random, like the jorōgumo grabbing anyone within proximity, and the zombies, but tricksters feed on fear, so a lot of the monsters it creates could be inspired by the fears it picks up from the community."

"You're saying these are designer monsters, created

from our nightmares?"

"Something like that. The trickster is visiting you in your dreams, so it's obvious that it's feeding from your fears, working with your fear of your succubus side causing you to do things you will regret, but I don't believe you are the only one it is playing with. Holden was just passing through, but stayed here because he was told about an attack he knew closely resembled that of a pontianak, which, after speaking to him, I can conclude is a fear of his. More accurately, losing someone to a pontianak kill is a nightmare of his. Ginger fears spiders, hence the jorōgumo."

"Yeah, that makes sense," I said, "but I don't think Daniel's had any fears brought to life."

Christian looked at me knowingly. "Losing you is that man's greatest fear, and he's had to worry about that constantly since this started."

I averted my gaze by studying the bracelets on the counter. "You know how he feels about me, don't you?"

"It's not exactly hard to see it."

Fear slammed into my chest. "Rider can't know."

"You really think he doesn't already?"

"What?" I looked at Christian to see him watching me warmly. "Trust me, he doesn't. He'd kill Daniel."

Christian's mouth curved into a gentle smile. "You'd think you'd know him better than that. Yes, the man is jealous when it comes to you, territorial, and even possessive, and he would kill anyone who even thought of harming one hair on your body in ways too horrific to even think about, but he will make any sacrifice it takes to keep from losing you."

"Wh… what?" I shook my head. "Are you talking about Rider or Daniel now?"

"Either, really." Christian shrugged. "There's no way Rider doesn't know how Daniel feels about you, but Daniel is a man of honor. He knows where the line is and he does not cross it. Still, he will do everything in his power to keep you safe, so what better guardian for you than a man who can't stand the thought of losing you either?"

I tried to respond, but found myself stammering. I took a moment to suck in a breath and release it slowly, calming the alarms ringing out in my head as I tried to process what Christian was telling me. "Rider knows."

"Rider knows, and he's not happy about it, and I'm sure there are moments when it absolutely kills him, but as long as Daniel doesn't cross the line, Rider will continue to shove down his own jealousy to allow that man to protect you when he can't." Christian finished his coffee and rinsed the mug out before putting it in the dishwasher. "He'd never kill Daniel either, not while you live, because he knows Daniel is your friend and that killing him will hurt you. He would never willingly hurt you."

My knees went a little wobbly, and I gripped the countertop. "A man like that wouldn't crush my heart."

"No, he wouldn't."

"The shower's all yours," Lana said, emerging from my room in black leggings and a matching tank top, showing off her perfectly proportioned body, which I now realized was kind of snake-like in the way it moved. Lithe, but coiled to attack if necessary. She towel-dried her long blonde hair with one hand, the other wrapped around her cell phone and switchblade. "I put my clothes in the hamper. I hope that's all right."

"That's fine," I replied, smiling as I realized the woman was absolutely stunning, and I wasn't jealous of her, a major milestone for me. And just like that, any negative feeling I'd had toward her fled. If she and Daniel had any issues between them, that was for them to work through. It wasn't my place to judge her for leaving him, because as he'd pointed out, I'd never been to Hell. I'd never been put through the trials those two had been forced to endure. "You can put your cell phone in this container. Hopefully, the rice will draw the water out."

She deposited her phone inside the container and listened to Christian's explanation of the dream beads before she selected one of the bracelets and slipped her hand through. She glanced toward the bathroom where Ginger's shower still ran. "You might want to get your shower in while there's still hot water left."

"Good idea," I said, my eyelids drawing heavier, "but I think I'll take the cold. I need to stay awake a little longer."

"You need sleep," Christian scolded me.

"I need to know what happened to the people we rescued," I called back over my shoulder as I headed toward my room. "I'll sleep after that."

I ducked inside my room before Christian could lecture me on the importance of rest, set my switchblade on top of my dresser, and pulled out leggings, underclothes, and an oversized T-shirt before heading to the shower to wash away the remnants of the night's ordeal.

I stepped under the spray, did a quick yet thorough scrub head to toe to get rid of all the nastiness I felt clinging to me, then leaned back against the wall, letting the water run over me as I closed my eyes and reached out mentally.

Everything all right? You don't often reach out to me this way.

I smiled, a natural reaction to Rider's voice, at least when it wasn't being used to boss me around. It was only a small smile though, as even across so many miles, I could sense how tired he was.

I miss you.

He was silent for a moment, and I thought I felt him sigh. *I miss you too.*

I wish you would sleep.

If I sleep, who else will scratch this stupid mutt's belly all damn day?

I laughed out loud, trying to picture the image his words had just put in my mind, and carried on our mental conversation, mostly talking about Kutya, who he pretended to be completely annoyed by, but I sensed he loved dearly.

After I'd finished drying off and getting dressed, I stepped out of my bathroom to find Christian sitting in a chair next to my bed. He pointed his index finger at me, snapped his fingers, and pointed to the bed. "You. Sleep. Now."

I laughed, but planted my feet and folded my arms across my chest in defiance. "I told you I'm not going to sleep until I know what—"

"Go to bed." Daniel leaned against the doorjamb at the entry to my bedroom, an apple in hand. "Gruff got some kind of non-addictive hallucinogenic herb from some hippie witch in town and doped up the survivors. He left enough of it around them so the medical team would think whatever wacky-sounding stories they tell them after they come to would be the herb talking. We got rid of all evidence of the spider webs and tied them up with rope before calling it in, then we left. Gruff stayed behind to wait on the police so he could spin a story about how he was out for a hike and stumbled on the people after he saw some crazy-looking guy with a knife running off from there. A little power of suggestion, and they'll think some psycho abducted them, doped 'em up, and unfortunately three died."

"Oh. I guess everything worked out then." I frowned. "The herb won't hurt them?"

"Nope." Daniel took a bite out of the apple and talked around it as he pointed to my bed. "Upchuck and Maryjane are safe now. We even rescued more than we'd set out for, so be a good girl and get some sleep so we can find out if that thing was the trickster or not. If you'll excuse me, Ginger finally got out of the shower so I'm going to wash the funk off me and try to get some sleep myself."

"Ew, you're eating when you haven't showered yet?"

"I washed my hands. I'm not an animal. Well… you know what I mean."

I watched him leave, chuckling to myself, then turned to see Christian watching me with a stony expression on his face. "All right, all right. I'll sleep now."

I immediately released a huge yawn and crawled into the bed. I plumped up my pillows, settled in, and pulled the cover up to my chin. "Are you going to tell me a bedtime story?" I asked with a grin.

"There once was a bratty vampire-succubus named Danni…" he began in a teasing voice, and the day sleep immediately pulled me under.

I smelled sulfur.

CHAPTER TWENTY-THREE

I kept my eyes forward, trained on the shadows toward the back of the cave where I sensed him lurking, while all around me bodies writhed together, their cacophony of moaning and groaning filling my ears.

Heat flooded my body, the seductive call of utter vulgarity crying out for my succubus side to rise and claim what it desired. I ignored the activities happening around me, ignored how good it had felt when I'd fallen into that pit of bodies during the last dream, and I thought of Rider and Daniel, how neither one of them would probably ever look at me the same if I gave in to the urge, and I thought of how I'd never again meet my own eyes in the mirror, which would be the reason they'd never look at me the same.

They wouldn't judge me for falling victim to a demon's manipulation, but they'd pity me, knowing how much I'd hate myself for it, and their pity was something I just couldn't accept.

"Are you sure you're not Selander Ryan?" I called out to the lurking shadow man, "because I have to tell you, this is some of the same tired-ass shit he likes to pull."

A wave of heat washed over me, this time having

nothing to do with what was happening around me. It didn't come from me at all. It came from the hulking figure moving toward me. He came to a stop about four feet in front of me and flung off the shadows as if they were a blanket.

"Do you know what I am?" he asked, his voice a thunder clap that echoed off the cavern walls. He towered above me, eight feet of blue muscle-bound pissed off demon covered in glowing tattoos that resembled Arabic symbols, including his face and cue ball of a head. His eyes were black as onyx as he glared at me, his nostrils flaring, reminding me of a bull. Then again, maybe it was those massive shoulders giving off the bull vibe. I could see his legs this time, and large as they were, they resembled tree trunks hidden away behind gold lamé pants. "I asked you if you know what I am."

I wondered why Christian hadn't pulled me out of the dream, and for a moment feared the dreamcatcher wasn't working, or maybe he'd fallen asleep, but I remembered he'd slept the night before, and even if he felt tired, he would have assigned someone else to watch over me. He had to know the entity was indeed a trickster, and it had not been killed at the stream. I had yet to be truly scared and thought maybe Christian knew this. Maybe he wanted me to find out what I could about the monster taunting us, as long as it was safe to do so.

"Umm…" I made a show of thinking. "I'm going to go with … a perverted Smurf with a steroid problem?"

Another blast of heat washed over me as the demon folded its massive arms, a deep growl rumbling up from its belly.

"You're obviously a genie," I said, my gut suggesting I shouldn't reveal all my cards by letting him know we were on to his true identity. "Unless you were on your way to Comic-Con and decided you'd just pop into my dream uninvited along the way. That's right, Sinbad McSmurf-Face, I know this is all just a dream. I've had two of them already, right? I'm catching on to the bullshittery. You can't screw with my head anymore because you're not even real. You're just a stupid nightmare, a product of my subconscious mind."

One inky black eyebrow raised. "You think I am just a dream? None of this is real?"

"I certainly didn't rub an oil lamp and ask for a giant blue turd to pop out." I fought the urge to take a step back as he snarled. "Genies aren't real. I'm tired, and I'm stressed, and I created you. Now, I'm telling you to go away."

He leaned forward, invading my space. "You know creatures that defy human logic exist."

"Well, of course I do. Without vampires, how else could we explain the never-aging beyond sexy perfection that is Lenny Kravitz and Keanu Reeves? Duh. But genies? Nah, not buying it."

He wrapped his meaty hand around my throat and lifted me from the cavern floor, dangling me in front of his face. "Are you buying my realness now?"

"No," I managed to croak out, "but I'll buy you a breath mint if you put me down, because *damn*, dude."

He growled and tossed me across the cavern. As I sailed across the open space, I noticed the succubi and prey they'd been enjoying had stopped their orgy, and were all huddled together, trembling as they watched the big blue bastard. It had just crossed my mind what a good effect that was if the trickster wanted to rattle my nerves when my back hit a wall and I slid down to the ground, thankfully not on top of anyone.

The trickster stormed toward me with a roar, his mighty fists clenched. I held my hands out in front of me as he reached me, halting him. "All right, all right. You're a genie. This is all real, but I didn't summon you, so who did?"

He cocked his head to the side, his black eyes glittering with rage. "Now, why would you think to ask me that?"

I hadn't been scared until that moment, feeling pretty much in control, but as his lips pulled back in a snarl and his eye started doing that galaxy thing, it occurred to me I may have said the wrong thing, and might have to pay for it.

"Danni!"

I opened my eyes, and was instantly aware that I was sitting up, clinging to Christian's arms and nearly panting.

"It's all right," he assured me. "You're awake now."

"What happened?" Daniel asked, standing at the other side of my bed, looking down at me, his eyes twin pools of concern before he directed a glare at Christian. "I told you she should have been awakened immediately."

"No," I said, willing myself to calm down. I released Christian's arms, allowing him to sit back on the bed, and focused on controlling my breathing until the final tremors of fear left me. "You wanted me to talk to it, didn't you? To find out what I could."

"If you could do so safely, yes." He reached forward and gave my knee a pat, his blue eyes watching me carefully. "Daniel got me as soon as the dreamcatcher made the demon's presence known, and we awakened you when the dreamcatcher told us things were getting dicey."

I turned to look at the dreamcatcher, but it hadn't seemed to change at all. "It told you?"

"It shook when you were dreaming about the demon," Christian told me. "The shaking intensified when you were in danger, then it stilled once you were awakened. We have our proof now that what has been entering your dreams is not a djinn, but a trickster posing as one. Were you able to speak to it?"

I nodded. "Maybe it was the dream beads, but as soon as I found myself in the same place it had brought me to in the last dream, I knew nothing was real there. You'd said it couldn't read my mind while wearing these so when it became clear it was going to try to put me through the same scenario as the last dream, I called it out to see if I could get it talking and avoid all that nasty crap it wanted to put me through again. I prodded it, told it I knew it wasn't real, but I tried to make sure I didn't clue it in to the fact we know it's a trickster."

"That's good," Christian said, giving me an encouraging nod. "Did you get it to reveal anything?"

I shook my head. "Honestly, I think I just pissed it off."

"You didn't tell the thing it fucks hobbits, did you?" Daniel asked, grinning down at me.

"No, but I called it a perverted Smurf and offered to buy it a breath mint."

Daniel barked out a laugh. "Ah, Danni, you never disappoint."

"What happens now?" I asked. "I tried to act like I thought it was just some part of my subconscious mind screwing with me because I was stressed out and tired, but then it seemed like it was going to get really violent in order to prove its realness so I said it was a genie, but I might have made a mistake when I pointed out I hadn't summoned it and asked who did. It seemed really suspicious, and really pissed when I asked that. That's when you woke me up, and if I'm being honest, that's when I thought I was about to piss my pants."

"Yeah, I wouldn't have cleaned that up."

I shot Daniel a look and fought the urge to grin back when the corners of his mouth curved upward. I expelled a breath and turned back toward Christian, noting the worried look in his eyes. "Did I just put us in deep dung nuggets?"

"No," he answered, grinning a little as he shook his head, then his expression went right back to pensive. "You confirmed what we suspected. A trickster is doing this, and someone summoned it. Not allowing it to control the dream may have raised the stakes, and may even force this thing to attack you outside of a dream like it's been doing with others."

"Great, so I made things worse."

"Not necessarily. If you can get this thing to manifest outside of your dreams, you can kill it, so there's a silver lining to it attacking you physically." He rubbed his chin as he thought. "Our best option is still finding who summoned it. Have either of you narrowed down any possibilities yet?"

"You're sure Danni would have to have this thing's DNA in her in order for it to invade her dream?" Daniel asked.

"According to the lore," Christian answered. "It can read anyone's surface thoughts, and fears are wide open to it, but it would still attack those people physically, even if that means creating monsters and siccing those on them. In order to do something as personal as actually infiltrating a person's dreams, there has to be a physical connection. Danni has to have somehow gotten this thing's blood or saliva in her system."

I grimaced. "Well, the only saliva I've had access to has been Rider's, and we know Angel and you don't have this thing's DNA to pass to me through your blood. I haven't drunk from anyone else since this all started."

"Actually, you have," Daniel said before muttering a curse. "Danni, you've been drinking from random people since we started working at Gruff's. You've been drinking bottled blood for weeks."

My mouth fell open, and I fought the urge to smack myself in the forehead. "You're right. I didn't even think of that."

"Where has Ginger been getting her blood while here?" Christian asked. "I saw only one bag of blood in the refrigerator, and I warmed that for Danni after her last dream."

"From Gruff's," Daniel answered. "She's been drinking the bottles too, but she doesn't have to drink as often."

"Could Ginger be in danger of this thing getting into her dreams too?" I asked.

"If she drank a contaminated bottle." Christian started rubbing his chin again. "The bottled blood seems a very likely source, but we need to establish if the contamination occurred during the bottling or after you had ordered it. Or the blood could have come from someone already contaminated themselves. We'll need to speak to Gruff about his inventory, and watch out for Ginger, but I believe the trickster would have visited her dreams already if it were going to."

"You're sure?" I asked.

"I would have sensed it in her just as I sensed it in you. I believe the jorōgumo may have been created because of her fear of spiders, which means the trickster is aware of her, probably aware of all of us through whatever information it was able to get from your mind before you put on the dream beads. However, it hasn't invaded her dreams, so I'm betting she didn't get a contaminated bottle of blood. This increases the chances someone deliberately laced yours with trickster DNA."

"So someone at Gruff's set me up to be stalked and terrorized by this thing after seeing what it did to Rob?"

"This person may have set up Rob too," Daniel pointed out. "Once the trickster has targeted someone, shared DNA or not, it doesn't have to stick to dreams to get them, does it?"

"No," Christian answered. "I believe it's messing with you in your dreams, Danni, because of what you are, and the fear you have. However, now that you've basically told it you won't be so easily fooled in dreams anymore, it may create special monsters for you as well."

"Oh, great," I muttered. I fingered the beads wrapped around my wrist. "Will this help in the physical world?"

"The dream beads have one power. They keep that thing from reading you. That's all they did in this last dream. You realizing it was just a dream, and that you could take some of the trickster's power away was all you. The beads will protect your mind from being read in the physical realm, but it won't prevent this thing from creating something to physically hurt you, or doing so itself depending on the type of binding that was done with its summoner."

"Speaking of realms," Daniel said, "Lana brought up something earlier. Is this trickster an entity that can access the Njeri realm? The Njeri realm is—"

"A dream realm," Christian finished. "I am very familiar with it, and I have been, although the witch who brought me to it wasn't a malevolent being. I am aware the mother of the werewolf race has used the realm as well to bring people to another physical location as they slept. It is hard to say which entities have access to it, and can use it in the way the mother of the werewolf race used it. It is vast, and it serves multiple purposes. It is possible the trickster could have the power to use the realm for evil."

"I'm still not understanding this Njeri realm thing." I looked between them, not liking the worry I saw on their faces.

"I believe Daniel's fear is that this entity can use the Njeri realm to create a world so similar to reality that you won't be able to tell the difference and kill you there. It is a possibility as your mind is more susceptible to illusions while sleeping, but the Njeri realm isn't just a dream. Dreams are what you create. The Njeri realm is a sandbox beings who possess certain magic can use to either create new worlds or merge dream worlds with the physical world their prey exists in. This could explain how the trickster creates its monsters, actually. Bottom line, if you are killed there, you die in reality."

I lowered my head and massaged my temples. "Yeah, still not wrapping my brain around that."

"Danni, you will not be left alone at any point while this trickster lives." I felt his hand lightly pat my knee. "Despite handing in my wings, I appear to still sense demons, so I will continue to watch over you as you sleep. You don't have to worry about it."

Yeah, right, I thought. I was being hunted by a demon that could get me in my dreams or while I was awake, and possibly had the power to distort freaking reality. Nothing at all to worry about.

I felt a surge of energy, the sun vanishing from the sky, and realized I'd slept longer than I'd thought. I tossed aside the covers and swung my legs over the side of the bed. "Night just fell. Let's get to Gruff's and see what we can find out about the blood."

I traded in my leggings for jeans, pulled on black leather shitkickers in place of the Adidas that were still soggy from the night before, and tossed a black sweatshirt over everything before grabbing a quick drink from Angel, just enough to make sure I didn't risk growing weak if we ended up getting into another monster fight, and headed out for Gruff's. I rode with Daniel. Ginger and Lana followed behind in Ginger's Mustang, and Holden had confirmed he would meet us there.

"What's that about?" I asked as Daniel pulled into Gruff's lot and parked.

"Holden got a call from Carrie early this morning while we were still with the jorōgumo survivors, and he walked away, but I heard them arguing. I caught her saying something about him being out with other women all night, and he didn't seem that happy after finishing the call."

We sat in the truck for a moment, watching Carrie and Pauline rant and rave in each other's faces, a very tired-looking Holden standing behind Carrie with his hands on his narrow hips, looking as if whatever the hell was going on, he was over it. Angie, on door duty, stood near Carrie's cousin, ready to jump in if needed.

We noticed Ginger and Lana walking up and got out of the truck as they reached us, both watching the drama unfold in the parking lot.

"Just think, Daniel, all that hot mess could be yours." Ginger laughed. "Wait. Didn't both those women ask you out?"

"Yup," he answered. "I knew Pauline was a little wacko, but Carrie is a bit of a surprise. She really seems to have gone a little crazy since Holden came to town."

"I thought they just had a casual thing," I said as we stood there, watching the women call each other a variety of colorful, somewhat vulgar names.

"Holden thought they were a casual thing too," Daniel replied, "but I think Carrie decided to change things up. I think she's about to be very disappointed though, because that right there is the face of a man who has had enough drama. I think we're about to have another roommate."

"That's it!" Holden threw his hands up in the air, having seen us watching, and judging by the red color crawling up his face, he was a little embarrassed by the display. "I've had it with this shit."

Carrie whirled around on him as her cousin's face spread in a wide, shit-eating grin. "What? What are you saying?"

"I'm saying I didn't sign up for this crap. I like you, Carrie, and we've always been real good friends, but you know that's all we've been. I don't stay anywhere long, and I damn sure don't report to a woman when I do. I'll get my things later, but… yeah, I'm not staying with you anymore while I'm in town."

"You sonofabitch!" She shoved him. "Just friends? Were we just friends when you were fucking me?"

"Oh, get over it, Carrie," Pauline said. "Did you really think he was going to marry you or something after you've been letting him hit and run for years? Think of how you even got him to stay h—"

Carrie launched herself at Pauline, ramming her fist into the woman's mouth before both of them transformed within the blink of an eye, not caring whether or not humans were around to witness. Thankfully, there weren't, or they would have been stunned stupid to see two brown wolves going for each other's throats.

We all rushed forward to pull them apart before they could kill each other. Angie sank a knife into one of their back legs as Holden shifted into his wolf form and clamped his jaws around the other's neck, yanking it off the other wolf by its scruff.

I had no idea which female wolf was which, as they looked exactly the same, and had rolled around in a tangle of fur and sharp teeth, biting and clawing at each other immediately after they'd shifted shape.

"You going to behave?" Angie asked the one she'd stabbed as it lay on its side, whimpering, unable to shift with the silver in its leg.

With a growl and a ferocious shake of his massive head, Holden released the wolf he'd pulled away, and she shifted into human form. It was Carrie. She backed away from him, tears pouring from her eyes as she rubbed the back of her neck. "You'll regret this, Holden. You'll regret doing me like this."

She turned and ran into Gruff's as Holden shifted back into his human form, looking as if he already regretted what had transpired between them. Angie pulled her knife out of Pauline's leg, and the woman shifted shape, healing the damage to her leg.

"Get out of here, Pauline." Angie stood. "Carrie's on shift tonight, but you don't work here, so consider yourself banned from the premises tonight."

"I didn't start this," Pauline said, picking herself up from the pavement.

"I don't give a shit," Angie told her, "and neither does anyone here. Now get out of my sight before I talk to Gruff and let him handle this."

"Good luck with Crazy Carrie," the werewolf told Holden before turning away. She glared at us, but said nothing as she walked off.

"So… that looked fun," Ginger said after a moment of

awkward silence.

"I don't want to talk about it," Holden replied, "but, uh, can I use your couch for a few nights?"

"Sure thing." Daniel clapped him on the back as they started walking toward the building. "We can go with you to get your things too if you think those women might pull some more crazy shit."

"I've known her for years," Holden said, almost to himself. "I don't understand why she's gone all jealous and possessive like this."

"It's probably because of everything going on around here," I told him. "I caught her and Pauline fighting the other night, and Carrie was really upset about Rob, and completely stressed out. This trickster thing is screwing with us all."

"Well, let's go check into this blood situation and hope that points us in the right direction of how to find and kill the thing," Daniel said. "I'm kind of ready for a break from the insanity."

We all agreed that we were too as we stepped into Gruff's and did our best to ignore Carrie's red-eyed glare as she stood behind the bar, tying her money apron on.

"I don't know how, but we are finding this damn thing and killing it tonight," I told the others, "before it turns this whole town and all of its people into something from a Stephen King novel."

CHAPTER TWENTY-FOUR

We entered Gruff's office to find the big guy sitting behind his desk, watching something on his computer. He looked up, his hard eyes narrowing on Holden. "What the hell was that just happened in my parking lot? And don't lie to me, because I didn't have sound, but I saw it right here on my monitor."

Holden shoved his hands into his pockets. "Carrie and her cousin got into it. We handled it."

"Looks like this fight of theirs had a little something to do with you, lover boy. Didn't I tell you some time ago that all that friends with benefits shit always leads to a bomb going off in your face?"

Holden took a deep breath through his nose, jaw set. I barely knew the guy, but from what I'd noticed, he wasn't much for his private life being widely discussed. "It was handled."

"They shifted shape right in the damn parking lot where anyone could have seen them, and from what I could tell, there wasn't any life or death reason." Gruff muttered an expletive under his breath. "I should fire Carrie."

"She's been under a lot of stress," I jumped in. "Rob's

murder, other coworkers going missing, having to work here knowing something's preying on the people around this area, and Holden's out every night fighting it. It's enough to make anyone snap."

"I can't have werewolves shifting shape all willy-nilly around here," Gruff said, and sighed. "But damn it, she's a good worker, and the way things are going around here, I never know when I'm going to lose somebody." He pointed his thick finger at Holden. "I don't need her pulling another stupid, anger-filled stunt like that in my establishment. Why don't you go out and help Angie watch the lot until Grady comes in? No offense, but I think it best you stay out of here until she calms her knockers."

"Yeah, I get that." Holden nodded, then looked at Daniel and me. "I'll be out watching the lot if you need me."

"Now, what brought the rest of you jackasses into my office today?" the surly werewolf asked as Holden left us. "You finally pull your heads out of your asses and figure out how to get shit back to normal around here?"

"You know, Gruff, it really gives me a tingle in my naughty place when you talk to me like that," I said, giving him a little wink.

He growled low in his throat as his eyes narrowed. "You must get on Rider's last damn nerve."

"He loves me, and so do you, you big cranky-butt."

"Actually, I often wonder how that man keeps from strangling you."

"I'm pretty sure her naughty place has something to do with it," Ginger said, and I elbowed her in the rib.

"Chrissakes." Gruff scrubbed a meaty hand down his scruffy face. "What do you need from me in order to be on your way and get the hell out of my office?"

"We need to know about the blood served here," Daniel said. He filled Gruff in on everything we knew, and what we suspected.

"Shit," Gruff muttered after Daniel finished. "The blood comes sealed in bottles from one of Rider's, uh, *distilleries*, so if there was any contamination, it'd be done there."

I knew enough about the very bloody marys to know the blood came from primarily pedophiles and rapists, or anyone else Rider's people killed and drained during the process of capture or interrogation. This was the first I'd heard of a distillery, and the image the word put in my head wasn't pretty.

"Where's this distillery you get the blood from?"

"Sweet-cheeks, you're the one sleeping with Rider. If he doesn't share that information with you, he damn sure doesn't share it with me. All I know is I put an order in through MidKnight Enterprises and I get the blood. I usually don't order much since we only have a few local reclusive vamps in this area, and a handful that pass through, but I increased my order when you and Ginger arrived, and now I have a few more vamps on the payroll who Rider sent up here to work so I'll keep it the same." Gruff's bushy eyebrows came together. "It comes in batches and it seems highly unlikely there'd be only one contaminated bottle in a batch or that only you would get any contaminated bottles."

"So it's more likely someone here spiked a bottle," Daniel said. "The bartenders and servers pop the caps off those bottles when they serve them."

"You're saying one of my employees spiked Danni's blood?" Gruff folded his arms over his barrel chest. "I got good people working for me here."

"It's that or some random person spiked it while she wasn't looking," Daniel said. "But we don't leave bottled blood just sitting around for humans to find, so the chances of that happening are pretty slim."

Gruff's phone rang, and he grumbled in annoyance before picking it up. "What?"

He jerked his head toward his monitor and let out an

expletive. "Help's on the way. Don't lose him!"

"What is it?" I asked, quickly rounding the desk to look at the monitor, which still showed the live feed of the parking lot. I caught a glimpse of Holden walking out of the frame, Angie following him.

"Angie said Holden just took off toward the woods in a daze and won't even respond to her." Gruff stood from his chair. "It's time to get this fucker and end this shit."

"You stay!" I ordered him. "Watch out for all inside and try to keep anyone from leaving."

We took off at a run, somehow managing not to knock anyone down inside the bar and grille as we raced out the front of the building and across the parking lot. A car almost hit me as the driver looked for a parking spot, but I jumped over the hood with an unhuman leap and kept going. I couldn't see Holden, but Angie was still within sight, so we went full-speed ahead, following her. Just as we caught up to her, the biggest dog I'd ever seen leaped out from behind a tree and snarled at us as it pawed the ground.

We all skidded to a stop, and I heard two gasps, one from Daniel, the other from Lana, whose eyes were wide open, glossed over in pure terror. Her mouth opened and closed, but sound didn't come out. Then her whole body froze except for tears pouring from her eyes.

"Fuck," Daniel said, his voice a strangled whisper. "It's a fucking hellhound."

I looked at the large animal. It resembled a wolf, except it didn't have fur, just smooth black skin, and its head and paws were massive, its claws long and curved, and its eyes flickered red as it pulled its lips back over viciously sharp teeth and released a growl that made the earth tremble around us.

"We have to get the heart," Daniel said, "but you can handicap it if you stab it in the eyes."

"But it's a doggy!"

They all swiveled their heads toward me, except Lana,

who was still petrified and sobbing in silence.

"Are you fucking serious right now?" Daniel asked.

The dog growled and smoke poured from its nostrils as it grew to double its size, and lunged toward us. We braced ourselves for the attack. Even I, who could see the demon resemblance better now that the thing was smoking and reeked of sulfur, but a blur of blondish fur caught the beast in mid-air and tumbled to the ground with it.

"Take Lana and find Holden," Daniel ordered. "Ginger and I will help Angie and catch up. Go!"

I grabbed Lana's arm as Daniel and Ginger unsheathed their knives and looked for a way to help Angie as she and the hellhound fought viciously on the ground and yanked the Imortian as I tried to move forward. When she wouldn't budge, I slapped her as hard as I could across the face. "Snap out of it, Lana!"

She blinked and shook her head, coming out of the daze. I saw her eyes start to move down to where the hellhound fought the others, and I gave her arm another good yank, getting her ass to move before she could take another look at the beast that obviously terrified her into a stupor.

"Hellhound," she said, sounding out of breath as we ran in the direction Holden had disappeared to. She suddenly dug her heels in and started to turn. "I can't leave Daniel. I can't leave him in Hell again."

The rise in octaves as Lana made the statement and the way her eyes still seemed about to bulge out of her head clued me in that she was about to go full cuckoo for Cocoa Puffs. I slapped her again. "Snap out of it! This isn't Hell. Daniel's fine. Angie and Ginger are with him. We have to get to Holden before the pontianak does." I softened my voice and gripped the back of her neck, forcing her frantic eyes to lock on to me. "You're safe, Lana. The hellhounds can't get to you anymore, but we need to help Holden."

The glossy sheen of pure terror evaporated from her eyes as she blinked, coming out of whatever mental hellhole the sight of that creature had plunged her into, then nodded. "Let's go!"

She took off running, and I quickly caught up. I smelled a strong aroma of flowers and knew the pontianak was near as we continued crashing through the woods, jumping over rocks and sticks, deftly avoiding trees, as we followed the scent. All the while, I prayed we weren't too late.

We found Holden standing right in the spot where Rob had been attacked. His hands were loose at his sides, none of his weapons drawn, and he stared ahead with a serene smile on his facc, his eyes not seeming to register anything.

"Holden!" I snapped my fingers in front of his face, but he didn't react. I shook him and got nothing. "Well, this explains how Rob was killed so easily. This bitch's prey must stay in this condition until after she takes what she wants. Let's cover him."

I stood tight against Holden's back, and Lana stood in front of him as we both continuously scanned the area, the sweet scent of flowers clogging my throat as my heart raced. "Just so you know, if this ghost bitch just pops right up in front of me, there's a good chance I'm going to piss myself."

"It happens," Lana said, seeming much calmer than she had been when she'd seen the hellhound.

I felt Rider pushing against my mind and knew he picked up on my fright. *I'm fine,* I quickly told him through our link, *but I need to concentrate. I promise I'll check in tonight.* I immediately sealed my mind, hoping he'd understand I couldn't be distracted.

Footsteps sounded the way we'd came, and we both jerked our heads in that direction to see Daniel, Ginger, and Angie arrive. Daniel and Ginger had a lot of black blood on them. Angie was clean, but she'd been dealing out damage in her wolf form, so her clothes were fine.

"What the hell's wrong with Holden?" Ginger asked.

"He's in some kind of trance," I answered.

"The hound is dead," Daniel said, holding Lana's gaze. The snake shifter nodded and recoiled as the smell of raw sewage washed over us.

"Block Daniel so this thing can't take his genitals!" I ordered, and Ginger and Angie immediately covered him the same way Lana and I covered Holden.

"Fuck," Daniel said, looking around. "I never thought I'd be the meat inside a chick sandwich and be too scared to enjoy it."

We all looked at him, and for a moment I forgot my fear. "Seriously, Daniel?"

"What? I'm a guy. I'm contractually obligated to be disgusting sometimes or else my man card gets taken away, then I'll have to drink pumpkin mocha everything, and piss sitting down."

I started to respond when I heard a startled gasp and turned to see Lana get shoved out of the way by a ghastly wraith in a white dress. Time seemed to slow as I took in the long, dark hair framing a familiar face. Dead eyes looked into Holden's as a skeletal hand reached low and a long, narrow lizard-like tongue unfurled from a mouth filled with sharp teeth. I could see through the pontianak's body, and knew when she was taking corporeal form to complete her gruesome attack, because her heart became solid first.

Moving purely by instinct, my arm shot out and my hand wrapped around the organ, snatching it out of the ether that was the rest of her body before I spun away, out of her reach. The vampire ghost's body flickered before becoming solid, and she let out a bloodcurdling screech as she looked down at the hole in her chest, then at me.

I removed my knife, flipped it open, and stopped with it hovering over the organ that beat in my hand, memories of my own heart beating in Rider's hand flooding my mind. The vampire ghost lunged toward me, her skeletal hand reaching out before her, and I knew I was going to die because there was no way I could destroy her heart.

Silver slashed in front of my face, and I screamed as pain filled my hand. The vampire ghost screamed too, rearing back as her entire body contorted in pain. Behind her, Holden fell to his knees, no longer under her spell.

I looked down and saw a silver knife had pinned the heart to my palm. Lana cursed a stream of obscenities around me, and I sensed myself being surrounded.

The heart and the knife that pinned it to my hand were yanked from my body, allowing a small geyser of blood to erupt from my palm. A dark head blocked my view of the injury, and I felt the pull of someone's mouth against my flesh.

"I'm sorry! I'm sorry!" I heard being said over and over as if from a distance as the world seemed to tilt on its axis, and I realized sound had been dulled. My brain felt like it had been stuffed with cotton. I felt like my head wasn't even attached to my body anymore. It was just floating in space.

Then the sound came rushing back, and I heard Holden yelling at Daniel to burn the bitch. I heard a large crash, and felt hands grab me as I was quickly dragged a foot over, a large tree crashing in the spot I'd been in, and there was Daniel in dragon form, releasing a stream of fire at a woman in white who seemed to dance in the flame until she burned to a complete crisp, her ashes floating away on the wind as Daniel shifted back to his human form and looked over at me. "Are you all right?"

I nodded, coming back to my senses. "What happened?"

"You froze with the heart so I stabbed it, but I accidentally stabbed you too," Lana said, her face a mask of regret. "I'm sorry. I really didn't mean to."

"It's all right," I said, raising my hand, which was now smooth and unmarred. "You didn't mean to."

"I sealed it up," Ginger said. "You're good, but you should drink soon."

"Okay." I nodded, something niggling at the back of

my mind. Why had I froze? The pontianak's heart in my hand made me remember my heart in Rider's hand, but I was over that, wasn't I? And I wasn't going to crush it. I was going to stab it in case the trickster was actually pretending to be the pontianak. But I knew her… and that's why I couldn't put a blade in her heart. "Did any of you recognize her face?"

"She kind of looked like that woman from the parking lot," Lana said.

"Pauline." I nodded and tried to sort through all the clutter in my mind as I started recalling things I'd overlooked and questioning oddities.

"Christian said the trickster could take on the appearance of someone else, or possess someone else," Daniel said. "The silver knife in the heart didn't kill the pontianak, so it wasn't the trickster possessing her. Do you think Pauline was made to be the pontianak, like those truckers were made to be zombies? Did we just kill her?"

I turned toward Holden as the puzzle pieces continued to come together in my mind. "Did Carrie ever date Rob? Was she involved with him in a romantic or sexual way at all?"

Holden's brow furrowed in confusion as he stared at me for a moment and shrugged. "We were never an actual couple. I didn't ask about who she slept with when I wasn't around."

"I'm pretty sure they slept together once or twice," Daniel said, watching me with curiosity. "When we first came here and she was flirting it up, he told me she was a nice girl, but took breakups bad. I kind of put two and two together. Why? What are you thinking?"

I took off running, tapping into my vampiric speed to cover the distance to Gruff's, fully aware the others were running after me, calling out to me, but I didn't slow down until I cleared the tree line, and only because there might have been humans in the area. I still covered the parking lot at a quick clip, ran past Grady, the short, but thick werewolf who'd replaced Angie on door duty, and nearly ran over a burly trucker on his way out after I pushed through the door.

"Your office, now!" I called out to Gruff, spotting him behind the bar making a drink. I raced to his office, not waiting for a response.

I was already standing behind his desk chair, tapping my foot impatiently, when he came through the door. "What in—"

"You still got that footage from the night Rob was killed?"

"Yeah."

"Put your ass in this chair and bring it up. Now!" I snapped when he seemed to stand there, stunned.

"All right, girl. Damn." He plopped down into his seat and started pulling up files on his computer. "Calm your gizzards."

I leaned over his shoulder, not caring that I was invading his space, as he pulled up the file from that night. "I only want to see the bar area, and take it to when I ordered a drink." He fiddled with the buttons and the video started speeding along in reverse, then fast forwarded. "There! Go back."

He fiddled with it some more and we watched as I approached the bar and asked him for a drink. Carrie walked past, tapped his shoulder, said something, then went around to where the bottled blood was stored under the bar. From where I'd been standing that night, I couldn't see her, and Gruff had been busy making drinks, but the security camera over the bar had just the right angle to catch her grab a bottle, uncap it, and remove a heart-shaped bottle from her money apron.

"Son of a…"

"Bitch," I finished for him as we watched Carrie work. "That psycho spiked my blood and sicced a demon on my ass."

CHAPTER TWENTY-FIVE

"It's Carrie," I said as the others spilled through the door, minus Holden, who'd apparently followed Gruff's previous order of staying outside.

"What?" they all said at once.

"Carrie spiked a bottle of blood with trickster DNA before giving it to me. A security camera over the bar caught it all, but we never thought to look at it before. I never suspected her until just now when I saw her cousin's face on that pontianak and it all just came rushing together. That jealous bitch must have summoned that thing for some kind of love spell and it got out of control. Then obviously she started siccing it on people. I'm going to gut that bitch." I moved toward the door, but Daniel grabbed my arm and pulled me back.

"We'll get her, but you had a decent amount of blood loss out there, and we don't know how hard it's going to be killing this thing. You need to feed."

"I'll feed later." I moved for the door again, but he held on tight.

"You'll feed now. Angie, you're the least likely of us that Carrie will get spooked by. Go out there and keep watch on her, but don't be obvious."

"Got it," she said, and moved toward the door. She stopped with her hand on the knob and looked back at us. "Carrie is the reason Rob was killed the way he was?"

I nodded.

"Take your time killing the bitch," she said, and left.

Daniel rolled up his sleeve. "Feed."

"I'm not feeding from you. I had venom just a few nights ago, and this trickster has me all out of whack."

"You can feed from me." Lana offered her wrist, and I felt my stomach roll as I looked at the tanned flesh, the estrogen flowing in her body practically forming a barrier. I dipped my head toward her wrist, but had to pull back. I'd just fed from Angel, and my succubus side could only take so much blood straight from a female vein. Lana lowered her hand. "I understand. I know snakes are—"

"It's not that you're a snake," Daniel cut in. "It's that you're female, and she already drank from Angel earlier. Her other half won't allow her to feed straight from a woman right now. Danni, you have to drink from me. Ginger will stab me if you have venom and it affects me."

"What the hell is happening here?" Gruff asked, moving behind us. "What's this venom and can't drink from a woman shit?"

"My other half is a succubus," I told him. "Sometimes if that side is dominant, I can secrete a venom that makes men very horny to the point they would sexually assault me, or if my succubus side is really revved up, I might assault them and kill them. I can't trust that the bottled blood isn't tainted, and sorry, Daniel, but I can't drink from you. You can shift shape and move faster than Ginger could stab you." And I honestly didn't know if stabbing him would pull him out of the venom's effect, not now that I knew he had feelings for me.

"Oh, for fuck's sake. Drink mine." Gruff rolled up the sleeve of his flannel shirt and held his wrist out. "Get those knives ready, you jackasses. If I go all horny balls and you don't stop me, I'm kicking all your asses.

Chrissakes, I'm old enough to be her daddy."

"You're sure about this?" I asked as I held his meaty wrist in my hand, and the others flanked him, silver knives out in case anything went wrong.

"Shit," he muttered, looking at the blades. "Yeah, just do it and go finish this."

My fangs lowered from my gum as I brought Gruff's wrist to my mouth. His blood came out in a rush, and held a good jolt of power, due to his age and bloodline. It wasn't spicy like Daniel's, but it had a flavor different from that of human or vampire. I almost wanted to call it a smoky mesquite. I drank just enough to get an energy buzz, withdrew, and sealed the wound with my tongue. "Thanks, Gruff. You feeling all right?"

"Yeah, that was weird, but I'm good. Now go handle that demon mess."

"She's gone!" Angie barreled through the door, Holden with her. "She ran out of here right after we all came running in, jumped in her car and left. She probably saw all the black blood on Daniel and Ginger, and got paranoid when we all ran in here. She has to know you all figured it out."

"Fuck!" I growled, my fists clenched and dying to swing at something. I was beyond ready to end this demon and get back home. "How good are you wolves at tracking?"

"Pretty good with scents, but not when she left in a car," Angie replied.

"I can follow the car by air," Daniel said, running out of the office.

"Let's go," I ordered. "Daniel will locate her and guide us where to go."

"Hey," Gruff called as I reached the door. "After you kill Carrie, tell her she's fired."

"Will do."

"How do you think Holden's doing?" Ginger asked as she directed the Mustang down the street. Daniel had ran out of Gruff's and taken flight the moment he was sure no one could see him shift, and flew high enough in the air we didn't have to fear freaking the hell out of the human people of Moonlight if they caught sight of him overhead. They might not be able to pinpoint what kind of big, weird bird they'd seen fly past, but they wouldn't recognize the bird they saw was, in fact, a dragon. Dragon eyes could see for miles though, so even from the high altitude, he spotted Carrie's car speeding away before she could get too far, and had been tracking her since, relaying directions to us telepathically.

I glanced back at the Impala trailing us, Holden at the wheel, and Lana riding shotgun, partly to ensure he stayed within the right headspace for what we needed to do. "It's hard to say when we don't have a mental link with him, but so far Lana hasn't alerted us to anything. I imagine it's got to be hard for him. He might not have been invested in a serious relationship with Carrie, but you can tell he cares for her, and apparently they have years of friendship between them."

"Why do you think she did it?" Ginger asked, her eyes on the road as she turned the steering wheel to the right, winding around a curve, then straightened out. "And how did you figure it out?"

"It just came to me when I saw Pauline's face on that pontianak. The trickster used Pauline to be the pontianak instead of just creating one, like it probably did when Rob was attacked. That suggested this pontianak attack wasn't just an attack on Holden. It was an attack on Pauline too because it's not like the trickster was going to just let Pauline go afterward. Carrie had just gotten into a fight with both of them right before. I remembered what Pauline said to Carrie before she threw the first punch and realized Carrie threw that punch to shut her up before she said too much."

Ginger frowned. "I can't remember what she said."

"She got cut off, but she was about to say 'Think of how you even got him to stay here.' She also said she didn't start this when Angie told her to leave. I don't think she was talking about the fight. She was talking about *this*, this whole demon mess. It all clicked when I saw her face on the pontianak. She and Carrie were fighting last night, and I saw Carrie take something from her and put it in her pocket. I'm pretty sure it was the same thing I saw her spiking my blood with on the security footage. I'm not sure if Pauline had any part in the summoning, but she definitely knew what was going on."

"How she got him to stay here? He stayed here because of the… Ohhhh… Oh *shit*. She didn't want Holden to leave, so the trickster created a pontianak attack so Holden would stay here to investigate, because Holden had all that history with his partner getting killed by one. There was no way he'd leave until that thing was caught. Why did you ask if she dated Rob? You think she intentionally caused Rob's death?"

"I don't think she intentionally caused anyone's death, but she definitely tried to cause mine. Remember what Christian said? The trickster can be intentionally targeted to a person if the summoner slips the target some DNA, as was my case, or it can be accidentally targeted by just a really strong thought or feeling." I glanced up at the dark form flying above us in the sky, outlined by moonlight. "Carrie strikes me as a lonely woman who's been left often. I think she may have tried a love spell and summoned the trickster instead. She wanted a man, and got Holden, but Holden doesn't stay in one place. She wanted him to stay here, and somewhere in her mind, which I'm sure the trickster has full access to, she was still licking her wounds over Rob not wanting her. According to Gruff, Rob would sleep with a werewolf from time to time, but would only get serious with humans."

"So the trickster made him the pontianak's victim."

"I truly think she regrets that, and never intended for it to happen, but she still made some pretty screwed up choices. She spiked my blood the night Rob died, before the attack. At that point, all we knew was some truckers had gone missing passing through. We were just security at Gruff's. She didn't spike the blood and sic that thing on me because I was investigating a death she'd caused. She sicced that thing on me for no reason but jealousy."

"What a crazy bitch," Ginger muttered, picking up a little speed. "Tell me again why we can't catch up to her and just ram her off the road."

"Because we want to know where she goes. At this point, we don't know if she physically has that demon trapped somewhere, or if it's trapped inside her."

"You're sure we don't need Christian?"

"Guardian or not, he's human, and this thing is not going to just stand there and let us kill it. He's best staying with Angel, protecting her from any bastard offshoots this thing might send out tonight."

"He sensed when a demonic entity entered your dream. Maybe he has some kind of demon-fighting superpower."

"Maybe isn't definite, and we don't have time to switch someone out with him. I am not leaving Angel alone. It would be too easy for this trickster to send something after her to get me off its trail.

"Do you think it would do that?"

"It had access to a lot of my thoughts and fears before Christian gave me these dream beads, and one of my fears is something happening to Angel while she's with us so there's a chance it could have picked up on that depending on how deep it was able to root around in my mind. This thing has to have a plan."

"I guess we'll find out soon enough," Ginger said.

Yep. That was what I was afraid of.

The house was small, and it had taken several winding

roads to get to as it was settled in the woods, at least three miles away from the closest other house. Carrie's Camry sat in the driveway, and she'd already left it. The house looked dark, but a sliver of light showed through the door on the large red structure behind it. Ginger and I stood on a hilltop debating if it was a shed or a barn as Holden pulled in behind the Mustang and got out.

A moment later, Daniel landed next to us, shifting effortlessly from his massive purple form. He rolled his head on his neck and stretched his arms. "She went in the shed."

"I told you it was a shed," I said.

Ginger stuck her tongue out at me before turning to Daniel. "Does your dragon form change color every time you shift? Last time you were green, and you were blue at the stream."

"Apparently, I do," he said before directing his gaze at me. "What's the plan?"

"Wait." Holden stuck his hand out. "Are you sure Carrie summoned this trickster on purpose?"

I expelled a breath, hoping the werewolf wouldn't prove to be a hindrance, as I turned toward him. "I don't know if she purposely summoned a trickster, but clearly she was messing with some kind of magic and that's what she got. I truly don't think she meant to have Rob killed, but she knew the trickster was behind the attack and didn't say anything to us."

"She was probably terrified." He looked at us as if searching for someone to back him up, but we all remained stony faced.

"Holden, she wanted you to stay and because of that, this trickster created the pontianak that killed Rob." I saw him wince and felt awful. "It's not your fault, not even a little bit, but you need to understand and accept that whether or not she planned the specifics of the attack, she brought this thing here and unleashed it on this town."

"How are you sure it was her? Maybe this thing

attached to her like it attached to you."

"I saw her on camera with my own eyes, Holden. She poured something into the blood I drank, and I saw her and Pauline fighting over that bottle just last night. Whether she summoned it or it attached to her, she sicced it on me intentionally before Rob was even killed."

"Before he was killed?" Daniel said, not having realized just how far back my blood had been spiked. "I figured it was after we started looking into his death. Why would she want to hurt you before then?"

"Because of you," I answered. "She asked you out, remember? Pauline flirted with you too, and I'm still unsure if Pauline was part of this or just knew what Carrie had done. I guess when you refused her, she realized we live together and spend so much time together, and thought I might be the reason you turned her down." I didn't bother pointing out that she might have been right, not with others around.

"Why didn't she spike Ginger's blood too then?"

"Because I don't like ding-dongs, you ding-dong. Catch on." Ginger rolled her eyes at him and shook her head. "I wasn't a threat to her getting what she wanted."

"I still think the jorōgumo was for you, G. And the hellhound for Lana. I just don't believe those were attacks Carrie wanted. They were the result of the trickster getting his kicks. Upchuck, Maryjane, all the others were just random victims, but I know Carrie purposely targeted me, and after that fight in the parking lot, she was angry enough at Pauline and Holden to trigger the trickster to create the second pontianak attack." I looked at the werewolf and saw the reluctant acceptance in his eyes. "She did it, Holden. Intentionally or not, she summoned that thing and there's not one person standing here who hasn't been at risk of death because of her actions. That includes you."

He sniffed as he aggressively nodded his head and palmed his silver knife. "In the heart, right?"

"Right." I sighed. "Holden, we don't know how she's bound the trickster, or how far it will go to save itself."

"I know." He sniffed again before lifting his gaze from the ground to meet mine. "Please, just… one of you get to her before me. Please don't make me be the one to have to do it."

I squeezed his shoulder as I saw his eyes water. "We'll try our hardest."

The others agreed, and patted the werewolf's back or squeezed his shoulder or arm, and soon he was able to gather himself with a deep breath.

"This is her grandparents' house," he said. "It's been abandoned for a while. I didn't know she ever used it, but I'm thinking everything's probably been cleared out of that shed. It would be a good place to summon a demon. It's not the most secure structure, but with the right sigils, it can hold one. There's only one way in, and it's through those two doors in front. I say we just rush in and quickly fan out, form a circle around it if we can."

"Okay." I nodded. "Do we know what kind of damage a demon can do if it's caught in some sort of binding?"

"Depends on how powerful the demon is," Holden answered, "but we all have silver knives. I know enough incantation to hopefully hold it still for long enough for one of you to ram a knife in its heart. That's all we need to do."

"All righty then. Sounds like the closest thing we're going to get to a plan." I looked at the others. "We ready?"

"Ready," Ginger said, her hands flexing. She was champing at the bit to dispatch the demon, and I was pretty sure she was remembering her time spent in a spider web, which fueled her vengeance.

"Ready," Lana said, moving to my side. Daniel took up my other flank, making it clear they were on Danni detail.

"Let's move." I started down the hill, and they came with me, all moving with supernatural speed and stealth, barely making a whisper on the grass. We threw open the doors, stepped inside, and fanned out, but there was no demon to circle.

The shed was bare. A series of LED shop lights hung in two rows across the ceiling, shining light on the dust that had gathered in corners, and the majority of the floor, except for the circle in the center, where some satanic looking symbol had been drawn around a support column that stood dead center in the room. Carrie leaned back against that column, her arms folded over her chest as she trembled. Tears ran the length of her face as she raised her gaze and locked eyes with Holden, who stood straight in front of her. "I didn't mean for all of this to happen."

"You didn't do anything to stop it," I said, noticing the pain in Holden's eyes. The guy wasn't going to be able to kill her if it came to it, and with no demon in sight, I was pretty sure it was going to come to it.

She slowly turned her head, running her gaze from Holden, past Lana, to where I stood at her left, outside the circle. "You think you've figured it out, don't you? How pathetic I am. How desperate I was to be loved."

"Carrie, I know what it's like to crave love, and to feel like you're never going to get it because you aren't good enough," I told her, and actually felt a little bit of sympathy for her because I was speaking the truth, "but you have to wait for it. You can't just summon a demon."

"I didn't summon a demon!" she yelled, then closed her eyes, her face pinched as she reined in her emotions. When she reopened them, she straightened from the column and forced a sad smile of defeat. "I thought I was summoning a genie who would bring me love. That's all I wanted. Someone to love me, a family… I didn't mean for anyone to die."

"You spiked my blood. I watched you do it on Gruff's security feed. What did you think was going to happen?"

"I didn't know anyone would die." She sobbed, shaking her head as she used the sleeves of her jacket to wipe away the tears. "It looked like a genie. It told me it would give me all I wanted except I had to share its blood so it could travel among others and help people. I wasn't sure about it so I… I slipped it into drinks of truckers who were gross to me, or people passing through who had attitudes and thought they could talk to me any way they wanted. Nothing happened to them after they drank thc drinks with blood, so I thought it was okay."

"Even when they started going missing?" Ginger asked. "News of those missing truckers was buzzing before the night Rob died, before you spiked Danni's blood. You knew it was because of what you were doing, and you did it to Danni."

"I just wanted her to go away!" She huffed out a breath before turning toward me. "I didn't know those people were dead. I just knew they were gone, and I wanted you to go."

"Why?" Holden asked.

"Because of you." She pointed at him. "You stopped over at my house, but you were already set to leave town. I didn't even know if you'd still be there when I got off work, and the whole night while I worked and wondered why the genie wasn't fulfilling my wish. I had to watch Danni and Daniel. I asked him out and he turned me down flat, but he could never take his eyes off her. And Rob…" She hiccupped. "I was good to sleep with, but he wouldn't give me a chance for anything serious, just like you, and I had to watch him flirt with some human bitch with bad hair all night. Why should they get what I wanted? Why were they good enough, but not me?"

"You spiked my blood, and the woman's drink," I said. "You did it knowing the people whose drinks you spiked were never heard from again."

"It's not like bodies were found," she snapped. "They could have just skipped the country. I didn't try to kill you, Danni. I just wanted you gone so maybe Daniel would look at me since Holden didn't act like he wanted to stick around."

"Until your pet demon killed Rob in a pontianak attack it created so Holden would stay," I told her. "Rob's blood is on your hands, and you knew that moment why he died."

"I didn't." She shook her head. "I didn't know. I never asked the genie to kill anyone. I never wanted it to do that."

"Fine. You wanted it to make people disappear, though, and you're not stupid enough to not know it made Rob disappear that night to give you what you wanted from Holden," I said. "But it didn't really, did it? Holden stayed for the case, not you, and that ate you up inside, so rather than come to someone and admit what you'd done so we could help stop this thing's reign of terror, you chose to let it keep killing people. You even sicced it on Holden and Pauline tonight."

"I didn't!" she screamed at me, her face reddening as fresh tears flowed. "By the time I realized what it really was, and what it was really capable of, it was too late. If I sicced anything on them, I didn't mean it. It knows everything I think and feel. Yes, I made sure it targeted you, but I swear I didn't send it for Holden and Pauline. I tried to stop her when she found out and wanted to use its power to make her frenemies disappear. That's why we were fighting." She looked around at all of us, her gaze landing on Holden. "Is Pauline dead?"

"Your demon buddy turned her into a pontianak and made her lure Holden right after your fight," I told her, ignoring her fresh burst of tears, however genuine they appeared. "We saved Holden, but had to kill her to do it."

"I didn't mean for that to happen. I tried to keep her out of it once I realized this thing was killing people, but she wouldn't listen." Carrie reached into the pocket of her money apron and removed a heart-shaped glass bottle full of crimson blood. "She took this and put it in a woman's drink at that party. I knocked the drink over and dragged her to the bathroom to get the bottle back."

"So you had a conscience attack," I said. "Why didn't you come clean with me in the bathroom instead of spinning me a story? You knew I was going after the thing."

"I know," she said, straightening her shoulders as she met my gaze dead-on. "You were hunting it, to kill it, and there's one very big reason why I couldn't let you do that."

"Wh—" I looked at the circle she stood in. I didn't know much about summoning demons or trapping them, but I was pretty sure if she'd trapped the demon in the circle she summoned it in, it would still be there. I didn't see a single spot where the circle had been broken either. All I saw was Carrie standing in the circle, and the blood in the bottle she held was dark, but still red. The hellhound had bled black, leading me to believe things from hell bled black. "Carrie, is that your blood in that bottle?"

"It's our blood," she said, before turning and raising her hair to reveal a satanic looking symbol carved into the back of her neck. When she turned around, her mouth spread into a smug smile, and her eyes bled to black as they connected to Holden's horrified gaze.

"You want to kill me," she said in a voice that belonged in my nightmares, not in her throat, "then you'll have to kill the stupid bitch so desperate for love that she bound me to her."

CHAPTER TWENTY-SIX

"Come and get it, bitches." Carrie, or whatever the hell she had bound to her body, pulled a switchblade free from her back pocket, and flipped it open before she surged forward, running straight for Holden, who stood frozen like a deer in headlights.

We all ran for her at once, except for Holden, who remained immobile, a look of sorrow on his face that showed he was absolutely gutted that the trickster had been bound to Carrie. Unfortunately, standing frozen was going to get him gutted physically too.

Lana reached Carrie first and dove for her midsection, not that afraid of the knife in her hand. Shifters could simply switch forms to heal themselves, so they tended to not care that much about getting slashed even though I was sure it still hurt like a bitch.

Before she could make contact, Carrie jumped straight up in the air and grabbed hold of one of the light fixtures in a move no human or shifter could make, causing Lana and Ginger to crash together and fall in a groaning tangle of arms and legs.

Daniel and I skidded to a stop, and looked up to see Carrie swinging from light fixture to light fixture until she made it back to the center of the room and dropped, landing on her feet as smoothly as a cat. She winked at us before shifting into wolf form.

Daniel shoved me behind him as the wolf ran toward us and moved to meet it head-on. I winced as I saw the wolf jump and sink its teeth into his shoulder before he grabbed its tail and slammed it onto the ground. Daniel dropped to his knee, silver blade in hand, ready to sink through the wolf's heart, when it shifted shape and punched him hard in the balls. Daniel grabbed his crotch as he sucked in wind and fell over, truly pissing me off.

"Hey, bitch! Only I get to punch my people in the balls!"

Carrie laughed as she flipped me the bird and backed up, using her other hand to make a come here gesture with her fingers.

On their feet again, Lana and Ginger joined me as we stalked toward the demon. Daniel was down, seriously hurting. He'd gone pale and seemed to be holding back the contents of his stomach. I had no doubt demons could throw a good punch. Behind us, Holden was still no help at all.

Suddenly, a hellhound appeared in front of us. Lana sucked in air and backed away, her face contorted in a mix of panic and terror. My blade was in my palm, but once the hound looked at me and made a whining sound in its throat, I lost my nerve to move forward and take it out.

"I got this mutt," Ginger said, rushing forward. Immediately, spiders fell from the hound's body and raced toward her. She screamed and jumped back.

"Having fun yet?" Carrie asked in the trickster's voice. "Sic 'em beasties!"

Doggy or not, I couldn't let the hellhound kill us. I raised my blade and rushed forward as it leaped for Lana, and sank the silver into its chest where I hoped the heart was. It let out a howl of pain before dripping black blood all over me and disintegrating.

Ginger had overcome her fear enough to stomp on the spiders, still crying out as some of the faster ones crawled up her legs, as they were doing to mine and Lana's, who had come out of her stupor with the death of the hellhound. The three of us stomped and swatted, and the moment we were through, three hell hounds appeared in front of Carrie, guarding her.

"Sonofabitch," I muttered.

"They're not real," Lana said, speaking to herself. "They're not real. This isn't Hell. This isn't Hell."

"Oh, honey," the trickster taunted us through Carrie's body. "It's going to be worse than Hell."

A dozen more hellhounds appeared, all drooling in anticipation as smoke rolled out of their flared nostrils. Their claws made deep grooves in the wooden boards beneath them.

"You couldn't shift in Hell," I reminded Lana, "but you can here. Eat them!"

Lana shifted shape as Ginger and I ran forward, the hounds coming at us with bloodlust in their red-flickering eyes. I forced myself to think of them as demons and not dogs as I sliced through any body part I could connect with as they jumped at me, attacking like the rabid, snarling beasts they were. Recuperated enough to join us, Daniel reached my side and used his blade to dispatch as many as he could as Lana wrapped her long snake body around the ones who jumped at her, squeezing them until their bones shattered. Ginger sliced away as well, crying out when one raked its claws down her leg, drawing blood.

A ball of fur flew past me and leaped at an approaching hellhound, rolling with it in a tangle of biting and growling. Holden was back in the game.

"Lana, clear the way!" Daniel ordered. "Danni, get ready to sink that blade into that bastard's heart."

Daniel disappeared in a shower of rainbow sparkles as Lana slithered her long reptilian body over the floor, going straight for Carrie. She moved so fast, and was so large, most of the hounds were knocked out of the way, and I was there running alongside her body to dispatch the few who managed to clamp their teeth into her scales.

As she reached Carrie, and the demon inside the werewolf's body braced itself to fight, Daniel appeared behind it. He grabbed Carrie's arms and pulled them back, giving me a clear shot. I jumped over Lana's reptilian body, knife held high… and felt myself get blown backward as the trickster released a deafening bellow of rage from within Carrie's body.

As I flew backward in what seemed to be slow motion, I caught sight of the others flying backward, as if the trickster's loud bellow carried the force of a bomb and we'd all just been blown up.

My head hit a light, and I saw stars, then my back connected with a hard surface, stopping my flight. The back of my head connected next, and everything went black.

I opened my eyes, and my body immediately flooded with pain. I hurt *everywhere*, but it seemed to radiate from the back of my head. I tried to lift my head, but it rolled right back until my chin rested on my chest. I heard laughter. Deep, evil laughter.

Feminine fingers came into view. They slipped under my chin and raised my head. It was Carrie, if Carrie had soulless black eyes. "You tried, but it wasn't good enough," she said, as her other hand appeared, holding a sharp blade. She placed it against my jugular. "Now I have to kill you and all your friends. Then, I'm really going to have some fun in this tow—ahh!"

Carrie's body jerked back and spun around, then dropped in front of me, a knife embedded deep in her chest right where her heart should be. She let out an enraged screech before smoke rolled off her body, and it went up in flames before poofing out. The body was no more, and Daniel stood over it, where he'd stood as he'd plunged his silver knife into the trickster's heart.

The column had stopped my flight, and now I rested my aching head against it so I could look up. "Daniel. Is it ov—"

He dropped to his knees, grabbed my face, and covered my mouth with his, cutting off my surprised gasp as he slid his tongue inside and kissed me with a wild, almost desperate passion. My heart raced and flooded with more emotions than I could handle. My brain was pure mush, a thick soup I couldn't make any sense out of. Panic, fear, excitement, surprise, and guilt assaulted me over and over as Daniel explored my mouth, and I realized my hands were on his shoulders, and I wasn't pushing him away.

He withdrew with a gasp for air, and rested his forehead against mine, his hands lowering to my collarbone as he closed his eyes and took several breaths. "I'm sorry," he finally said as I scrambled to sort through the tangle of thoughts that had entered my mind and process what had just happened. "I'm sorry. I know you're with Rider, but I thought that was it. I thought I was going to lose you, that I was going to fail you, and I just couldn't… I love you, Danni, and I can't lose you. Even if you're not mine. I can't lose you."

I didn't know what to say. His kiss had been electric, sending a shiver of desire down my spine, but Rider's name was a splash of ice cold water. "Daniel."

"I know I can't have you. I just had to say that. I just had to… tell you. Just once." He kissed my forehead before standing and offered me his hand.

I hesitated for a moment, afraid that if I gave him my hand, I might be persuaded to give him even more. My lips still tingled from his kiss. My heart still raced. I heard the others groaning, though, and knew whatever we'd just shared wouldn't be repeated in their presence. I gave him my hand and allowed him to help me to my feet.

The room spun for a moment, but I otherwise seemed

fine. Ginger and Lana, back in human form, limped over, rubbing their heads. "I guess we all got blasted," Ginger said.

I nodded and looked for Holden. I found him standing in the now open doorway, looking up at the moon. I walked over to him and placed my hand on his shoulder. "I'm sorry for your loss."

He looked down at me, and nodded, but said nothing, and I didn't force him to. Soon we all stood around him, offering support as he grieved in silence.

"That seemed too easy," I said a little while later as we watched Holden get in his Impala and leave, headed out of town, on to his next case somewhere far away from the memory of what he'd lost in Moonlight, West Virginia.

"Sure, if you thinking fighting through an army of hellhounds was easy," Ginger said, causing Lana to shudder.

"Hey, you got over your fear enough to help save the day," I told the Imortian.

"Daniel did all the saving," she said. "If he hadn't come to when he did, we'd all be dead."

Daniel shrugged off the praise as the two women clapped him on the back and smothered him with accolades, even Ginger who usually withheld praise in favor of busting his chops, and stared at me, holding my gaze as something unsaid and truly problematic flowed between us.

"I'm ready to go home," I said, still holding his gaze, then forced myself to say what came next. "I need to get back to Rider."

I saw the little flinch before he closed his eyes, took a breath, and nodded. "I'll take you."

Home.

It seemed a little intimidating as Daniel pulled his truck into the lot beside The Midnight Rider, but I told myself that was just my subconscious guilt. Daniel cut the engine, and we sat there for a moment, neither speaking. It was daylight, but I had my sunblock on, so that wasn't what caused our hesitation in getting out of the truck.

"I've made things weird between us," Daniel finally said, his voice soft, regretful.

"No."

"Yeah, I have. I'm sorry. I shouldn't have said anything at all. I just saw you hit that column, then I woke up, and you looked dead. Then that demon lifted your head, and I saw you were alive, but not for long. I just got flooded with so many fears and emotions at once, and I couldn't stop myself. I'm sorry."

I reached over and took his hand in mine. "You mean so much to me, Daniel. If Rider and I weren't—"

"Don't." He released a mirthless little laugh and shook his head as he lowered it, avoiding my gaze. "Please don't. You belong with Rider, and I am not the selfish asshole that's going to screw up you being with who you're supposed to be with. I love you, Danni. I love you enough to make sure you're happy no matter what."

He opened his door and stepped out of the truck, then waited for me to do the same. My eyes burned, so I took a moment to wipe them with my sleeves and get my emotions under control before I stepped out and joined him, but I couldn't leave things so awkward between us. I grabbed him and pulled him into a hug, and held him there for a moment, long enough for both of us to take a few very much needed deep breaths.

"I love you too, jerk," I whispered before pulling away, and the little smile he wore said we were good.

"Let's get you to your man," he said, and led the way into the bar.

Tony was at the bar, filling bowls with peanuts as we stepped in. He looked up and gave a little smile. "Welcome back."

Tony wasn't much of a talker, so the greeting instead of

just a nod of his head was a big deal. The smile was a rare phenomenon. I looked around the bar, seeing only a few people scattered about. It was during the middle of the afternoon, and things wouldn't pick up until later. I saw a few servers I didn't know, and I hadn't recognized the muscular guy posted at the door either, but I knew Rider had hired some new people since I'd left.

"Boss is in his room," Tony said.

"I'll hang out here," Daniel said, and slid onto a barstool before tapping on the bar top. "Gimme a beer."

I took a breath and moved through the bar, pushing through the door in back that connected to the hallway that held the staircase leading to Rider's private quarters. I tried to sense him as I took the stairs up and only felt peace.

I stepped through the door and was shocked to find him in bed, sleeping. Yes, it was daylight, and he preferred getting as much day sleep as he could given the energy he often had to expend in his job, which was basically keeping the entire area safe from those who chose to play on the wrong side of the paranormal spectrum.

"Rider." He didn't budge, so I moved over to him and gave him a shake. "Rider!"

He opened his eyes and smiled. "Danni."

"I'm sorry if you just got to sleep, but…" I stopped. He looked well rested, not as if he'd been struggling to sleep at all. Very well rested, I realized as he stood from the bed, naked and *very* healthy.

"Danni," he practically growled my name, his voice full of hunger as he lowered his head and kissed the side of my neck. His body immediately stiffened, and not just the part that had woken up that way, and inhaled deeply as he moved his head around to the other side of my neck, his nose hovering just over my skin.

When he pulled back, his eyes had darkened until they were almost black. "Did you think I wouldn't know?"

I gulped, reading the rage in his eyes. "Know what?"

"I can smell him on you," he said before forcing a hard kiss against my mouth. He released me and spat. "I can taste him!"

Oh no. "Rider, nothing—"

"Don't say another damn word." His eyes filled with golden light as his power poured out of him, and I knew he was calling his people, giving them orders. He shoved me back onto the chaise and quickly dressed in black.

"Rider, calm down."

He grabbed me by the back of my neck, and walked me out of the room, forcing me down the stairs, then walked me around the staircase where he opened the door leading to the sublevels, and forced me down those stairs until we reached a floor that filled me with dread.

"You don't have to do this," I said, knowing where we were headed and who I would find there.

"You're right," he said as we reached the interrogation room. Two armed guards stepped aside as he opened the door and shoved me inside. "*You* have to do this."

I nearly fell, but righted myself in time to see Daniel strung up spread eagle on a rack against the far wall, his wrists and ankles chained to the rack, a silver blade in his thigh so he couldn't shift and escape. The tight set of his jaw showed his pain, but his eyes registered his fear… for me.

"She did nothing wrong," he said. "Just kill me if you have to."

"Let him go!" I turned toward Rider. "This is cruel, and you're not cruel!"

Rider glared down at me, the corner of his mouth curving into a grin. "Am I not? Have you not seen me do horrible things in this very room, Danni?"

"Not like this." I shook my head and took a breath, trying to calm my nerves enough to clear my head and think. This was wrong. The whole thing was wrong. "This isn't you. Daniel is a friend."

"He's your friend," Rider told me. "Not mine. You've

always known this would happen, Danni. It's why you struggled so hard to resist him. Do you think I never smelled your arousal around him, never noticed the way you looked at him, lusting for him right under my nose?"

"She only wants you," Daniel said, coming to my defense, forcing words out through the pain and agony that had crept into his voice. "I crossed the line. I kissed her, but that was it. She did nothing wrong. Don't punish her."

Rider's blue eyes smoldered as he leered at Daniel. "So considerate of you to worry for her sake, dragon. Don't fear. I'm giving her a chance to prove her loyalty."

Rider turned those cold, dark eyes toward the table, where I saw several knives had been set out. Then he turned his eyes to me.

"No," I said, instinctually knowing what he was going to ask next.

"Yes." He grabbed my chin and forced me to meet his gaze. "You are mine, yet you allowed another man to put his mouth on you, to touch you."

"It was just a kiss."

"Take your fucking hands off of her and fight me like a man," Daniel bellowed, struggling against the chains binding him to the rack. "This is between us."

Rider released me and walked over to Daniel. He shoved the knife deeper into his leg, causing my friend to cry out in agony.

"Stop it!"

Rider turned toward me. "You know no one leaves interrogation alive. He dies fast, or he dies slow, depending on who does it. The choice is yours."

I gasped and looked down at the weapons on the table. "You mean you want me to…"

Rider walked over to me and grabbed my chin again, forcing my eyes back to him. "You asked for this man to be your guard and allowed this to happen. You claim it was just a kiss, then prove it. Prove this man means nothing to you. Prove that you are mine."

I would never ask you to prove anything to me, and Danni… I would never hurt you.

Rider's voice filled my mind, reminding me of his promise. The room spun. This was wrong. This wasn't Rider. This wasn't who he was. Rider loved me. Rider assigned Daniel to me despite his obvious moments of jealousy *because* he knew Daniel cared about me, and would protect me with a dedication no one else in his nest would.

"Danni!"

I looked up at him to see him handing me one of the sharp instruments from the table. I backed away, took a breath, willed myself to calm enough that I could make sense of the thoughts flooding my brain.

Would Rider kill Daniel? He'd said he would more than once. He'd said he'd kill any man who touched me, but would he make me do it? No. I shook my head. Rider wouldn't hurt me. I knew that as clear as I knew my own name. Rider Knight loved me, and although he could be gruesome in the interrogation room, he'd never hurt me by killing my friend in front of me, or worse, making me do it.

So what the hell was happening?

"Are you going to do this, or am I?" He towered over me.

I looked into his face, a face I knew every inch of, and it matched perfectly, right down to the specks of light blue surrounded by the darker blue in his irises. It was him, but it couldn't be.

Something's wrong… something's wrong…

I looked past him to where Daniel pulled against the chains, desperate to get free and defend me. Rider grabbed my chin, forced me to look into his eyes, his cruel eyes that were full of evil, and so very well rested. Far too rested for a man I'd known hadn't been sleeping.

Who the hell was I looking at?

This thing is a master imitator, and can survive for eons because people aren't likely to go for a kill shot if they think there's even the slightest possibility they may be killing someone else, I heard Christian say in my head.

No. We'd killed the trickster. Daniel had stabbed it and it disappeared. I'd seen it happen right in front of me after I'd… Holy shit. Was I still unconscious?

"All right, then," Rider said, spinning the blade in his hand. "I'll get started, and your friend can die slowly. Feel free to jump in and finish him off if you'd like to prove your loyalty, otherwise it's going to be one hell of a long day and night for him." He chuckled. "Hell, maybe we'll make it last longer than that. I have the time."

Time. Time moved differently in the Njeri realm. The dream realm. I was asleep. The trickster knocked us all out. I was in the dream realm, where time moved differently. None of this was happening, except it was. I was still there in the shed, knocked out, but I was here, and maybe Daniel… I looked at Daniel as his eyes widened, watching Rider stalk toward him with that sharp blade.

Was that really Daniel or another illusion? The trickster had a connection to me. I'd drank its blood, but Daniel… Daniel had been bitten by Carrie, who was bound to the trickster. He could have been infected then, just as Pauline had been infected when they'd fought, enabling the trickster to turn Pauline into the pontianak, and the trickster could have brought Daniel and I to this dream realm to play out this sick mind game, to force me to kill my best friend, absolutely killing me inside, before revealing itself and killing me for real because anyone who died in the dream realm died in reality. I reached behind me and pulled free the silver switchblade I still had in my pocket and quietly flipped it open.

"Let's see if it's any easier for her to kill you once we take away your pretty face," Rider said, raising the weapon in his hand.

I started to lunge, but froze. What if it really was Rider, and his jealousy had just driven him mad? He was jealous, and controlling... but he loved me. He loved me. He wasn't the kind of man to do this. As much of a cold, calculating front he put on to appear all powerful before his nest, as much as he put in to the reputation of being a cold-blooded killer no one should dare attempt to try, he was still the man who'd taken me to Pigeon Forge, who'd worried himself to a state of not being able to sleep over me, who'd grumbled, yet given in to keeping... *the dog.* Where was Kutya?

As Rider swung the blade toward Daniel's face, I drove my own silver blade through his back, piercing his heart.

He swung his head around, eyes wide in pain, surprise, and betrayal. "Danni?"

CHAPTER TWENTY-SEVEN

"Rider!" My heart stopped as I stared into the wide, hurt-filled eyes of the man I loved and watched him slowly turn toward me. What had I done? Had I just killed Rider?

"Danni…" Tears spilled from his eyes, each drop seeming to suck out a piece of my soul. What had I done? "Danni… I loved…"

I screamed as he crumbled to dust in front of me, and continued screaming as everything went blinding white, then exploded in a giant fireball.

I still screamed as I found myself back in the shed, Carrie writhing in front of me, flames licking up her body as it flickered between her image and that of a humanoid shadow, but it really wasn't a shadow. It was some kind of entity that no light could penetrate.

I continued to scream as the flames devoured it, and the silver knife I'd plunged into its heart dropped to the ground among the blackened ash left from what was the trickster. I still screamed as Holden ran forward and lifted me to my feet, and as Daniel reached me, gripping my arms before giving me a shake.

"He's all right," I heard him yell into my face as he shook me. "It wasn't him." He kept repeating this until I realized I wasn't just screaming. I was screaming Rider's name. "Danni, calm your mind so you can reach out to him! He's fine!"

I sucked in air, as much as I could take in, and forced it back out, forcing my heart to stop racing, repeating this as Holden and Daniel held me up, my knees too weak to keep me on my feet. Finally, my head cleared, and I felt Rider's presence.

Rider?

Chrissakes, baby, what is it? What's happened? Tell me you're fine.

I fell apart, more tears than I could imagine containing in my body releasing as my knees buckled and the guys lowered me to the floor, allowing me to melt into a puddle of relief and cry until I couldn't cry anymore.

I didn't bother returning to the cabin. I helped take care of the cuts the hellhounds had inflicted on Ginger's thigh, while Daniel flew back to Gruff's to get his truck. By the time he returned, Ginger had fed from Lana. The blood, along with my saliva used to heal her cuts, had her well enough until the day sleep could completely heal her damage.

I explained to them what had happened, leaving out the part where Daniel had kissed me, and the real reason Rider, or the trickster posing as Rider, had wanted me to kill Daniel. Ginger watched me knowingly as I told my version of the story, her gaze flicking over to Daniel enough times, that I knew she realized what had happened, and as I caught Daniel often looking away, I wondered again if he'd really been there with me.

"Are you sure you don't want to rest a bit first?" he asked later as we watched Holden drive away, ready to get as far away from the place his friend had died as possible.

"I can sleep on the ride," I told him, although I had no intention whatsoever of closing my eyes until I was with

Rider and one hundred percent sure it was really him. "I need to get home now."

We said our goodbyes to Ginger and Lana, then got into our vehicles, Lana and Ginger heading back to the cabin to pack, promising they'd wrap everything up with Gruff, while Daniel and I headed for Louisville, where Rider waited.

"Daniel," I asked hours later as I saw the sign announcing we'd just entered Louisville, and thought we'd gone long enough without talking, only the music on the radio breaking the silence.

"Yeah?"

"Were you there? Were you in the dream realm with me?"

I watched him out of the corner of my eye, saw his jaw clench as he white-knuckled the steering wheel. He swallowed hard. "I was knocked out with the others."

I released my breath and returned to looking out the window, deciding not to push the fact that he hadn't said yes or no, and we'd all been knocked out, even me. At least he hadn't outright lied to me. Maybe it was best we didn't speak of it again, and just pretended it had never happened at all.

It was early afternoon when we reached The Midnight Rider and hurried inside. My body was tired, but my mind was far too wound up to sleep. I saw Tony at the bar, filling bowls with peanuts, and got a little woozy as déjà vu swept over me.

Daniel grabbed me from behind, holding me securely. "Are you all right?"

Tony looked up, his face remaining expressionless as he nodded a greeting, then went right back to what he was doing.

"Yeah, I answered. I'm good." I rushed over to Tony, grabbed him by his stoic face, and planted a kiss right on his forehead.

"What the hell was that for?" he asked, wiping the back of his wrist over the place my lips had touched.

"Just for being you," I said as I hurried to the back hall and ran toward Rider's office, where I felt his presence.

I burst through the door, finding him sitting behind his desk, Rome lounging back in one of the seats before it, and a gorgeous dog resting in a very plush looking dog bed on my left.

"Danni!" Rome said, smiling broadly as relief flooded Rider's face and he stood from his chair. "What up, baby girl? You finally back to—"

I grabbed Rome by the ears and popped a big kiss on his forehead, stunning him into silence before I rounded the desk to reach Rider. I grabbed his face and looked deep into his red-rimmed eyes. "You look awful!" I cried out with glee before kissing him, then turned for the dog, dropping on my knees to rub my fingers through its dark fur. "What a beautiful, wonderful dog."

"Um, thanks for that," Rider said. "Glad the dog at least looks nice enough for you."

"Boss, I think she done went a little nuttier than usual while she was gone," Rome said. "I'll let you handle that."

I giggled as the dog, an absolutely stunning beauty of a dog, licked my arm, then got back up, turning for Rider. "Oh, you look just wonderful," I told him, kissing him again, this time taking the time to savor it as he pulled me tight against him and returned the kiss, expressing how happy he was to have me back without having to utter a word.

"Uh, I just wanted to make sure all was good."

We withdrew and turned to see Daniel standing in the doorway. I thought I saw a brief flare of sadness in his eyes before he blinked, and it was gone.

"Daniel." Rider stepped around me and the desk and

held his hand out. "Good work keeping my girl safe."

Daniel glanced at me before accepting Rider's hand and shook it firmly. "That's my job. I do it with pride."

And love, I thought a little sadly as Daniel glanced my way again and turned for the door.

"I'm exhausted so…"

"Go," Rider said. "Go get some rest. You've earned it."

Daniel nodded, then left.

"I look awful, huh?" Rider turned toward me, grinning. "That's the first thing you say to me after scaring the hell out of me?"

"You're gorgeous as always," I said, walking into the arms he held open for me. I touched his face. "You just look like you really need some sleep."

"Yeah," he said, and kissed my forehead. "What happened out there, Danni? I've never felt that much terror in you. I had already started to call Rihanna to transport me there to you when I realized it wasn't just terror. It felt like…"

"Like I'd just seen someone I love die at my own hand?" I finished for him as I rested my cheek against his chest and breathed in the beautiful midnight rain scent of him.

He withdrew just enough to see me, and tilted my chin up with two fingertips before moving my hair out of my face and running those same fingertips down my cheek. "What happened? It looks like neither one of you bothered to even clean up after what must have been one hell of a bloody fight."

"I couldn't wait to get back home to you." I told him the same version I'd told the others, leaving out the feelings, and that kiss, that had been shared between Daniel and I, suggesting the trickster had created the whole senseless jealousy of Daniel just because I'd returned with him, and explained how I'd realized the man who looked like Rider wasn't him, but how the trickster had looked so much like him after I'd stabbed it in the heart, the vile creature still torturing me as it died.

"I'm so sorry you had to go through that." He gathered me to him. "How did you figure it out?"

"It wasn't right," I answered. "Everything looked the same, but Tony was a little too happy to see me, and you were far too cruel. I remembered you told me you'd never make me prove anything to you, and I knew you wouldn't make me do anything you knew would hurt me, even if you were absolutely enraged." I chuckled. "The real clincher was I remembered the dog."

I looked over at the beautiful animal, who watched us with its large head tilted to the side. "Kutya wasn't there. I remembered I still wore the dream beads so the trickster couldn't read my thoughts. I hadn't feared the dog or even thought about it in the dreams it had invaded before, so the trickster didn't know anything about Kutya, and since I was wearing the beads when it brought me into the dream realm, it had to create a world using only information it had already received from me prior to me putting the beads on."

Rider grinned and looked over at the dog before patting his thigh. "Good dog, Kutya. Good boy."

The big dog rushed over and raised up on its hind legs before barking. I laughed and patted its big head as Rider scratched it under its ear. Okay, so I guessed I could accept the dog's name. It seemed so happy when Rider called it.

"Auntie Mo was right, as usual," Rider whispered softly.

"What?" I looked up at him. "You spoke to Auntie Mo?"

He nodded. "She called Rome just after you hung up on me, right as we were getting ready to leave the garage to go get you, and told him to give me the phone. She warned me she'd just seen you die in a dream, and I'd done the killing."

I gasped. "Surely, you didn't think you'd—"

"I didn't know what to think. Auntie Mo hasn't been wrong about anything yet. I asked how it happened, and how to prevent it, all the while knowing there was no way possible I'd ever kill you. But if she saw it, then it had to be. She said it happened here, which is why I didn't drag you home with me, and she said in order to prevent it, I needed to make sure you knew who I really was, and that I loved you and would never make you prove anything to me." He closed his eyes and took a deep breath. "I have been so worried, so afraid I failed to do that, and that I was going to lose you because of it."

"You did it. I heard the real you in my heart when I was in that realm with the trickster, but can you do something else for me now?"

He returned his gaze to me again, and held me tight against him as Kutya dropped down to all four paws. "Anything."

I cupped his cheek with my hand, and looked straight into his beautiful, but oh so tired blue eyes. "Can you sleep now?"

His expression grew almost sad. "I'll try."

"You'll try?" I scoffed. "I'm home now, and I'm not leaving, so you will *do*. Come on. I don't care what you're working on. I don't even care about that witch who tried to kill me locked up somewhere here. You are going to bed right now."

"Yes, ma'am." He laughed, and allowed me to pull him by the hand all the way to his room, Kutya merrily wagging his tail as he followed behind.

"I'm taking a shower," I announced, "and when I get out, I want to come out here and find you asleep in that bed."

"Seriously?" he asked, pulling me against him so tight I had no choice but to feel how happy he was that I was back. "You think I can sleep knowing you're in the shower? After so much time apart, you're not going to invite me in there with you?"

"Fine," I said, trying to fake disappointment and failing miserably, "but then you sleep."

"What's wrong?" I asked almost an hour after we'd showered together and continued round two of what we'd started in the shower, under the sheets, Kutya whining from where Rider had ordered him to go wait in the bathroom, giving me privacy after I'd been unable to do all the naughty things I wanted to do with the dog watching. Now we were together in bed, completely sated, Kutya resting on the chaise so no longer begging to come back in. Still, Rider was awake.

"Nothing. I'm glad you're back. I'm excited."

"Hmmm…" I rolled onto my side and grabbed his chin, forcing him to look at me. "You are exhausted. I can see it in your eyes. You should be asleep."

He smiled. "You go to sleep first. I'll catch up."

"I don't believe you." I sat up, covering myself with the sheet, as Kutya sat up on the chaise and whined, as if trying to tell me something. I remembered Christian mentioning the dog had adopted Rider because it sensed his pain, how he'd hoped the dog would help him sleep. I thought for sure Rider hadn't been sleeping because I'd left. He'd told me before that he slept better with me at his side, so what else could it…

"No," I whispered as I realized it wasn't just the night I left that Rider stopped sleeping. He'd stopped sleeping after what had spurred me into leaving.

"What is it?" Rider sat up and reached over to cup my face.

I turned toward him. "Why can't you sleep? Tell me now."

He lowered his eyes and sighed. "It's nothing. I'm just having a little trouble."

"What do you see when you close your eyes?"

His jaw clenched, and he dropped his hand as he pulled

away from me.

"Uh uh. What do you see?" I grabbed his face and forced him to look at me again. I forged forward when he just stared at me, not wanting to answer. "You see my heart in your hand, don't you?"

He closed his eyes and let out a ragged sigh before nodding. I thought I'd been all cried out, but new tears formed. I'd been so caught up in what seeing my heart in his hand had done to me, I'd never thought what it had been like for him to see it, for him to *do* it. I knew now though. I understood. The quick thinking I'd had to do in the dream realm, the fear of actually killing him mixed with the fear of dying or allowing Daniel's death, had to be right up there with what he'd felt that night deciding whether or not to pull my heart from my body in order to save me without hurting me by killing my sister.

He'd had to work through so many thoughts at once, so many fears… he'd had to protect me and free me of a curse by doing the same thing he'd done to his brother, the same thing that had *killed* his brother. He had to have been afraid of something going wrong, and he had to have feared me being upset with him, but he'd forced himself to do it because, in the end, it saved me. And I had done nothing but hold it against him ever since.

"I forgive you."

He looked at me, hope in his eyes. "What?"

"I forgive you. I know why you took my heart. I know you had to do it because you love me, and you would do anything to protect me and save me. I'm sorry I didn't understand then, but I understand now, and I forgive you."

His eyes narrowed as he studied me, doubt settling in.

I took his hand and placed it over my temple as I opened my mind to him. "I forgive you. See for yourself."

Relief filled his eyes as I flooded him with all my feelings of love and complete forgiveness. He laughed, so overjoyed as the weight that had been crushing him since the night my sister tried to kill me was lifted.

"Now, please, go to sleep," I begged. "It would make me so happy."

He nodded his head and allowed me to wrap my arm around him. A moment later, I sensed the day sleep take him as I cradled his upper body against my breast, and rested there, listening to the sweet sound of absolute quiet.

Kutya jumped from the chaise, then onto the bed, stepping over Rider. He crawled over my legs and settled himself on top of my thighs, staring right into my eyes.

"He belonged to me first," I told the dog. "You and I are going to have to come to a few agreements about some things."

The dog raised one of his massive paws, and I shook it.

I stretched as I came awake to find Rider propped on his elbow, watching me, one finger running the length of my thigh. "Tell me you didn't wake up right after I drifted off."

"I slept like a baby." He kissed my nose. "In fact, I just woke up about ten minutes ago, just as the sun went down."

"Good." I turned toward him, missing the weight that had been on my legs when I'd fallen asleep, and looked over to see Kutya back on the chaise.

"I've just been informed Ginger and Lana arrived safely, and they have your things. They're down in the bar. Angel was dropped off at your apartment, which is still under my protection, so don't worry about her safety."

"Ginger healed fine?"

He nodded. "She slept while Lana drove them back."

I raised my eyebrows. "She let Lana drive her Mustang?"

"You really think Ginger is above letting an attractive woman drive her car? Ask her nicely and she'll let you drive it too. Daniel or Rome, on the other hand, would have to pry her keys out of her cold, dead fingers."

I chuckled. "I guess we should go down there and welcome them."

"Hmmm. Later." He moved over me. "Kutya, out!"

The bar was full of people as we entered a couple of hours later, fresh from another shower that had lasted longer than it should have. Kutya followed on Rider's heels as we crossed the bar to where Ginger sat alone in a booth, nursing a dark mug of what I knew to be blood. A few people looked at the dog as we passed, and I pitied the fool who dared suggest the animal not be allowed inside Rider's bar.

We settled into the other side of the booth, and Kutya sprawled on the floor next to us. Across the room, Daniel and Lana talked closely at the bar as the two Imortians sipped from beer bottles.

"Might be a love connection going on over there," Ginger said, jerking her head in their direction. "They've been talking close like that for a couple of hours now."

I looked away when Daniel's gaze lifted to mine. "I don't know about that. They have history, and I get the sense it's not all that great. They just have things to work through, that's all."

I felt Rider's gaze on me and looked over to find him watching me curiously. He looked over at Ginger. "All healed up and ready to start another job?"

"Good to go," she answered. "What do you have for me?"

Rider and Ginger's voices droned out as I looked back over at the bar and saw the two Imortians continue talking, their bodies turned toward each other, and their heads close. If they were a random pair of strangers, I'd think they were into each other, maybe already an established couple. I couldn't look away as I watched them converse. Daniel said something that pulled a genuine smile out of Lana, and she covered his wrist with her hand. I felt a little jab of pain in my chest.

"Danni?"

I jerked at the sound of Rider's voice so close to me and looked at him. "I'm sorry. What?"

He looked over at Daniel and Lana, then at me, his brow furrowed.

"Danni London Keller!"

I cringed as I turned toward the sound of the sharp, grating voice, and saw my mother pushing past Rome at the entrance, a short, shady-looking man at her side.

Ah, sonofahobbitfucker.

DANNI KELLER WILL RETURN IN PEACE, LOVE, AND FANGS IN 2021

***

IF THIS IS YOUR FIRST TIME MEETING CHRISTIAN, AND YOU'D LIKE TO SEE WHAT HAPPENED THE FIRST TIME HE MET DANNI, CHECK OUT VAMPIRE'S HALO (BLOOD REVELATION #5), WHICH TAKES PLACE AFTER SUCK IT, SISTER!

ABOUT THE AUTHOR

Crystal-Rain Love is a romance author specializing in paranormal, suspense, and contemporary subgenres. Her author career began by winning a contest to be one of Sapphire Blue Publishing's debut authors in 2008. She snagged a multi-book contract with Imajinn Books that same year, going on to be published by The Wild Rose Press and eventually venturing out into indie publishing. She resides in the South with her three children and enough pets to host a petting zoo. When she's not writing she can usually be found creating unique 3D cakes, hiking, reading, or spending way too much time on Facebook. Find out more at www.crystalrainlove.com